Looking for Trouble

S. MIA MCCROSKEY

ISBN: 0-9963040-4-5

ISBN-13: 978-0-9963040-4-7

DEDICATION

For my father, Adrian Aubrey McCroskey.

CONTENTS

ACKNOWLEDGEMENTS

As a teenager I made the pre-dawn hike up Mount Rubidoux for the Easter Sunrise service with church youth group. Like Beth, my recollection of the other members of the group has faded, but I thank them nonetheless for empowering me to do something that was pretty far outside of my wheelhouse. I also believe it's important to acknowledge the real-life publication that inspired my fictional *Gunkholing* magazine: *Cruising Outpost* (formerly *Latitudes and Attitudes*). The dinghy raft-up at the end of this novel is a typical activity at the gatherings that the magazine organizes, although I don't think they've ever put together a treasure hunt. If they ever do, you'll know who thought of it first. Thanks also to Charlotte Chappel for reading and providing valuable corrections.

ONE: SOUTHERN CALIFORNIA

"Beth! Over here!"

"Aunt Beth!"

"Hey Aunt Beth!"

The chorus of voices was impossible to ignore, and drew looks from several passengers arriving in the baggage claim area. Trish and her children, Sammy and Eli, were standing in the prime spot next to the baggage carousel where the bags from Beth's flight would come sliding down a chute onto the rotating belt. Beth grinned and waved as she hurried past the last security exit and crossed to them.

"Hello everyone!" she crowed, arms wide offering a group hug. Sammy had to be four inches taller than she remembered – his head brushed her bust now. Eli, who had been little more than a toddler when Beth last visited, was a young lady in a Disney princess costume. Beth's sister Trish looked alarmingly like a stereotypical soccer mom in her yoga pants and light weight hoodie over a cotton tank top, and were those actual Uggs on her feet? Beth recalled how when she lived in New York, Southern Californians' colorful clothes had seemed jarring when she visited. Now Trish's yellow, coral, and black outfit didn't seem outlandish at all. She fit right in with the other passengers from Miami all around them.

As Trish and Beth engulfed the children between them Beth's tattered blue nylon daypack slid off her shoulder and banged into her sister.

"Sorry!" Beth groaned, breaking the hug so that she could set the bag down.

"It's so wonderful to see you Sis. We are all so excited!" Trish gushed. At her sincere welcome a sense of well-being suffused Beth, and she realized how tense she'd been since leaving her boyfriend Terry to board

1

her flight in Miami. She had delayed this visit to her family for months, missing all of the winter holidays, out of guilt and fear. Guilt over not being nearby as her father's health declined. Fear of what she would find when she did visit. She and Terry had spent too few days sailing Beth's sailboat, *Double Trouble*, in the Caribbean before her guilt and his business commitments had forced them to put the boat in a marina and fly together back to the U.S. In Miami he'd seen her away on her flight to Los Angeles then went to catch his own flight to his home in Washington D.C. Now Trish seemed to be doing her best to make her arrival happy and she was very grateful.

Behind Beth a loud buzzer sounded three times and the baggage conveyor jerked to life. She turned to face it and felt little Eli's hand slip into hers. She smiled down at her niece.

"What does your bag look like?" Sammy asked, eying the first bags sliding down onto the conveyor belt.

"It's a navy blue duffel bag."

"Is that it?" Eli asked, pointing at an enormous blue roller suitcase coming down the chute.

"No sweetie, that's much bigger than my bag."

"That's a suitcase, silly. Aunt Beth said it was a duffel." Sammy's tone was typical big brother. "Mom?"

"Yes Sammy."

"What's a duffel?"

Beth shook her head and laughed, suddenly thrilled to be spending some time with the children.

Trish explained what a duffel was as more bags slid down onto the moving belt. The first bags had made their way back around by the time Beth's faded navy blue canvas sea bag half slid, half rolled down and hit the edge of the carousel right in front of her.

She and Sammy both reached for it and they lifted it together off the belt and onto the floor. Sammy was grinning.

"I knew that was yours!" He crowed proudly.

"Is that all?" Trish asked, her tone clearly conveying skepticism at Beth's one small bag. It was true that her bag was almost small enough to carry on the large cross-country jet.

"I live on a boat, Sis. I don't have much."

"Well, you're looking great. You can probably borrow some things if you need them."

"I'll be fine. Shall we go?"

Trish's offer to share her wardrobe wasn't intended as a backhanded compliment. In fact, Beth knew, her "you look great" was sincere, even if it did include the unspoken "you used to be fatter" that Beth heard loud and clear. The funny thing was, when she'd bitten the bullet and stepped on the scale in the gym at the hotel she and Terry had stayed in for one night in Miami, it had told her that she had not lost any weight at all. That surprised her, since her body certainly had changed over the months since she started her sailing journey from New York to the Caribbean. Some of her shorts were loose enough to need a belt, and the arm holes of some of her tank tops were so large they easily revealed whatever she had on underneath, which was often nothing. No matter, her size six sister was nuts if she really thought Beth could borrow any of her clothes. Maybe an oversized t-shirt would just fit.

Navigating out of the airport parking lot, Trish started listing all of the activities she had planned for them during Beth's visit. It started before dawn tomorrow when they would be climbing up Mount Rubidoux for the sunrise Easter service. Beth had fond memories of making this hike a couple times as a teen. The trail was well worn, steep in places but not difficult, and there were hundreds of other climbers as well as volunteer trail monitors along the way. But she couldn't quite imagine that Eli would be able to do it. She wasn't sure that she wanted to do it either, but she squelched her reservations as Trish moved on to other plans for the next couple weeks. These included day trips to both Disneyland and Knott's Berry Farm, a day or two at the beach, the San Diego Zoo, and – a misguided concession to Beth's lifestyle – a walk around the marinas on Balboa Island. Omitted from the list were any tasks related to the relocation of their parents, getting their house on the market, and all of the associated emotional trauma. Beth held her tongue, certain that Trish was avoiding the topic because of the kids in the back seat.

During the past month, while Beth was sailing her boat *Double Trouble* down the Caribbean island chain, Trish had selected and made arrangements with an assisted living facility for their parents. This included what, to Beth, was a terrifying task: evaluating their financial situation and working with the facility to finance their stay. Beth had been living on her meagre savings and on scraps of income from temporary jobs for nearly half a year. Her precarious financial position made her instinctively shy away from looking too closely at it. She knew that learning about her fathers' pension and other retirement finances would make her feel like a middle class failure. Trish, a working mother with a working husband and, no doubt, a couple of retirement accounts to which regular contributions were made, was in a much better place to organize their parents' finances.

To make up for avoiding the money, Beth had taken every opportunity to research their father's condition — which meant an hour at an Internet café every few days. While Mom was in good health, Dad had been diagnosed with Alzheimer's disease last fall. He was being treated, but his symptoms were becoming too difficult for Mom to manage on her own. She had been a reluctant collaborator with her eldest daughter in finding a place to move. As she'd come to understand that they could live in their own apartment with minimal intrusion by medical staff she'd become more interested. Her phone calls with Beth had started to include phrases like "I'll be glad when I don't have to worry about this pool," and "the lawn man charges us twenty-five dollars just to mow the front lawn, I can think of so many other ways to spend that money."

No, Beth did not envy Trish the chore of sorting out their finances and reviewing the contracts with the facility. But now she had to face her part of the deal: organizing their parents' move, including the disposition of their house full of possessions. Trish had made it very clear that she had already collected everything she wanted from the house, so Beth expected to be having at least one garage sale, and coordinating with charities and, ultimately, a removal company. And then there was the challenge of making Mom understand just how much less space she was going to have. Amusingly, that was a job for which Beth was particularly suited, having gone from an apartment to a boat herself, and having made plenty of poor choices of what to keep in the process. Beth had plenty to do for the next few weeks without fitting in any fun excursions.

Even though it was Saturday afternoon the traffic was dense, but once Trish got the minivan onto the freeway they started to move and Trish's listing of her extensive plans wound down.

"God, let me shut up so you can talk. Is there anything you really want to do while you're here?"

Beth had to think for a moment, she was so overwhelmed by

everything Trish had already mentioned.

"I guess I assumed that taking care of mom and dad would take a lot of time," she said, hoping Trish would not be annoyed at her for getting to the point. Her sister glanced in the rearview mirror, presumably looking at the kids.

"I just don't want your visit to be all depressing and serious," she said, flicking on her turn signal to go around a truck that did not seem to Beth to be going especially slowly.

"Oh I agree. But we do need to get certain things done. Anyway, I hadn't even thought about fun stuff. I would love to go to Disneyland and Knott's, it's been so long. How much do they cost these days?"

Trish made a strange grunt and took her eyes off the road to look at her sister for a second.

"You can't afford it. That's what you're saying."

"I didn't –."

"Hush. We have season passes. My treat for your tickets."

"That's not –."

Trish raised her right hand, palm toward Beth. "No. Be our guest. If we came to visit you, wouldn't you want to do some nice things for us?"

Beth's protest died in her throat. Trish had a point. Although Beth's living arrangements alone were comparable, for someone like Trish, to an adventure.

"Good." Her big sister said with finality. "Now, the kids are off this week, so Mike and I are splitting the week and we're both taking Thursday and Friday off work. We thought we'd do the parks then. In any case, we'll set you up with the van so you're not tied to us," she patted the dashboard. "But we may have to ask you to do a few errands."

"That's no problem Trish," Beth replied, not surprised that her sister's seeming suggestion of Disneyland and Knott's had really been far more concrete plans. It was spring break, after all. "I'd be happy to help out with anything. It will be great to have wheels. I want to stock up on stuff at Trader Joes and ship it to the boat, so I'll need to get a box and get it shipped."

"You do still have a valid driver's license, right?"

Beth frowned, then opened her daypack to find her wallet.

"Seriously? You have to check?" her sister croaked.

"I'm ninety-nine percent sure," Beth said, finding the wallet and pulling it out of the bag. Trish was shaking her head. Beth found her

New York driver's license buried in a seldom-opened compartment. It was good for another four years.

"I never use it as ID anymore. I use my passport all the time."

"Well that might be inconvenient in SoCal, so you probably want to keep that in a more accessible place."

"Good idea." Beth replaced the license in a slot next to her credit card and put her wallet away.

Trish exited the freeway and rolled to a stop at a traffic light. In the back seat Sammy looked up from his Nintendo.

"Mom, don't forget dinner. You promised." He said.

"I didn't forget Sam I Am," Trish said, looking in the rear view mirror at her son. Then she turned to Beth. "Marie Callender's. Mike's meeting us."

The mention of a favorite local chain made Beth realize that she was actually hungry. She'd bought a sandwich at the airport early that morning and eaten it on the cross-country flight, but that had been several hours ago.

"It's getting near nine o'clock in my time zone," she said. "I'm definitely ready for some dinner."

"We thought you would be."

The light changed and Trish turned left.

"At least you're only one hour earlier there." Beth rolled onto her side on the sofa bed, looking for a position where the thin mattress actually padded the metal frame. Her internal clock said it was midnight, but it was just eight in Southern California. Beth had excused herself from another round of the board game that her sister's family was playing in order to call Terry before it got too late in Washington.

"True, but I had a longer layover in Miami. Airport waiting time counts double."

"Silly."

"I miss you already."

"Me too, you. But I'm glad I came. I'm glad I'm facing up to all this."

"I want you to call me any time it gets hard, okay?"

"Okay. It's wonderful to hear your voice. And sad too, since that's all I get."

"Yeah. But every day we're apart will make the reunion better."

"That is so cliché!"

"Sorry."

"No, I love cliché," Beth sighed. "But I should get back to the family. I love you."

"I love you too. Good night Bethy."

"Night."

Beth flipped her phone shut to end the call and rolled over again to plug it in. She'd had to unearth her U.S. cell phone from the bottom of a dry storage locker on *Double Trouble*. She had not used it in several months, ever since she reached the Caribbean and bought a phone for use with the local carriers. She'd charged it in the hotel in Miami, then spent an hour on it getting her account reactivated. When she grabbed it to call Terry when they got to her sister's house it was dead again. After an hour of charging it was good enough to make the call, but she feared that months on board, even in a watertight container, had done in the battery. Another item for her to-do list: get a new battery.

Just one of life's little curve balls, she told herself as she got to her feet and headed back out into the family room.

TWO: EASTER

The sounds of young voices gradually replaced a delicious dream of sailing across a calm sea and Beth realized that she was awake. *Oh God, Easter.*

She had not found the courage last night to tell her sister that she didn't want to do the pre-dawn hike. More than once Trish had commented on how physically fit she looked, and how she envied Beth's active lifestyle. Clearly Beth had an image to live up to, or risk losing her sister's respect. Did Trish think she got up every morning and hiked up some island mountain to get breakfast?

Beth allowed herself to admit for a brief moment that it would be cool to watch the sunrise over Box Springs Mountain. But did it have to be today? After traveling all day yesterday? Why hadn't she thought this through when she booked the flight? She could have come a day earlier.

Eyes half open she dragged on her nylon pants with the zip-off legs – she didn't even have a pair of jeans on board *Trouble* – and layered one of Mike's sweatshirts over a t-shirt and long-sleeved cotton shirt.

"Weather's perfect," Trish informed her as she trudged into the kitchen. Her sister looked totally put together in her jeans, pink and black plaid flannel shirt, and black puffy vest. Her light hiking boots looked new. Beth's had done a lot of walking across a lot of islands. Watching her sister pour hot coffee into a stainless steel thermos, Beth smirked inwardly. At least she knew that she wasn't going to develop any blisters this morning.

Cars lined the suburban streets at the base of the diminutive "mountain" in the middle of town, but Mike steered the minivan into a parking lot where people waving flashlights with colored plastic covers directed him.

"There are more people every year," Trish observed. "The paper said last year it was nearly three thousand. And some people parked the night before and slept in the car."

Beth bit back the observation that first came to mind: *nuts!*

"That's a lot of people. Is there enough room up there?"

"It's a spectacular crowd," Trish replied. Those were two words that Beth did not typically put together, and she silently cringed at her sister's wide-eyed admiration of the gathering, which seemed rooted in the Christian nature of the event. Beth's relationship with God was clear to her, but her appreciation for organized churches had never been strong. The latter seemed to her to insert a lot of bureaucracy between the two entities in the former. At least, as far as she remembered, no one church had a lock on this event. It was a non-denominational celebration of Christ's rising. It was Christian, for sure, but not any more specific than that.

Trish and Mike each took a child's hand and they joined a stream of people walking quietly toward the base of the mountain and the trailhead. Beth followed, her small flashlight in hand, although for now there were plenty of others lighting the way.

They were no more than five minutes up the trail when Eli demanded to be carried. Mike picked her up without comment. Beth absently wondered whether the four-year-old would remember the experience, leaving the related question "why do it?" hanging in her consciousness. Her mind drifted back to when she and Trish had made this hike as teenagers with a church youth group. Her memories of that group were vague — clearly it hadn't had much of an impact on her at the time. She'd done it because Trish did and Mom expected it. The charity drives and activities were fun and she liked helping others in this organized, acknowledged way. She'd known that the prayer sessions were designed to keep the kids on the straight and narrow, a path that she'd never been strongly tempted to veer off of. So she'd treated them with respect, but with a vague idea that they weren't really meant for her.

She hadn't made any lasting friendships in that group. Really most of the other members had been Trish's friends, two years ahead of Beth in school. Why hadn't she found a group her own age? She wondered as she pushed up a steep bit, planting her hands on a trail-side Boulder. Who *were* her friends back then?

It startled her to realize that she couldn't remember. Was she a freak, that there was nobody in her home town who she wanted to visit while she was here, other than her family? She thought about high school. Did she want to try to see any of her teachers? There was an idea: she'd loved her senior year history teacher, Mrs. Bra – Broo – damn. Then there was the phys ed teacher – what was her name? – who'd had Beth help teach swimming during senior year.

It was as if she had dropped into New York City whole and unattached. She was still in touch with friends that she'd made there – heck, some of her belongings were stored in a friend's mother's garage on Long Island. But jump back to her life before moving east and there was nothing, other than her family. Soon there would be a high school reunion. Who would she come back to see? Nobody, apparently.

She had dropped herself into a trench of guilt for her imagined failure to connect with people in her life when she realized that the ground had leveled and she was following her sister, now holding Eli while Mike carried Sammy, across a plateau toward the back of a crowd gathered below the mountaintop cross. The hike was over and she'd hardly noticed it. Even though she could be pleased that she was more fit than she'd been as a teen, it still felt wrong: the journey was supposed to prepare her for the dawn, and she'd wasted it fretting about her past.

The dawn service was a non-denominational sequence of bible readings, short sermons, and hymns. It culminated with a hymn that Beth didn't know heralding the resurrection of Christ as the sun emerged from behind the distant mountains to the east. She tried to divide her attention between reading the lyrics on a paper program that she'd been handed and watching the sun, but quickly gave up in favor of watching the dawn and listening to the others singing. She had forgotten how "Bible belt" Southern California could be. She recalled now the tide of "born again" high schoolers that she'd basically ignored. They were here this morning in force, all grown up, swaying and singing and clapping their hands. She was sure that she heard a tambourine somewhere.

The few church services she'd been to in the Caribbean had provided their own creole flavor that she enjoyed. She had never understood the Evangelical attitude that was prevalent in this crowd.

She often watched the sunrise from *Trouble*'s deck, usually with her hands wrapped around a mug of coffee, listening to the susurrus of nearby surf, and the early cries of seabirds, roosters, and goats. As the voices of the crowd around her swelled in Christian praise for their Lord she felt a wave of smug pleasure that for her this wasn't a once-a-year devotion. That was followed instantly by another wave of guilt, especially after all of the sermons about humility and loving her fellow man. Certainly many other people here regularly got up before dawn.

The crowd burst into applause as the hymn ended. The sun was fully up now, the enormous white cross gleaming against the strikingly blue sky beyond. Whatever southern California's reputation, there was no smog on this beautiful morning.

"Over here," Trish said, tugging on her sleeve and then weaving through the now moving crowd. People were moving in groups, talking and walking toward the trailhead and the road. Trish, Mike, and the kids wove their way through them to the Eastern side of the mountaintop. They stopped at a railing with a view of the valley below and the distant Box Springs Mountain where a huge cement letter C indicated the location of the University of California campus. Mike produced a pair of binoculars from the daypack he'd worn. He used them to scan the suburban neighborhoods below.

"Can you see it? Lemme see!" Sammy demanded while Mike was still searching.

"Just a second honey," Trish said. "He has to find it."

"I want to see," Eli put in sleepily. Trish turned to Beth.

"We always look for our house, and mom and dad's," she explained. "It gives the crowds a chance to clear."

Beth nodded and looked out into the valley. She was surprised when it wasn't that easy to identify the familiar avenues of her youth and follow them to her parents' house – her childhood home. But gradually the streets below resolved into familiar patterns and she found the high school and the development that had been an orange grove when she was a child, and then their street and the familiar blue shape of the swimming pool in their backyard. Her breath caught in her throat and she had to fight back a sob at the sight of her old neighborhood. Shocked at herself, she pulled her eyes away toward the distant mountain and stared at it, gathering herself. In a few hours she'd be down there facing her father for the first time since he was diagnosed. She was terrified.

They took the descent slowly, Trish and Mike helping the kids down the steeper parts, but refusing to carry them.

"Mom, did the Easter Bunny come to Gramma and Granpa's house?" Sammy asked as Trish fastened him into his car seat.

"Yes he did Sam I Am. But first we're going to get a special Easter Breakfast."

"I want to see my Easter basket," the boy whined.

"Patience my dear," Trish replied firmly. "It's too early to go see Gramma and Granpa. They're not up yet."

"But the Easter Bunny −."

"Nope," Trish held up a single finger in front of her son. He closed his mouth.

Trish moved out of the sliding doorway and Beth climbed into the seat behind the kids in their car seats.

"Aunt Beth?" Eli's voice came over the sound of the front doors shutting.

"Yes Eli?"

"Does the Easter Bunny visit your boat?"

"Yeah, does Santa Clause come to your boat?" Sammy added. Craning his neck around to look at her from the extra elevation of his "big boy" booster seat.

Beth thought about last Christmas, spent with Terry aboard *Trouble* at anchor in a tropical paradise.

"Santa definitely comes to my boat, Sammy," she assured him. "As for the Easter Bunny, I hope not, because the chocolate will melt before I get back!"

"Oh!" Eli replied thoughtfully. "Maybe he brought your candy to Gramma and Granpa's."

"Maybe Eli. But really, seeing you guys is enough of an Easter treat for me."

Beth glanced up at the rear-view mirror and saw her sister smiling happily back at her.

By the time they finished a diner breakfast where the portions looked gigantic to Beth it was late enough − nearly nine o'clock − to go to Gramma and Granpa's house. Beth downed the last of the endless cups of coffee that the waitress had poured her and pulled out her wallet to cover her share of the meal. Mike scooped up the check and waved her away.

"Forget it. Yours is a drop in the bucket," he said as he headed for the cashier.

Beth took bills from her wallet anyway and placed them on the table. A minute later she intercepted Mike on his way back to the table with cash in hand – clearly planning to leave it for their waitress.

"I got the tip," she said firmly.

"Thanks!" Mike pocketed his cash with a smile.

Although she knew it was not, it felt to Beth as if the breakfast stop was a stalling tactic by Trish, who must know how nervous Beth was about seeing their father. His Alzheimer's diagnosis had come shortly after Beth had set sail south from New York. At the time Beth had not been in a position to leave her boat somewhere and come here. She'd been operating on a shoestring, and she didn't have the money to pay a marina to look after her boat, let alone buy an airline ticket to California. Her parents and her sister all realized this – they had probably understood better than Beth had at the time how tight her budget was. They had all urged her to carry on in her trip down the east coast before considering a visit. There were plenty of good reasons for this: It was November, and the marinas in the northeast were hauling the boats for the winter, not taking in transients. She had a good weather window, and that could change any day. Once in Miami there were many marinas to choose from. And in Miami there were many more air travel options than in the small coastal cities. So she'd kept going, keeping in touch with her family along the way, ignoring her proximity to Baltimore, Washington D.C., and then Norfolk and their airports, as Trish helped her mother get her father to his medical appointments and did the bulk of the grunt work learning about their options.

Beth had met Terry during her brief stop in Annapolis, Maryland. She'd been smitten with him, but played it cool because she wanted to sail her boat single-handed, and also because he seemed just too good to be true. But she had taken his card when he offered to help her get *Double Trouble* to the islands. She had eventually called him and accepted his offer after she'd had to hire a crewman to help her get through the long, boring Intracoastal Waterway, the protected inland passage along the coast.

Beth had broken up with her last boyfriend a couple years before setting sail, and it had not been her intention to start a new relationship while still getting the hang of living on and sailing a floating home. But there he was, a charming, handsome man who loved to sail. He'd told her, after they'd admitted their mutual attraction and affection, that he had not been searching for a girlfriend when he offered to sail with her, but by the time they got together in Miami, after dozens of phone calls while she was underway with her hired crew and he was tied up with work, he'd grown more and more interested in her. And she had become somewhat obsessed with him. Their eventual transition into a cruising couple had seemed inevitable on some levels, but for Beth it had been hard to work out their roles in the relationship and aboard her boat. One of Terry's finest virtues was incredible patience, and she knew she'd tested it in their early days. Somehow, somewhere between Miami and the Virgin Islands, she'd found her way to equilibrium as both the captain of her boat and the girl in their relationship. But even now, when he'd fronted her the money to fly to California because everything she'd saved working in the islands in January and February was going to pay the marina to look after *Double Trouble*, she still harbored concerns that he'd grow tired of the challenges that she presented in the relationship. Even if Terry had never once accused her of causing problems. She was, she smiled thinking about the loving way he said it, "sometimes a bit challenging."

When Mike pulled the minivan into her parents' driveway Sammy had shot out the sliding side door before Beth could get her seatbelt off. Then Trish blocked the door while she leaned in to release Eli from her seat. Sammy ran to the front porch where he stuck his finger on the doorbell and didn't let up. Exiting the car with just a little bit more dignity, Beth slid the van door shut with a clunk that sounded flat in the warm, dry air. She tried to conceal her survey of the familiar old neighborhood: The next door neighbor's house with the shades always drawn. It was gloomy inside, she knew, from the one or two times she'd been admitted. They were a lonely seeming, childless couple about her parents' age. Beth wondered if they still lived there. Judging by the window shades, they must. The house across the street sat on a high front lawn with a steep driveway up to a closed garage door. The Andersons had only been cordial with whoever lived there back then.

Next to it was the former home of a childhood friend. He was long gone, living somewhere in Northern California, and his parents and younger sister had also moved away. The house on the other side of her parents' had the same slightly neglected look that she remembered. It had been inhabited by a succession of families who had mostly kept to themselves. Beth had the idea that it was rented out, and there had been rumors at one time about drug dealers invading this quiet, suburban neighborhood. Even as a teen she'd attributed those to adults who were afraid of change and the cultural shifts of the seventies and eighties.

By the time Beth, Trish, and Mike had walked across the lawn the front door had opened and Beth's mother was cheerfully scolding Sammy for "ringing the bell off the hook" — whatever that meant. Mom had always been good at inventing gibberish phrases that got her point across.

"Happy Easter!" Trish called out, hurrying to the door to embrace her mother. Beth followed, and as Trish released Mom she moved in to give and receive a hug.

"Beth, it is so good to see you. Come inside," Mom said, guiding her daughters in and sparing a free hand to reach for Mike. The kids had disappeared into the house. "How was the service? Do you want coffee? Or is it time to move on to iced tea?" She was interrupted by delighted squeals from the children. "That will be their Easter baskets. We also hid eggs in the yard for them."

Beth absorbed her mother's monologue as they walked through the large living room with its clerestory windows high on the long wall. The carpet was just as springy underfoot as she remembered, due to her mother's choice of a very good pad when they'd had it installed. It had been a point of contention in the household for nearly a week.

As usual, the heavy drapes were drawn over the floor-to-ceiling wall of windows at the back that looked out onto the patio and swimming pool beyond. The furniture was unchanged since Beth's last visit: an long floral couch, a couple comfy chairs, a heavy wooden coffee table, and a wooden cabinet from the nineteen sixties that housed television, turntable, and radio receiver. Beth wondered if any of it still worked.

The wall of windows extended into the kitchen where lighter curtains were pulled aside to allow the backyard view and admit natural light.

Sammy and Eli were standing – hopping up and down, actually – at the kitchen table in front of enormous Easter baskets.

"Yum yum yum yum," Sammy was chanting as he eyed the assortment of candies through the clear cellophane.

"Mom, those are huge," Trish groaned.

"Easter Bunny, Mom," Sammy snapped, eyes sliding sideways toward his younger sister. *So*, Beth thought, *he's playing along for his sister. That's sweet.*

"Yes, sweetie," Mom said to Trish. "You just tell the Easter Bunny if you think they're too big."

Beth's father was seated at the round table in between his two grandchildren. Belatedly looking up as the adults came in, he stood up. But Beth did not miss the bewildered look on his face.

"Hello Dad," she hurried to him, wrapping her arms around him as he watched her curiously. Suddenly his arms wrapped around her.

"Hello Bethy. It's so good to hold you again. How have you been? Where have you been?"

"Dad, you remember, Beth has been sailing in the Caribbean. Look at her tan!" Trish said. Released from his hug, Beth looked at her sister and saw tight lipped frustration. She looked at her Mom and saw resignation and a sad smile.

"That's right Dad. I have some great pictures. You would love to look at the stars out there. You can see so many more."

"I hope you have some pictures of your boyfriend," Mom said pointedly, but not unkindly. Beth nodded. "Of course." Then wondered how they'd react to the pictures being on her computer, not physical prints. Of course she had emailed photos of Terry, but she had a feeling her mother didn't think of those as real pictures.

"Mommy? Can we open them?" Eli pleaded, obviously growing upset that the focus had drifted from the youngest generation.

"You and Sammy take those into the living room, right there in front of the TV so we can watch," Trish said, pointing. Sammy and Eli wrapped their arms around the baskets and carried them there, Mike standing by to help Eli if she needed it.

"We'll sit here to watch," Trish added, moving to one of the chairs at the table. Beth took another, sitting next to her father who resumed his seat. Mike stayed in the family room, sitting on the edge of one of the chairs to watch the great unwrapping.

While the children tore off the cellophane and scattered jelly beans and colorful plastic grass on the carpet Mom set glasses of iced tea in front of her daughters, then took one to Mike. Mom's sun-brewed iced tea was as good as Beth remembered, mild and flavorful and poured over lots of ice. The first sip brought her back to hot summer days lazing in the pool on a lounger with Styrofoam floats covered in blue woven nylon fabric chafed through in places. She'd read so many book out there, sipping cold tea until the ice had diluted it too near water. When that happened she'd paddle over to the steps in the shallow end, put her book on the coping, and roll off the lounger. The cold water on her hot, dry skin would make her shiver. She'd dash across the hot concrete into the shade of the patio to refill her big, plastic cup from the cooler that was always sitting on the table. Then she would force herself to get into the water and swim a little before resuming her lounge and reading. So many days like that, when Trish was off with her friends, and then away at college. Mom had, occasionally, suggested that Beth was wasting her summer, she should go do something. But Beth had been doing something – she'd been traveling all over the world and through time in her books.

She made a mental note to make sun tea on board *Double Trouble* – she certainly had abundant sun, and the tea was nothing special, just ordinary Lipton.

The squeals and giggles in the living room soon quieted when each child unwrapped and bit into a chocolate egg.

"Sammy, Eli, bring a few jelly beans over here for your Aunt Beth."

"They're mine!" Sammy snapped, then dropped his gaze to the floor.

"Samuel!" his father growled. The boy's shoulders hunched a little as he reached for a trio of jelly beans that had landed on the carpet.

"It's okay–." Beth started.

"It is not okay. Sammy, Eli, we talked about this last night. And what did they talk about on the mountain this morning? Sharing? Generosity? Do you remember?"

Beth did not recall much in the morning's sermons about sharing and generosity, but she kept her mouth shut.

"Yes Mom," Eli said in a saintly tone that was obviously intended to be as far from Sammy's obviously bad behavior as possible. The little girl scooped up several jelly beans and a small chocolate egg and climbed to her feet. She carried the candies to the table and set them on the violet plastic placemat in front of Beth.

"Here you go Aunt Beth. Happy Easter."

"Thank you Eli. Happy Easter to you," Beth replied, although the situation had become so strained her words felt empty.

Sammy followed his sister and presented his handful of jelly beans to his aunt. There was no chocolate in his offering. Beth half expected her sister to make him go back and get one of the medium sized chocolate eggs – and she would have loved to have one, they were a favorite from a local candy maker. But she was relieved when Trish let it end there.

After that the children were allowed to focus on the goodies in their baskets, which included stuffed bunnies and other small toys. Beth noted that Sammy's had toy cars while Eli's had dolls. She wondered if Trish regretted leaving the choice to their mother.

Mike remained in the living room, joining in the adult conversation, but also joining in the children's play. Beth suspected that this was Trish's doing: require her husband to keep the children busy so that the Anderson family could reunite. Beth felt bad for being the cause of his exclusion, but she did appreciate the chance to focus on her father for the first time since learning of his illness.

At Mom's urging Trish described the sunrise service, resuming the slightly awed, beatific tone that she'd used back in the pre-dawn darkness to describe the crowd. Beth watched for Mom's reaction to her daughter's tone and saw a familiar expression that blended slight impatience with sincere interest. Mom didn't buy the Christian awe, but she was looking past it to the facts about the event that Trish was providing.

Satisfied that Mom had not been brainwashed by the Evangelicals, Beth looked to her father. He was staring across the table in the direction of the kids in the living room. But he didn't seem to be actually watching the children. His expression was painfully empty.

"Dad, you would have loved the hike," she inserted when Trish had finished her description of the "amazing" sermons on the mountain top. It was a dumb thing to say – their father had never been a hiker and certainly couldn't do it now.

To her surprise, he turned to her and asked "Was it hard?"

"No. I thought it would be harder than it was."

"You've been living outdoors. You don't realize how much you've changed," Mom said.

"I live indoors," Beth countered. "*Trouble* has a main saloon and two separate cabins. With doors."

"You know what I mean. You're out in the sun all the time, walking everywhere."

"I walked everywhere in New York City, too, that's not different," Beth countered, wondering what the hell she was doing arguing about it.

"Well whatever you're doing differently it suits you," Trish said, glaring at her sister for a moment, then glancing pointedly at their father.

"I do love living on a boat," Beth said quickly. "It is very different, even from the small apartments I had in the city. I can't just decide to try a new hobby like I used to, there's no room to spare and *Trouble* always needs me. I have to spend any spare time on her."

"Well that's no different from owning a house," Mike put in, reminding them that he was listening.

"I guess so." Beth acknowledged.

"No yard, no furnace," Trish said, "It's not nearly as much to care for."

"Your house doesn't have a diesel engine, mast, running rigging, standing rigging. And probably most importantly, your house isn't floating on water."

"The washer cold inlet broke last year," Mike replied with a grin. "We've experienced flooding."

"But your home didn't sink," Beth replied, also grinning.

"You got me there. We only had to replace some floors."

"But come on, how likely is it that your boat will sink?" Trish asked still trying to discount Beth's assertion that the boat required as much maintenance as a house. Apparently that reality would destroy her vision of Beth's life was one of no responsibility or duty.

"It almost did between Florida and the Islands," Beth asserted, annoyance with Trish causing her to forget her plan not to mention that particular episode.

"Really?" Mike piped up again.

"Really. The bilge pump broke and we had a leak around the propeller shaft."

"You were sailing?" Trish asked, her previous dismissive tone gone. "Or were you using the engine?"

"We were sailing in the middle of the Florida Straits. If I'd been alone I would have had to call for help. Since there were two of us we took turns bailing until we got to shore."

"And you never mentioned this before?" Trish said with restrained anger.

"And that's why," Beth countered. "We dealt with it just like you dealt with the washer flood, which you never mentioned to me."

"But Beth, you said it yourself: Trish and Mike's washer flood couldn't have destroyed their home. You're saying that your boat could have sunk to the bottom of the sea." Mom said. Beth was grateful that she didn't sound as angry as Trish, just concerned. And that she hadn't carried the narrative to the possible conclusion of her younger daughter drowning.

"I'm glad that you're not sailing alone, Bethy." Dad's words instantly calmed the tension.

"Me too Dad. I originally planned to do it that way, but having Terry aboard has turned out to be pretty wonderful ."

"Maybe because he's pretty wonderful," Trish retorted with an apologetic smile.

"Do you have any photos?" Mom asked.

While Beth retrieved her laptop from the tote bag she'd left in the car, the party moved out to the patio table where the old green-tinted fiberglass roof provided watery shade from the morning sun that had warmed the yard. The children brought their goodies out and claimed two of the lounges. But they didn't stay settled for long.

"You know, Eli, Sammy, I saw the Easter Bunny poking around out here in the yard early this morning. I think he left some more Easter eggs." Mom said innocently.

"What?" Eli's delight was so endearingly genuine that for a second Beth wanted a little girl of her own.

"Come on! Let's look," Sammy declared, standing up and spinning in place, obviously planning his attack on the poolside shrubbery. Mike stood up, waving the rest of the adults toward the table.

"I'll help them," he said quietly.

"They'll be busy for a while," Trish said. "Let's see some pictures."

Beth took the open seat in between her parents and used the computer's track pad to launch the photo application. She had prepared several different slide shows, separating her life in New York from the trip down the east coast, life on St. Thomas, and the brief time with Terry in the islands. She'd realized when compiling the photos, that she'd hardly taken any pictures during her trip from St. Thomas to St.

Hillaire to find her friend Ori. That just meant she had to go back to all the islands she'd visited.

When the photo application was up she turned to her Mom.

"Want to see some pictures from New York? Or do you want to see the islands?"

"I want to see this boyfriend of yours." Her mom said firmly. Trish, who was standing behind her, chuckled.

"Me too," she said.

"Okay fine," Beth had to chuckle. "That okay with you Dad?" She looked to her right.

Her father was staring intently at the computer screen. After a moment she also turned to it and saw that her background wallpaper was a sunrise shot taken somewhere at sea. The dark water in the foreground had a single, orange stripe pointing straight at the camera. The horizon was clear, the clouds above it tinted from red at the center to orange, pink, and yellow at the edges. The sun itself was a bright blob in the lower third, centered. It wasn't a great photo, but Beth liked it.

She looked back at her father's profile, wondering whether he was looking at it, or not looking at anything. Trish put her hand on Beth's shoulder and squeezed gently.

"Okay, Terry it is," Beth said. She didn't have a slide show of photos of Terry, although in retrospect she realized she should have anticipated the demand. Instead she used the software's facial recognition tool to instantly compile pictures that included him.

"Oh my," Mom said.

"Isn't he gorgeous?" Trish gushed. Beth craned her head around to glare at her sister. "Well he is Beth. Do you not see it?"

"I see it, I see it. He's really handsome. His eyes are amazing."

"Let's see them," Mom said, squinting at the array of photos. Beth realized that, other than the one or two close up shots, most were too small to really see the details of Terry's face in the thumbnail view. She clicked on the first one, a shot of her and Terry on the bow of *Trouble* that a fellow sailor had taken. She tried to look objectively at Terry as her mother and sister did, but it was impossible. She remembered that moment, and the silly comment she'd made that had triggered the devilish grin that reached his eyes. She adored the sunbaked crow's feet at their corners. She could practically feel the roughness of five-o'clock shadow on his cheeks and chin. The strands of grey at his temples amid his brown curls lent him a maturity that she knew did not reach his heart, nor his sense of fun. He wore a loose cotton shirt, the top three buttons open to reveal his throat and a bit of his sparse chest hair. The light yellow fabric enhanced his deep brown tan.

"He looks kind," Mom said.

"And smart, you can see it in his eyes," Trish added.

"He is both," Beth nodded, switching to a different photo, a group shot of a bunch of cruisers sitting around enjoying a potluck beach party.

"This was on St. Martin. Cruising sailors regularly bring dinner to a beach for a party."

"Just another Saturday night, huh?" Trish asked with a smile.

"I think it's wonderful. Are they all nice people Beth?"

Beth thought briefly about the range of people she'd met since moving aboard *Double Trouble*.

"There are all different kinds, like any community. But I guess that's the thing: they *are* a community. I haven't yet met a really unpleasant cruising sailor. Some are more friendly than others, or more or less polite. But I haven't yet met one who wouldn't lend another sailor a hand."

"Really? No grumpy neighbors? No 'get offa' my lawn' geezers?"

Beth thought again.

"Well, there's a guy on St. Thomas who seems to socialize just so that he can collect gossip to repeat. He's not the first person I'd turn to in a bind. But I think what happens is that if someone is really unpleasant or doesn't help out in an emergency, they get ostracized. They're probably out there sailing, but they don't come to the beach potlucks or say hello at the dinghy dock." She trailed off, running out of scenarios that her family would understand.

"Seems like when I was growing up," Mom said. "The whole neighborhood looked out for one another. Not like today."

Beth glanced up at Mom, then at Trish, who's lips were pursed. She turned back to the computer and flipped over to the slideshow of her and Terry's recent sailing. As the pictures started to cycle, the strains of a Jimmy Buffet tune coming from the speakers.

"What's that?" Dad asked, looking around the patio.

"It's coming from the computer Dad. It's music to go with the pictures," Beth replied, finger hovering over the volume key. "I can turn it off."

"No, it does go with them," Mom said. "Just relax honey. It's nice."

A dozen or more photos had come and gone, Beth providing one-sentence descriptions when the scene changed, when Sammy's call from the far end of the yard interrupted the mood.

"Mom look! Mom!"

Trish sighed as she directed her gaze from the screen out into the bright yard. The others at the table did the same. Sammy was holding up his basket. He'd removed all the original goodies, which were piled on the patio lounge, and filled it with eggs that he'd found around the yard. Beth was relieved to see that they were the colored plastic kind, not real eggs that could have turned rotten by now.

"That's great Sammy. How many has Eli found?"

The little girl was with her father, half way around the pool from Sammy looking through the dormant vegetable garden next to the garage. She turned and held up her basket to show them that she had nearly as many as her brother. Beth suspected that Mike had a lot to do with that.

"Nice," she called out to Eli, who smiled proudly before dropping to her knees to feel around under the rosemary bush that Beth remembered planting during her gardening phase. To think that it was still there, quietly growing all these years, felt both reassuring and sad to Beth. She'd abandoned it here, and yet it kept on growing, living its own life.

"Where did they go?" Dad said, pulling Beth back to the laptop where the slideshow had ended.

"Sorry Dad. Let me show you some more." Beth navigated to photos from her trip south before Terry joined her in Miami, and started that show.

"It got colder all of a sudden," Mom observed.

"This was my first night out. It's late October, anchored at Sandy Hook New Jersey," Beth explained her sweater and jeans. "Feels like an eternity ago."

"It sort of is," Trish nodded, smiling at her sister.

The photo changed to Barnegat Bay and Beth told them how she'd been uncomfortable in the very shallow water there, but how now she was used to finding her way in water barely deeper than her boat. And then they were working their way past Atlantic City and Cape May and into her passage up the Delaware Bay. Beth knew that to non-sailors the sites along the Intracoastal Waterway looked much the same, so she'd been very judicious in her selection of photos, making sure that every one that she included was either really beautiful, or included a point of interest that a landlubber would recognize. So they leapt from the Cape May Canal to boats on the Delaware River to the St. George's Bridge over the Chesapeake and Delaware Canal to a distance shot of the Aberdeen Proving Ground, which looked like any other stretch of wooded coastline. And then there was the Chesapeake Bay Bridge followed by the shining white dome of the Maryland State House in Annapolis.

"This is it. Here's where you met Terry!" Trish declared.

"Yes, but I didn't take any pictures of him then," Beth replied as the image changed to a shot of *Trouble* at anchor. She'd taken it from the water taxi.

"Oh, but hey, look at that," she paused the show so that she could point at a dark-hulled boat in the background. "That's *Grace*. That's Terry's partner Jeff's racing boat. Terry and I met aboard her."

"Wow," Trish said, an empty utterance because the dark smudge of *Grace* was barely perceivable as a boat, and the image Beth had tried to conjure hadn't worked. Beth restarted the show.

It ended a few pictures later in Nag's Head, North Carolina. That's where Beth had hired Kenny to be her crew to Miami. So the short trip they'd just watched had been the extent of her solo sailing career, which had seemed to Beth to deserve its own slide show. Of course, she'd done a lot more solo sailing last month when she sailed from St. Thomas to Guadeloupe to find her friend Ori, but that was a story she didn't want to get into with her folks.

"Before we see more, let's get lunch organized," Mom said as Beth moved the mouse to the next slideshow. Beth glanced at the clock on the computer and was surprised to see that it was approaching one o'clock.

"Okay. What can we do to help?" Trish asked.

Trish and Beth took orders from Mom to bring place settings and more glasses of iced tea out from the kitchen. She carried out a large bowl of chicken salad with apples and cilantro, Dad trailing her carrying a package of potato rolls and a smaller bowl of buttered pasta that Mom said was for Eli the picky eater.

Shortly they were all seated at the table, the kids reluctantly leaving their Easter hauls over on the lounges. Mom asked Sammy to say grace, which he did in an artificially deep voice that made Beth smile.

The chicken salad was so good Beth insisted that her mother give her the recipe. She wondered aloud if she could substitute canned chicken and dry cilantro, which spurred a discussion of provisioning and cooking on a boat. She explained that sometimes fresh food was hard to find, so they kept a rather large supply of canned meats and vegetables and dried herbs. This surprised Trish, who had envisioned baskets of fresh greens and colorful tropical fruits always to hand. Beth assured her that yes, whenever they could they bought, or traded for, fresh produce from the locals, but sometimes the locals had none to spare.

That stopped Trish cold. Clearly the notion of poverty in paradise didn't fit in with her mental image.

"Well you don't see that on the commercials for Caribbean cruises," Mike observed pointedly. "Is the economy that bad all over the Caribbean?"

"No. A lot of the islands have developed their tourism, but that's a mixed blessing. The cruise ships bring in lots of money, but that attracts international vendors. The passengers don't necessarily do business with the locals. On so many islands I've seen huge cruise ship terminals with bars and jewelry stores, endless t-shirt shops, and pseudo local craft shops where most of the merchandise has "made in China" stamped on the bottom. But a couple streets over there are local grocers scraping by and farmer's wives selling homemade jewelry on the street. The passengers who step out of the bars are scooped up by the tour operators – at least they're usually locals – and loaded onto busses that take them on tours that stop at other touristy places on the island."

"Wow. Tell us what you really think," Mike chuckled.

"We were thinking of taking a cruise," Trish added ruefully.

Beth shook her head, embarrassed. "Just make a point of getting past the terminal to see the real island. And spend some money there," she said.

When the kids started bickering Beth noticed a silent exchange of glances between Trish and Mike and correctly interpreted it as "time to go." As Mike got up to intervene in the fight, Trish rose with a "well, we were up awfully early."

"Let me help," Beth added, jumping up as Trish reached for the bowl of chicken salad. They carried the lunch dishes into the kitchen.

"Put them in the sink. Let her deal with the dishwasher. She's been getting picky about how to load it," Trish said.

"And then she'll complain that we only did half the job."

"Yes. But if we load it, she'll complain that we did it wrong. Your choice."

"Fine."

THREE: DAD

The next morning Beth took command of Trish's minivan. Mike had moved the kids seats into the back of his Subaru Sunday evening so that he could take them on a secret adventure while Beth used the van.

She was disturbed to discover that her once honed California driving skills were extremely rusty. When she lived there, she'd been able to thread her little Toyota from lane to lane, gauging speeds and distances with tight accuracy to beat the average traffic speed, which, at rush hour, was that of a snail. Learning about sailboat racing on Long Island Sound she had recognized the similarity of her freeway technique to that of racing boats – but with an added dimension: sailboats don't have brakes. This makes them more predictable, and once she'd made this mental connection she'd never been frightened maneuvering a boat in close quarters. Back in a land-bound car with brake lights all around her she felt not fear but annoyance.

After dropping off her sister at work Beth felt a rush of freedom that she hadn't felt since the last time she hauled the anchor and set *Trouble*'s sails. All of a sudden she realized that since leaving her boat in Pointe-à-Pitre, Guadeloupe, she'd felt restrained by her familial duty. For the first time since leaving New York on her boat she had to set aside her own activities in favor of the needs of others. It was startling to realize that she had so thoroughly spoiled herself, but it was true. Every move she'd made since last fall had been entirely her choice. Sometimes none of the options were great, but even so the choice had been hers and she'd owned each one and the outcome. She'd come to feel that she deserved any success she had because she took responsibility for the missteps.

Meanwhile, Trish had been here making decisions based on their parents' needs, and her childrens' needs, and her husband's, not to mention dealing with the demands of her job and commitment to the church, the PTA, and other organizations.

By the time Beth got to the trailer rental shop to buy a supply of packing boxes she was working on converting her guilt into renewed determination. Tucking the receipt for forty dollars' worth of cardboard and packing tape into her wallet, she swallowed her alarm at the expense and got back in the van. Her goal today was to get started on what she had taken to calling "The Great Sort."

The previous afternoon Mom had showed her and Trish her efforts at making a "discards" pile. It was a stack of eight books and three coffee mugs on the floor in Trish's old bedroom. Trish and Beth had stood staring at it for longer than was appropriate, Beth finally realizing that her work was truly cut out for her.

Pulling the minivan into their driveway she was filled with trepidation. She was about to invade her parents' space and start going through their belongings. These were things that she had grown up with, that she respected, that were a fundamental part of who her parents were, and therefore who she was too.

Mom came to the door when she rang, shaking her head as she said, "Ringing the bell? You know you can just come in sweetie."

"Good morning Mom," Beth replied, deciding not to point out that the door had been locked – she'd heard the deadbolt when her Mom opened it.

"Can I get you coffee? I'm on my second cup. Dad's not allowed."

"I would love it. We can talk about how to get started."

"Oh, I've already started sweetie, you saw. I'm so glad you came to help."

Beth's trepidation grew as she sat at the kitchen table listening to Mom explain that every single pot and pan in the kitchen was essential. Dad was in the living room watching the ancient television which did, in fact, still work. Mike had, she'd learned last night, attached the necessary digital to analog converter required since all broadcasts were now digital. The picture wasn't bad for a thirty-year-old television, he'd declared. *More like forty years*, Beth had thought, but didn't say it.

The sound of gunfire and neighing horses filtered into the kitchen. Was the broadcast also forty years old?

"You know, when I moved aboard *Trouble* I brought my favorite pans because I had to have them. And then some of them wouldn't even fit in the oven or on the stove. And I was just cooking for myself most of the time, so I didn't need the big ones – I hadn't needed them in my apartment either, for that matter. Don't you think some of your pans are bigger than you need?"

"Oh but Bethy, I still have Trish and the family over. I cook a lot!"

"Okay. Fair enough. But maybe if we dig into the cabinets we'll find some older stuff that you haven't used in a long time."

Mom looked uncertain. "Maybe."

"Your new kitchen is going to be quite a bit smaller Mom. This is a chance for a fresh start. You might actually want to buy some new things, so you're going to need room."

Mom's face brightened at that notion. "I have always wanted matching copper pots hanging up."

Beth stopped herself from pointing out that copper pots had to be polished.

"Okay, then let's take another look at what you've got here."

Beth hadn't dared bring in the folded boxes right away, so she and Mom made more piles on the kitchen floor. Mom kept getting confused about which was the "keep" pile, and Beth had to check it continually and discretely move things to the other pile. After an hour they were through two of the cavernous bottom cabinets, but at least the "keep" pile was no larger than the "discard" pile. Beth knew that it was still too much stuff. She needed to get the discards out of the house before she even hinted that they needed to do another round.

By mid-day they had tackled all of the lower cabinets and stalled out on the everyday dish cabinet. It was stacked with place settings for eight of mom's colorful Fiesta ware dishes. Beth took out a dinner plate and turned it over.

"It's original, except for three pieces that I've had to replace. You know what it is, right?" Mom said.

Beth shrugged. "The dishes. We've had them forever."

"That's right. That's why they're valuable! Except for the replacements."

Beth peered at her mother, trying to decide what "valuable" meant. She had been about to suggest that they split the set in half and eliminate some of the more esoteric pieces. But something told her to do some research first. She took the plate to the table and set it face down, then took her camera from her bag and photographed the back. Mom watched her curiously.

"Let's see how valuable they are. So you know," Beth said.

"But I do know. I get the price list from the replacement people every few months."

"Oh," Beth was nonplussed. There was a replacement service? They must be valuable. "Listen, I'm going to get some boxes from the van. We'll pack up these discards to make some room in here, okay?" Beth consciously omitted any mention of taking the boxes to Goodwill. If she could get them out into the van she'd have won the day.

Coming back into the house with a half dozen collapsed boxes under her arm and the heavy-duty packing tape dispenser she'd invested in under the other she stopped in the living room at the sound of her father's raised voice.

"Who is she? Why is she making this mess?"

"Hush sweetheart, it's Beth. She's helping us."

"No no no no no! She's making a mess! She has to put this all away! How can you make dinner in this mess?"

Beth leaned the flat boxes against the side of the sofa and dropped the tape on the cushion where it bounced silently.

"Mom?" she called out gently, realizing as she approached the kitchen that she was actually afraid of her father, or at least afraid of the man in the kitchen arguing with her mother.

"In here Bethy. Everything is fine."

"Is it?" she asked tentatively, stopping just this side of the divide between the living room carpet and the kitchen's linoleum floor. Her father was standing between the "discard" and "keep" piles, faced off with her mother who stood near the kitchen sink. For the first time in Beth's life her father's height – especially contrasted with her mother's petite size – felt menacing.

She'd learned after moving across the country and meeting people from diverse backgrounds and places that the childhood that she'd thought was normal really wasn't at all. She and Trish had never suffered abuse, their parents had never even considered divorce, as far as she knew, and nobody had struggled with addiction. Her father had remained gainfully employed throughout his working life and her mother had raised their daughters and pursued charity work and hobbies.

Certainly there had been family disagreements, occasional loud arguments and slammed doors – especially when Trish and Beth were teenagers. But Beth had never felt afraid of the man of the house. He was a gentle spirit, a lover of plants and star gazing, a salesman by choice, but at home as sincere and genuine as a priest.

"Dad?" She said softly. "Let's talk about this? Can we?"

Her father pivoted to look at her. His anger-contorted features made her recoil, stepping further back into the living room. This wasn't her daddy.

"You!" he growled.

"Yes, me Dad. It's Beth. Your daughter." The words came automatically, an obvious response, but not the one she wanted to make.

Out of Dad's line of sight Mom waved her to come closer. Despite every instinct to stay away from the angry man who should be her father, Beth took two steps into the kitchen, eyes on his contorted face. With each step her heart broke a little bit more.

"Dad? I know I look a little different – it's the boat, and the sun. My hair is lighter, and I'm always tanned now. But it's me. Beth." She wanted to yell at him, tell him to snap out of it and be reasonable. To stop breaking her heart. It was nearly impossible to treat him this way, like some mad man who had to be pandered to. He was supposed to be her Dad, he was supposed to comfort her, to be rational through her tantrums.

"Beth? Where's the woman who made this mess? Did you see her?"

Beth's eyes darted to her mother, who shook her head, mouthing "no."

"I didn't Dad. She must have left. I'm going to help Mom clear it up right now. Do you want to help us?"

His expression softened and he reached for her with both hands.

"Dad," she whimpered, stepping to him. "It's me." And then she was shivering in his arms, his little girl seeking comfort from a freight. Except he was what was frightening, and she knew that he would do it again and again and he was never going to be her safe daddy again.

Beth was still shaken, her heart still aching with the loss that she had dreaded for months but only today begun to understand when she picked up Trish at work that afternoon. She didn't mention what she was thinking of as "the incident," but she wasn't surprised when Trish brought it up. Of course Mom had called Trish the moment Beth had left the house.

"I'd tell you that you get used to it," Trish said. "But I haven't yet, so I don't know. Everything I've read says it only gets worse."

"We have to get them moved. Mom needs help."

"Yes. Now you truly see."

A flash of resentment colored Beth's cheeks, but she kept her mouth shut in order to drive safely through rush hour traffic. It was heavier than she remembered it ever being when she lived here.

"And I'm here now to help." She yanked the wheel, swerving the van into the left line right in front of a faster-moving BMW. It's angry honk accompanied Trish.

"Beth! Watch out. Jesus!" and then, only calmer with a seething edge, "I know you're here to help. Finally."

"What the hell Trish, for month's it's been 'you stay there, we can handle this, we know you're thinking of us.'"

"What else was I going to say to you? I know you're broke. We all know that you're running away. You've been running away since you graduated from college. What would be the point of throwing more guilt on you? You've always been irresponsible. It's just you."

Beth's mouth hung open, ready to spit forth her indignation, hurt, and anger. But her brain couldn't form the words. So many words and fragments of thought swirled in incomprehensive patterns that she snapped her mouth shut again to prevent herself from simply wailing. Both hands gripped the steering wheel and she stared straight ahead, but her awareness was focused on her sister sitting next to her.

"You have to hear it, Beth. I've been playing along with Mom and Dad for too many years, but I'm over it. It's your turn to be a grownup and deal. Dad is going to die. But before that he's going to become a zombie. And before that he'll forget all of us. That's what we're facing. All of us, including you. But wait, I know, you're just going to run away again, aren't you? You do have a return ticket to your little boat, don't you?"

"Hell yes I have a return ticket, and I'm going to use it. This isn't fair, Trish. None of it is fair. Not Dad's illness, not our having to take over our parents' lives, and not you. Most of all not you."

"Oh yeah, that's our Beth. Always expecting life to be fair," Trish growled, head shaking.

Beth turned the van onto their street and focused on slowing down, watching for the kids and pets that abounded in the suburbia that she had run away from, according to her sister. They rode the last two blocks in hot silence. Beth turned into the driveway and all the way up to the closed garage door before stopping the van.

"I think I should go stay with them."

"Fine. Mike can drive you."

Shocked that Trish had called her bluff, Beth looked over at her sister in time to see her back as she got out of the van and slammed the door.

How is this going to work? Beth wondered, still sitting in the driver's seat. I need the van to move their things. I can't afford to rent something.

She was still sitting there, her cheeks wet with tears that she couldn't stop, when Mike came out the kitchen door and walked over to her window. He tapped on it. She touched the button to roll it down.

"Hey Beth. Trish said I should drive you back over to your folks. I think you should come in and talk it out."

Beth looked at him, disgusted with herself for how she knew she looked: eyes red and puffy, cheeks damp. He didn't seem to notice – but why would he? He was Trish's husband and had no business showing any interest in her sister.

"I was afraid something like this would happen," he went on. "I know she's been telling you everything's fine, she and your Mom are coping. Then she rants about you after she hangs up the phone," he said, and Beth wondered if the thought that helped somehow. "She's always done that, though."

Beth frowned at him. "Always?"

He nodded, then shrugged with a wry smile. "Big sister, little sister. You pursing your dreams at her expense, the usual crap. My sisters always fight, so I've never thought much of it. But this is important. You two have got to work this out for your parents' sake."

Beth hadn't gotten past the idea that Trish was jealous that she had moved away. It wasn't a new notion, but it shook her that Mike said it, that Trish had said it to him.

"She chose to stay here. She didn't have to," she said, offering him a confrontational stare, as if it was his fault. He didn't succumb to her tacit accusation.

"Of course she did, she never wanted to move away. But the fact that you did hurt her – you didn't realize that? You abandoned her and your parents. They weren't good enough for you."

"What? That's nuts."

"No, that's Trish. Have you met your sister? She's just a bit single-minded. Do I really have to tell you that she doesn't deal with contrary opinions?"

"No. You don't. I never thought my moving away for a job was abandonment, though. I was trying to take care of myself, earn a living without any support from Mom and Dad."

Mike put his hand on the door handle and stepped back to open it.

"Come on," he said. "You can be mad at her, but you've got to find a way to get along and get through this for your parents."

Beth swung her legs out to the ground and grabbed her backpack from the floor between the seats. Holding the button to raise the window, she felt trapped by circumstances and she hated it. She wanted to refuse, to be the stubborn little girl that Trish said she was. After all, what was the point of acting mature about this if Trish wouldn't change her opinion? Her subconscious – that was where it had to come from – flashed the memory of her mother's anxious face and she caved. That was the point. To help Mom. And Dad.

"I don't know what else to say to her," she said, yanking the keys out of the ignition. "I'm not going to apologize for my life choices. Especially since when I made them she told me they were good," she asserted as Mike shut the van door behind her.

"Did she really? Or did she tell you it was okay?" He asked.

Beth frowned, pressing the button on the key fob that locked the van as they walked to the kitchen door. *It isn't fair to accuse me now if she wasn't honest back then*, she thought. But she kept it to herself.

Inside, Trish was slamming the blade of a kitchen knife through a stalk of celery, dicing it to smithereens. Beth could hear the kids in the family room singing along with the television.

"I thought you were leaving," Trish said, eyes on her blade.

"That won't help us get through this, Sis. So let me have it. Let it all out."

The knife dropped to the cutting board next to the pile of celery and Trish half turned. Going for calm and in control, Beth walked over to the kitchen table and pulled out a chair. Eyes on her sister's, she sat down and waited.

"No. I promised," Trish said, turning to face the counter. Beth studied her back, contemplating what that meant.

"Promised who?" she asked. And then before Trish could answer, added "Mom wouldn't want us to have this between us. We can disagree, but we have to be able to work together." Beth silently thanked Mike for that advice, only then noticing that he'd managed to disappear. *Sure, and left me with the woman with the knife.*

"Did Mike tell you that?" Trish snapped, back still turned.

Touche. "It's the truth Trish," Beth evaded.

"Mike doesn't know everything."

"Nobody knows everything, Trish. And no two people always agree. So let's agree to disagree. But can we talk it out? I don't like being accused of running away."

"You deny it? Seriously?"

"Hell yes I deny it. I moved to New York for a job. Do you remember how many resumes I sent out around here? I was interviewing in Los Angeles, and I even went to San Diego for one interview and did a phone interview with a company in Santa Barbara. Then I tried New York and I got an offer after a telephone interview. Have you forgotten that? Oh, right, maybe you didn't notice what was going on with me then, since you were a newlywed and all." She instantly regretted her vaguely sarcastic tone.

Trish had turned around when Beth was half way through her diatribe. She shoved her hands into the pockets of the demure cotton apron that Beth only now noticed. It made Beth wonder if she would have enjoyed staying here, getting married, having a kitchen like this and a white cotton apron. But no chance she'd ever wear that knee-length muted plaid skirt.

"I struggled in New York. I fell in love. I broke up. I got laid off. And all along the way I relied on talking to you to help me through. Now you're telling me that the whole time you thought I was a flake, a runaway. You didn't mean any of the encouraging things you ever said to me. Thanks a lot Sis. Love you too."

"Beth, stop. That's not right. It's not true." Trish paced across the kitchen to the French door refrigerator and pulled one side open.

"Isn't it?"

"No! I meant everything I ever said to you when you lost your job over and over again –."

"Just twice! And the economy is in the toilet."

Trish opened the crisper drawer and took out a bag of salad greens, a cucumber, and a bunch of scallions. She shut the refrigerator and turned with the produce cradled in one arm.

"— and when you broke up with that guy," she went on as if Beth hadn't interrupted her. "It was just when you went nuts and moved onto the boat that I started questioning your decisions. You became so self-centered. It was all about Beth and her boat. I couldn't begin to imagine it, living on a thing floating on the water!"

"So that made it irresponsible?"

"It made it — weird. Other. You'd become something different."

"Yes. And you can't tolerate anyone whose different from you."

"But you're my sister. We come from the same roots. How could you change so much?"

"I haven't changed! At least, not the parts of me that matter!"

"I don't know what to think about you anymore."

"Why do you have to judge me? Because that's what you're doing. Mom doesn't do that. Neither did Dad." Beth heard her use of the past tense and flinched just as she saw Trish do the same. It was a tiny reaction that ran soul-deep. Dad didn't. Now he couldn't. He never would. She couldn't stop tears from running down her cheeks. Across the room, arms around her salad makings, Trish stared at her with accusing eyes.

"Stop it. You don't get to do that. You haven't lived it for the last six months."

"What?" Beth croaked, shocked.

Trish stalked across the kitchen to the stretch of counter where she'd been working and plopped the vegetables down next to the cutting board.

"When you've put in the time dealing with him, then you can start grieving over this."

"I have to earn the right to be upset about his Alzheimer's? Are you kidding me?" Beth stood up, finished trying to be reasonable when Trish wasn't making the slightest effort. When Trish didn't respond, Beth grabbed her bag and headed for the hall and the guest room. She wasn't sure what she was going to do: pack? Indulge in a crying jag?

She refrained from slamming the door, but shut it and stood in the room staring into space while she tried to make sense of her emotions and thoughts.

Trish's blame ran much deeper than she'd believed. Beth had been imposing guilt on herself for not being around to help, but had thought her collaboration over the phone and this trip made up for it. Clearly it didn't come close. Possibly nothing ever would, even if she were to stay here, sell *Trouble*, break up with Terry, and basically devote her life to helping their parents. Which, of course, was absurd. Sighing, she unzipped her bag and dug around in it as she moved to the bed and sat down. She didn't give any thought to the time back east when she speed dialed Terry on the cheap phone that she'd picked up that morning when she'd learned that she couldn't get a new battery for the old one.

"Hello beautiful."

Beth shut her eyes and basked in the warm embrace of his voice. "Hi," was all she could manage to squeak out.

"What's wrong?"

She smiled. He knew her well enough to pick up on her distress from one syllable.

"You know how guilty I've felt about not being here for them?"

"Yes. But Beth –."

"No matter how guilty I made myself, Trish blames me a hundred times more."

"Come on, it can't –."

"Yes, it can."

"Why don't you tell me what happened? Why has it all hit just now?"

Beth mentally rewound the hours since they'd last talked. Then she described her father's sudden memory lapse and how much it had upset her. He made soft sounds of commiseration, but didn't interrupt. Then she described the drive home with Trish and the fight in the kitchen. So that he'd know she wasn't being a raging bitch, she made sure to add that Mike had been a rational influence, but didn't mention that he'd disappeared once his wife and sister-in-law were together in the kitchen. Even as she reconsidered it she realized that Mike had no choice. He couldn't afford not to side with his wife, but he clearly knew she wasn't being reasonable.

"So are you going to your parents' house?" Terry asked when she had described everything up to her pulling out her phone.

"What? Oh. I don't know. No. That was an impulse to get away from Trish. But think about it – how would Dad react to someone suddenly

37

living there who he doesn't know half the time?"

"It might help, being there all time. Does he recognize your Mom consistently?"

"I guess so. Wait, no. Sometimes not."

"Oh. Well, maybe you're right then."

"It's interesting that your first response wasn't 'you have to make up with your sister.'"

When he didn't respond a wave of apprehension washed over Beth. *Too personal. He doesn't talk much about his sister. Now he's going to dump me.*

"You've got a point there." When he finally broke the tense silence on the line his voice was thinner, strained. "But can we put off dissecting my interpersonal relationships until we're together?"

"I don't know. I kinda think we're in the middle of a very interpersonal relationship. Should I be worried?"

Great. First Trish, now Terry. Who else can you ostracize today?

"Beth, our relationship is nothing like any other one I have, or have had. I certainly don't think of you like I do my sister."

Something about his tone reassured her. He wasn't angry, if anything there was a touch of amusement, a hint of something just slightly improprietous. She couldn't repress a smile.

"Well that's reassuring. Yes, let's put that aside. Let's assume you think I should make things right with Trish."

"I do think that. I didn't mean to say –." He stopped for a second, then started over. "I was trying to be supportive of your decision to get out of her house. That doesn't mean I think it's best."

"Okay. So how do I get through to her? She just told me that I have no right to grieve over the loss of our father because I haven't been here to experience his slow decline. She's not being fair."

"Because she's still grieving herself. She's in the denial phase, or accusation, if that's one of the phases, I don't know. She's certainly not ready for acceptance. Neither of you are."

"Okay. So what do I do?"

She heard an exhale, one of his little nasal sighs that were a sign of frustration. Why was he frustrated? She was the one with the rabid sister.

"Does she know how much research you've done over the last few months?"

"I doubt she realizes. And she'll just say it's less than she's done, on top of helping them in person."

"Right." His tone was agreement with her assessment, which made her feel a little better. "What can you do with what you've learned that's different from, but as useful as, what she's done?"

"I'm doing their move. That's what I can do, and it's a lot."

"I know, I know. But that sort of balances out her finding the facility and taking them to the doctor and all that. You need to make use of the knowledge you've gained in a way that helps all of you, even though you just gained it for your own understanding. Maybe talk with the doctors at the new place? Maybe there are programs for families."

"That I won't be here to participate in," Beth pointed out, then quickly added, "But I get your point. In our phone calls over the months I often found information on line before she did and sent her links. I just don't know how I can make her see that as my contribution."

Through the closed door Beth heard Trish call the children and Mike to supper. She was noticeably omitted. A knock on her door startled her up off the bed.

"Hang on Terry," she said, lowering the phone from her ear as she crossed the room to open the door. Mike stood there.

"Dinner's ready," he said with a smile.

"I don't think I'm invited."

"Don't be ridiculous. I say you are. Come on."

"Hey Beth?" Beth and Mike both heard Terry's faint voice coming through the phone's speaker. She put the phone to her ear, eyes still locked with Mike's.

"Yeah."

"Go have dinner. Tell Mike he's right."

Phone still to her cheek, Beth said to Mike, "Terry say's you're right. Okay. You guys win. But it's going to be uncomfortable."

"Love you. Talk to you later. Call, even if it's late."

"Bye."

Beth was surprised to see a place for her at the table, and she wondered if the kids had set it automatically. She suspected so as her sister managed to get them seated and food on their plates without speaking to or even acknowledging Beth.

Beth served herself a piece of baked chicken from the platter in the middle of the table and took the salad bowl from Mike after he had placed small portions on each of the kid's plates and a larger portion on his own. Trish asked him to hand her the bowl of corn, clearly heated in the microwave after being dumped from a can. Realizing that nothing on the table included celery her sister had chopped, Beth frowned.

"What's wrong?" Trish asked. Beth's head jerked up to look across the table at her sister.

"Nothing's wrong. I just – I wondered what the celery was for," Beth blurted the last part, unable to be anything but honest.

"Oh." Trish's eyes dropped to her plate with what looked like contrition. Beth was amazed. "No, I – I decided not to use it."

"Good," Mike said with forced cheerfulness, "I hate celery in my food. So does Eli."

"That's right!" Eli declared, oblivious to the tension and eager to participate in a grown-up conversation.

"You don't even taste it," Trish muttered, stabbing some lettuce with her fork.

"I do," Eli insisted. "It's icky."

"I know, right?" Mike added with a smile at his daughter. "So we're glad you changed your mind Honey."

Trish's gaze rose to meet her husband's. Beth wondered what silent communication passed between them, because Trish turned her head to look at her sister.

"After dinner, I have some newsletters I'd like to show you. I don't think they have on-line versions of them."

"Okay. Great," Beth replied, meaning it. Anything was better than the silent treatment: even going back to mutually suppressing their fundamental differences.

Beth was deeply grateful to Mike after that for keeping up normal conversation at the table. He encouraged the children to tell Trish about the fun they'd had that day with him. Their inventory of outings – the park with the miniature train that they got to ride three times, the mall where both children got new shoes, a matinee where they shared popcorn, and back to the local park for some post-movie jungle-gym activity – sounded exhausting and made Beth feel guilty for being tired after her seemingly slow day of sorting stuff. She looked at both Mike and Trish with renewed respect. Their kids were a lot more work than she remembered being.

Trish never managed to address Beth directly through dinner and that was okay with Beth. They were both too close to erupting all over again to risk it in front of the kids.

Everyone helped clear the table, and then Mike ushered the children into the family room for a round of some childish game Beth had never heard of. Trish disappeared down the hall, but returned in a few minutes with a thick file folder. She set it on the table and went to the refrigerator from which she removed a bottle of white wine, the cork pushed part way in.

"Yes?" she asked, holding it up.

"Yes," Beth replied.

As Trish got stemware from a high cabinet and poured, she explained the contents of the folder that Beth had pulled closer and opened.

"It's a support group. Those are issues of the local chapter's newsletter. They mail it out. They don't have anyone who knows how to put it on line, or at least is willing. But they do send it to a larger organization and some of their articles are published in that group's newsletter. I think you sent me a link to them. That's how I tracked down the local group."

"Right, I know the national group's website. I look at it all the time." She stopped herself, realizing that her definition of "all the time" was a lot less frequently than Trish's. "When I'm in an internet café," she added, immediately regretting it. She scrambled to change the subject. "Their articles about coping are very interesting. They have some very realistic suggestions."

"Yes they do." Trish set the wine glasses on the table and sat down. "And it's because they're coming from real people. Not just the local group here, but all over the country. That's where the national group gets their stories."

"Right. I remember reading this on-line," Beth indicated the lead story on one of the printed newsletters in the folder. "I noticed it because it was about a husband in Southern California coping with his wife's dementia."

Trish was sipping her wine and watching Beth expectantly. Beth sipped from her glass and looked at another issue of the newsletter in order to avoid that look. Clearly Trish expected something, but Beth couldn't figure out what.

"What do you do well, Beth?" her sister finally asked.

Beth looked up, frowned slightly, then said, "Sail."

Trish shut her eyes, shook her head, and emitted a throaty "harumpf."

"What else do you do well. That you get paid for?"

"Oh. Well, writing marketing copy."

"Writing."

"Oh."

"I can barely write an email. But you're a good writer Beth. I know you didn't lose those jobs because you can't write."

Beth sucked in a deep breath followed by a gulp of wine to keep her temper in check. Trish couldn't help it. She really couldn't.

"You want me to write something for them."

"I want you to write something for us, Beth."

FOUR: ORANGE GROVE WELLNESS

Beth stood in her old bedroom, which was stripped of everything that had made it hers other than that dark spot on the wall above where she used to burn a candle on her dresser. Soon that would be gone too, when the painters came next week. Her furniture had gone to a consignment shop along with much of the rest in the house. Gone, gone, gone.

She wondered if she'd regret not taking some things. But who was she kidding? She couldn't afford a storage unit. Trish had taken the three pieces of any value: a cedar chest, a delicate tip-top candle stand that had been passed down from their maternal grandparents, and a lone ladder back chair that had once been part of a set belonging to their father's grandparents. Beth had packed up the mantle clock that chimed ships bells when someone remembered to wind it. She was determined to make a spot for it aboard *Trouble*, although she suspected the swaying of the boat would affect its ability to keep time. The other good antique, their father's beautiful carved rocking chair from his mother's family, was going to the apartment along with enough of the rest of the furniture to make it comfortable, but not cluttered.

She moved on to Trish's room, also bare except for the vinyl flowers stuck to the ceiling. The painters were charging an extra fifty dollars to get them off. Their shared bathroom was clean, the medicine cabinet empty of old shampoo and dental floss for the first time in her memory.

Back in the kitchen, scene of the most difficult fights these last three weeks, the cabinets were all empty. The refrigerator, too. Trish had taken care of moving its contents to the new place last night. Beth walked over and pushed the junk drawer shut. The goodies they'd unearthed from there had made for an amusing hour a couple weeks ago, and Beth had tossed a bottle opener that felt like an old friend into her box to be shipped to *Trouble*.

She walked through the living room, double checking that the furniture to move was properly labeled, and went into her parents' bedroom. Trish had gotten them up and out this morning, leaving Beth to strip the bed and pack the sheets and duvet into a waiting box. Their clothes were in three wardrobe boxes lined up against the closet doors. Beth made a mental note to check in the closet after the movers took the boxes out of the way, just to be sure they hadn't missed anything.

The special seat with handles over the toilet in their bathroom was still in place. Beth lifted it out of the tiny room and checked that it had been tagged to move. Then she noticed the toothpaste and brush on the counter, which inspired her to check the medicine cabinet and gather up her mother's face cream and a tube of hemorrhoid medication. She dropped them into the box with the sheets.

That was it. Her childhood and much of her parent's life together packed up and ready to go. She still had thirty minutes before the movers were due. She passed back through the kitchen and out the back door to tour the yard. She would miss knowing that the swimming pool was here for her, even though she lived now right on top of the ocean that, throughout her childhood and youth, she'd imagined this pool to be. The pool toys had gone to Goodwill, and thinking about it made her realize that Sammy and Eli would probably miss the pool the most. Trish and Mike might just have to give in and have one put in.

She stood for a while looking at her father's garden. They'd uprooted and potted some of the plants that could stand it, like Beth's old rosemary. Mom and Dad's new apartment had a small patio adjacent to the facility's larger common garden. But the fruit trees would be left to the care of the real estate firm engaged to sell the house. She tried not to think about how that felt like abandonment, and decided to finish her tour with the garage.

This had been the hardest. She'd found her father's workbench mostly neglected since the illness had started. He couldn't be allowed to tinker with hand tools unsupervised, and Mom drew the line at sitting in the garage watching him. Mike had come and taken everything he wanted, and Beth had put a few familiar tools, like her dad's old pliers, in her box. She'd sold more than she'd expected in her two garage sales.

Everything else, from old hubcaps to a trio of broken lamps that had never been rewired, would be picked up by a salvage service later today.

She examined the remains of the garage, knowing that she'd searched every nook and cranny but still harboring a concern that there was something valuable tucked away somewhere in the rafters. On impulse, she lowered the garage door and checked once again for anything tucked up there above it. Just a black widow's nest and lots of dust. The rumble of a truck outside interrupted her search. She opened the garage door to see the moving van adjusting position in front of the house.

This is it. Time to move.

It took the three-man crew an hour and a half to load the furniture and boxes that were going to the apartment. Beth stood watch at the front door, checking each item that went out for the right tag. The last thing she wanted was to have to bring things back later. When the lead mover announced that they were done she walked with him through the house to check. They found one more box marked to be moved on the stack in the kitchen. He picked it up without comment and carried it as they visited the rest of the rooms.

"See you there," Beth assured him as he carried the box to the truck and she turned to lock the front door. It wasn't the last time she'd come here – there were still the salvagers to let in later – but the gesture had a feeling of finality that forced her to stop, hand on the knob, and catch her breath. Once more the rumble of the truck returned her to action, and as she walked to the driveway and Trish's van she wondered if she would forever associate the sound of a truck's engine with the act of opening or closing a door.

Thirty minutes later she drove up to the gatehouse at Orange Grove Wellness and was waved through by Teddy, the guard on duty. A retired police officer, he looked like many of the residents, which made Beth wonder about the point of such a guard. Sure, he could try to turn away solicitors and other unwanted visitors, but if they really wanted in he couldn't stop them. On the other hand, he was certainly up to stopping any of the residents who tried to get out. Maybe that was his real purpose.

Beth parked the van in the visitor lot and carried a shallow box containing three potted plants with her in to reception. Trish and Mom had selected an apartment with monitored entrance, or more to the point, monitored exit. Dad would have to get past the receptionist and several other staff, or set off an alarmed exit, should he try to wander off.

"Good morning Miss Anderson," Liz, the receptionist said as Beth entered. "Your parents and sister got here a few minutes ago."

"Thanks. How about the movers?"

Liz shook her head with a knowing smile. Beth sighed. No matter how hard she'd tried to plan this day to go off like clockwork, something was bound to gum up the works.

"You'll send them in as soon as they get here, won't you?"

"We have them on our schedule for today honey, don't worry. But I've never seen a moving company keep to a schedule. You can all go get lunch in the cafeteria. I can call there if they arrive."

"Thanks. I'll let you know if we do."

Beth headed down the corridor that led to her parents' new home.

It was pleasant enough in a California casual sort of a way. The walls were light peach, the floors some commercial product that looked like hardwood. There were ivory baseboards and chair rails. Above it there were framed pictures of old California: orange groves and carts full of orange crates being pulled by weary looking horses, ladies in elaborate swim costumes sitting on the beach, a row of palm trees in front of the setting sun.

Shifting the box of plants onto her left forearm Beth knocked with her right hand on the door of her parents' apartment. It swung open a moment later.

"Knocking again Beth!" her mother teased. "Come in, we're here waiting."

"Let me take that," Trish reached out to take the awkward box in both hands.

"How's Daddy?" Beth asked. Trish and Mom's exchanged look was a partial answer.

"He's confused," Mom finally said. "Seeing his things arrive will probably help.

"I hope so," Trish added from across the pastel living room. The walls were almost the same color as the corridor outside, with the same ivory baseboards. There was a gas fireplace faced in white painted brick with a marble tiled hearth. The carpet was very light taupe and extended down the hall toward the bathroom and bedroom. It ended at the open entrance to the kitchen where another hardwood floor began.

Trish had carried the box to a sliding glass door that stood open. Beth could see Dad standing out on the brick patio looking further out beyond the low fence into the larger garden beyond.

"Look dad, here are some of your favorites," Trish said.

"He has no idea this is permanent," Mom told Beth. "You know how many times we've told him." She shrugged, raising her hands as well.

"I know. I think you're right, once you're settled he'll be okay."

"I didn't exactly say that," Mom replied with a chuckle that felt wrong until Beth looked curiously at her face. Acceptance, and, to Beth's surprise, real amusement. She realized that her Mom must be relieved to be here, where there were other people — trained people — to help her. That look, and that chuckle, went a long way toward easing Beth's fear about how her parents would do here and guilt for not being around more to help.

"He'll do better," she corrected herself, returning her Mom's smile. "Liz suggested that we go to the cafeteria for some lunch. She said she'd call there when the movers arrive."

"I wouldn't want to get there and have to rush back out —."

"You wouldn't. I'll come take care of them. You guys could come when you finish."

"But you would have to leave your lunch —."

"That's okay, I don't mind. I think it might be better for Daddy not to be here as they're bringing everything in.

Mom nodded. "Sam," she said, walking across the living room toward the open door. "It's time for some lunch. Trish, we're going to the cafeteria."

"Oh. Okay," Trish replied, making eye contact with Mom for a moment. Beth couldn't see what passed between them, but imagined it was a silent agreement about Dad. Trish wrapped her hands around her father's upper arm. "Dad? I'm hungry, aren't you?"

"Yes," he replied, smiling at her.

"We're going to try lunch in your new cafeteria, okay?"

"My cafeteria?"

"Yes, you can go there whenever you're hungry. Isn't that cool?" Trish was guiding him back into the living room.

"I guess so, but I — Beth! Where did you come from?" Trish let go of his arm as he hurried over to his younger daughter. "It's been ages. It's so good to see you." He engulfed Beth in a hug. She relaxed, enjoying it, and squelching her distress at his lost short term memory.

"Hi Dad. I'm glad to see you too. Come on, we're going to lunch."

She paired up with him following Trish and Mom out the door and down the hall toward reception. Beth sent a wave at Liz, who nodded, holding her hand up to the side of the face to indicate that she would call.

The cafeteria was not as horribly institutional as Beth had feared. There was a wide range of choices organized in separate stations where cooks prepared hot and cold dishes. In between were refrigerated cases and racks of packaged foods and pre-made salads and sandwiches. A soft-serve ice cream machine near the exit was stocked with sugar-free, fat-free, and full-of-everything choices. Carrying a tray with a chicken Caesar salad, a sourdough roll, and a diet Coke, Beth approached the cashier. As she set her tray down and stuck her hand in her pocket to find her wallet she noticed that nobody else was using cash. The elderly residents presented cards that the cashier swiped through a reader.

Beth turned to Trish behind her, "How do we pay?"

"How —? Oh, Mom has the card."

"Mom shouldn't pay for us."

"It's just lunch on their first day. It won't break their budget. Move up. I'll get the card from Mom."

Reluctant, but resigned after a long morning, Beth moved up to the cashier and looked back along the line.

"Here, this is for all four," Trish extended the brightly printed card over Beth's tray to the cashier, who took it without comment.

They found a table for four near the windows that looked out on a bright green lawn. Off in the distance a four-story building was the full-time care facility for residents who could not get along in an apartment. Elsewhere on the property there were townhouses with separate entrances for "active seniors" who didn't need anyone looking in on them or monitoring their egress. The contract Trish had negotiated planned for their parents to transfer to the building across the lawn when the time came. The idea of living so close to the next step had given Beth the shivers when Trish had described it. But being here with her ailing father and struggling mother she understood that it reassured Mom. For Mom the next steps were no longer a frightening unknown. And that was all that really mattered, not what Beth thought, or even what Trish thought. Beth found new respect for her sister's mature decisions.

Beth had crunched through half of her salad when the cashier sent a spry female resident over to their table to relay a message that Liz had called.

"I'll go meet them," Beth said, dropping half of her roll on top of her salad and putting the lid back on the plastic bowl. "Don't rush. I think it's best to let them get a lot in."

"Well, I for one want some of that ice cream I saw inside. How about you Dad?" Trish asked helpfully, giving Beth her chance to escape carrying her leftovers.

The rest of the afternoon went by in a whirl. The movers had all of the furniture and half of the boxes in before the rest of the family came strolling back. Trish handed Beth an ice cream cone, which she immediately started to lick even though she hadn't found time to finish her salad.

"Lots of activity here," Dad observed as he and Mom came in to the apartment followed closely by a mover carrying a box marked "kitchen." "What's going on?"

"They're bringing all of your things Dad. You'll be comfortable by tonight."

"Oh, my albums!," he said as if he Beth hadn't spoken. Off he went to the cabinet below the wall-mounted flat screen television. His albums were visible in the open box on top. Beth had opened it for exactly this purpose.

"They're all moved in – not all unpacked, but completely moved." Beth told Terry that evening. "The salvage guys took away everything else. I was so glad to get out of the house after that."

"Eerie feeling?" Terry asked.

"Very eerie. It didn't feel like home anymore, with everything gone. That's sort of a good thing, I suppose. I don't harbor any notion that I can go home again."

"You've never struck me as the homesick type."

That made her smile. Her days here in her home town had definitely confirmed that for her. She'd driven out of here five years ago and never looked back, at least not with the longing of homesickness. Maybe she'd been cut out for the vagabond life of a sailor all along, and just hadn't realized it until last summer.

"Well, I don't have a huge bunch of friends here. That's something I realized when I got here. I saw a couple over the last few weeks, but there's no 'old gang' pulling me back."

"It seemed to me that you were too busy dealing with your parents place to do much socializing anyway."

"That's for sure. I think Trish had no idea how much work there was left to do. She had all these plans. We did go to Disneyland one day, but there was no way to fit in the rest of it. I'm glad. Disneyland was hard enough with Mom and Dad."

"I can imagine."

"And I certainly didn't need to go to the beach, I mean really."

"Really!" he laughed. "Your life's a beach."

"And then you die…" Beth added.

"I really miss you." Terry said after a chuckle.

"Me too. I'm arriving on Guadeloupe day after tomorrow. Any change to your plans?" she asked this with bated breath, fearful that he'd say yes, that he would be delayed.

"No ma'am. I'll see you on Guadeloupe in a week."

FIVE: TOBAGO CAYS

"Hello Missus."

Beth's eyes popped open at the startlingly nearby voice, belatedly reaching for the towel she'd left beside her on the deck. Her hand fell on bare fiberglass.

"Over here," the voice came again. Beth sat up reluctantly, looking for the source of the voice, and the towel, her arms instinctively crossing in front of her bare chest. The voice was coming from somewhere aft.

"Be right there," she called out, wishing she could avoid drawing attention to herself, although she knew that he knew where she was and that she was sunbathing topless, he'd obviously seen her before calling out to her. At least he'd brought his small boat around to *Trouble*'s stern rather than right alongside where she was stretched out on the bow.

He was Ricky, the local fisherman with whom she and Terry had been doing business for the last four days. This morning she had ordered lobster, fresh caught and barbequed. He was probably here to deliver it.

She spotted her towel half hanging over the toe rail, saved from a watery grave by virtue of snagging on the cotter ring in a turnbuckle of the forward shroud – a ring she'd been meaning to tape before it snagged and ripped the sail. Shaking out the towel and wrapping it around herself, she thanked her own procrastination for preventing her from having to put on a show – more of a show – for Ricky.

He barely cracked a smile as she accepted the warm paper sack in exchange for a handful of rumpled Eastern Caribbean dollars. His eyes seemed to bore right through the faded terrycloth as he asked if there was anything else he could get her today. She said no, knowing he'd be by in the morning to ask again. She adjusted her towel as he pushed off and started his outboard engine. His look had no meaning – he always appeared to be on the point of rage – but it was jarring nonetheless. When he was several boat lengths away she turned toward the companionway and dropped the towel, picking up the heavy sack to take it below.

It was one huge lobster, split lengthwise on the underside from head to tail. The shell was charred in places from the fire, the ends of the small legs scorched black. Rich white meat curled out from the nooks and crannies. Beth sighed sadly at the sight of bright orange roe inside the body cavity. It was a tasty treat, but she hated taking a breeding female from the sea. She had tried to instruct Ricky on this point, but as with so many Caribbean fishermen his grasp of environmental concerns was heavily influenced by his ability to support his family. Taking the creatures of the sea was his birthright, and although he complained that there were fewer fish, he did not connect his own activities with the loss.

The lobster smelled wonderful. Beth re-wrapped it in aluminum foil and opened the oven, thinking to store it there. But it was too big, so she put it back into the brown paper sack and set it out in the cockpit.

At thirty-six feet long *Double Trouble* was a comfortable size for two people to share, but her accommodations could not be called spacious. The galley comprised a U-shaped counter to the right of the companionway steps with a small sink set into it and the stove mounted into the short side of the U. A hatch in the counter top opened to reveal the top-loaded refrigerator, and cabinets with sliding doors above the counter contained food and dishes. There were drawers for cooking and eating utensils, and a cabinet under the sink for pots and pans. A small net hammock suspended from a support pole to a handhold contained produce that did not need refrigeration, currently two mangos, three onions, a pair of spotty bananas, a lemon and two limes, and a forlorn looking kiwi.

Beth took down a mango and an onion and set to work peeling and chopping, improvising mango salsa to go with the lobster. Her largest pot – four quarts – was already sitting on the stove half full of water and two ears of corn waited on the counter. She had boiled potatoes first thing in the morning with the idea of making potato salad, but the mayonnaise had smelled funny so she'd left them in the refrigerator until inspiration struck. It was an elaborate meal, but it would probably be their last in this particular slice of paradise: they were planning to sail to the nearest town tomorrow for fresh water and supplies, and from there they would head *Trouble* north toward St. Vincent. Ricky could provide most supplies – for a fee – but refilling *Trouble*'s water and fuel tanks meant visiting a marina.

Rubbing at her teary eye with her forearm Beth scraped the chopped onion and mango from the battered wooden cutting board into a plastic bowl, then rinsed her hands and the knife and slid open a cabinet to find salt, pepper, and olive oil. She dressed the mix and lifted the lid of the refrigerator, nestling the uncovered bowl in among the plastic wrapped items inside. Glancing at the clock on the shelf she decided it was too early to cook the corn. Her laptop sat open on the saloon table, the screensaver's tropical fish cruising endlessly back and forth past coral and anemones. It was plugged in to a twelve-volt outlet, the cord strung across the saloon to the electrical control panel on the navigation desk. Beth stepped over to the desk and leaned close to the panel to look at the gauges that reported on the boat's battery power. She could not suppress a smile: the solar charger that she had installed months ago continued to keep them charged under normal load, which meant she did not have to run the engine to do so.

The boat rocked gently on a small wave and the attached mouse rolled a few inches. The laptop blinked to life, seascape replaced by the stark whiteness of an open word processing document, a few lines of text at the top. Beth stared guiltily at it for half a minute, then sighed and sat down on the settee across from the table.

She took the laptop into her lap, then put it back on the table and reached for a t-shirt that was draped on the back of the settee and pulled it on over her bare bosom. Taking the laptop back she crossed her legs and wiggled her bottom into the thin cushions. The settee was just wide enough for her to sit that way.

She had stayed on board today for the express purpose of working on the article that was open in front of her. And then instead she'd gone for a swim, ordered dinner, read – for inspiration – and stretched out on the bow topless for a restorative nap. Terry would be back in another hour at the latest and she had written a total of two sentences.

She knew what the problem was, why she had allowed herself to procrastinate most of the day. She had long ago developed the self-discipline to sit down and write cleverly about things that did not interest her all that much, and about things that she did not know all that well. It was as skill that had kept her employed in marketing for several years, until she'd jumped ship from corporate New York and landed aboard her own little ship and the wonderful world of un-, or at best under-employment. But this project was different from the enthusiastic descriptions of books and financial products and services that she had specialized in. This was deeply personal, bordering on painful, and she would do almost anything to avoid having to organize her thoughts and feelings into cogent sentences.

She typed a few random letters, hoping that her fingers would take off on their own. *This is all Trish's fault.* She stared at the sentence, then pressed the backspace key and watched the blinking cursor consume the letters one by one. Blaming her sister was wrong on every level and she felt even more guilty for having put the thought into writing, no matter how ephemeral. What was happening in their family was nobody's fault, it was just the course that life took. And although this writing project had been her sister's idea, she had agreed to it for altruistic reasons: she would do anything to help others cope with the horrible disease that her father and their family were battling. And one thing she could do was write.

Writing about their experience was a small way – insufficient, really – to make amends for her physical absence. Trish had even presented it that way – "since you're going to run back to paradise, how about if you contribute to the support group?" Beth had come to realize through the later part of her stay in California that although Trish expressed it that way, her feelings were not as bitter as they sounded. No, most of Beth's guilt was self-imposed, and writing this article was self-imposed penance for her chosen lifestyle.

Frustrated, she opened the photo application and brought up an album of family photos. That was something she'd been able to do, too – while closing up their parent's house she'd shipped the boxes of pictures and albums to a service that had scanned everything, put them on compact discs, and shipped them back. Trish had willingly paid for the service. Now it was Beth's job to work her way through renaming the images and adding notes. Someday Trish's kids might want to see their mother, aunt, and grandparents. Someday maybe Beth would have kids who'd want to as well.

She scrolled through the old photos, pausing on images of her parents as a young couple, then moving through the years to the father she knew, the man she always pictured, frozen forever at a time when she was ten or twelve. As happened all too often her throat closed and she swallowed hard, shutting her eyes against the tears that welled up.

She was still reeling from the month spent clearing out her parents' house. It had felt like an invasion of their privacy. Hard as she'd tried to get her mother to reduce their wardrobe to apartment size, she had finally had to barge into their bedroom and do it herself. Everything about it had felt off-limits, and the very necessity of it had made Beth's heart ache.

Until the ugly fight she'd had with Trish, it had seemed like nothing about the bizarre role reversal fazed her older sister. When the acrimonious feelings had cleared, Beth found herself feeling relieved to know that Trish was as upset as she was by it all, and had simply had more time to develop the matter-of-fact mindset. Because she'd promised Trish, Beth was sticking with her commitment to write their story for the Alzheimer's support group newsletter. She was struggling to emulate their stirring stories of support and triumph over pain. The pain part was coming out easily. The triumph part was impossible because she hadn't felt it yet. But Trish continued to assure her that seeing their story in print would mean a lot, particularly for their mother.

Beth had wanted to do it. She'd contacted the newsletter and received encouragement along with some guidelines for submission. The editor had stipulated more than once that they had no budget for writers, which had not surprised Beth. She'd started making notes in between the other tasks of parental relocation and care. This was physically tiring and emotionally draining, and in the evenings Beth had found it comforting to focus on her notes.

But then her visit had ended. She'd left the house ready for repainting and whatever else the real estate agent dictated. Trish would take over from there. Beth had paid a final, tearful visit to her parents in their new apartment and found herself clinging to her mother as she never had before. Her father had been warm and lucid, holding her hand, his eyes communicating volumes as he failed to blink back tears that ran down his sunken cheeks.

Trish had taken her to the airport assuring her that everything would be okay, and thanking her for all she'd done even as Beth was thinking that she'd done nothing, that she was leaving the burden of everything on her sister. Again.

And then she'd landed in Point-à-Pitre, taxied to the marina, and walked down the dock toward her sailboat. At the sight of the neatly coiled lines and canvas covered sails her confusing, painful, backwards world had all fallen back into order.

She'd enjoyed scrubbing the decks and cleaning out the refrigerator, changing the diesel engine's oil, and washing every piece of fabric she could remove from the cushions, berths, galley, and her clothes lockers. The box she'd shipped herself full of goodies from Trader Joes and the few items from her parents' house arrived and she spent a half a day trying to stow it all. How amazing that what had seemed like a small box in California had turned into an enormous crate that took up the entire dining table. She found a place for the beautiful mantel clock on the shelf on the starboard side. It's soft ticking and tinkling chime was remarkably comforting that first night.

A few days later she took a taxi back to the airport and watched through the security glass as Terry climbed down the boarding steps and crossed the tarmac to the terminal.

Together they'd returned to *Double Trouble*, provisioned, and set sail for islands to the south. Terry had pushed to get to this anchorage in the Tobago Cays where the daily fee to use the moorings had made Beth wince and where the local fishermen insisted on providing supplies to the visiting boats and charged close to New York prices. But she'd watched Terry pay the fees and the fishermen without giving voice to the feeling of inadequacy it caused. There was no getting around the differences in their fortunes: he had just sold a business. She was an unemployed marketing copy writer.

No. Right now I'm an unpaid freelance writer.

She clicked from the photo program back to the word processor and held her fingers poised over the keys. Eyes shut she started to type – real words, not statements of guilt or grief. The real story of two sisters and their magnificent, loving, fatally ill father.

SIX: TREASURE!

"Hey Beth, come see this," Terry's voice came an instant after a thump on the hull signaled his return.

"Yeah Beth, you really missed it!" a younger voice put in. "Come see!"

Beth saved her file – six full pages – and unfolded her legs, grabbing a railing as her knees complained at having been folded for so long.

"Coming," she called out.

Terry was sitting on the combing facing outboard, his dive bag dripping on the cockpit seat behind him. He glanced over his shoulder at her, blue eyes flashing with excited amusement beneath windblown brown curls. Beth knelt on the cockpit seat and leaned in beside him, looking over the edge of the boat and down into the inflatable dinghy that was floating alongside.

"What *is* that?"

"It's a treasure chest!" Michael, the possessor of the younger voice, replied. "Seriously!"

Beth looked to Aiden, Michael's older brother, who was sitting in the rear of the dinghy beside the idling motor. He shrugged, smiling noncommittally.

"It's an old footlocker," Terry explained. "We found it half buried over on the other side of Petit Rameau.

"Underwater?" Beth could see the footlocker now, camouflaged in weeds, barnacles, and other attached sea growth. She felt sorry for the unfortunate creatures who'd been dragged out of the water with it.

"Yeah, right where we anchored the dinghy!" Michael said.

"So what's in it?"

"We haven't opened it yet."

"It's locked," Terry added, drawing Beth's eyes to his. She smiled, suddenly aware of the closeness of his damp body, rubber wetsuit pulled down to his waist. She put her right hand on his shoulder, ostensibly for balance as the boat rocked gently. His skin was warm.

"My dad has tools," Michael explained. "We're going to take it back and open it. But Terry gets one third of the treasure, for sure."

"That's great," Beth said, hand sliding across Terry's shoulders. "We could use some gold doubloons."

"Yeah, maybe that's what's in it!"

"Come on," Aiden said, grinning at his brother. "Sit down so we can get back. Mom's going to be mad."

Enthusiasm undimmed, Michael sat down on the side of the dinghy with his feet on either side of the box. Terry and Beth waved as Aiden revved the motor and the dinghy moved away, heading toward the boys' sailboat a few hundred yards away.

"What do you think is in it?" Beth asked, her still stiff legs complaining as she stood up.

"Gold doubloons," Terry replied, swinging his feet around into the cockpit. He caught her waist and pulled her close, forcing her back onto her knees on the cockpit seat. "What have you accomplished while I was treasure hunting?"

"I did some writing," she replied, head tilting to the side in an invitation to be kissed. Terry accepted it, wrapping both arms around her as his mouth found hers. He tasted salty, and his day's growth of beard scratched her chin. She kissed him back, wishing she weren't wearing the t-shirt as she stroked the hard muscles of his upper arms and shoulders. Their lips parted and she placed another little kiss on his nose, then looked into his eyes.

"Really, it's an old foot locker. Do you think it fell overboard?" she asked, having caught a bit of Michael's enthusiasm.

"Maybe someone threw it — maybe it has a dead body in it," Terry teased, easing his arms from around her in order to reach for his dive bag.

Beth wrinkled her nose. "It's too small."

"Well, I'm sure we'll hear about it later," Terry said, getting to his feet. "I hope Michael isn't too disappointed."

"So it was a good dive?" Beth asked, turning toward the

companionway. Terry pulled his mask and snorkel out of the bag and set them on the cockpit floor.

"Very good. The boys did great. No problems with the decompression stop, and they stuck with me."

Beth nodded. Terry had offered to take them diving on a whim without really thinking through the responsibility. Only after their parents had agreed and the boys had been in a state of high excitement had he considered all the things that could go wrong.

"Laurie and Joe sent this, to thank us," he added, pulling a bottle-shaped brown paper sack from his bag. He handed it to Beth, who opened it to find a bottle of white wine from California.

"Nice," she purred. "I'll put it on ice and we can have it with dinner."

"I'm starved," Terry observed, dropping his fins next to his mask and snorkel, followed by his weight belt.

"Then I'll go finish it. Are you going to shower?"

"I'll rinse off out here."

Beth glanced down at the pile he was making on the cockpit sole and understood that he would be showering both himself and his gear, and that she would have to wait to set the cockpit table for dinner. She started down the companionway ladder, scooping up the lobster still in its bag as she went.

A few minutes later Terry climbed down and passed behind her toward their cabin in the front of the boat. Only belatedly did she realize he was stark naked, or she might have made a grab for him.

She lit the oven and had to crack off the claws to force the oversized lobster into a baking pan to warm it. While the corn boiled she put everything they needed to eat dinner on a tray and stepped up on the ladder to set it out in the cockpit. She got out the mango salsa and had a taste, deciding it was acceptable. Then she pulled out the cooked potatoes and stared at them as if they might form into something appetizing on their own.

"How hungry did you say you are?" she called out.

"Famished," came the muffled reply.

"I hope you're shaving," she added, stroking her abraded chin. There was no reply, and she looked toward the forward bulkhead, smiling. If he hadn't been, he was now.

Terry, a grown man in his thirties, had the metabolism of a growing boy, a fact for which she sometimes hated him. The active lifestyle of a cruising sailor had gotten her to a size fourteen after a few months, and occasionally allowed her to try a twelve. But she had to work at it, consciously monitoring her diet. Terry could eat all day, and eat almost anything, and he kept the same relatively fit build. At home in Washington, D.C. he belonged to a gym and went every couple days. Even so, he had a small tummy that Beth rather liked – it meant he wasn't perfect, which would intimidate her, and it was very comfy to rest her head on.

She had to feed him the potatoes in some form tonight, or he'd be back in the galley looking for snacks when she hoped to have his undivided attention. Finally she found the olive oil and some vinegar, onion, and bacon bits and made a pseudo German potato salad. Terry was a bit of a gourmet, but he was also willing to try almost anything and rarely turned down her creations. She tasted her concoction and decided it would do in a pinch, although some dry mustard would really help.

Eventually Terry emerged freshly shaven, hair combed, dressed in a nearly clean polo shirt and cargo shorts. Beth dug the bottle of wine out of the refrigerator and handed it to him along with the corkscrew.

"Will you set the table outside?"

"Whatever you need," he replied, leaning in to kiss her on the cheek. She reached up and stroked his face, smiling.

"We'll get to that later."

With a devilish grin he climbed the ladder and was soon rattling plates in the cockpit.

The lobster surprised him, and he dug in to his portion with enough enthusiasm to overlook any shortcomings of the potatoes. He told her more about the dive while they ate, and explained why finding the footlocker had caught Michael's imagination so intensely.

"They told me that *Gunkholing* magazine is sponsoring a treasure hunt and the boys have convinced Joe and Laurie to participate. Michael is absorbed by the idea of finding lost pirate treasure."

"So the magazine wants its readers to search for pirate treasure?" Beth asked.

"No, I don't think so. That's just his imagination running wild. It sounded like they've planted the treasures for people to find. You have to hunt for a bunch of them, leading up to a big party on Antigua in August."

"So is there a treasure map or something?"

"Aiden said the magazine published the first clue – the issue that just came out has it. You follow it to someplace where you get the next clue, and you get something as well – you have to collect points to prove you actually solved each clue."

"And where are the treasures? What island?"

"The islands, that's all the boys said."

"All of them?" Beth chuckled at the notion of a treasure hunt all up and down the island chain.

"Probably not," Terry shrugged, watching her closely. "You're interested, aren't you?"

She looked a bit sheepish, "I'm curious. Can't pass up a challenge, I guess."

"Well we know that," he smiled, softening the tacit reference to her recent expedition to save her friend from unknown danger.

"What's the point, anyway? Is there a prize, other than the party?"

"I'm not sure – the boys were more interested in the hunt itself. But I'd guess there's something. It would cost a bit to traipse all over the islands hunting, so it has to be worth it."

"Unless you were planning on going there anyway."

"Unless you were," he nodded, taking her point. What else did they have to do?

"Maybe Joe and Laurie will let us have a look at the magazine," he suggested and saw Beth's face brighten.

As the lobster disappeared he insisted on hearing more about her day. She admitted to her procrastination, but only because she could conclude by claiming six pages of solid writing after all. She told him about her errant towel and Ricky's visit, hoping that the mental image of her lying topless on the deck would have the desired effect. From his crooked smile she thought that it did.

Not that it took much to seduce him, or her for that matter. They had met in the fall, and become lovers just before Christmas. Their romance had been conducted entirely on and near her sailboat in the warm tropics. Sometimes she felt sure it wasn't real – and her recent month back home had only reinforced that. His real world was in D.C. Hers was, well, wherever she took *Trouble*. Or was it? Just how tied to Terry's life was her own?

Almost six months ago when she'd set sail from New York she'd planned to sail to the Caribbean on her own. That had been the initial challenge, made by her friend Ori who was doing the same on a schedule about three months ahead of her. She'd followed Ori down the east coast meeting Terry in Annapolis, and hiring a crewman in North Carolina. In Miami she'd traded the hired crew for Terry and together they'd brought *Trouble* to the Virgin Islands, where he'd had to leave her to go back to work.

The uncertainty of his return had contributed to the next decision she made: her friend Ori had sent a puzzling email implying that she needed help and Beth had pulled up her anchor and set sail for Guadeloupe. She still couldn't believe that when she'd admitted her actions to Terry over the phone he hadn't been livid. But instead he'd been impressed with her solo sailing and as soon as he was able he'd come looking for her. She supposed that he'd been more worried than he let on, although they'd never discussed it. In any case, he had come to the rescue only to find that she had things pretty much under control. She had found Ori and gotten her to needed medical help, saving both her life and that of her newborn child. But still his timely arrival had been the best moment of her life. They'd seen Ori and her new son with her parents and spent a few days exploring Guadeloupe and its neighboring islands. But Beth's family needs and Terry's business had cut short their interlude. They'd left *Trouble* in the marina in Point-à-Pitre with a local friend promising to look in on her, and they'd both returned home – Terry to Washington to conclude the deal to sell his business, she to her parents in California. And throughout that visit, right up until he landed at Point-à-Pitre, she had still suspected that this entire romance was a dream. Her life had never been fairytale perfect, and she couldn't quite believe that a wealthy businessman would arrange his life around her sailing plans.

But he had, and Beth felt as if their relationship had moved in to a new phase. Sailing half way down the islands alone had been invigorating, fulfilling, and sometimes frightening. Sailing the rest of the way as a couple had been even better. Terry had pushed to get to this anchorage because, he said, it was one of his favorite places on Earth. Now they were planning on a slow northbound trip with plenty of stops to really visit each of the islands where initially Beth alone, and then the two of them, had barely stopped. During their first cruise from Miami to the Virgin Islands they had mostly occupied separate cabins, Terry in the small aft cabin and Beth in the bow. They maintained this formal arrangement even after they'd become lovers during an emergency landfall in Cuba. Coming together for a few hours or a night was not the same as sharing the same small cabin – they both knew that it was all too new and they weren't ready to move in together.

They'd stepped on to the boat in Guadeloupe after a month apart and stood awkwardly for a moment. They were about to settle in for their first extended cruise as a couple and they had to decide where to sleep, and somehow it seemed imperative, as if once settled the decision could not be changed.

"Terry," she'd said, then stopped, looking from him toward the door to the forward cabin, then back to him.

"Whatever you want Beth," he'd nearly purred, his smile just the right degree to convey affection without being a leer. She'd reached for him, desperate for physical intimacy.

"I want you."

"I want you too." He'd let his bags fall to the deck and held her, nuzzling her hair, hands caressing her tired back. And then he'd loosened his hold and looked her in the eye.

"But do you want me in your space? Be honest."

Her mouth had opened, but words to express her wishes did not come easily. She thought she did, but what if things didn't go as well as before? What if it was infatuation and it wore off? What if –.

"Yes. If it's not going to work let's find out now," she'd finally said. Hardly the romantic lover's response she would have wanted to hear. But Terry had nodded, expression impossible to read.

"Good idea," he'd said, releasing her entirely to pick up his bags. Beth had done the same, shouldering her day-pack and turning toward the cabin door. "But there's nothing to worry about," he'd gone on. She'd glanced over her shoulder to see a devilish grin. "It's going to work," he'd shrugged at her uncertain expression.

"Really?"

"I'm certain," he'd nodded again. "I'm going to marry you Beth."

She'd dropped her bag on the cabin floor and forced herself to look at him, fearing beyond all else that this was some mean joke. But he'd been smiling warmly, and seeing her shock he'd dropped his own bags and brought both hands up to cup her face.

"You'll see."

Terry stacked the dishes back on the tray and carried it down to the galley, then returned with the cold wine bottle. His body was tired from the dive – wrestling the heavy tanks from Laurie and Joe's boat into the dinghy and helping the boys put on their gear and get in and out of the small boat had been a lot of work, even if the dive itself had been easy and fun. But Beth's little hints – the special dinner, that kiss earlier, and her topless sunbathing story – were crystal clear, and he was not one to turn down an open invitation.

He had only lived with a woman once before, and it had been a difficult relationship with frequent spats and slammed doors and sleeping in the guest room. It had come as a revelation that sleeping in the same bed on a permanent basis did not automatically mean sex all the time. There were still little signals, rituals to be observed, and privacy to be respected. In fact, that – privacy – was even more important. That's one reason why he'd taken the boys diving and left Beth to herself most of the day. She'd been in a strange emotional place since their return to *Trouble* and he knew she was still struggling with her situation with her parents and sister. Their relationship could only progress so far until she found emotional balance. The article she'd promised to write sounded like a good step. He didn't think it mattered if she never sent it to the newsletter, so long as she wrote it. Beth was a closed person, rarely expressing extreme emotion. The guilt, fear, and who knew what else she was holding inside was robbing her – robbing both of them – of what he intended to make an extended romantic trip. He had meant what he'd said from the bottom his heart: he wanted to marry her. But he knew full well that until she was ready, or at least until she felt that her other family obligations were fulfilled, or manageable, the last thing he should do was exert any pressure. It had taken a great deal of thought to say what he had, to lay it out there that first day, like a ground rule or a long-term goal. And he suspected that she didn't entirely believe him, which made him sad.

"Let's go up on the bow and look at the stars," he suggested. *Trouble's* cockpit was shaded by a canvas cover – a bimini – that made it comfortable during sunny days, but blocked the view of the tropical night sky. Beth picked up their empty wine glasses and followed him out along the side deck to the tapered flat area on the bow above their cabin. Terry handed Beth the cool wine bottle, then crouched to open the forward hatch. Stretching out on the deck he leaned the front half of his body inside to grab the light blanket from the bunk. He dragged it out and spread it on the deck to soften the rough fiberglass surface and provide a little insulation as the evening cooled.

From horizon to horizon the Milky Way was a brilliant swathe of twinkling pinpoints, so many stars that the ones forming familiar constellations were difficult to find amid the rest. Lower in the southern sky an undeniably multi-colored pinprick was a satellite, probably in orbit over the equator. Every now and then a fast moving streak was the luminous death of a bit of space dust, a meteorite burning into the atmosphere far, far away from their perch on the tiny deck. Slower moving lights were airplanes crowded with travelers making their way to distant lands. Beth always wondered if anyone up there looked down at the water so far below and wondered about the invisible sailors there.

Much nearer *Trouble*'s anchor light rocked back and forth on the mast head fifty feet above them.

They sat for a while sipping wine and talking quietly as the sea breeze ruffled their hair and played with the edge of the blanket. Eventually they tucked the feet of their plastic wine glasses under a line for safe keeping and stretched out. Stargazing soon gave way to caressing and gradually clothing was shed, dropped down through the hatch. They made passionate, unhurried love, reveling in the exposure of it, protected by the darkness and the unspoken respect of their neighbors on other boats. No one, seeing the shadow of moving bodies on the bow in the dark, would approach.

The wind caressing bare skin gradually cooled them, and they traded their starry bed for the coziness of the cabin below. Terry snuggled Beth against himself, spooning behind her, face nuzzling her neck, and whispered the secrets of his heart. She had touched him in ways he had never thought possible. He could not imagine life without her. He loved her unconditionally. Beth wrapped her hands around his at her chest and listened to his words, wanting to believe, knowing he was sincere, and doubting herself.

SEVEN: CLIFTON

"Morning Beth. You two are heading out today?" Laurie leaned one hand on the soft side of her dinghy as it drifted beside *Trouble*. Beth had just finished sluicing out the cockpit with several buckets of seawater. She dropped the bucket into the lazarette and closed it, then knelt on the seat to look out at her neighbor.

"Yes, we need water, and more provisions than we want to pay Ricky for."

"Joe and I wanted to thank Terry again for taking the boys yesterday. They talked all evening about the dive."

"Hey Laurie, did they get that footlocker open?" Terry had come up through the companionway behind Beth and now he stepped out from under the bimini, one hand resting on the canvas covered aluminum frame.

Laurie squinted up at him, shading her eyes with one hand. "That dirty thing," she groaned, "Joe pried the latch open with a crowbar. It was solid. It had some tools in it — pliers, screwdriver, some other junk."

"I bet Michael was disappointed," Beth said, feeling a flash of it herself.

"You know, that kid will make the best of anything. He's calling them his pirate tools, and he cleaned the box out. He wanted to bring it into the cabin to store treasures or something but that's where I put my foot down."

"Good for him," Terry said. "Say Laurie, the boys were talking about this treasure hunt in *Gunkholing* magazine."

"You too, huh?" she laughed, shaking her head ruefully. "They managed to talk us into starting it, but we withhold the right to call a halt at any time, if it gets too crazy."

"We're curious about it. Do you suppose we could see the magazine?"

"Uh oh, competition?" she laughed again.

Terry shot her his most flirtatious innocent expression. "I guess we caught a little of Michael's treasure hunting bug."

"Well if you want to come over before you leave I can let you copy down the information, but you know I can't give you the magazine – Michael wants it."

"Of course," Beth put in, glancing up at Terry. She was tickled that he'd asked about the magazine, she'd been thinking about it, but had been unsure whether to bring it up again. "But we'd love to read about it – see what it's all about."

"Well, I think it's going to be tough to win the big prizes – there are a lot of cruisers in these islands who'll work hard at it. But it could be a good time, and I think you can go to the party even if you just get a few points, if you want. Personally I wouldn't make an effort to be there if I hadn't won – it's bound to be a huge crowd – but maybe you'll want to. Like I said, come over and I'll show you. Maybe you can find an issue over in Clifton."

"Good point," Terry said. "But just in case, I'll come over in a few minutes."

As Laurie motored away he climbed back into the cockpit where Beth was stowing the long handled brush she'd used to clean the deck.

"Unless you want to go over," he said tentatively.

"No, you go ahead. Just get all the information. I'll finish stowing things below and we'll go as soon as you get back. And Terry, thanks."

"Thanks?" he paused half way out of the cockpit.

"For asking about it. I'm really curious."

"I guess I am too. I won't be long."

"God this place is crowded," Beth complained from behind *Trouble's* wheel. It was midafternoon and they had just completed the sail from their idyllic anchorage in the Tobago Cays to Clifton on Union Island. Terry was moving around the deck securing dock lines to cleats and placing the cylindrical fenders on the side decks ready to be deployed depending on how they docked. He came back into the cockpit and picked up the hand held VHF radio, hailing the Anchorage Yacht Club for the third time. That seemed to be the charm, for a female voice responded instructing him to change from the hailing channel to one of the recreational communications channels.

Beth divided her attention between navigating the crowded anchorage and listening to Terry's conversation. The marina dock master told him where they should tie up to fill their water tanks. He set the radio down and he climbed out of the cockpit to finish preparing the lines and fenders.

"There it is, see?" he called, standing near the mast pointing at the open stretch along one of the marina's crowded pontoons. Beth nodded, too focused on boat traffic, water depth, and the effect of the breeze on *Trouble* to speak. Terry watched her for a moment to be sure that she was simply focused and not losing control. She was so ultra-cool under pressure he sometimes missed those moments when she actually needed his support. She had told him about a motor cruiser that cut in front of her at the fuel dock in St Kitts. She had scraped it with *Trouble*'s anchor, unsuccessfully trying to turn away in time. Approaching unfamiliar docks was always a little stressful, but that experience had definitely played on Beth's nerves. Even so, she had handled *Trouble* through a lot more anchoring and docking than he had, so on the whole he was very comfortable with her at the helm and happy to handle the lines.

A male attendant in a navy blue polo shirt and khaki shorts stood on the dock with hands raised to catch the line Terry held coiled and ready to toss. Beth angled *Trouble* sharply toward the dock, keeping the engine in gear against the strong breeze that was blowing against them. If she turned broadside to the dock too soon *Trouble* would be blown away from it before Terry and the man on the dock could get the lines secured. But if she waited too long to turn *Trouble* would impale her bow on the dock. At the last possible moment Beth turned the wheel and *Trouble*'s bow and anchor skimmed past the man's belly. Terry tossed him the line, then hurried along the deck to the gate in the lifelines and stepped off onto the dock himself. As *Trouble*'s hull slowed alongside the dock he walked back and grabbed the stern line that he'd prepared. As *Trouble* began to slide away sideways with the breeze he threw the line around an oversized cleat on the dock and stopped her.

"Heave her in," he called to the man, who heaved on the line he held. The boat snugged up against the dock, her fender slightly squashed between fiberglass hull and wooden dock.

Ten minutes later the water tanks were full and Beth was peeling off Eastern Caribbean dollars from a thin wad. She handed exact change to the attendant and tucked the rest back into the pocket of her shorts.

"Anchor?" Terry asked her as she stepped back on board *Trouble*. That had been their plan, but he wanted to be sure she hadn't changed her mind. The yacht club had berths available, although they were rather expensive, according to the cruiser grapevine. Beth squinted into the afternoon glare as she looked across the anchorage. It was populated by all manner of boats from big shiny charter sloops to the usual fleet of ragtag small cruisers, a pair of enormous white motor cruisers looked like stately guardians over near the harbor entrance, balanced by a dozen or so colorful little local boats in the shallows off to the left. There were few open spaces amid the crowd. It would be a far cry from the privacy of their spot in the Tobago Cays.

She turned her attention to the detailed chart of the harbor provided in a cruising guide. She had studied it during the sail over, but comparing the drawing to the real place always brought into focus details that were not obvious.

"It's deep," she observed, not for the first time. The deeper the water, the more chain and rope needed to secure them. *Trouble* only had enough to anchor in water about thirty-five feet deep. The harbor was mostly deeper than that. If their anchor wasn't well set, when a squall blew through – and they did just about every day – *Trouble* might be blown backward into whatever boat was behind her.

Terry freed the stern line from the dock and gestured to the attendant to hold the other line for a moment.

Beth looked back out at the anchored boats and back at the chart.

"How about over there," she said, pointing to the far side of the harbor. "It looks pretty open." Terry looked where she was indicating and noted that it was fairly close to the town dock where they would land the dinghy. That was convenient.

"Okay, let's go check it out."

Beth got behind the wheel and started the engine and Terry nodded at the attendant to release the line. As *Trouble* slid away from the dock on the breeze Beth put the engine in gear and turned her bow out into the anchorage.

"I'll meet you at the grocery in a half hour," Beth told Terry as he gave her a hand up onto the dinghy dock. *Trouble* was securely at anchor a couple hundred yards away in twenty-eight feet of water, occupying a surprisingly clear area of the anchorage.

"See you there," Terry replied, shouldering the canvas tote that contained several more that they used to haul provisions. Beth clasped her own bag containing *Trouble*'s papers, their passports, and her laptop under her arm. "You have enough cash for the fees?" Terry belatedly asked. Beth pressed her hand to the pocket where she'd tucked her money and did a mental calculation.

"Yes, plenty."

Terry placed an impromptu kiss on the corner of her mouth and started up the dock. Beth followed, glancing back at the anchorage and then at a group of locals sitting at the head of the dock. As she passed, fragments of their conversation caught her ear:

"De mail boat ..."

"... ya mon, dat gonna' happen."

Deciding that they were not looking to vandalize or steal the dinghies on the dock, and specifically hers, she turned up the road toward the customs office. Terry had already gone down a side street toward the small grocery. The cruising guide had not promised any place with Internet access, but she'd brought her laptop anyway, just in case some enterprising businessman had set it up since the book went to press.

The customs officer asked the usual questions about how long they had stayed in St. Vincent, the island nation of which Union Island was a part, and their next destination.

Terry had transcribed the treasure hunt information from Laurie's magazine that morning. The first clue was latitude and longitude coordinates. Contestants had to go to those coordinates and receive the next clue, along with a card representing the number of points they'd earned. There was no limit to the number of contestants who could participate, but the first three to claim the clue at each destination got more points than the rest. The winner would be the contestant with the most points. There were prizes for second, third, and fourth, and some undescribed special prizes, and hats for everyone who brought at least one clue to the party. There were a lot more rules to ensure safety and guard the magazine against liability, but Terry had not transcribed those.

During the sail they had discussed it and plotted the coordinates on *Trouble*'s charts. They were surprised to find that the location was somewhere in St. Georges, the capital of Grenada – surprised because of the remoteness of the location at the southern end of the island chain, and pleased because they had been planning on going to Grenada next anyway. Therefore, they were going to make as quick a passage as they could over to Carriacou, the nation of Grenada's northern-most island, as soon as they finished their errands.

The officer assured her that if they were detained here and unable to get out this afternoon, they could spend the night at anchor so long as they did not leave the boat and they left first thing in the morning. Beth was thanking him for his lenience when a dark face appeared outside the office's open window.

"De mailboat mon," the man said, looking directly at Beth.

"I'm sorry?" she asked, looking from the stranger to the customs agent.

"De mail boat commin'," the man looked at the customs agent as if for help. The officer looked out the window past the man, as if deep in thought.

Beth followed his gaze and saw the crowded anchorage.

"De mail boat commin'," the man repeated, looking expectantly at Beth.

"I don't understand," she said, shaking her head slightly. "What does that – ?"

"Your boat in de way," the man added in a tone that suggested he thought she was addled.

"You anchored in the harbor?" the customs officer looked back at her.

"Yes. We found room just off the dock – ," she stopped, realizing all at once why there had been open space there and what "de mail boat" was.

"Please forgive me, I have to go," she said to the officer, shoving her completed papers into her portfolio.

"You got to go to the airport for immigration," he reminded her.

"Yes yes, I will, but I think I have to go move my boat first."

He did not respond, at least not before she was outside his office and trotting down the street along the waterfront.

Out at the harbor entrance a huge blue-hulled wreck of a boat was slowly passing the big white cruisers. It was headed for the town dock, where it would have to turn ninety degrees to maneuver alongside. *Trouble* was anchored right where the boat would need to make its turn.

The local man was following her, and as she broke into a run a couple more locals fell in with them shouting "De mail boat, de mail boat," as if it were some weird local ritual.

A familiar figure crossed the road ahead of Beth, going toward the dinghy dock.

"Terry!" she shouted breathlessly. She saw him glance over his shoulder toward her as he climbed down into their dinghy. He didn't stop, but rather dropped his empty bags into the small boat and scooted to the stern to lower and start the engine. A moment later she climbed in and uncleated the line from the dock, pushing them off hard into deeper water so Terry could put the engine in gear.

"How did you know?" she shouted above the roar of the outboard, eyes locked on the looming blue hull.

"People at the grocery said that there was a sailboat in the way of the mail boat. Something just clicked."

"A local came to the customs office. They saw us anchor. I heard them saying something about the mail boat when we got out of the dinghy. I didn't even thank him."

"It probably happens all the time," Terry said, slowing the dinghy for the approach to *Trouble*'s side. "They probably make bets on whether the mail boat will win."

He shut off the engine and stood up, grabbing *Trouble*'s rail to steady the dinghy while Beth climbed up the ladder and into the cockpit. He didn't meet her eye, regretting his casual comment about the possible destruction of her boat. He secured the dinghy painter to the rear cleat while Beth started *Trouble*'s engine. She was already motoring slowly forward when he climbed up the ladder and went up to the bow to haul in the anchor.

He spared a glance at the mail boat as he hauled in the rope anchor rode using his shoulders and flexing his knees to drag it up in six foot lengths. The rust pocked dark blue hull proceeded with unrelenting persistence. It seemed to be taking an awfully long time to pull in the anchor. The blue hull was just a few a boat lengths away when his hands grasped chain. He swallowed hard and heaved with all his strength, forcing himself to focus on his job as foot after foot of chain dropped into the anchor well. Sweat dripped into his eyes and he was gasping from the intense cardio workout when, finally, the anchor itself rattled and banged onto the bowsprit. He allowed himself to look up, dashing sweat off his brow with the back of one hand. The rusty blue hull was a bare boat length away. A froth of water at her stern indicated that it was reversing, probably to avoid hitting *Trouble*.

"We're away!" he yelled to Beth, dropping the anchor well cover and heading back to the cockpit. She had been watching and already turned the bow away from the looming hull. Only now did Terry see crewmen on the bow of the blue boat looking down at them, their expressions a mixture of contempt and annoyance. Then he looked to the stern of the boat and saw the pilot through the bridge window. He was holding the VHF radio microphone to his mouth, talking quickly into it.

"He's on the radio," Terry said as he stepped down into the cockpit. The companionway was locked, the radio stowed below. Glancing up again at the mail boat, which was further away now, he dialed the combination and unlocked the companionway, slid open the hatch, removed the washboards, and climbed down. He switched on the radio and tuned it to the hailing channel.

"… anchored off the Clifton dock, sailing vessel that was anchored off the Clifton dock, come in."

Terry looked out at Beth. She shrugged.

"Don't answer. We're out of his way now."

Terry looked at the radio in his hand, torn between settling the matter with the other captain and following Beth's very reasonable advice. She was scanning the anchorage once more. Terry climbed up into the cockpit and set the radio down. Presently the hailing stopped, but by then Beth and Terry were focused on finding a new spot for the night.

They settled unhappily for a spot between two other boats of about *Trouble*'s size, with two more close astern. They dropped the anchor in almost forty feet of water just behind a coil of two-inch diameter rope floating on the surface. They assumed it was adrift, a bit of industrial grade flotsam working its way through the anchorage.

Once they were sure the anchor was holding well enough, at least for a couple daytime hours, they set about returning to their errands. Beth still had to visit the immigration office at the airport, about a mile out of town. Terry had left a hand basket of groceries on the floor in the market when he'd understood that *Trouble* was in jeopardy. Once again they locked up the boat and climbed down into the dinghy.

"Can we wait until the mail boat leaves?" Beth asked as Terry started the engine. He looked up, concerned, and saw that she was smiling. "It's just a bit embarrassing."

"I was joking before, when I said they probably take bets. But I'm sure it happens. Think of it as a rite-of-passage for Union Island."

Beth sighed, gazing out across the anchorage as Terry steered them through it toward the dock. He was right, but it didn't stop her cheeks from coloring as they secured the dinghy and walked past the same group of locals at the head of the dock.

"I guess if I don't get back in a half hour or so you should go on out to the boat," she said. "You never know how long these guys will take."

"I'll take the food out, then come back and head toward the airport. Worst case I'll keep you company there, or maybe I'll just meet you on your way back."

"That would be nice. Thanks."

Walking along the road toward the airport Beth began to feel the weight of the long day with more still to come. The adventure of the mail boat had sent a spike of adrenaline through her system that was wearing off. The prospect of sailing another seven miles and checking in with customs on Carriacou was no longer as appealing as it had sounded that morning. Likewise, staying in the crowded anchorage where she was not entirely confident that the anchor was secure did not sound good either. Torn between conflicting bad choices she did the only thing she could: plodded along the road past grazing cows and curious goats.

The grocery proprietress gave Terry a broad grin when he entered her shop. She set his abandoned basket of goods on her counter with a nod.

"Thank you," he said, retrieving it. "I had a little emergency."

"Yah, mon. De mail boat. I know."

"Happens a lot, I'll bet, in this crowded harbor," he ventured. Her eyes narrowed as her smile broadened.

"Not so often as all dat," she said.

"Well, thanks," Terry replied ruefully, turning toward the shelves.

Returning to the counter twenty minutes later with two full baskets he noticed a small magazine rack behind the woman, the current issue of *Gunkholing* magazine prominently displayed. Taking it as a sign, he bought the magazine along with the provisions, which cost about the same as they would have in the bodega near his townhouse in Georgetown. During their trip from Guadeloupe Beth had trained him to shop for price, not brand. If he'd selected familiar labels his canvas bags of groceries would have cost half again as much.

He wasn't quite sure how he and Beth had gotten sucked in to this treasure hunt, but he had to admit that it was seductive. They had several months of cruising ahead of them, based on his informal plan to spend six months before returning to Washington and his partner to begin discussing another business venture. The treasure hunt lasted for three, and it would give them a goal – a series of goals – that would provide structure to their voyage. He had not expected to need structure on what he'd been envisioning as a long, romantic vacation. This was his opportunity to get to really know Beth, and she him, and to lay the foundation for what he dearly hoped would be a long term relationship. He had naively thought that was enough. But he had realized, once they reached the Tobago Cays, that although he'd left the office behind, he had not shed his innate goal-oriented personality. And Beth was the same: she had set the goal of sailing from New York to the Caribbean, and once there she had found a new goal – helping her friend Ori. She was as lost as he was without a plan. So no matter what the outcome of this silly treasure hunt, playing the game in order to have something to do could be exactly what they needed to keep their relationship on an even keel.

He wasn't surprised that Beth wasn't at the dinghy when he got there. The walk to the airport was hot and dusty, not a quick trip. He ran the groceries out to *Trouble* and hastily stowed them below, taking the time to put the perishables in the refrigerator lest they spoil in the tropical heat. As he tied the dinghy at the dock for the third time he ignored the curious looks from the locals. Half way to the airport he spotted Beth coming back. She looked worn out, with wisps of hair sticking to her face and dust caked on her shoes and bare calves. His heart went out to her, and he hurried along the road to reach her and offer succor, even if it was just in the form of moral support.

"Everything okay?" he asked as they came together. He fell in beside her, slinging his arm around her shoulders for a quick squeeze. She leaned into him for a moment, then straightened, not, he realized, because she didn't enjoy the hug but because it was hot.

"We're all set. Did you find everything on the list?"

"More or less."

She gave him an amused glance. "I was thinking," she said, clearly changing the subject.

"Uh oh."

"No, it's nothing. Just a thought. We could stay here tonight — we just have to pull out first thing in the morning. I wish we had more anchor rode, but it is five to one scope. That ought to be okay."

"Is that all?" Terry forced a laugh, pretending he had expected something much more serious. In fact, he had hoped she would suggest staying. "Sure, let's call it a day when we get back. No romance on the bow, but we can just take it easy."

"I'd really like to get away from this place," Beth said, still not comfortable with the decision and the change of plans it represented. "But I'm not sure we can make it to Carriacou before sunset, and I don't want to find my way in to the anchorage in the dark."

That was common sense as well as good seamanship. For all their being a paradise, the islands were severely lacking in navigational aids, and lighted ones were virtually nonexistent. Entering a new harbor after dark was an act of desperation, or of the foolhardy.

"No, you're right. We'd be cutting it very close. And their customs and immigration offices would definitely be closed by the time we got there, so we couldn't check in until the morning anyway. Let's make dinner — we have plenty of provisions now — and we can read the fine print about the treasure hunt."

Beth half turned, face brightening. "You got the magazine?"

"Yup. Our very own copy."

EIGHT: ST. GEORGE'S

"Look over there!" Beth grabbed Terry's upper arm, steering him to look across the narrow street.

She had torn the full-page advertisement for the treasure hunt out of their copy of *Gunkholing* and pinned it to the small bulletin board above *Trouble*'s navigation desk. The same colorful ad with its intricate logo of tropical flora, fauna, and sights, was reproduced poster size and displayed in a shop window across the street. She and Terry both looked above it at the same time to see that the shop was actually the Grenada tourist bureau. Terry looked back down at the portable GPS in his hand.

"Signal's jumping all over the place, but we're close enough that that could be it."

Beth groaned at his unnecessary attachment to technical precision and looked up the street for oncoming traffic before dragging him off the sidewalk and onto the street with her.

"Of course that's it," she said, stepping up on the opposite sidewalk just before a girl on a moped, blonde hair flying out from beneath a scratched white helmet, materialized out of nowhere at high speed and nearly bowled them down. Terry jumped up beside her and reached for the door to the shop.

"Good afternoon," a woman in a colorful print blouse, hair styled in a neat chignon, rose from a desk behind a counter. "How may I assist you?"

"Good afternoon," Beth replied, "we are looking for the *Gunkholing* treasure hunt – that is, we're starting the hunt, and we saw the poster in the window. Do you have any idea what I'm talking about?"

The woman's smiled widened and she nodded. "Congratulations. You have found the first stop." She took a step back in order to look under the counter. Finding what she wanted she withdrew several pieces of paper and stepped back, laying them out in front of Beth and Terry.

"Here is your point ticket for this stop," she said, tapping one finger, the nail long and crimson, on a glossy card printed with the treasure hunt logo, the location of this first stop, and a big, bold number one. "You are not the first ones here, unfortunately, so you only receive one point."

"We didn't expect to be," Beth said, knowing even as she spoke that this woman didn't care, but unable to stop herself. There was a hint of apology in the woman's tone and she wanted to assuage any guilt the woman might feel for awarding only one point. Beth knew it was ridiculous; but the need to take responsibility was overpowering. As expected, the woman went on without acknowledging Beth's comment.

Moving her finger to the next document, she said, "This is an entry form and release – it was mentioned in the rules. Did you read them?"

"Yes," Terry put in before Beth could speak. The fine print in the magazine advertisement had explained that all hunters had to submit an official entry when they found the first treasure. The fine print in the release would absolve the magazine of any responsibly for anything that happened to anyone or their vessel, or any vessels they came in contact with, or their extended families and friends, during the hunt. During their trip down the west coast of Grenada Terry had tried to think up as many possible scenarios as he could and present them to Beth, to be sure she understood. Not that he thought she would want to sue the magazine over damages or injury. But people could behave oddly when something awful happened.

He had no reservations about signing away his right to legal action because he had no intention of doing anything more dangerous than he would have done anyway were he not on this hunt. And besides, a good lawyer – and he had one – could usually find holes in any of these liability waivers. But it was Beth's signature on the form that mattered: she was the boat owner.

"Good. You can fill it out and leave it with me to forward," the woman went on. Moving her finger to the third document she smiled again, "And this is your next clue."

It was another glossy sheet, folded in thirds, printed with the hunt logo. Beth reached for it, but the woman slid the release form on top of it pointedly.

"I must ask for release forms from everyone in your crew, except minor children," she said, the apologetic tone back.

"Yes of course," Beth said, taking the form. "It's just us. Two forms."

They filled out and signed the forms and were given the point card with an admonishment not to lose it and the second clue. Beth was unfolding the clue as they stepped back out into the late afternoon sun.

"It's a map!" she said, excitement growing as she tried to recognize the locale. Terry looked over her shoulder at it.

"Pretty cryptic," he said. "But it has to be identifiable. Either it's close by, or those place names," he pointed at a mysterious label on a point of land, "are genuine."

"I bet they're genuine. And I know how to find them." She turned her face to his and placed a kiss on his cheek, then set out at a brisk walk. Terry took a quick step to catch up and caught her free hand.

"Oh you do, do you?"

"I'm particularly good at identifying islands based on cryptic clues," she said, shooting him a bright smile.

"So you are," he agreed, realizing she was referring to her identification of St. Hillaire based on her friend Ori's very indirect descriptions in a series of email messages. Beth had correctly interpreted them as a cry for help. "Where do we start?"

"We could go back to the boat and start looking at charts," she said, her pace not slowing even though the harbor was in the other direction.

"Or?" he prompted.

"We Google them."

Beth had developed a habit of researching key resources before arriving at any new island town. These included a laundry, grocery store, liquor store, cruiser's hangout, and Internet access. At first Terry had been impressed with her ability to find these places – once ashore she rarely referred to whatever map she had, although she always carried it in her bag just in case. He'd come to realize that she had an excellent sense of direction, both at sea and ashore, and a knack for remembering key landmarks on a map and matching the map symbology to reality. She said she didn't like to pull out a map because it branded her as a newcomer. He thought she was sincere, but he was still impressed with her skill.

In a few minutes she was ordering two coffees and a slice of spice cake in an Internet café on a tiny side street. Rather than use one of the provided computers, which were not only filthy but also so old their operating system and browser must be a decade out of date, she plugged her laptop into an available connection and entered the access code provided by the server.

One by one she entered the place names from the map into Google's search field, getting a wide range of hits, many not geographical. She added the word Caribbean to narrow the scope and things started to make more sense. But they were still all over the search results map.

"Try all three?" Terry suggested tentatively. Neither of them expected any results with all three in them, but in fact, there at the top of the list was an item from a website about Grenada.

"Brilliant!" Beth declared, turning to give Terry a quick kiss.

"My pleasure," he purred, squeezing her shoulder with one hand. She followed the link to bring up the website and they both read the brief introduction about local pirate legends. Scrolling down they saw the three locations highlighted in a link to one of the legends.

"It's almost too convenient," Beth said as she followed the link.

"Like maybe the magazine put this site up?"

"Yeah, it seems possible."

"As long as we don't think they'd intentionally try to confuse us …" Terry's voice trailed off as a map that matched the one in the clue filled the screen.

They both stared at it for a moment, noting how well it matched the simpler line drawing of the clue map that Beth was holding in her hand.

"Look, there's one place name that's not on the clue map," Terry said, pointing to the screen. "This waterfall. The line leads up from the beach to the X. That's where the waterfall is on the map on the web."

"Remember, Indiana Jones said that X never marks the spot," Beth quipped. "Except when it does. I'll bet we could get a taxi to take us to that waterfall, if there isn't a tour."

"Shouldn't we take the boat to the bay?"

Beth looked at Halifax Harbor, the tiny indent in question, on both maps. "I think it's a lot further than it looks to the waterfall from there. And there may not be any roads. The rules say you must use a vessel to get from island to island, they don't say you have to sail to the closest possible point before going ashore. I think they expect you to go overland from here to there."

"How about this — we try going by car, but if we get there and find out we needed to bring the boat, we come back and sail."

"Assuming there's some way to know," Beth considered. "I mean, there could be some clue on the beach that we'll never know about if we don't sail there ..."

"We'll ask around about whether it's walkable from the beach."

Beth nodded. "Okay." But she didn't sound convinced. It looked like a long uphill walk through the humid jungle. Terry pursed his lips in frustration at her indecisiveness. It was not like her to waffle; that she was doing it meant something was bothering her. It could be a simple as fatigue or, he frowned, then caught himself and schooled his features, it could just be her monthly cycle. He did not believe she could be having second thoughts about the treasure hunt itself, not after her enthusiasm over finding the first stop.

They finished their coffees while taking turns checking their email. Terry downloaded long messages from his partner Jeff, his sister, and his father and responded to a couple short ones from his nephew and a couple friends. Beth downloaded and saved three messages from her sister and one from her friend Ori, all of them too long to read and respond to before the coffee ran out. She glanced at the subject lines on Trish's messages to assure herself that none of them reported any emergencies, knowing that if something had happened to her father Trish would have called.

They walked hand-in-hand back to the visitors' bureau where the woman who'd awarded them their first prize had been replaced by a compact man in a pressed short sleeved white shirt. They presented their dilemma — whether to sail to Halifax Harbor or hire a driver to visit the waterfall. At the last moment Beth added that they were going because of the treasure hunt, on the off chance that he would offer specific advice about the rules.

He grinned, displaying an alarming gap where his right canine should be. "Everyone hire Tobias to run them up there."

"And is Tobias a taxi driver? Or a tour guide?" Terry asked.

"Yah mon. He have a little van, drives people around the island. Wherever they want to go."

Disregarding the fact that this wasn't really an answer, because in the islands a taxi driver often was also a tour guide, Terry asked for his phone number.

"There are probably dozens of men who'd take us," Beth pointed out as they strolled down the street toward the harbor. "He probably gets a kick-back from this Tobias person."

"Could be," Terry agreed amiably.

"So shouldn't we pick someone ourselves?"

"Do you have any criteria on which to judge them? Or any other phone numbers?"

"Well, no …"

"And I figure if this guy Tobias was a total screw up it would reflect badly on the visitors' bureau. These people have a lot of pride about their island."

Beth dug in the pocket of her shorts and pulled out her phone, extending it toward Terry.

"Just call him," she said with a conciliatory smile. He shot her a mischievous grin and took the phone. They stopped in the shade of the awning on a shop displaying gaudy tropical clothing targeted at cruise ship passengers. He made the call, arranging to be picked up at the marina entrance in an hour.

"You know, just because other contestants have hired him to take them doesn't mean we're not supposed to sail to Halifax Harbor," Beth observed as they continued on their way to the boat.

"Good God woman, will you stop?" Terry groaned.

Beth stopped short, stricken by the frustration in his tone.

"Sorry," he mumbled, half turning toward her from a step ahead, reaching out to take her hand. "Is it the treasure hunt? Or news in your email? Something's eating at you love, and I don't know what to do to help."

Beth sucked in a sharp breath, suddenly seeing herself as he must. All afternoon she'd been feeling uncertain, uncomfortable with any decision she tried to make. She knew that he was not used to seeing her question herself so much – not that she didn't do it, but she usually kept it to an internal monologue, only verbalizing her final decision once she was ready to live with it. And the monologues were usually very short – from a few seconds to make an easy choice to a few hours to mull over something larger.

"I don't know. I guess I feel off center, do you know what I mean?"

His smile was intensely understanding as he slipped his arm around her shoulders and started her walking again. She was glad to let him steer them.

"I do, although I'm not sure that I understand why, and I want to. If there's something about what we're doing here, about us —."

"No! Terry no, 'us' is the best thing I've got going right now and —."

"Woah," he squeezed her shoulders. "You can't really think that. Look around you, look where you are and how you got here. That's all you, love."

"Not all," she mumbled, following his instruction and looking around at the marina office and adjacent shops.

"Okay, not all. But we wouldn't be at this end of the Caribbean if you hadn't brought *Trouble* more than half way on your own. And forget about that for a minute, go back further. Aren't you the woman who cut herself loose from New York and headed south all on her own? You're making it, girl. You have a lot to be proud of."

"But was it the right thing to do?"

He inhaled a long breath and stopped her again in the shaded passage from the street to the docks where *Trouble* was berthed. He turned to face her.

"Why are you questioning it now?" he asked. *This is serious. She needs more than friendly encouragement.*

"I always question it. I guess I'm just doing it a little more for some reason."

"That's what I want to know — I mean, what I want you to figure out. Why are you questioning yourself now? What's going on?"

Beth glanced around, then made for a bench positioned with a view of the boats in the marina. She sat down, the searing wooden slats burning the backs of her thighs. She shifted forward to get more of her bare skin off and leaned back, her upper back propped uncomfortably on the hot back of the bench. Terry sat down beside her, his longer shorts protecting him. He half turned to watch her expectantly.

"I can't write it, Terry. Every time I try I just start weeping."

"You said you wrote six pages, before we left the Cays."

"I did. But it was all background. History. I thought that would get me going on the current story, but now I'm stuck."

"You can't find words at all?"

"No, I can. But I just cry and cry."

"So cry," he shrugged, trying to reduce the significance of her emotional malady, to make it something she could conquer. "Cry while you type."

"That's so — weak." She wrapped her arms around herself and stared out at the forest of masts. Her cheeks were reddening.

"It's human, I think. Why don't you just try it? Let the tears flow, and see if the words flow too. It's just possible the result will be very good."

"Or complete drivel," she sighed, dashing at her eyes with the backs of her hands.

"Either way, you'll get through it. I really think that will help. If you go on being conflicted about this you'll never — how did you put it? Find your center again."

She took a deep breath and shut her eyes, turning her face to the sun for a moment, which only made her feel redder and hotter. She plastered both hands over it and rubbed, brushing her hair back, then turned to look at him.

His rueful smile reflected her shattered appearance.

"I need to wash my face before this Tobias gets here," she said with a tentative smile.

NINE: TOBIAS

"You de seventh people I take to de falls for dis contest," Tobias told them. As he spoke he glanced at Terry in the passenger seat, his hands turning the wheel to the right as they moved with his head. Fortunately he looked forward and corrected the van's direction before it veered into the deep gully at the side of the road.

"So this is the best way to get there, then?" Beth asked from her perch in the middle of the second seat. Tobias looked up into the rear view mirror and grinned at her.

"Yes ma'am. Dis de *only* way."

"We thought we might be supposed to sail to Halifax Harbor and hike up," Terry said, studiously not looking at Beth.

Tobias's genial smile transitioned into laughter. Now Terry did look back at Beth and they exchanged puzzled frowns.

"Dat not a nice walk," Tobas said between guffaws.

"Why?" Beth asked.

"Halifax Harbor is de island dump, mon."

"They dump garbage in the water?" Beth asked, incredulous.

"No, no. De dump just behind de harbor. De harbor is full of flies, though. Ugly. You want to hike through de dump?"

"No!" Terry and Beth laughed now too, although Beth couldn't help but think that the dump couldn't completely surround the bay. Still, it didn't sound like an idyllic anchorage. She wrinkled her nose reflexively just as Tobias glanced at her in the rear view mirror.

"She got it right," he laughed, directing his comment to Terry. "It very smelly."

A half hour later Tobias turned his van in at a small parking area half full with local cars and two large tour buses.

"We walk from here," he said, getting out of the van and rounding the front to open their doors. Beth shouldered her daypack and reached for Terry's hand as they crunched across the graveled road and entered the jungle on a well-worn path. Not twenty feet along the lush greens and browns of the jungle canopy blocked the sun and the chatter of insects and creatures created a wholly different environment from the sunny beaches and marinas they were used to. The air was close and insects swooped around their heads, making Beth blow out, trying to make them veer away from her face.

They weren't alone in the jungle for long. Within five minutes of their setting out voices carried to them and presently they rounded a bend and found themselves facing a long line of people coming from the other direction. They were a typical tour mix – some jovial, some unreadably silent, a few kids talking excitedly to their parents, a few older people shooting disapproving looks at younger children who were darting in and out of the jungle fringe. They trooped along in ragged order, loosely following their guide, with whom Tobias exchanged a curt nod. The path was barely wide enough for two to walk side-by-side, and not wide enough for a third to pass if they did, and yet repeatedly Beth, Terry, and Tobias had to stand sideways as pairs and even threesomes pushed by without a word of apology. When they finally cleared the last of the tourists Beth emitted a heavy sigh that drew Tobias's attention.

"Big group, from de bus," he said. "Not on your hunt, though, so don't worry."

"Oh I know," she replied. "I've just never understood why people chose to travel like that, in a big pack."

"You've never taken a bus tour?" Terry asked.

"I have, actually. That's why I know I don't want to do it again. Except in extreme circumstances."

"What would those be?"

"I guess if there was nobody like Tobias around," she smiled at their driver, who grinned back. "And I didn't feel safe renting a car myself, or couldn't."

"So if you really wanted to visit some place and that were the only way, you'd do it?"

"What do you have in mind?"

"I don't know, just testing your limits, I guess."

Beth rolled her eyes and he grabbed her hand, raising it to his lips.

Three more tourists trotted by, nodding greetings as they passed.

"The stragglers," Beth observed. "I like them already."

"They're the ones who'll get left somewhere along the line and have to fend for themselves," Terry said.

"And be happier for it."

Terry laughed.

The jungle trail transitioned into a wide, paved area with a small cement block structure painted in bright reds and yellows.

"You buy tickets here," Tobias explained. "You go ahead. I wait for you dere." He nodded toward an adjacent structure that was less decorative, made of wood slats with a window and counter. Two men stood at the counter with glasses in front of them, talking animatedly with a young man inside.

"Do we need to get tickets to get the clue?" Beth asked.

"All de others did. There are some ladies selling things by the falls. I think you see one of dem."

"Come on, we should see the falls in any case, since we're here," Terry prodded, pulling his wallet out of his pocket. Beth followed him to the ticket office. There was no evidence of the hunt there, as she had hoped, so she decided that Tobias must be right. Terry handed her a pre-torn ticket and they passed through a squealing wooden turnstile and into a maelstrom of tourists, visitors, and thundering falling water.

"I didn't expect Disneyland!"

"I know, it didn't look like that many cars."

They made their way toward a row of vendors backed up against the overhanging jungle. The first stand displayed baskets of spices and dried herbs, with rows of jars above them and creatively packaged gift packs above those. Beth imagined the elderly native women carefully tying scraps of green ribbon around the necks of small canvas bags full of Caribbean saffron, mace, and whole nutmegs. She loved buying spices from the local markets, but this product was aimed squarely at the cruise ship tourists. She saw no sign of the treasure hunt, so they moved on.

The next stand was much the same, but with different products. Hammered steel cut into fish, bird, and leaf shapes and painted in gaudy reds, oranges, blues, and greens were arrayed above woven baskets, carved figures, and baskets of trinkets intended for small children's amusement. Beth really wanted to pick up one of the multitude of small toys to confirm the "Made in China" stamp she was sure was there, but she refrained. Still no sign of the treasure hunt. They moved on.

A t-shirt on a hanger rotated in the light breeze at head level. Beth started to duck under it but stopped, peering up at the treasure hunt logo on the reverse side. As she watched it rotated again and she saw the waterfall on the front. The stand's proprietress saw her looking and came over.

"You like it?" she asked.

Beth drew the map out of her bag and showed it to the woman, who nodded. "Congratulations. I am the next stop."

"Thank you. What do you have for us?"

"You got to buy de shirt. It got de clue."

"You don't have something to give us?"

The woman nodded and went to her mechanical cash register. From behind it she took a creased, stained manila envelope and withdrew a card like the one they'd received from the visitors' bureau.

"You get this. But you gonna buy de shirt? Dat the clue."

Beth looked to Terry. She had not expected to have to buy anything and wondered if the woman was selling what she was supposed to give away. Terry shrugged and brought his wallet back out.

"Two – one large, one extra-large."

"Terry –."

"Don't you want a commemorative shirt? I do."

Beth shut her mouth. He was right. Pleased, the woman located two of the shirts and handed them over in exchange for Terry's cash. Beth stuffed them into her daypack and took Terry's hand, leading him on through the crowds toward the edge of the paved area where it overlooked the pool and waterfall.

They leaned on the damp railing and watched tons of fresh water plunging over rocks and past ferns to splash exuberantly into the deep pool below. Beth lost herself in the sound and the notion of water passing. Born somewhere high in the jungle as condensed dew, or rain, each droplet had made its way downward, joining with others to form tiny puddles, then larger pools, and then to spill over into rivulets and run along to find streams. Streams had met and merged and reached this rocky place where the droplets tumbled over the edge, some seriously flowing, others gleefully dancing up and out. Their journey was far from over, would not be until, sometime later today or late tonight they tasted salt and merged with it, entering the vast sea. Was it like Nirvana? Was it like death when the river water reached the sea? Were the droplets reborn as mist drawn into the clouds and rained back down on another jungle on another island?

Someone jostled Beth from behind and she instinctively pulled her pack in under her arm, mentally shaking herself from her reverie.

"We should have brought swim suits," Terry said, looking across the pool at some water-level rocks where a group of giggling children were daring one another to jump in.

"It never occurred to me," Beth sighed. "Mental note: Always bring a bathing suit to a waterfall."

"Shall we get back and study those shirts?"

"I guess so." Beth cast one last glance at the streaming, thundering water, and turned away with Terry toward the entrance.

"I don't get it. We have to go back," Beth declared. She was sitting in *Trouble*'s main salon with her t-shirt spread on the table in front of her. Terry was at the opposite end with his shirt. They had both been examining them for the past hour. Beth had even studied the tag sewn into the collar, but found only the usual iconic washing instructions and the useful clue that the shirt was a cotton polyester blend.

"At least it won't shrink much," she'd muttered, dropping the garment on the table.

"Let's rethink our assumptions," Terry said, rubbing his temples with his left hand, elbow planted on the shirt on the table. "We don't think we need to disassemble them — there are no secret hiding places like you might have in a lined jacket or something."

"Right."

"There is a clue in or on them. I mean, the card she gave us is just like the first one, right?"

"Right. The only difference is that is says 'Annendale Falls, Stop Two.' It's only worth one point, by the way."

"I don't really expect us to get to any of these in the first three, do you?"

Beth sighed, still looking at the points card from the falls. "No. And definitely not at this rate, if we're already stumped. It can only get harder."

"Well, the first two were awfully easy."

"Hey, you said I was good at figuring out clues to places!" she smiled across the table at him. He looked up at her, returning her smile, glad to see it.

"No, you said that. I just agreed."

She snorted derisively and looked again at the card in her hand. Terry watched as she set it down on top of her t-shirt and planted her hands on the table, lifting herself to put one knee on the settee. At first he thought she was just changing position, but she stayed up, staring straight down at the card and the t-shirt.

"What is it?" he asked, hope sparking.

She looked up, face radiant with excitement. "They aren't the same!"

"What aren't?" He got up and came around the table to look at the two items from her angle.

"The two logos. The one on the shirt is different from the one on the card."

"No kidding? Sneaky. Unless it's just a printing error."

"Look at this," Beth pointed at details in the logo on the t-shirt, then at the same area in the logo on the card.

"It's a flying parrot on the card," Terry said. "But on the shirt it looks like a building. Is that a building?" he bent low, focusing on the screen-printed image.

"It's better to get back from it," Beth advised. She was reaching into her canvas tote. Terry straightened and looked again from a distance. It was definitely a building.

Beth placed the first point card from the visitors' bureau on the table and they compared all three logos.

"The two cards are definitely the same. And they're like this one," Terry stepped over to the navigation desk and pointed at the ad tacked up there, staring at it to be sure as he spoke. "They all have the bird."

"This building is definitely the clue. But what the heck does it mean?"

"Look for other differences. Isn't this different?" he dragged his shirt off the table and held it up next to the ad on the bulkhead. "Upper right, isn't that a beer bottle on the shirt, behind the palm fronds? That's not in the one on the ad."

"You're right. And it's got a label. It's a red label with green and yellow details. It looks familiar."

"It is," Terry lowered his shirt and turned toward her. "Why don't we go get some dinner at the bar next door?"

"What?"

"I'm getting hungry, aren't you?"

"Well I —," Beth paused, realizing that she hadn't eaten since the spice cake at the Internet cafe several hours ago. "I am. That's a good idea. We've made progress here, and we may need to go online anyway."

"Right," Terry's face was a mask, but she was sure she detected amusement behind it. Curious, she reached for her daypack, which was sitting on the settee next to her.

"I'll be ready in a sec."

Terry was decidedly non-communicative as they strolled up the dock, only mumbling responses to Beth's speculations. They passed out of the marina and turned toward the waterfront restaurant and bar next door. It was a cruising sailor's hangout, attracting a few tourists and locals, but mostly filled with the familiar faces of the sailing set — familiar in a generic way, for when they entered they did not see anyone who they actually knew.

"Hey!" Beth paused just inside, eyes locked on a neon sign over the bar. It was green, red, and yellow, promoting Petit Quaff beer. She looked toward Terry and saw from his delighted grin that he must have known it was there. "You rat!" she declared, playfully punching him on the upper arm. He laughed and caught her fist, eyes sparkling. "You knew!" she added, allowing him to capture her in a bear hug.

"I stuck my head in here earlier when I dropped the trash."

"For a beer?"

"To see if it looked like a good place to get one later. It did, by the way."

"More so now. Let's see what the bartender can tell us about Petit Quaff."

"It's brewed on Petit Martinique, the last four or five years I guess," Cyril the bartender explained as he placed a foamy headed glass of lager in front of each of them, wiping the bar with a white cloth before stepping back to lean on the rear counter. He looked more than ready to give them the low-down on Petit Quaff.

Terry raised his glass and took a sip through the foam. It was more bitter than he expected, but refreshingly cool. Beth followed his example and took a healthy mouthful, closing her eyes to savor the flavor before swallowing.

"I like it," she said, taking another gulp.

"It's refreshing," Terry concurred.

"Not your American Budweiser," Cyril observed.

"Thank goodness," Beth replied.

"We both like our beer to have some substance," Terry added, taking another sip. "So does the brewery offer tours or anything?"

"On Petite Martinique?"

"Yes. We might stop in on our way north."

"You're sailing – charter boat?"

"My boat."

Cyril nodded, silent acknowledgement that this put them in a slightly different league from the many short-term bareboat and crewed charter sailors that passed through town.

"You watch the shoals coming in there. You may want to anchor at Petit St. Vincent – PSV – and dinghy over."

"And we could visit the brewery? I mean, it's worth the trip?"

"I don't know about that – being worth it. A brewery is a brewery. But I think they have a bar and some free tastings. But Petit Martinique is a pretty place, with some good restaurants. It's worth a visit."

"Thanks Cyril. That's useful information," Terry raised his glass, nodding at the bartender. After taking a sip he looked at Beth. "Shall we get a table and something to eat?"

"Yes let's. I'm starving. Thanks Cyril." She slid off the bar stool, turning toward the dining room.

"Don't mention it. Good luck finding the treasure."

Beth and Terry both looked back at the bartender's sly grin. Beth laughed. "Well at least we know we're on the right track!"

TEN: PETIT QUAF

After a short discussion over dinner and frothy glasses of Petit Quaff, they decided to spend another day in St. George's. It was an effort, at first, to calm themselves after finding two of the treasure hunt stops in one day. But after a second beer their focus began to shift back to their original plan for the cruise. As Beth had put it months before, she wanted to get to know each island she visited. On her trip south she had barely set foot on many of the islands where she'd stopped, and sailed right on by several. When she and Terry had returned to *Trouble* a month ago he'd set the pace, heading them south again to get to the paradise of the Tobago Cays with the briefest of stops on Dominica, Martinique, St. Lucia, and St. Vincent. "We'll come back slowly," they'd agreed as they bid farewell to one enticing harbor after another.

Beth hadn't questioned his drive. Shell-shocked from her time with her family and desperately glad to be back in his company, she'd simply gone along. And when they were finally settled in the Cays and she began to regain her sense of self she'd been glad to be there. She didn't resent his choices at all.

But now, spending only one day on Grenada, and that engaged in the treasure hunt, seemed like cheating the island of its due. So the additional day was a compromise of their old plan and the new one. They knew that they were behind in the hunt, and although they did not expect to catch up to whoever was finding the next clue first, they were both too competitive not to make an effort.

In the morning they contacted Tobias and arranged for a tour. He drove them around the island, showing them the jagged east coast and idyllic bays of the south where a big charter company kept its fleet of sparkling white sailboats. They visited the northern tip of the island, and then wound through the mountainous, jungle interior on sometimes terrifying roads. In banana plantations they saw the odd sight of blue plastic bags tied around the bunches of tiny bananas. Insect protection, Tobias explained. At one of the island's several waterfalls Tobias picked a fruit like a nectarine and sliced it open to reveal the mace-covered pit. He smashed this open with two rocks and a whole nutmeg tumbled out. Soon Beth's daypack was weighed down with the fruit, which Tobias assured them would make tasty preserves. They'd remembered their swim suits this time, and plunged together into the waterfall pools, gasping at the unfamiliar chill after swimming so much in the warm sea.

They concluded the perfect day with a romantic supper at a restaurant on the Grande Anse, the endless white beach south of St. George's. They dug their toes into cool sand beneath the table while sampling one another's flying fish and grouper along with a crisp French white wine that was amazingly cheap. After a decadent but irresistible dessert of caramelized bananas and vanilla ice cream their waiter placed shot glasses of amber liquid before them. At their curious look he explained that it was a local rum compliments of the gentleman at the large table. They raised their glasses in a toast to him, and he nodded acknowledgement as they sipped the strong beverage. It was as smooth as the best whiskey Beth had ever had, smoky, but with a surprising sweetness.

"That's Mr. Callwood," the waiter said quietly, seeing their appreciative expressions. "He own the distillery. This is the best they sell."

"I can taste why," Beth said, looking at the liquid remaining in her glass.

"Do you think he does that often?" she asked Terry when the waiter had gone.

"Maybe. It's good business to get the tourists tasting the product. I'd buy some now, whereas before I'd never even heard of it."

Early the following morning as Beth carried a small bag of trash up the dock like a parting gift for the island she caught sight of a familiar hull over on the next pier. After dropping the trash bag in a dumpster she made her way over and found Laurie sitting in the cockpit sipping coffee. She could hear a commotion going on below.

"Hey there!," Laurie called out. "Fancy meeting you here."

"I was going to say the same. Did you come in yesterday?"

"Yup. The boys were driving us nuts. When they found out you'd left the Cays to join the hunt they couldn't believe we let you get a head start. Have you found the first clue?"

"We did. And the second," Beth said proudly.

"Uh oh. Hey boys, Beth's here with news," Laurie leaned into the companionway to speak to the rest of her family.

"What?" Came Michael's young voice as his head appeared in the opening. Prodded from behind, he climbed out and was replaced by his father Joe.

"Hello Beth. How was your voyage?" he asked as he climbed out after his son.

"It was a great sail. We stopped in Clifton and Carriacou, then came here."

"And you found the first stop?" Michael asked.

"We did. And that led us to the second one. Now we're getting ready to head out for the third."

"So two are here," Joe said with a sly grin and Beth realized that she'd inadvertently given them a hint. Oh well, it was such an easy clue they'd have figured it out without help. And besides, they were still at least a day behind.

"Two are here," she nodded.

"So where are you headed?" Aiden asked, coming up the companionway ladder. He'd obviously been listening.

Beth shook her head with a smile. "Oh no. You're on your own buddy."

They all laughed.

"Enjoy your stay here. We did. But I'm sure Terry's wondering what happened to me – I was on a garbage run when I saw your boat here."

"Thanks Beth. We'll see you soon," Laurie said, shooting a grin at her boys.

"Not if we see you first!" Beth crowed as she hurried away along the dock.

ELEVEN: TYRELL BAY

"I'm glad we found out about the dump at Halifax Harbor," Terry said. He was stretched out in the cockpit, head and shoulders elevated by a couple cushions just high enough to see out across the water to either side. Beth, sitting up on the cabin top with a book, was responsible for keeping an eye on the waters ahead as *Trouble*'s autohelm, "Otto" steered.

Beth glanced down at Terry, then followed his gaze toward shore, where a break in the dense green foliage indicated the entrance to the small bay. It looked lovely – a tempting anchorage, all the more so for the lack of other boats there.

"I might have suggested we leave the marina yesterday afternoon and come here for the night," Terry went on.

"Probably would have been really unpleasant with the breeze blowing from the garbage," Beth concurred.

"I hope the hunt takes us to some of the other Grenadines," Beth said a while later. She had closed her book, a page-turner mystery, resolving to get out the computer and try again on her article. If she was going to weep, she might as well do it out here at sea so that only Terry would see her bloodshot eyes and blotchy red face.

Terry opened his eyes to look up at her, making her realize that she had to sit out here, since her partner seemed on the verge of a nap. He was allowed, she reflected with a private smile. They had not slept all that much last night after returning to *Trouble* from their romantic dinner.

"If it doesn't we'll go anyway," he observed. Seeing her conflicted expression he went on. "We know when the final party is — it's more than two months away. I know we won't get the rest of the clues as fast as the first ones. But we did agree not to forget what we came for originally."

Beth noted that he did not suggest that this was a "once in a lifetime" opportunity to see these islands. They had not discussed their plans beyond the six months Terry had managed to arrange for this cruise, other than, Beth realized with a shiver, his declaration that he wanted to marry her. And the truth was she did not have a plan. For the first time in her life she was living in the moment, or at least in the half a year. She could not contemplate the end of this cruise and possibly parting from Terry. And on a deeper level she knew that she tied that timeframe with her father's health. She had subconsciously decided that his condition would change by then, that — she swallowed hard and forced herself to think it — he would die. And when that happened she believed her life would change, although she did not know how. She would go to California, of course, although there was no reason to think she had to move back there. No reason to think that her relationship with Terry could not weather the turmoil of burying her father, either. But when she forced herself to contemplate that moment she was filled with fear. And trying to describe in writing her family's experience so far forced her to do just that. She had chosen the independent life far from her roots, and now she was paying the price for it through fear of abandonment and loneliness; feelings that were entirely imagined, she reminded herself harshly.

In any case, she refused to consider that this tour of these islands was her one and only visit. She would come back here, one way or another.

"PSV was on my list anyway," she added, realizing she'd been quiet for too long, although Terry had simply shut his eyes again. "I want to see the fancy resort."

Terry shifted up onto one elbow and looked around as if awakening to realize he'd been derelict in his duties. His eyes finally fell on her where she had ended up sitting in the far corner of the cockpit.

"I don't suppose I could convince you to check in for a day or so and raise the 'do not disturb' flag."

"Only after raising the 'bring champagne and oysters' flag," she laughed at his sudden leer beneath tousled hair and sleepy eyes.

"Of course," he purred, dragging himself to a sitting position and craning his neck to look at the waters ahead. There was nothing in their path, and the island continued to block the breeze. "We could go further off shore and try to sail."

Beth peered off to the west at the open Caribbean. "The forecast was for light air. We could go a long way out and end up motoring anyway."

"Boy, this treasure hunt is really changing you," his tone was amused. "Preferring to use fuel over sails."

"I'm a pragmatist. I'll bet we can sail when we get north of Grenada."

"I'm sure we can. So what about PSV?" he tried again.

"About...?"

"The resort. I've always been curious."

"Isn't it ridiculously expensive?" She knew it was. There were no phones, no televisions. The guests communicated their needs to the staff by raising multi colored flags on poles outside their private bungalows.

He shrugged. "Jeff went, on his honeymoon."

"That sounds like the right time to go," Beth replied, only as the words left her mouth considering their various meanings. Terry's mouth quivered, with mirth or something else? She could not tell.

"It does, doesn't it?" he replied softly. And for a terrifying moment she thought he might be about to suggest something crazy. He stood up, stretching his arms wide over his head, his hands brushing the canvas bimini. Beth's eyes were drawn to the thatches of dark hair in his armpits then followed the lines of muscle down his ribcage to his waist and bellybutton just peeking from the shadows at the top of his shorts. He was watching her, a shadow of the earlier leer playing around the edges of his expressive mouth.

"Do you want anything below?" she asked, breaking the tension.

"My water bottle from the fridge," he said, resting his hands on the wheel and inspecting the instruments, checking up on Otto.

Beth climbed down the companionway ladder and went about collecting her computer and their water bottles. For a horrible moment a wave of emptiness washed over her and she stood, hands on the galley counter, eyes shut tight. It was a strange sort of grief, born, she realized, from what Terry had not said. She had feared a sudden proposal of marriage, but now that he had not made it she felt irrational sorrow.

You're a wreck, girl, she told herself. *Whatever the hell is wrong, you have to get over it or you'll ruin everything.*

For the next two hours while *Trouble* made her way to the northern tip of Grenada Beth struggled to record her family's experiences at the onset of her father's ailment. She let the tears flow, pressing her face into a sun-warmed towel now and then. Terry remained at the back of the cockpit, watching the water and sky around them for obstructions and signs of change in the weather. He also watched her, but he did not interfere. This was a way of life on small boats – privacy must be granted and observed even between people who were occupying the same small physical space.

She had written three difficult pages when Terry stood up, catching her eye as he peered ahead. He glanced down and saw that she was watching him through red-rimmed eyes.

"We're coming to David Point," he said, referring to the northern tip of the island. Beth understood his unspoken message and immediately saved her work. She stowed her computer in the navigation desk, leaving it on and plugged in to the twelve-volt outlet from which she'd strung an extension cord to the cockpit. Up on deck Terry was preparing to sail, sliding the chart book – open to the page showing Grenada's north end – under the flotation cushions he'd been sitting on and then climbing up on the cabin top to remove the sail ties from the mainsail.

When Beth came back out he was ready at the main halyard, winch handle in hand. He had altered the course Otto was steering to point *Trouble* directly into the light breeze. She nodded, reaching for the main sheet. As he raised the mainsail she eased the sheet, allowing the boom to rattle and bang until the fabric of the sail began to pull it up with it. As Terry made the last few turns on the winch she cleated the sheet and went to the back of the cockpit to get behind the wheel. She turned off Otto and took control, slowly turning *Trouble* so that the breeze struck her starboard bow and filled the sail. The boat heeled over a little and surged forward, the drive of the wind augmenting that of the propeller.

An uncontrolled smile filled Beth's face at the feel of her boat finding the wind, which was stronger than she'd expected. She reached down and turned the key to shut off the engine. On the port side now Terry was juggling two lines – grinding the winch to pull on the jib sheet while keeping tension on the reefing line that was slowly rolling up on a drum at the base of the sail up on the bow.

"I'll take the reef line," Beth said, reaching for it from behind him. He passed it to her and together they finished pulling out the forward sail. It filled and *Trouble* seemed to leap forward with enthusiasm.

"This is what I needed," Beth sighed, settling on the combing on the port side of the cockpit, one arm extended to hold the wheel. Terry, standing at the forward end of the cockpit separating and coiling the mess of main halyard and sheet, grinned back at her.

"That was slick the way you slipped in there behind the wheel as soon as the wind came up," he teased.

"Do you want to steer?" she asked insincerely.

He chuckled. "No, I think I'm off watch for a while. Are you hungry? We should have gotten food out while we were in the calm."

He was right. They'd be heeling for the rest of the afternoon, battling their way almost into the wind to get to Carriacou, Grenada's northern neighbor. Tyrrel Bay on its western end was their destination for tonight. Tomorrow morning they would sail around to the northern side to check out of Grenada at Hillsborough before heading for Petit Martinique, further to the northeast and home of Petit Quaf brewery. In fact, they planned to anchor at Petit Martinique's neighbor, Petit St. Vincent, because, as the bartender in St. George's had said, the anchorage was well known to be more secure. Since Petit Martinique was part of Grenada, technically they should visit it first and then return to Carriacou to check out of Grenada with customs and immigration. But the majority of cruisers they'd talked to had assured them that coming from the south they checked out of Grenada, then visited Petit St. Vincent and Petit Martinique before making the upwind trip to check in with customs and immigrations for St. Vincent and the Grenadines. "Everyone does it, and the officials look the other way" was the common message.

Beth particularly liked this plan because they might be able to skip Union Island entirely and sail all the way to St. Vincent from PSV, if that's where the treasure hunt clues took them. Or they could stop at one of the other islands that had a port of entry. She had gotten over the embarrassment of the mail boat incident, in fact the phrase "de mail boat, mon" was making its way into their vocabulary to indicate looming peril, but she still disliked Clifton's deep, crowded anchorage. Fortunately, their fuel supply was ample, and they'd topped off the water tanks in St. George's. They could go for several days without visiting another marina.

They smelled Tyrell Bay's vast mangrove swamp long before they could make out the details of the harbor. Landfalls were one of Beth's least favorite things after a long, relaxing sail. With their destination in sight she felt a powerful need to get there and move on to the next stage of the voyage, but the land was deceptive, seeming to move farther and farther away as they approached. Sailing in to an up-wind bay meant they had to tack back and forth, making far more sideways progress than forward, while the island seemed to hover just out of their reach. And then quite suddenly they were much closer to the mountainous coastline on the north side of the bay and the wind was gusting randomly, distorted by the island's contours.

They inched their way southeast along the point matching sparse landmarks on shore to the chart. Finally they were in the last stretch, screaming along on a close reach past the mangroves to the north, aiming for a slot between reefs that would force them to round up and turn on the engine, or short tack back and forth up the channel.

Beth could tell Terry, who was steering now was tempted, but she could think of no good reason and plenty of bad ones. Without consulting him she bent down and turned on the engine. She saw him nod slightly out of the corner of her eye, then glance over his shoulder looking for traffic astern before gently turning *Trouble* head into the wind.

"Drop the sails?" he asked.

"At least the jib, for now. I can get it."

Terry held *Trouble* steadily into the wind while Beth hauled in on the reefing line that rotated the head stay, rolling the jib up around it like a giant vertical window shade. Grunting, she took a final few heaves on the line and cleated it. While she tidied the lines Terry turned *Trouble* onto the course that would take them straight in between the reefs and eased up the throttle to cruising RPMs.

"I'll turn on the fridge," Beth said, heading for the companionway. The steps for coming in to a harbor were automatic for both of them; informing one another of what they were doing assured that they both knew what was going on.

They found a good spot to anchor and traded places, Beth handling the helm while Terry deployed the anchor and directed her to reverse and dig it in using hand signals. They were still tidying up, refolding the mainsail, recoiling and stowing lines, when a local rowing a small wooden boat approached and called out a hello.

"Welcome to Tyrell Bay. I am James."

Terry draped the jib sheet around the winch and leaned out of the cockpit toward the visitor. "Hello James. I'm Terry, and this is Beth."

Beth waved from across the cockpit. She still found the friendly formality of the islanders alien to her protestant upbringing and in stark contrast to her New York experience. Failure to introduce themselves when James had offered his name would be considered insulting, and she was glad the proper response rolled right off of Terry's tongue.

James proceeded to offer them all manner of services, including taking them, in their dinghy with its motor, over to the mangrove swamp to gather mangrove oysters. Beth could tell Terry was tempted by this one, perhaps the most unusual service they'd yet encountered. But it was late in the day and this man was a total stranger. And what the heck were mangrove oysters anyway?

"You get to rig the motor," she said, assuming that would be enough of a deterrent, when he looked his question at her.

"Okay James, you're on," he said, shooting a smile at her before turning back toward their visitor. Beth retreated below, suppressing her annoyance that he hadn't understood her unspoken message.

James helped with the motor and told Terry to bring a bucket and some gloves for the expedition. Encountering Beth in the galley when he went to get gloves he paused, putting his hands on her waist and a kiss on her forehead.

"You sure you don't want to come?" he asked.

"I think I should try to write a little more."

"You made progress earlier."

"I did. In a lot of ways."

His second kiss was deeper, his lips parting hers as he engulfed her in his arms for a moment. "I love you Beth. I won't be gone long."

She stared after him, startled by his sudden declaration, as he climbed the ladder and disappeared over the side into the dinghy where James was already waiting.

Beth hit Control-S to save her work and stretched her arms above her head. She had just written two pages about her father without crying a tear. She glanced at the clock in the upper right corner of the computer screen. Her eyes widened in alarm: Terry had been gone more than an hour. She set the computer on the desk and went to the companionway ladder to poke her head out and survey the world.

Evening clouds were forming on the western horizon: *no green flash tonight*, she thought, disappointed but not surprised. Conditions for the mysterious phenomenon when the setting sun flashed bright green had to be perfect, and rarely were. She turned toward the mangroves hoping to see a small boat carrying two men toward her. No sign of them. She allowed herself a moment of regret for not going, wondering what it was like in between those trees. She'd walked through a mangrove swamp once in a park in Florida, along a boardwalk that gave it the feel of a Disneyland attraction. Going in to a wild swamp by boat was authentic.

Concern growing as the sun crept downward, she forced herself to turn away from the trees and survey the rest of the anchorage. There were twenty or so boats at anchor in the broad harbor. It was the least crowded place they'd been since the Tobago Cays.

Out of habit she picked up the binoculars that were hanging on the binnacle and scanned the other boats looking for familiar names. The boats in the big bareboat charter fleets were easy to identify: all French made and nearly new, uniformly bright white hulls, with unfaded canvas biminis and dodgers, and a flag in the rigging or painted logo on the hull or boom identifying the charter company. There were small charter firms too, but their fleets tended to blend in with the private boats: older looking, well used, with no markings to call them out as short-term visitors to the islands. Beth guessed that about half the boats anchored today were bareboat charters. She skipped over them easily and focused on the rest one after another. She saw three that looked familiar. She would have to check her log, where she recorded the names, makes, and owners of boats she met. She skipped over a big, ostentatious bareboat at least fifty feet long, and landed on a decidedly familiar vessel: *Great Escape.*

She had last seen the French-made sloop three months ago in the anchorage at Charlotte Amalie, St. Thomas. As she studied it through the binoculars she remembered the puzzle that had formed around it and its owners. Maggie and Bill Hartford were not quite the typical cruising couple: Bill had made his fortune in business and they'd bought the boat and escaped to the tropics. Beth had not been that close to them, but she recalled that unlike many cruisers who had done a complete disconnect, Bill sometimes returned to the states to deal with business matters. Perhaps he had left a business under someone's direction, or maybe he was managing a large financial portfolio that could be left to itself for long periods. In any case, they had seemed well-funded – perhaps more so than the myriad shoestring cruisers who'd saved up a budget for a year's worth of cruising and lived frugally to stick to it.

The puzzle had centered on Bill's whereabouts. Just before Beth upped anchor to leave St. Thomas he had seemed to be missing, for Maggie was taking care of chores that were normally his. And she had lied about it to Beth. She'd told her that Bill had taken the dinghy engine for repair; later on other cruisers mentioned seeing Maggie hauling it awkwardly up the street. And then there'd been the late night departure from the boat – hardly sinister, but unusual in that someone had climbed over the side into a dinghy rather than using the open transom that was a standard feature on the modern French cruising boats. Beth had seen that the night before she left. She hadn't given more than a fleeting thought to Maggie and Bill in the months since then.

She put down the binoculars and moved toward the companionway to get her shoes: she should go say hello. Then she realized that Terry had the dinghy. James's sun-bleached wooden rowboat was tied to *Trouble*'s stern. She was capable of rowing to *Great Escape* – she made a point of rowing regularly so she would be able to if the dinghy motor died on her. But she was loathe to borrow someone else's boat, particularly a local's, when it wasn't an emergency.

Her concentration on her article broken, she went below and made herself a rum and tonic. She added a generous squeeze of lime to compensate for the slightly flat tonic from yesterday's leftover open can, then returned to the computer to review her logs from those last days in St. Thomas.

Hearty male laughter interrupted her reading a short while later, followed by a gentle thump against *Trouble*'s hull and the telltale rocking as Terry climbed the ladder up her side. Beth looked up from the computer to see his shadow fill the companionway. He descended the ladder and turned to the galley.

"Why are you sitting in the dark?" he asked, opening the refrigerator. "Is everything all right Beth?"

Struck by the concern in his voice Beth nodded, illuminated, she knew, by the light of the computer monitor.

"I hadn't noticed," she said. "I was reading."

Terry set two beers on the counter and shut the refrigerator, his eyes still focused on her.

"I promised James a beer," he said by way of acknowledging her explanation. "Want one?"

"I have this," she lifted her cup from the seat cushion where it was leaning against her leg.

"Um, good idea," he said, clearly realizing it was a run drink. He turned and carried the bottles up the ladder.

James had transferred into his own boat and was standing in it holding the bucket of oysters that was their prize for the expedition.

Back among the mangroves he had shown Terry how to slice open the soft shells. Now he held the bucket up in exchange for the beer Terry offered him.

"De missus at home?" he asked, sitting down in his boat. Terry put the bucket on the deck beside himself and opened his own beer.

"Below," he nodded, then took a long gulp.

"She like dose oysters," James glanced at the bucket. Terry cracked a wry smile, not at all sure he agreed. They had tried the sample that James had cut open back in the mangroves.

"Mon you gots to make her have some, you know what I mean?" James went on. Terry did. James had waxed eloquently about the effect of the oysters on the women in his life. So much so that Terry had grown uncomfortable with the topic.

"She'll try them, James, don't worry about that," he said. "So these were red mangroves, right?" He struggled to change the topic. Fortunately the question was successful and they finished their beers discussing the use of the trees other than as host to aphrodisiac shellfish.

Beth stood at the base of the companionway ladder, at first thinking to climb up and join them, but stopping at the sound of their conversation. She couldn't quite make out what they were discussing, but something about the quiet tone in the early evening twilight seemed private. Marshaling her sudden, inappropriate resentment she turned back to the computer. After all, he had done exactly what he'd said he would and was not intentionally excluding her – if anything she had excluded herself. Feeling foolish she refocused on her old notes about Maggie and Bill.

A few minutes later – about the length of time it took to drink a beer, she felt the boat rock slightly as Terry rose and moved around. Then the fresh water pump came on, a dull hum from beneath one of the settees in the salon. Realizing he must be rinsing off in the cockpit she shut down the computer and climbed the ladder.

He had set the bucket on the floor behind the wheel right next to the cockpit drains. Rather than rinsing himself, he was using the cockpit shower to rinse mud from a few flat, grey ovoid objects that were on the floor next to it.

He glanced up at her as she sat down on the lazarette just in front of the wheel.

"They're awfully small," he said, holding up one of the oysters. She reached through the spokes of the wheel to take it. It was cool and damp, not much bigger than a fifty-cent piece, the surface mottled greys and creams, the shades of granite if not the texture. Holding it between thumbs and fingers she flexed it gently.

"They're soft," Terry confirmed. "Here." Using the rigging knife he always had attached to his belt he sliced into another of the oysters, lifting the top shell with the point of the blade, then slicing beneath the contents to sever the muscle. He held it out to her.

She handed him the closed one in exchange, and studied the unfortunate creature in her hand. It was a tiny glistening lump of pearl grey tissue.

"You'd need a lot of them to make stew," she observed.

"Try it," Terry urged all too enthusiastically. Beth pursed her lips, then raised the little shell to her mouth and slurped the raw oyster off of it.

"It tastes like salty mud!" she declared, tossing the empty shell over the side. "And you knew it!" she added at the sight of his devilish grin.

"I thought it was just me," he tried with a shrug, dropping the oyster he was holding back into the muddy bucket.

"You tried one out there, but you still brought these back?" she went on, looking into the bucket.

"Come on now Beth, if I'd come back here saying they were awful you'd have been disappointed."

"You mean I wouldn't have believed you," she admitted, unable to contain a laugh.

"Something like that," he agreed, lifting the bucket and standing up. "Want another one?"

"No, thanks."

He nodded, then held the bucket out over the stern and upended it, sending the rest of the oysters back to the sea.

TWELVE: MAGGIE

"So you thought that Bill was gone and Maggie was covering it up for some reason," Terry summarized.

After discarding the oysters they had retired to the galley and reheated leftovers from last nights' dinner. They were sharing the last of a piece of key lime pie out of a white Styrofoam container, two forks competing for the bits with both whipped cream and graham cracker crust attached.

Beth had told him about seeing *Great Escape* in the anchorage and that she'd reviewed her log entries from those last days in St. Thomas.

"I wouldn't have thought anything of it if Maggie hadn't lied about Bill not being on board. Why wouldn't she just say that Bill was away and she had to deal with the motor herself?"

"Who knows? There could be hundreds of reasons. None that I can think of right now," he admitted, putting down his fork. "Take it," he nodded at the last bite of pie. "Let's ride over in the dinghy in the morning and say hello."

"He took you into the mangroves for oysters, didn't he?" Maggie Hartford's clear laugh challenged the tolling of bells in a church someplace just inland. Their peals fluttering across the anchorage had been the only reminder to Beth and Terry that it was Sunday morning as they breakfasted early on cereal and coffee before getting into the dinghy to pay their planned visit on *Great Escape*.

As they'd approached Terry had pointed out that *Great Escape*'s dinghy was missing. Maggie had greeted them from the cockpit as they puttered up, outboard motor on low so as not to disturb the neighbors. Beth had felt like they were sneaking up on the Hartfords, and was startled when her old acquaintance appeared before they got close. Maggie invited them aboard as far as the cockpit and after warm greetings steered the conversation to their travels, deftly preventing them from asking about the obviously absent Bill without seeming rude.

Still, this was not out of character for Maggie, who always struck Beth as a very social, outgoing person. Only now she began to consider that these traits could also be used, as now, to shield herself. As long as she kept her guests talking about themselves they couldn't ask about her.

"I was curious," Terry shrugged, unwilling to be embarrassed at having been drawn in to what was most certainly a local prank. "The forest was neat – so dense and quiet. There are alligators in there, or crocs – I have to look up which live here. And tons of birds."

"Well it sounds like you didn't mind taking Tobias for a ride then. Look at me, talking away here without offering you coffee!" Maggie stood up and climbed down the companionway ladder. Beth saw her chance.

"Thanks Maggie. So I guess Bill's not aboard – he must have gotten an early start," she asked, leaning forward from her seat on the lazarette to look down into the boat where Maggie had stopped.

"No, he's not here," she looked out at them from the shadows of the cabin below. "He's back in Michigan taking care of business. Again." She rolled her eyes, smiled, and turned toward the boat's spacious galley. Beth straightened and met Terry's eyes from across the cockpit. He shrugged, his expression suggesting that it was a plausible answer. But Beth wasn't convinced. Carriacou was a small island to leave a wife and valuable boat alone, and it didn't have an airport. Bill would have had to catch a ferry to Union Island or Grenada. And where was the dinghy? Her expression must have conveyed her objections because Terry leaned forward to speak into the cabin where the clanks of stainless steel indicated a coffee pot being readied. But Maggie went on before he could.

"When he retired and he called it 'semi-retirement,' I didn't realize that the 'semi' was his excuse for hanging on to almost half of his responsibilities. I've been pushing him to get out. Maybe he'll do that this trip. When I retired I went cold turkey. He doesn't seem to understand how great that feels."

"What did you do, Maggie?" Terry asked.

She moved into view and stood looking up at them, obviously planning on waiting below for the coffee to perk. "I'm a certified life coach."

"What's that?" Beth asked. She'd never heard of it. "Did you help people sort out their careers?"

"No, that would be a career coach," the other woman replied. Her tone was gently pedantic, but it left Beth feeling stung. "A life coach helps clients set life goals and work toward them."

"My sister hired one for a while," Terry said, glancing over at Beth as if inviting further discussion. She smiled at him and filed the invitation away for later. Instead she looked down at Maggie.

"I should think you'd have insisted on going to St Vincent or Grenada before Bill left. Not a lot to do here," he said.

Maggie's replied with no hint of surprise or concern at this comment or the change of subject, "He left from St. George's. My brother Steven joined me there. He's always wanted to sail the southern Windwards."

"That's great," Beth tossed out, watching Terry, who sat back looking satisfied. He shot her a warning look and shook his head a little. *Let it go.* There might be problems between Maggie and Bill, but nothing suspicious.

While the coffee perked Maggie described her cruise down the islands, mentioning Bill's involvement just enough to be convincing. There were places and even people she'd met who Beth knew as well and they continued comparing notes over the coffee Maggie served.

"Well I can't imagine where Steven's gotten to," Maggie finally said, craning her neck to look toward shore where they could all see a black dinghy beached. "He just might have snuck off to church."

"The service can't last much longer," Beth observed.

"And we should get going," Terry added, the sudden urgency in his tone reminding Beth that they had a bit of sailing to do.

"It's been great catching up, Maggie. We have to get to customs in Hillsborough and they're only open for about an hour today," Beth explained as she and Terry made to get up.

"Can't linger another day?" Maggie asked. "I'd love for you to meet Steven. He'd want to pick your brains about the islands. He does it to everyone he meets."

"We're on a bit of mission," Beth reminded her. They had described the treasure hunt earlier.

"Of course. You always have been a bit driven, Beth. Not sure it's a good trait in a long-term sailor. But listen to me! What do I know? You obviously love it, and you're a good sailor."

"I do my best ..."

"Off with you then. Have a great sail and I'll look forward to seeing you both again."

Feeling dismissed but relieved nonetheless, Beth and Terry climbed into their dinghy and headed back toward *Trouble*. Looking back at the shore Beth saw someone launching the beached dinghy. She pointed it out to Terry, who didn't look at all surprised.

"There's nothing in her story that doesn't make sense," he pointed out.

"Still, I'd like to meet this Steven."

"Do you want to hang around here?"

She shook her head and focused her attention ahead on *Trouble*.

"Ahoy *Great Escape*." The call from a short distance across the water brought Maggie to the back of the cockpit.

"Ahoy," she called, stepping onto the swim platform as the dinghy approached.

"Ready for a quick trip?" the man driving the dinghy asked. "Shall I hand these up first?"

"Yes, thanks. Come along side."

The man complied, using the outboard motor to swing the little boat broadside to the swim platform. Maggie grabbed the boat's bow line and the man took hold of a handle on the stern of *Great Escape* with one hand. With the other he reached down by his feet and one-by-one listed six gallon jugs of water up onto the swim platform. As he placed each one Maggie lifted it through the opening in the back of the cockpit and gave it a shove so that it slid forward on the floor toward the companionway. When they were all loaded Maggie sat on the swim platform and threw her legs into the dinghy, then slid her behind onto the inflated gunwale.

"You good there?" the man asked.

"Sure. Drive on."

Maggie and the man both pushed the small boat away from *Great Escape*, then he pointed it across the anchorage at an unkept cruising boat anchored not far away. Maggie studied the half-inflated dinghy spread across the cabin in front of the mast.

"Did you find what you needed in Hillsborough?" she asked, shouting over the motor.

"Sort of. You know how it is: you find something similar and you figure out how to improvise. I think I'll be able to patch my dinghy."

"That's good. But if not and you need more help, just give me a shout."

The man brought the dinghy alongside his boat with practiced grace. Maggie reached up and grabbed the base of a stanchion forward of the boarding ladder that was hanging over the side.

"Go ahead. I'll move back once you're out."

"Sure I can't offer you a beer?" he asked, grasping the toe rail of his boat as he stood.

"It's a little early for me, and I just had coffee with a couple other cruisers. I'll take a rain check."

"You got it Maggie. Thanks again." He set a canvas bag on the deck of his boat, then mounted the ladder. As his weight left the dinghy Maggie lifted her legs over the rigid seat that ran across the center of the dinghy and then started sliding her ample behind aft. When his foot left the little boat it started drifting away from the larger boat. Maggie got into position at the motor and watched him get both feet on the deck. She put the motor in gear and turned back toward *Great Escape*.

"So long. Thanks for picking up the water," she shouted, waving as she motored away.

THIRTEEN: PETIT MARTINIQUE

The customs and immigration officer in Hillsborough looked to be about to close his office for the day when Beth and Terry walked in at four minutes to twelve. They had pushed *Trouble* hard around the north west tip of the island. They'd passed inside of The Sisters, two offshore rocks, and Maboya and Sandy Islands. Beth studied the latter with the binoculars as they motored by. It looked like the model on which every desert island story and cartoon was based – a lump of crystalline white sand topped with a Mohawk of shrubs and a half dozen palm trees leaning in various directions. Later in her log she noted that it would be nice to plan a day there pretending to be castaways.

They were extremely courteous in their request to check out of Grenada and endured a relatively short scrutiny of their documents before the officer, clearly anxious to get home to Sunday dinner, made his cryptic notations in their passports and forms and bid them bon voyage.

Two or three restaurants beckoned as they walked back to the dock and their dinghy. From the number of boats in the anchorage and obvious volume of visitors on the streets of the small town, it seemed likely that they could find a tasty lunch. But the sea miles to windward ahead loomed large and they returned to *Trouble* and sandwiches under sail.

"This was faster than I expected," Beth said as they approached the open anchorage on Petit St. Vincent's south side. Like the Tobago Cays it was protected to the east by extensive shallow reefs, but only a narrow spit of the island that extended a little to the south. So the potential for heavy swells rolling in from the Atlantic was minimal, but there was nothing to cut the wind should it come from the southeast. Fortunately, the prevailing breeze was a little north of east and the island itself provided shelter, making the anchorage delightfully calm. Petit Martinique lay close by to the south, a second peak of the same submerged mountain, with its anchorage more open to the northeasterly wind and whatever swells could build up across the open water between the islands. That made it slightly less popular as a stop for cruisers. Beth and Terry were comfortable with the idea of taking the dinghy across: after all, it wasn't even a mile.

Their sail from Carriacou had been perfect. The breeze in the high teens was exactly what *Trouble* liked, and she'd dug into the sea with gusto, working to windward easily under Terry's constant adjustment of the sails and other rigging. Beth had been in heaven pointing her boat across the water, navigating to the turning points by GPS and confirming it with dead reckoning using landmarks on the surrounding islands and the charts.

Terry went up to the bow and prepared the anchor as Beth motored into the anchorage and looked for a good spot. He looked as well, and pointed to suggestions as they meandered between the boats already there. They soon picked their spot and dropped the hook, which dug in on the first try. Feeling comfortably tired after a perfect day on the water Beth tugged at the open fingers of her gloves and gazed across the water at Petit Martinique.

"You know, we didn't check to see if this brewery is open on Sunday," Terry said, stepping back into the cockpit. Beth's head snapped up, eyes wide.

"It never occurred to me!" Even after months in the islands she was still taken aback by how conservative some of them could be. A tourist attraction would never be closed on a weekend in the states. But some islands were like micro-time machines with lifestyles from an earlier age.

"Easy enough to find out," he replied unzipping the cooler to fish out a dripping beer bottle. He held it up toward her in inquiry and she nodded. "I'm sure they have wi-fi in the resort." He found another bottle and zipped the cooler shut, then used the opener hanging on its handle to open both bottles and reached across the cockpit to give Beth hers. Both were only slightly cool.

"Here's to a wonderful sail," she said, tapping her bottle against his. He nodded agreement and they indulged in long gulps.

"Now about this resort," he said, a sly smile spreading across his face.

As it turned out the resort was fully booked, but the receptionist who spoke to them over the VHF radio offered the option of dinner. She had one table left at their seven-thirty seating. Dress was casual. She was also able to tell them that the brewery on Petit Martinique was indeed closed on Sunday.

They booked the table for dinner and Beth dove into her drawers to find her best outfit: casual here would be a cut above the same definition at most of their stops. Fortunately she kept a few things folded into sealed plastic bags, dryer sheets tucked in with them, for such occasions. After a swim and another beer they bounced off one another in their cabin and the saloon trying to dress at the same time.

Typically, Terry turned out in khakis that looked freshly pressed and an aqua polo shirt that combined with his deep tan to make him look rather god-like. Beth felt inadequate in her white cotton skirt and floral print short sleeve blouse with the deep v-neck until she saw his appreciative expression. Whether it was automatic or not, it sent a shiver of warmth through her as she climbed carefully down the ladder and into the dinghy.

After dinner they slipped into a lounge off of the bar and used a computer provided for resort guests to research the Petit Quaff brewery. Beth was relieved to confirm that it was open for visitors starting at ten o'clock in the morning.

Later, sipping rum in the cockpit, snuggled against Terry's chest and watching the lights on the other boats swaying gently, she wondered if any of them were there for the same reason. But Terry soon banished the question from her thoughts, nuzzling her neck as his hands roamed over her body.

"I may not be in one of their exclusive rooms, but that doesn't mean I can't have the same experience," he muttered, his lips and warm breath tickling her ear. She reached up and slipped her fingers into his hair and he turned his face to kiss her palm.

"No reason at all," she agreed.

The Petit Quaff brewery was housed in a group of buildings that looked like a big city architect's idea of a quaint old Caribbean establishment. The office and pub were housed in a half-timbered structure that appeared to be trying to look like a transplant from some alpine village. The building housing the brewery proper was round and faced in stone to make it look like an old sugar mill. But the giant fins mounted near the top were stationary and the location, near the base of Petit Martinique's central peak, would have been a poor choice for a real mill using wind power.

To Beth and Terry's eyes – which had seen a lot of genuine Caribbean construction – it was unconvincingly new and solid. Even recent construction in the islands tended to be less substantial than this, with the exception of the heavily financed resorts.

In retrospect they decided that none of this was particularly surprising. Clearly some developer had seized upon the brewery idea as a way to attract wealthy visitors to the island. The townhouse development near the shore to the west was the likely suspect. That the resort on PSV sent regular tours over by boat attested to the success of the scheme. Given that, the brewery's participation in the treasure hunt made perfect sense.

They didn't immediately see any sign of the treasure hunt: there was no poster on the front door nor banner across the parking lot. Since it was early in the day and they were curious, they purchased the inexpensive tickets for the tour and joined a few other guests in the walk through the facility, dutifully admiring the huge vats and pipes snaking overhead.

"You know, I've read some discussions on line about brewing beer on board sailboats," Terry observed as they followed their guide past yeasty-smelling vats.

"You're kidding?"

"No, really. One guy described storing the carboy – that's the jug you store it in while it ferments – in the bilge where the temperature is about right."

"Yuck."

"Well you wouldn't mix in bilge water," he laughed.

"Still," she groaned, hoping she was correct in thinking he wasn't seriously considering it.

"We'd need a bigger boat," he mused. She rolled her eyes and moved more quickly to keep up with the group.

The tour ended at the brewery pub. Terry gave the guide a couple Eastern Caribbean dollars as a tip before opening the door for Beth to enter. They had seen no sign of the treasure hunt during the tour, so the pub was the last possibility.

"Burt?" Beth strode across the tile floor of the pub making a bee-line for a robust red-headed man seated on a stool at the bar. Terry shut the door and approached at a more conservative pace. Burt Adams was a member of the cruising community who he had mixed feelings about knowing.

A retiree from an undisclosed intelligence agency, Burt worked now as a charter boat captain running his own luxurious cabin cruiser among the islands. Beth had met him during her trip down the islands to find her friend Ori. They had struck up a friendship, which did not surprise Terry: who wouldn't want to befriend Beth? Burt presented himself as a gentle giant, the type of person that Beth, in her lonely quest, would have gravitated toward. Their friendship had proven valuable when Beth had made some risky choices and Burt had been concerned enough to look for her. Terry had also been looking for her by then, and when his and Burt's paths had crossed they'd joined forces.

Terry knew jealousy was irrational, but he couldn't shake a slight tinge of it. He had been in Germany on business when Beth had needed a friend and she'd found Burt. Fair enough. But there was more to it: at the time, Beth had been concealing her expedition from Terry, sailing alone from island to island. Terry could not have joined her if he had known – salvaging the German deal had been critical to the impending sale of his business. But he might have talked her out of her headlong rush into what had turned out to be a dangerous situation.

"Is that you Beth? And Terry? Wonderful! Great to see you again!" the ebullient former spy got to his feet and offered Beth a friendly hug, then extended his hand to Terry, who stepped up and shook it.

"Let me guess," Beth said, "You're charterers are touring the brewery? I didn't see *Sandcastle* in the anchorage, but I wasn't looking for her."

The big man nodded, eyes twinkling. "Two couples. I am very much the proverbial fifth wheel this week. She's out there, over at PSV. I'm sure you paid no attention to the stink pots in the anchorage. How are you two? No, wait, let me buy you a round," he turned to the bartender who had moved within discrete range. "Samuel, two tasting flights for my friends."

"Generous of you," Beth chuckled, for the tasting flights – four small glasses of the brewery's product – were free with the tour.

"To the core," Burt agreed, hoisting his behind back onto the bar stool. Beth took the one next to him and Terry sat beyond her, left elbow on the bar as he half turned toward the other two.

"So let's see, when we left off you had parked *Double Trouble* in Pointe-à-Pitre. That was – what? – two months ago? I looked in on *Trouble* a couple times while she was there. "

"Something like that," Beth agreed. "We both went home for a while, as planned. I had family business to take care of, and Terry had real business."

"Yours is no less real," Terry put in, placing his right hand on Beth's lower back. She glanced over her shoulder at him, noting for the first time his mood change since entering the pub. They had never really discussed Burt, but she had assumed he understood her friendship with him. It had started awkwardly, with Burt and his charter guests seeing her enjoying the sun while sailing *Trouble* toward St. Martin. She'd repaid the embarrassment by nearly getting his boat inspected by customs through an offhand remark in the customs office. But Burt's good nature and Beth's honesty had prevailed and they'd bonded over cruising stories.

She had opened up to him about her quest to find her friend Ori before she'd told Terry, a fact that she was still a little guilty over. That, combined with the reticence Burt seemed to inspire – doubtless a talent very useful in his former career – had kept her from bringing him up over the last weeks. Seeing Terry's closed expression now she realized that the subject should be addressed between them, and that perhaps Burt himself was not as important as the manner in which she'd met him.

"Your father," Burt was prompting, drawing her attention back to him. She nodded.

"He's doing okay," she said, thinking it was a lie. She didn't want to discuss California.

"Glad to hear it," Burt replied unconvincingly. She suddenly felt uncomfortable under his searching gaze. But he let the matter lie. "How about you, Terry? How's business?"

"Blissfully over," Terry replied, removing his hand from Beth's back in order to reach for one of the four glasses that had just been placed on the bar in front of him.

"Ah, the beer. Now, I recommend starting on the left and working right," Burt said, indicating the lightest brew. "That's the lager."

"We had that in St. George's," Beth said. "It's okay."

"Then drink up and move on to the ale. Too bad it's not as widely distributed. It's much better."

Their conversation moved from the beer to their reason for visiting and when Beth mentioned the treasure hunt she elicited a barking laugh from Burt.

"Samuel," he called to the bartender, who was serving other tourists down the bar. "You should have mentioned it earlier. He has something for you."

"Yes sir?" the bartender strolled toward them. "Another round Mr. Adams?"

"Samuel my friend, it seems that these two rag boaters are here on a mission. In fact, my friend Beth seems to always be on a mission," Burt grinned teasingly at Beth.

"Treasure hunters?" Samuel asked, studying Beth and then Terry.

"Precisely."

"Congratulations, you have found the third stop." Samuel moved a few feet along the bar and reached beneath it, returning with a pair of beer glasses. "Which beer do you prefer?" he asked.

"Ale please."

"I'll have the Porter."

He nodded sagely and filled a glass with each.

"Thanks. Do you have a clue for us?" Beth asked, wrapping her hand around the cool glass.

Samuel nodded at her hand. She lifted the glass and rotated it, a smile widening her lips when she looked at the colorful logo printed on it. She did not immediately see any differences from the official logo, but she was sure that was what he meant.

"And this," Samuel added, producing a glossy point card.

"Are we very far behind the leaders?" Beth asked, taking a sip of ale.

"About a week I guess," the bartender replied. "I've given out about fifty of those."

"Fifty!"

"I wouldn't worry," Burt put in, patting her shoulder. "Most of 'em will drop out soon enough. If I know you, you'll stick to it right to the end."

"Why do you think they'll drop out?" Terry asked.

Burt half turned to look at him. "Some of them started it in St. George's because they were there – bareboaters with a week or two to spend. They'll never be able to go the distance. Others are independent cruisers who will decide they don't like being herded from place to place. Then there are the challenges."

"Meaning?"

"Well, I have it on good authority that some of the clues will require some tricky navigation. And some require rock climbing, scuba diving, that sort of thing."

"Don't the rules say you can hire someone to do things you aren't certified to do? I took that to mean scuba."

"Well they can't have people who aren't qualified trying to dive, not that any dive shop would rent them gear, but determined people can be resourceful. Still, those who can't dive and can't afford to pay a diver will drop out."

"We're both certified," Terry said, immediately regretting how defensive he sounded.

"But I don't have my card yet," Beth added, tossing Terry a smile and half shrug. She had completed her certification just before leaving St. Thomas. She'd arranged to have her card delivered to the dive shop where she had worked.

"How are you at rock climbing?" Burt teased.

"Never tried it," Terry admitted. "How about you Beth."

"A couple times at the gym," she said, thinking for the first time in many months about her ex-boyfriend Peter, the reason she had learned to sail. There was another subject she'd never discussed with Terry.

"Oh yeah?" he said, curious.

"Yeah. It was nothing like real rock climbing," she tried to minimize it, but she could see he was curious, and he would certainly bring it up again later. Well, if she had to talk about Peter, then he could just tell her something about his former girlfriends. She knew he had them. A sly smile curled the corners of her mouth and she saw that he noticed, his eyes narrowing ever so slightly. She purposefully turned back toward Burt.

"What's your next port Burt?"

He'd been watching their exchange, a friendly bear of a voyeur, doubtlessly well aware that he was watching their relationship develop. Her question, obviously changing the subject, took him by surprise.

"A stop at Bequia then back to St. Vincent," he said. "That's where this lot started."

"What happened to Guadeloupe?" Beth asked. Burt was based there.

"Well, when they offer an extra ten percent to be met somewhere else I don't say no."

"Makes sense," Terry said. "You charge for fuel on top of that?"

"There's a fuel surcharge. I adjust it depending on costs," Burt nodded. "It's worth my while, usually. And I was getting tired of The Saintes – Marie Galant – Deshais circuit."

"Oh yeah, the dull old French islands," Beth said, her accompanying laugh infecting the others.

"Well, too much of anything can become dull," Burt tried, but she shook her head.

"Now you just sound jaded," she scolded. "Look, will you have to baby-sit them tonight, or can you get away for dinner?" Terry's hand landed on her lower back again, but she wasn't sure if he objected or supported the suggestion she was about to make.

"They have reservations across the water," he said, referring to the resort restaurant. "I'm on my own."

"Not anymore. Please have dinner with us on *Trouble*."

She noticed him give Terry an inquisitive look and wondered what he saw behind her on her boyfriend's face, but didn't dare turn around to look without being terribly obvious.

"I'd love to. Thank you. I'll ferry my lot ashore around six."

"Then come on over after that."

FOURTEEN: BURT

"I bet this is the last of the fake logos we see," Beth said, rolling the glass back and forth to examine the logo. She had rolled a sheet of white paper and put it inside to provide a solid background. Terry was quietly impressed with her practical solution after being frustrated by the transparent glass and distortion of the curved surface for several minutes.

"Why?"

"It's an obvious trick now, too easy already. They'll have to switch to some other type of puzzle."

"I guess you're right. None of these are going to be just 'go to such and such a place.'"

"Okay, so where the beer bottle is on the t-shirt, we've got a different bottle. Looks like liquor." Beth had the magazine ad and her t-shirt spread on the table for comparison with the glass.

"Gotta be rum," Terry said.

"That would make sense. The flying parrot is back where the brewery building was on the shirt, though. There has to be something else – I can't read the logo on the bottle."

"No, it's definitely not detailed enough to read. All I can see is that it's tan with some red."

"So what else is different?" Beth mused, eyes darting from the glass to the ad to the t-shirt and back. Terry looked over her shoulder doing the same, struggling to keep his focus on the puzzle before them and not the scent of her hair, which was vaguely floral with an undercurrent of the sea.

"Look to the stars," he murmured, giving in and pressing his face into her frizzy locks.

"Humm?" she sighed, straightening against him, distracted now too.

He nibbled on her ear, smiling. He'd seen the rest of the clue and knew their next destination. It was amusing to keep it to himself for a moment.

"Look to the stars?" she repeated, leaning over again with renewed interest. Terry stroked one hand up her spine, smiling wryly. It had been a glorious moment, however short. "Orion," she said, turning her head to look at him for confirmation. He nodded, suddenly proud of her for seeing it so quickly. The logo contained a small patch of night sky filled with twinkling stars. In the real one, the big dipper shone clearly. But in the one on the glass Orion's belt and knife were distinct, his shoulders and heels at the edges of the starry field.

"Orion Distillery is on St. Vincent, I think," he said.

"What part of the island? Do you know?" Beth asked stepping away from him to go to the navigation desk and get the cruising guide.

"No idea."

She turned to the advertiser index and was not surprised to find a listing for the brand. Turning to the ad itself she pursed her lips in annoyance.

"No address?"

"No, it's for the rum, not the distillery. They have a P.O. box in Kingstown." She held the guide out to him open to the ad.

"Well we can't take the time to write to them," Terry joked, taking the guide. "I think we should go to the anchorage in Calliaqua Bay first and see what we can find out," he said, flipping through the pages to find the start of the section on St. Vincent.

They had both read the guide several times: it provided critical details about entering every harbor as well as useful information about facilities ashore and even warnings about potential dangers unrelated to navigation. These were usually disguised as positives, but every sailor got to know how to read between the lines. A suggestion that you lock your dinghy and dinghy engine meant they tended to go missing. Advice to carry small change in your pockets meant that the locals were particularly poor and particularly aggressive in asking for handouts. Florid descriptions of the "helpful" boat boys meant you'd be approached by many and they would not accept no for an answer in offering their services.

"We can always go ashore and Google them," Beth said, moving toward the galley. "I'd better get started on dinner."

"Right," Terry's response came out too sharp. Beth looked across at him from behind the galley counter, a slight frown creasing her brow. She remembered the look Burt had given him back in the pub, and how she couldn't see Terry's expression. She had assumed from Burt's enthusiastic acceptance that it had been welcoming, but now it seemed like it might have been negative after all. She had no idea whether he objected to Burt, or to the idea of a dinner guest, or some other aspect of her invitation. Better get this settled, she thought.

"Kingstown is a couple bays over from Calliaqua, west of it. I remember now, we decided not to go in to Kingstown harbor because it's very commercial," Terry said, eyes focused on the book in his hands.

His easy switch back to the treasure hunt made Beth doubt her interpretation of his previous comment. Had she heard a sharpness that wasn't there?

"That was a lovely anchorage. I wouldn't mind going back if we can get to town from there," she said, pausing to look at him again before plunging head and shoulders into the refrigerator to find a package of chicken pieces. When she emerged victorious she looked at him again. He was sitting at the table, the book open in front of him. She reconsidered, and then decided to plunge in as aggressively as she just had into the refrigerator.

"Do you mind that I invited Burt for dinner?" she asked in as non-confrontational a tone as possible.

He looked up, his expression unreadable as he studied her.

"You sounded – I don't know, annoyed, a moment ago. Is something wrong?"

His eyes dropped to the book, then returned to her, softer now, a hint of contrition behind the weakening mask.

"I guess I worry a little about getting too close to Burt Adams," he said.

Beth opened the refrigerator while she considered this. Rather than jump to conclusions – he was jealous of her friendship? That would be intolerable. He was concerned about Burt's past? That was possible. Did he know more about Burt than she did? Could be.

"Why?" she finally asked, not wanting to make assumptions.

"How do we know that he's really retired?" Terry asked. "He's got a perfect cover, roaming around these islands, hanging out in local bars..."

"The brewery is hardly a local bar –."

"And why are you being defensive?"

Beth was taken aback by the sudden accusation, the anger she'd sensed at first had returned in spades.

"I'm not being defensive. I'm pointing out that Burt was hanging around in a touristy spot today waiting for his tourist customers." She opened the knife drawer and found her favorite chef's knife.

"But that isn't the point. You know he knows the locals everywhere. He could be active with some intelligence agency."

"So what?" Beth removed the cork from the tip of the knife and positioned the half of an onion she'd taken from the refrigerator on the cutting board over the sink. "Are you worried about guilt by association?"

"No. I'm worried about being in the wrong place – with the wrong person – at the wrong time."

"What is that supposed to mean?" she started to chop the onion, fingers curled carefully back from the blade. *He doesn't want to be with me?*

"If he has enemies who come after him while we're with him, you'll be in danger."

"I'll be – ," Beth stopped speaking and chopping, staring in surprise at Terry. "What about you? You'd be in danger too," she said more quietly. "Besides, I respect Burt. He's a cautious man – remember he tried to talk me out of going after Ori. I don't think he'd place us in danger. If I did think there was slightest chance that you're right about him." She resumed chopping.

"Which you don't."

She paused again. "I guess it seems a little too, I don't know, adventure story-ish. This is real life. Guys retire from the CIA. Don't they?"

Terry's knowing smile threw her.

"Don't they?" she repeated, knife poised over her onion.

"A friend of mine was in the marines, got into intelligence and really liked it. When he got out he went to work for the CIA. He's said that they never really cut anyone loose. A guy like Burt is useful to them, that's all I'm saying. He may have officially retired, but if they want him they'll call on him and he'll have very little choice."

"You mean they have something on him?"

"Don't have to. They know him inside and out. They'll find something to use to coerce him if they have to – threaten to seize his boat, maybe."

Beth shut her mouth around the words that she wanted to say: that would be wrong, they can't do that. She was not that naive.

"Maybe he was a screw-up. I mean, what do we know about him?" she suggested, although she didn't believe it. Burt struck her as very competent, and beneath the warm exterior she suspected a core of rather frightening steel.

"I don't think they let screw-ups loose on the public."

"Oh." She finished dicing the onion and reached for the partial clove of garlic in the produce hammock. "Well, I like him Terry. He's been a good friend. Do you dislike him?"

"No, no. He's a nice guy," Terry managed. He didn't want to let it get personal. But watching Beth smash a garlic clove and deftly remove the papery skin he couldn't find a way to lie.

"I just regret that I wasn't here for you, and he was," he said. *There. Couldn't be simpler.*

Beth held the smashed garlic on the cutting board, knife ready to slice it, eyes locked with Terry's. Her expression surprised him: guilt.

"I wanted to tell you what I was doing, but I was afraid you'd be mad at me – tell me I was nuts to go on my own and goodbye. Or you'd try to talk me out of it and we'd have a horrible fight. I was dreading having to confess to you, and the longer we went not being in touch the worse it got."

"But you couldn't wait," he said, not a hint of accusation in his tone.

"I was so worried about her," she replied. "I was worried about – ." She stopped, realizing what she had been about to say.

"You transferred your concern over your father to Ori."

"No. Of course not. That's silly."

"Beth, it's normal –."

"That's not what I did. I was worried about Ori."

Terry sighed, lowering his eyes to the cruising guide on the table.

"Should we call and tell him not to come?" she asked. Terry looked up, pain-filled eyes stabbing at her. She winced inwardly.

"No, an invitation is an invitation. And as you said, you like him."

Objections, apologies, pleading explanations all froze on her lips. She swallowed hard and focused on the garlic as Terry returned his attention to the cruising guide.

She had failed, and it was such a simple test. *Admit your emotional confusion. Admit that he's right. You chased Ori down the islands because you wanted to make everything better. If Ori was okay, Dad would be too. He can't accept me unless I do, because I can't love him free and clear with all this other crap going on. He wants me to be honest with myself.*

In simple sentences Beth asked Terry to set up and light the barbeque grill, which mounted on the stern railing where it hung out over the water. He complied without a word, not even meeting her eyes as he picked up the lighter she'd set on the counter and climbed the ladder to the cockpit.

This is going to be a miserable evening.

But then Burt came aboard bringing a bottle of red wine and enough friendly warmth to melt the frost between his host and hostess. They sat in the cockpit sipping the wine and nibbling on cheese, Terry tending the chicken on the grill, brushing it with marinade now and then. Bert easily filled space and time with stories of his charters since they had parted company in Guadeloupe weeks ago.

When the chicken was done they moved below to the main dining table. Burt's stories had run down, so Beth recalled something he'd mentioned as an aside in one of them.

"So this guy you ran into on Martinique," she said, hoping she was remembering right, although it didn't much matter. "You said you knew he had a past or something?"

Burt's naturally narrow eyes closed further as he gazed at her, and for a moment she expected him to tell her he couldn't discuss it.

"Oh right, Jimmy Kang," he said, and she realized he had just been trying to remember. "Now there's a piece of work. Unfortunately you run into that type all over the islands – all over the world, for that matter. They thrive in loose communities like ours.

"Loose?" Beth asked, although she thought she knew what he meant.

"Impermanent, then," he offered. "When you think about it, we boaters are just street people with better resources, for the most part," he grinned, silencing Terry from the response on his lips, that some cruisers were hardly financed at all. That might cut too close to Beth's home, and there was no need for it. "We see one another here and there, form up into groups for a while, then break apart when our paths are no longer mutual. I don't know what you've really been doing since we last saw one another, nor you me. Nor do I know what's going on below decks in all those boats out there," he gestured at the side of the cabin, indicating the anchorage beyond.

"But we can't be suspicious of everyone," Terry said, eyes darting to Beth and then back to Burt. She felt like he'd read her thoughts. *Maggie.*

"No, but you take precautions. You don't even realize you're doing it. I didn't see Beth latching on to anyone else when she was sailing south. Lord knows she could have used company, or even crew, but she knew she was better off relying on herself than trusting a stranger who she didn't have time to get to know."

"You really think that?" Beth asked, distracted from her thoughts of Maggie Hartford by his compliment.

"I know it. You've got good survival instincts, Beth."

She caught Terry's expression before he hid it behind his wine glass: admiration shone in his eyes. He may have concerns about Burt, but he valued the man's opinion of his girlfriend. Beth felt herself smile inwardly. The rift between them could be mended.

"But what about this Jimmy Kang?" Terry asked, lowering his glass. "What sort of a bad seed is he?"

"Papaya – round and slimy, but looks like a delicacy," Burt's rumbling laugh filled the saloon making Beth groan and Terry smile. "Papaya seeds look like caviar," he added unnecessarily.

"Yes," Terry assured him. "Although not royal sturgeon. So this guy's slimy but looks good?" his eyes met Beth's again, this time with a hint of warning. *I'm not the one pursuing it*, she thought wickedly.

"He's slick all right. But I know he's run at least four cons in the last five years, gotten away with about half a million, all insurance fraud."

"How has he gotten away with it? I mean, if you know about it –."

Burt shook his head at Beth's objection. "I know because I'm observant. I recognize the type, I can see the patterns, and I've talked to some of the cruisers he used – offered a shoulder to cry on. But I'm not an insurance investigator and I have no evidence to give if one came asking."

"So he's stolen from insurance companies," Terry said. "Not other cruisers?"

"He sets up the accidents so that his property – usually his dinghy – gets damaged. He gets whoever his latest buddy is to fake an injury, or he fakes it himself. And he pushes for a huge settlement not to sue. The people who 'caused' the accident," Burt curled two fingers of each hand in the air, implying quote marks, "don't pay out of pocket, other than in increased insurance premiums."

"And we all pay because all the rates go up," Beth added. Insurance on herself and her boat were her two largest regular expenses. Burt nodded, acknowledging her point.

"There's no law enforcement agency that would expend energy going after someone operating like that out here. I'll bet he pulls each con in a different island nation," Terry observed. Burt nodded again.

"That's right. Nobody is getting hurt hard enough to flinch, except the insurance companies themselves. That's his biggest risk – hit any one of them more than once and they'll spend the time and effort to go after him.

"So beware of slick men who ask who your insurance is from," Terry said to Beth with a genuine smile.

"Just be judicious in who you associate closely with," Burt added, his bright eyes surprisingly serious as he looked from one to the other.

"Including you?" Terry asked, equally seriously.

"Especially me!" Burt laughed, slapping his hand on the table and getting to his feet. He looked back down at Beth's shocked expression. "Oh don't fret, I'm no con man. It's too much work and I know too much about the ways they could catch me."

"You said nobody's trying to catch them."

"I said nobody's making an effort. For a scam to be worth my trouble it would have to be big. Huge. And foolproof because once I pulled it off I'd be out of here for good. And I assure you there are those who keep an eye on things down here who would put a stop to a big operator."

"Law enforcement?" Terry asked, looking skeptical. Burt took a step toward the ladder.

"More like the opposite," he said, and Terry nodded as if that's what he'd been thinking.

"Geez, you're scaring me Burt," Beth said. She had never considered that organized crime had an influence in the islands. Both men looked surprised.

"Drugs, Beth. Or rather, the drug runners," Burt said. "Why do you think the officials are so scrupulous about drugs and guns?"

"Of course," she felt foolish.

"I don't see any reason why you two would get mixed up with that crowd, or any of the petty criminals. You're clean, and smart. I've got to go collect my group. Thanks for dinner and the intelligent conversation."

He mounted the ladder, Terry and Beth following. As they watched him climb into his dinghy Beth wondered how he knew she was "clean." Was he just assuming, or had he checked up on her?

Stop it! She mentally scolded herself, then headed back down the ladder to clean up.

Terry followed and at first she feared that the silence of the late afternoon had returned. She just wanted to forget about their fight, to move on as if it hadn't happened. It didn't have to matter, did it? She was silly to feel guilty, he was silly to be envious. Burt was a nice, knowledgeable guy, but certainly not an active intelligence agent.

"You don't still think Maggie Hartford is pulling something, do you?" Terry asked out of the blue. He was gathering the plates and pans from the table and stacking them on the galley counter for washing. Beth pulled her head out of the refrigerator where she'd been stowing a foil-wrapped bundle of leftover chicken.

"I don't think she's pulling an insurance scam like – what was the name? Jimmy Kong?"

"Kang."

"Right. I don't know Terry. She's probably exactly what she claims to be – a sailor wife whose husband can't completely let go of his work, or won't. She probably doesn't like not being like everyone else down here, so she covers for him."

"Like everyone else?" he asked, placing the pan that they'd served the buttered macaroni from on the counter and placing himself close beside her. It was a strong signal that he wanted to make up, but her hands were deep in a sink full of warm, soapy water. She turned her head to look at him, still clutching a dinner plate in the water.

"You know," she whispered, "Happy couples."

"My folks taught me never to go to bed angry," he whispered back.

"And are you angry?" she asked, returning her attention to the dishes as much as she could.

"No. I've reformed my opinion of associating with Burt. He's full of useful information."

"What about my behavior – how I met him?"

"What about it?" he was nuzzling her ear, arms suddenly around her waist making her feel warm all over.

"What you said earlier, about why I did it," she said. "That I was going after Ori because of my father." She took a deep breath and allowed herself to lean into his embrace. He had stopped nuzzling her and simply held her, waiting. "You're right. I felt powerless about him. I had to do something for someone, to prove to myself that I cared."

"And now? Are you satisfied that you care enough?"

"How much is enough?"

"From what I've seen, what you've said, your family wants you to live your life. I know your sister has her issues. I'd have to meet them to form more of an opinion."

It hung there for a moment in the tiny space between them, an unformed request full of possibilities. And then Beth turned her head and let her mouth find his, kissing him lightly at first, and then harder as a surge of powerful need took over. She took her greasy hands from the water, but stopped herself from touching him. He loosened his embrace and leaned away, looking curiously at her hands held in the air on either side.

She smiled, feeling foolish again. "Let me finish the dishes," her voice came out as a seductive purr. He smiled back and released her.

"I'll check the anchor," he said, releasing her and grasping the ladder handles. She smiled as she plunged her hands back into the water: checking the anchor was a euphemism for urinating over the side under cover of darkness.

FIFTEEN: ORION

"We're a week, and fifty other people, behind. And how did it go from seven – that's how many Tobias said he'd taken to the waterfall – to fifty?" Beth sighed, exhibiting anything but interest in continuing the hunt as she shifted position with a soft grunt. She laid her open book over her face as an impromptu sun shade and let her arms flop down on the deck on either side. The sound of small bristles scrubbing a hard surface was unnaturally loud. She blamed it on a trick of acoustics; sound waves bouncing off hard fiberglass somehow channeled right to her ears.

Standing in the shaded cockpit a few feet away Terry was using an old toothbrush to clean the inner workings of the main winch. The cover and parts he'd removed were laid out on a plastic bag, some clean, others awaiting their turn under the brush covered with gasoline from the dinghy fuel jug.

Beth wrinkled her nose as a breeze picked up the odor, lifting the book and rolling her head to the side to watch his hands as he worked. Beth had started the morning with a trip ashore to use the resort's wi-fi to research the Orion Distillery while Terry attended to the winch, which had been squealing and rattling for the last week. When she'd learned that the distillery was near Kingstown, St. Vincent's capital at the southern end of the island she'd hurried back to *Trouble* thinking they needed to get going. They'd looked over the charts and quickly realized that if they set out this late they were destined to spend the night at Union Island. Alternatively, they could skip customs and immigration at Union and sail directly to St. Vincent and take care of customs and immigration there. But the trip was almost seventy-five miles: more than a full day of sailing. If they set out now they would have to navigate between the many islands of the Grenadines in the dark. An overnight passage across an inter-island channel was one thing, but when there were reefs, rocks, and islands in the way it was a risk they weren't willing to take for the sake of the treasure hunt.

"If we leave at dawn we can get to customs at Union Island when they open, and then sail as far as we can and stop at whatever island we want – maybe even get to Young Island Cut before dark," Terry had proposed, referring to the big, safe harbor near Kingstown. Beth had known he was dangling a carrot in front of her, but that they were unlikely to get all the way to St. Vincent before dark in the twelve hour Caribbean day.

Treasure hunt aside, the prospect of spending the rest of the day right where they were had been tempting enough to settle the matter. Now Terry was finishing the winch he'd started before they packed a picnic and snorkeling gear into the dinghy to explore the local reefs.

They'd watched Burt maneuver *Sandcastle*, his boat, out of the anchorage an hour ago, exchanging waves with him when he tooted his air horn as he passed.

"Tobias wasn't the only cab driver in St. George's. We should have realized that there were more ahead of us. I'm about finished." Terry said, noting that Beth was watching him. She sat up groggily, half asleep from the enervating sun.

"I'll get ready to go then."

They returned to *Trouble* hours later, exhausted from an afternoon of swimming against strong currents over the reef on the northeastern side of the island. The forest of living coral had also contributed to Beth's breathlessness. Schools of immature tangs, snappers, and the perky black, white, and yellow striped sergeant majors flitted across the sun-streaked bottom. Brooding barracuda watched the swimmers right at the edge of visibility, toothy mouths slowly opening and closing as if in rehearsal for a meal to come. Terry teased the soft, purple sea slugs making them reform into hard, self-defensive balls that he tossed slow motion through the water to land a few feet away on the sandy bottom. Once a ray darted away from Beth, scattering its sandy disguise in its wake as she dove to look more closely at the bottom. Terry nearly stepped on a flounder similarly concealed. It wobbled off, its two eyes swiveling wildly.

They spotted the telltale antennae of lobster hiding in rocky crevasses, but let them be. They weren't sure if permits were required and it was not worth the risk. Beth was tempted by a seemingly empty conch shell until it began moving across the surface of a brain coral. She saw Terry laugh at her startled reaction to the slow moving creature and had to join him.

"Early start, right?" Terry confirmed, holding his mult-function wrist watch in front of him. Beside him Beth grunted, face buried in her pillow. He turned his head to look at her in her t-shirt and underpants, a few red welts on her thighs evidence of a brief encounter with some rough coral that afternoon.

If only every day could be like this one. If life could be all exploration and fun, with a little simple labor for variety, he examined the rime of winch grease around his fingernails, persistent even after the hours of swimming. Alarm set for a pre-dawn awakening he put the watch on the shelf just above his head, switched off the light, and rolled onto his side, his left arm across Beth's back. She lifted her head and turned her face toward his, a sleepy smile gracing her sweet face. He stroked her back, letting his hand roam down to cup the roundness of her behind.

"Sleepy," she sighed, sounding it. And then: "Love you."

Terry pressed in past the knob of her shoulder and kissed her mouth, then withdrew, rolling over onto his other side, giving them both some space in the warm cabin.

The stop at Union Island was blissfully brief and uneventful even with the trudge to the airport. By nine-thirty they were on a fast reach slightly west of north past little Mayreau. Late morning they tacked and Terry trimmed *Trouble*'s sails until they achieved a heading just a few points south of due east. They cleared the north coast of Canouan with a mile to spare and kept going until Mustique was abeam far to the north. As they neared them they spotted the tiny islets trailing in a line south of Mustique so they tacked. On their northwesterly heading Isle a Quatre and Bequia were dead ahead.

As the afternoon wore on the wind shifted to the south, which presented a decision – pass to the east or west of the two islands ahead? – and a possibility: The southern tip of St. Vincent was just a few miles beyond. Could they make it?

Unfortunately, as is often the case the wind shift was also a slackening. Their bid for St. Vincent out of reach, they motored up the eastern coast and around the northern end of Bequia. They pushed *Trouble*'s engine as the seemingly endless northwest coast slid by, finally slipping into Admiralty Bay with the sun setting off their stern.

The call of Bequia's famed nightlife wasn't strong enough to draw them ashore. They dined on leftover chicken, chips and salsa, and cuddled in the cockpit watching the lights of vehicles, restaurants, and hotels on shore. It had been a long day of companionable sailing. They had talked little but communicated volumes about the boat's position, speed, and response to the conditions. Beth had sailed with enough different people to realize that this natural affinity for one another and the boat was something special. She believed Terry had too. As they enjoyed the evening neither of them broke the spell of the day with spurious conversation. Long before the lights ashore began to go out they were deeply asleep below.

"This is narrow!" Beth complained, comparing the entrance to Young Island Cut just off her bow with the chart on the seat beside her. Terry did the same, studying the face of Young Island, a petit rocky lump in the mouth of the harbor, topped with an abandoned fortress. He didn't bother to offer suggestions for how to navigate it. Complaints aside, Beth knew what she was doing. As expected she steered *Trouble* through the channel and into the wider harbor beyond.

"Moorings," she said simply. He nodded and rose, climbing out of the cockpit to pick up the boat hook that was tucked in under the teak monkey rail on the deck. They had discussed it earlier – whether there would be a mooring available in this anchorage and if so whether to use it. They had decided yes. The fee was small and they'd been economical the last few days. To Terry it was an easy answer – the cost was negligible and anchoring amid a mooring field could be problematic. But Beth's wallet was slimmer and he made a point of respecting her wish to keep expenses at a level where she could pay her share.

Trouble slowed to a glide as she approached one of the floating white balls. Terry spotted a length of line floating in the current and waved to Beth to adjust course slightly so that he could hook it. In a moment he was dropping the boat hook and hauling in on the line, which in turn brought up a harness of heavier lines that was attached to the underside of the float. He secured one of the two harness lines on a bow cleat, gesturing with his left arm for Beth to stop the boat. He felt her shift into neutral and then reverse, then neutral again and the strain on the line eased. They had arrived.

Beth joined him on the bow, watching him arrange the two lines on the two cleats, a typical Y configuration that would hold *Trouble* through a gale, should one materialize. That seemed unlikely: yesterday's calm had continued overnight and through their short morning motor from Bequia.

"I guess we're all set," he said, wiping damp hands on his t-shirt.

"Let's see if we can find a way to Orion," she replied, briefly scanning their neighboring boats in the harbor before heading back to the cockpit. This was a paradisiacal harbor, the location, she recalled reading, for some scenes in a nautical thriller movie she'd seen a couple years ago. The grey-green fringe of palms was backed by wave upon wave of rolling dense jungle on ever steeper mountain slopes. At the shoreline bright red roofs topped white, taupe, and turquoise wooden buildings with an occasional old stone one in between. The seawall along the inner side of the harbor reminded her of new England. In places green lawns extended down to it from hotels and restaurants set back from the water. In the other direction Young Island stood sentinel, the scar of a path wrapped around it, leading from a small dock up to the old fortress.

Holding the safety line while Terry attached the motor to the dinghy she watched a dive boat coming in through the channel she'd just navigated. Once in the narrow section it slowed, angling toward a marina to the east where she now noticed a dive flag hanging limply on a pole.

Presently Terry had the engine secure and she joined him in the small boat, her day pack on her back and his over one shoulder.

He drove them to a dock with a crowd of other dinghies already tied to it. They shoved their way in between and climbed out, then tied theirs on a long enough lead that it could be moved aside as well.

"It's early and I could use a good walk," she said. They had not discussed how they would get to the distillery. "Why don't we walk to the airport and see if we can get a taxi or rent a car there? I'm still not sure where the distillery is exactly."

"I can handle that," Terry replied, extending his hand for his pack.

As so often happened, what started out seeming like a good idea soon became mildly unpleasant in the tropical heat. Almost an hour later

Terry and Beth ambled across a shaded cement sidewalk into a car rental office at the airport. The over-active air conditioning immediately cooled the sweat on their t-shirts, sending a chill down Beth's spine. Wrapping her arms around herself she followed Terry to stand behind a short man in a Hawaiian shirt and Bermuda shorts waiting his turn at the counter.

"I don't know which is worse, the humidity outside or the chill in here," she murmured, rubbing her hands on her arms. Terry wrapped his arm around her and held her close to his side in the name of providing body warmth.

"People coming off flights are hit in the face by the heat," he said. "They run in here for relief and end up renting cars."

Beth scowled and studied the man in front of them until he was finally called to the counter. Their turn came soon after as the other agent became available.

Terry took charge, providing his credit card before Beth could object, and asking for her driver's license so that she could be added to the rental agreement. Soon they were sitting in a blue Isuzu Gemini, Terry in the driver's seat exploring the controls. Beth smiled wryly as she tried the radio pre-sets, each of which was tuned to one of the island's three high-power radio stations.

"Do you mind?" Terry groaned as the car was alternately filled with pulsing dance music and irate accented voices.

"Sorry," she gave him her most apologetic smile as she lowered the volume and used the tuner to look for a less dominant music station.

"Let's see that map."

Beth pulled the cruising guide with its sketch map of Kingstown out of her pack and handed it to him. The spiral bound book was folded open to the correct page.

"The address is on the sticky," she added, indicating the yellow note stuck to the page. "I think this is the street, but there are no addresses on the map." She pointed to a street that ran north-south and seemed to peter out at the northern outskirts of the town, which was only about four blocks wide.

"I bet it keeps going into the hills," he said.

"That's what I was thinking," she agreed, turning off the radio in defeat. He smiled victoriously, although he didn't look at her. He didn't tend to listen to music on the radio, preferring to program his own entertainment. He particularly disliked strident radio commercials, which were very common on island radio stations.

"Let's explore," he said, starting the engine and gently shifting into first gear.

They spent a laughter filled hour navigating the car over underdeveloped Caribbean roads and through St. Vincent's capital. It was a great change of pace to drive rather than walk, sail, or be driven, and Terry put the poor rental car through its paces trying to drive it like he did his BMW at home.

"We could have taken the bus!" he said, watching a brightly painted vehicle, loaded down with passengers, cross through an intersection ahead.

"If they go over to the anchorage," Beth agreed absently. She was glad they hadn't. She wasn't in the mood for overcrowded public transportation. "This is the street!"

"Left or right? I'm turned around."

"Left! Left!"

Glancing over his shoulder Terry switched lanes and made the turn, missing having his bumper shaved by an oncoming car by just a few inches. Beth swallowed hard and took a slow breath.

"It's number 843. I haven't found any addresses yet."

"There's 200." She followed Terry's quick glance at a building on the left with the number prominently displayed.

She soon spotted 209 on the other side. "That makes sense. If the numbers were going down as we go inland, then number 843 would have to be in the water behind us," she said, for they had turned onto the street just two blocks from the harbor.

The addresses crept upward as they left the town proper behind. Soon they were on what in most parts of the U.S. would be considered a country lane, but was actually a major thoroughfare here. Buildings were infrequent, and few displayed addresses. But they were still in the 600s when the road took a turn and began a series of switchbacks into the hills.

"I guess they don't want the pedestrian tourist trade," Terry observed, downshifting to push the car up a steep stretch.

"Are we gonna' make it?" Beth asked as the engine roared in protest and the car slowed.

"I hope so," he replied, sounding uncertain. The car eased up over the hill at a crawl and Terry coaxed it back to an acceptable speed on the next level stretch.

"Look at that," Beth pointed ahead and to the right. On the other side of a deep ravine there was a group of buildings under a sign for Orion Rum.

"Nice. But how do we get over there I wonder?" Terry replied as the road turned to the left, away from the distillery and down into the ravine.

"I think I know," Beth replied, seeing a ribbon of asphalt on the opposite side. It looked impossibly steep. "We may have to walk."

"The road's not wide enough to park and leave the car," Terry countered, accelerating down the hill.

"There's a hairpin turn at the bottom you know," Beth pointed out, hands landing on the dashboard in front of her. Terry's wolfish grin actually calmed her a little: he had it under control.

The car's soft suspension slewed around the tight curve and Terry downshifted, giving it more drive early to maintain speed as they started up the other side.

"Nice move," Beth observed as they continued upward at cruising speed.

"Just had to get to know her better," Terry replied so flirtatiously Beth burst out laughing.

Even so, the car was back to creeping speed as the road flattened at the top of the ravine. Terry once again coaxed it forward and turned into a parking area in front of what seemed to be the distillery's main building.

"Thank goodness," Beth declared, and Terry thought she was commenting on his driving until he saw that she was peering out through the window at the front of the building. He followed her gaze and saw it too: a poster version of the treasure hunt ad.

"I was a little afraid that we were on the wrong track. We could have been supposed to go to a bar somewhere."

Terry had never doubted that the distillery was their target. He was surprised at Beth's uncertainty about it, expressed only now.

They entered an air conditioned reception area where a professionally dressed woman greeted them with cool formality, stepping out from behind her desk to meet them mid-way from the door. Her hair was swept up in tight knot on the back of her head, a severe look that was oddly softened by bright pink lipstick on a full mouth. They explained their mission, holding up the glass with the clue logo that Beth had tucked into her pack. The woman looked puzzled.

"There's a poster outside, on the wall by the door," Beth said, an unintended whininess in her tone.

"That is just decorative, advertising a local event."

"But the event is here," Beth protested, plunging her hand back into her pack.

"It's promoting a treasure hunt," Terry put in. "Every other place we've been to that has displayed the poster has been one of the stops. Perhaps someone else knows about it?"

"What do you mean by 'treasure hunt'?" she asked, moving back toward her desk.

"The sponsor has made arrangements with businesses like yours to provide clues to participants when we visit."

Beth withdrew the wrinkled magazine ad from her pack and extended it toward the woman.

"You see? Just like the poster outside."

The woman was shaking her head, although her eyes were still on Terry.

"I have not been instructed to give you anything," she said, belatedly glancing at the paper in Beth's hand, then up at Beth's face. She did not take the ad from her.

"Our ads also appear in many magazines and on posters around the islands. It signifies nothing," she said. Beth's hand lowered to her side and she looked at Terry. But instead of the frustration she expected to see his face was a congenial mask.

"Does the distillery offer tours?" he asked through an amazingly broad smile. The woman brightened just a bit.

"Yes. You may visit our visitor center. It is in the next building, to the left when you exit this office. Perhaps you can purchase something for your treasure hunt."

"Thank you miss –."

"Mrs. Lee. It was my pleasure to assist you."

Terry gestured for Beth to precede him and reached past her to open the door. Once out in the humidity and heat Beth groaned out her annoyance, harshly folding the magazine ad and stuffing it into her pack.

"Calm down. It's okay," Terry murmured, guiding her with a gentle pressure on her back to the left and the next building over.

"She was so — you sure charmed her!"

Terry laughed, his eyes flashing with what Beth recognized as affection — for her.

"That was my salesman persona, do you like it?"

"I'm not sure. A little slick, isn't he?"

"When in Rome."

"When in Kingstown, or whatever damn town we're in now."

He opened the door under a sign that said visitor center, noting that one of the eight glass panes in the door was filled with a smaller version of the poster.

"Welcome to Orion Distillery!" a man dressed as a nineteenth century bartender from the American west, with garters holding up his shirt sleeves and a bright red waistcoat, nodded toward them from behind a massive wooden bar.

"Where are we now?" Terry murmured near Beth's ear before stepping over to the bar and extending his hand. The barman shook it, grinning widely to reveal over-bright white teeth.

"Good afternoon. We're hunting for treasure," Terry said.

"Yes of course," the bartender replied, putting his hand on the top of a bottle of rum standing on the bar in front of him. "You are here for this."

Terry's expression turned even brighter as he picked up the bottle and held it so that both he and Beth could inspect the label.

"This is for the *Gunkholing* treasure hunt?" Beth asked, wishing she didn't need further confirmation. But the rum bottle did not have the hunt label like all the other clues had.

"Yes ma'am. Congratulations. I understand you've come all the way from Petit Martinique just for that."

"Yes that's right. Have many others already been here?" Terry asked.

The bartender looked thoughtful. "Two yesterday, a lot more last week. A lot more," he nodded as if still mentally calculating.

"How many bottles like this do you have to give out?" Beth asked. It was a question she had thought of after receiving the glasses. They would not have made up an oversupply of the clue items.

"Oh, I've got five, six more cases I guess."

"Wow." Beth was surprised. If he'd given out fifty bottles, based on the bartender at the brewery's estimate, then he'd started with nine or ten cases. The magazine expected a hundred and twenty participants. Or maybe more — the brewery had given them each a glass, but they were only getting one bottle of rum. So that was a hundred twenty crews, and few would be just one person. *I guess it will be a big party.*

"Would you like to tour the distillery?" the bartender was asking.

"Certainly!" Terry replied before Beth could collect her thoughts. *Why not, we're here.*

Terry stowed the bottle in his pack as they were handed off to a distillery worker who guided them into the bowels of the rum making facility.

"Are you sure you're okay to drive?"

"Yes."

"That over proof was good."

Terry laughed, starting the Gemini's engine. The distillery tour had concluded back at the bar where, over two or three samples, Angus, the bartender had admitted that Mrs. Lee had telephoned to warn him of their arrival. From the way he'd spoken of her they could tell that she was not his favorite person. Beth heartily agreed.

"Where to now?" Terry asked, backing the car and turning to position it to exit the parking area.

"We haven't figured out the next clue."

"Forget the clues. We have a car on St. Vincent. Let's see the island."

"Oh. Yeah. Good idea." Beth found the cruising guide and turned to the island map. "Let's just go to the coastal road and drive around," she suggested, memories of their difficult climbs returning.

"If we can get through the ravine," Terry grinned, turning out onto the road back the way they'd come. "In any case, we aren't going to drive up Souffriere," he added, referring to the volcano that formed the northern end of the island.

"There's only a hiking trail," Beth said, looking at the map.

"I know."

"Oh. I get it."

"I think we better start with some lunch."

The rum had made Beth feel a little stupid. She dug around in her bag for her water bottle and gulped half of it down, then braced herself for the downward plunge.

"This is why I bring my own computer," Beth grumbled as she backspaced and retyped for the tenth time on the non-US keyboard.

Beside her Terry's smile was indulgent. He put both hands on her shoulders and kneaded them lightly. She instinctively leaned into him as she hit Return and waited for the computer to respond to her input.

After lunch and a wild driving tour around St. Vincent that Beth was convinced had nearly ended several times in the waves at the bottoms of steep, rocky inclines they'd stopped back in Kingstown at a computer center that rented Internet access time. They had studied the rum bottle and concluded that it contained only one possible clue: an internet web site address on the label that was not the same as the Orion Distillery web address in their advertisements. The fact that the address was "orionclue" had made them certain.

The web browser showed that it was working for a moment, and then the window cleared to a blank page. Beth frowned, noting that the browser said it was done loading the page.

"Buggy?" she wondered.

"Scroll down." Terry lifted a hand from her shoulder to point at the right side of the window where a blue scroll bar was displayed. If the page was truly blank there would be no scroll bar. It's presence meant that there was something below the open window's bottom edge.

"Sneaky." Beth used the mouse to scroll down and reveal two rows of numbers in a very familiar format.

"Latitude and longitude," Terry said, reaching for his pack for pen and paper.

Beth scrolled the page up and down again to be sure that was all there was. Then she clicked on the numbers, even though the simple arrow pointer confirmed that they were not a link to some other page.

Behind her Terry copied the numbers and read them back to confirm he had them right.

"Map them," he suggested.

Beth painstakingly entered the Google Maps website address and entered the numbers as Terry read them. The mapping website responded with an error message.

"That was the right format, wasn't it?" Beth asked, looking at what she'd entered. Terry frowned, then understanding showed on his face.

"It wants decimal and these are in hours, minutes, seconds."

"We can find a conversion program —," Beth started to enter search criteria.

"The GPS can do it. Look, it's too late to go looking today anyway.

Let's return the car and go back to *Trouble*. We'll plot these on the GPS and see where we're going next."

"You think we'll need to sail?"

"If we don't we can just get another car. If we need it."

Beth recalled the rather exorbitant price of the rental and realized he wanted to return it before it clicked over to another day. Fair enough. She rather hoped they could sail to the next clue too.

"Okay. Let's go."

Terry plotted the coordinates on the chart the old fashioned way while Beth entered the numbers into the GPS, a painstaking process as the device had no keyboard, just buttons to scroll through the digits for each position in the long string of numbers. They reached their conclusions at nearly the same time.

"That's the bay we bypassed on the way down," Beth said, setting the GPS with its tiny map display on top of the chart. The coordinates indicated a spot just inland from the beach in Wallilabou Bay, just short of half way up the west coast of St. Vincent. The chart indicated an adjacent road that intersected the main road that they had driven on that day. "We should have researched it before we set out today."

Terry shrugged, dismissing the lost opportunity. "We can sail around. It's a port of entry, so we can check out there, assuming we have to sail to another island from there. In fact, the trend so far has been northward, so we'd be at an advantage to leave from there."

Beth couldn't argue with his logic. Instead she sat back and looked around the harbor at the other boats, the nearby jungle, and the colorful buildings. She was ready to move on.

"Let's go in the morning. We should stop over at the marina and take on water."

SIXTEEN: WALLILABOU

"Is that a dinghy?" Terry asked, squinting far ahead at a dot in the water. He had his right foot up on the lazarette watching the water ahead and steering with his left hand on the wheel. Beth, sitting with her laptop in the shade at the front of the cockpit, looked up at him, then stood up and looked forward toward where he was staring. There was something there, but she couldn't tell what. Months of experience on the water had taught her that the flotsam and jetsam of fantastic movies – floating bodies, castaways in need of rescue – were just that: fantastic. What looked like a bird, or a dolphin, or a chunk of debris always was. What looked like a guy in a dinghy probably was just that, too.

She set the computer on the cabin top safely under the dodger, wedged between the jib halyard and Terry's deck shoes, and reached for the binoculars.

"Yup, it's a guy in a little boat," she confirmed. "Rowing like hell."

"What is he doing that far out?" Terry wondered, glancing at the chart on the lazarette then the shoreline to their right. Beth was studying the shore up ahead.

"I think he's pretty much outside of the entrance to Wallilabou. I remember them saying back in St. Thomas that the guys here are particularly aggressive."

"Define 'aggressive.'"

"You know what it means," Beth replaced the binoculars and sat back down. If they were to be approached by a determined boat boy there was nothing for it. But she'd be sure her computer was out of sight before he got close.

"He's got one hell of an upper body," Terry mused a while later. *Trouble* was cruising toward him at a comfortable four and a half knots. The man was rowing his wooden boat fast and steady, closing the distance at surprising speed.

When she heard him shout Beth saved her writing and took the computer below. She returned just as *Trouble* came alongside the rower, who had spun around and started rowing back the way he had come to match the sailboat's course.

"Going to Wallilabou?" he called out as sailboat and rowboat bows were side by side. His dark face was glistening with perspiration, but his arms and shoulders worked like mechanical parts, each dip and pull shooting the boat forward in a great bound. Beth, who had done her share of rowing her own dinghy, was impressed.

"Yes," she shouted back.

Faster than she could believe the man had shipped his oars and thrown a loop of line around *Trouble*'s mid-ships cleat. The wooden hull thunked against fiberglass and *Trouble* shuddered as she took the weight of his boat.

"Hey!" Terry shouted angrily, stepping behind the wheel to grasp it with both hands as the sailboat turned, suddenly unbalanced.

But the man was undeterred. Relieved of self-propulsion duties, he stood up in his boat grasping a stanchion, eyes scanning *Trouble*'s deck curiously. Beth caught herself checking to see that the six inch dive knife that they kept strapped to the binnacle was in place. The man's ebon features were all angles: prominent cheeks, a heavy brow, a lantern jaw. His lips were a slash of chapped red that did not look capable of a smile. His eyeballs gleamed unearthly white as he turned his inquisitive stare on her.

"You need a boat boy," he said, a statement, not an offer. "I show you where to anchor. My wife sell you what you need."

"You untie that line from my boat before I cut it!" Terry growled, reaching to turn on the auto helm so that he could leave the wheel, then stopping himself, not sure the system could compensate for the awkward extra weight.

But the man put his hand on the cleat and looked back at Terry, expression somehow softening.

"I'm Horace. You tell them you hire me. I come show you where to anchor. Okay?"

"Okay," Beth said, then looked at Terry too, because clearly Horace wouldn't accept her answer. Scowling, Terry nodded.

Expression grim once again Horace dragged his boat forward a bit using *Trouble*'s toe rail, then flicked the loop of line off the cleat. He sat down as his boat rocked sideways away from *Trouble*, and rocked some more on the sailboat's wake. Terry controlled the helm as *Trouble* reacted to the sudden absence of the extra burden.

"Jesus," he growled. Beth sat down, inhaling a deep breath.

"That was scary," she managed, eyes riveted on the man in the boat in their wake. He was already rowing again, not keeping up with *Trouble*, but not losing that much ground either.

"I imagine he counts on that," Terry said, glancing back over his shoulder. When he turned back his expression was more thoughtful than angry, though.

"It could be a good thing," he said.

"How?"

"Well, if he's the scariest bastard in the harbor, then we want him on our side." He concluded with a grin and a quick, nervous laugh. Beth smiled too, but she was not comforted by his logic.

"That's assuming we really do have him on our side. Did you see the way he looked around? Like he was putting a dollar value on everything he saw. I'm glad I took the laptop below."

"What do you want to do?"

"I don't think we have much choice. It would be even more risky to go back on our deal with him."

They sailed in silence for a few more minutes, until Terry nodded, a knowing look in his eyes all of a sudden.

"What is it?" Beth asked, standing up to look ahead where he was looking. There were nearly a dozen small boats arrayed across the entrance to Wallilabou Bay.

"His competition," Terry said. "He's probably the local success story – beats out the competition through sheer brute force. The next boat that comes along will go to one of these."

"Maybe they just take turns rowing out, like a cab line."

Terry's grin infected Beth as they both visualized a long row of taxis at an airport.

The nearest boat boys shouted offers of service as *Trouble* passed between them, but Terry waved and shook his head firmly. It was obvious that they knew Horace had closed the deal and were trying to cheat the system. One persistent fellow followed them as they dropped the sails and switched to motor power, easily keeping up with their slower speed. He took advantage of their distraction with *Trouble*'s needs by calling out a running patter of services he would render. Terry kept interjecting that they had already made arrangements with Horace, to which the newcomer offered other specific services that they could pay him to do: "Did he offer to take your line ashore? No, so I can do dat. Did he offer you fresh bread? You buy dat from me."

Finally the sails were stowed and Beth stepped back into the cockpit, her eyes locking with Terry's in sympathy for his growing irritation with their visitor. She looked out at the entrance to the bay. Suddenly the sight of Horace stroking toward them, energy seemingly undiminished, was very welcome.

"I'm sorry, but we only want to do business with one man, and Horace got to us first," Terry said to the man in the small boat.

"Dat a mistake mon," the man replied, shaking his head sorrowfully. With one last longing look up at them he spun his boat around and aimed for the bay entrance. A few minutes later they heard an angry shout and saw that Horace had paused in his rowing to point at the other man.

"They are either very greedy or very poor," Terry observed, taking a gulp of the beer Beth had fished out of the cooler. As usual after a warm day it was not very cold. "We can send Horace for ice."

"I think we'd better send him for something," Beth agreed.

Horace performed as promised, guiding them to a spot off a long stretch of creamy sand beach backed by rocks and trees. There were two other sailboats already secured stern-to the shore and Beth imagined that they'd be watching the newcomer from the shade of the awnings they both had rigged over their cockpits. They were private cruising boats with some dings and lots of gear lining the decks. Beth would try to see their names and check her log later.

The depth gauge read sixty feet – far too deep for the anchor and three hundred feet of chain and rope to hold them. That explained the offers of taking a line ashore – the deep anchor would hold the boat off shore while the line tied to something on land would keep her from going adrift. Horace asked them for their long line, clearly assuming they had one, and instructed them to anchor with the stern toward shore. Beth hauled out the rarely used two-hundred foot line – actually a spare anchor rode – and secured one end to one of *Trouble*'s stern cleats, leaving the massive coil of rough brown line on the seat beside Terry.

They anchored, Terry fighting with *Trouble* to keep the stern pointed at the shore and into the breeze. The boat naturally wanted to point its bow into the wind. Terry had to rev the engine in reverse to move the boat backward and ensure that the anchor had caught. While he continued to use the engine to keep her facing the right way Beth passed the long line to Horace and he started rowing, using his feet to hold the line in his boat as it paid out.

The competition seemed to be suspended now, for two other men joined him on the beach and helped carry the line into the trees, heaving on it together to take up as much slack as they could. By the time they were done the line was stretched from the boat to a large tree, dipping to brush the water then rising as *Trouble* rode up on a swell.

"Satisfied?" Terry asked, watching Horace and the other two men return to their boats.

Beth grimaced, not comfortable with the unconventional situation. But she knew it was not that strange, and on some levels she was glad to experience it, having read about it many times.

"I'd like to have a look at the tree and his knots when we go ashore," she said. "And I'm going to take some anchor bearings."

Terry nodded, acknowledging her plan as good basic seamanship.

"This reminds me of Deshais," Beth said as she studied their surroundings, looking for landmarks to use for her bearings.

"Where's that?"

"It's a bay like this on the north end of Guadeloupe. I had a rough passage from the north, and when I got in there it had this spooky feel. And aggressive boat boys, although nothing like Horace and his friends."

Terry snorted a laugh and said, "Do you think they all go drinking together at night?"

That made Beth laugh too, and then Terry began suggesting landmarks and they quickly took three bearings that could be checked later to see if the boat had moved in relation to them. Terry augmented this with an anchor position on the GPS. If the boat moved much, it would show on the screen.

During this process Horace returned and asked what else they needed, saying he was going to go fetch his wife. Surrendering to the local procedure, Terry put in his order for ice.

"I really want to go ashore," Beth said when they had stowed the sailing gear and made *Trouble* ready for an evening at anchor. It was early afternoon, plenty of time to look for the clue. But they felt obliged to wait for Horace and his wife, uncertain of what might happen if they were not aboard when he returned.

Within a half hour they were locking the boat and climbing into the dinghy anyway. Shortly after Horace had paddled away they'd been the target of a swarm of locals, mostly women and children, who seemed to appear from nowhere, in and on a huge array of water craft. These ranged from long narrow boats, obviously handmade from local trees, to battered surfboards. The boldest visitors stood up alongside *Trouble* and placed their wares right on her side deck. Beth felt her heart fall as a skinny little girl no more than eight years old offered a handful of colorful shells obviously recently collected from the beach a few yards away. She was standing in the bow of a little rowboat. An older child, a teenage boy who'd paddled out on a surfboard, offered a crudely carved leering coconut, husk hair flying off in all directions.

The crafts were uniformly simple – strings of seeds, wooden figures with scraps of fabric glued on, and things made of shells. One thing was certain, none of it had a "Made in China" sticker on the bottom.

Because of their deal with Horace, and to some extent because of his frightening demeanor, they chose to flee.

"I'm sorry, we need to go ashore," Beth explained as she climbed first into the dinghy. They had left the motor on for the relatively short sail from Calliaqua Bay, so Beth slid back along the gunwale toward it. She glanced up and saw that Terry was closing the gate in the lifeline, something they almost never did when going off in the dinghy. Somehow it gave the impression of an "off limits" sign.

Already some of their visitors were moving away, many with unhappy scowls. As Beth started the dinghy engine all the rest followed their neighbors, except for one enterprising teenager.

"You need a guide ashore?" he asked, one hand resting on their dinghy, the other on one of his oars.

"We're going for a walk," Terry replied somewhat curtly.

"I can show you the waterfall."

"What waterfall?" Beth asked, nodding at Terry to release the painter from *Trouble*'s cleat. She was just talking to fill the time until they could drive away.

"We got a beautiful waterfall. Up de road. I show you. Horace, he just work for you on de water. I work for you on shore."

"We're going up the road," Terry said, shoving the dinghy away from *Trouble* and coincidentally away from the boy's boat.

"De waterfall up de road," the boy persisted.

Beth and Terry exchanged a look, challenging one another to either send him away or accept.

Terry turned toward the boy. "You come show us then," he said. The boy's grin was infectious as he grabbed his oars and swung his boat around to follow them ashore. There was no sign of Horace, and Beth hoped that his neighbors would tell him that they had honored their agreement and not bought from anyone else. Not that there had been anything she wanted, but the huge-eyed children had been hard to deny and she'd very nearly ended up with a handful of pretty shells in exchange for a few Eastern Caribbean dollars.

As they got to the beach Beth slowed the motor for a moment, waiting for a bit of a swell to lift the dinghy. She revved it up to ride the swell as far in as possible, simultaneously killing the engine and lifting it out of the water as the little wave deposited the boat on the hard sand. They both jumped out, Terry with the painter line in hand, and waited for the next little swell. As it rolled in they dragged the boat further up the beach.

"One more," Terry said as their momentum gave out. The next swell came and he pulled while she pushed until the boat's momentum was dragged down by soft dry sand.

"That ought to do it," Beth gasped, hands planted on the gunwale. Terry was scanning the area for somewhere to tie the painter. He settled for a large rock settled into the sand, making a tight loop low down on it, hoping it would not slip up and off. The tropical tidal range was only about a foot, so they were most likely well above the range of the water.

As he finished their new guide came splashing ashore. He had tied his boat to a bit of line they'd seen floating in the shallows and assumed was debris.

"I'm Terry, what's your name?" Terry asked, shouldering his day pack.

"I'm Eugene. And you miss?"

"Beth. Nice to meet you Eugene."

"You need to go to customs?"

"Umm," Beth looked at Terry and he shrugged. "Not yet."

"Well dey closed for lunch now anyway. He back later."

"How late does he stay?" Beth asked.

"Oh, six o'clock, maybe seven."

"That's great. We'll know what we're doing by then."

"Then we go to the waterfall?"

"Sure, let's go.

As they followed him to the start of the paved road leading up into the hills Terry took the handheld GPS out of the front pouch of his daypack and studied the screen. Beth glanced over, but couldn't read the screen.

"We're heading the right way," he told her, then handed it to her.

They were represented by an arrow in the middle of the little screen. A thin line extended out ahead of it indicating the course to the location indicated by the coordinates. She zoomed the screen out until the location, marked by a black dot, was visible. But the GPS was programmed for use on the water and lacked any useful information about the land. Beth pressed a button to cycle through the various displays on the device, stopping at one that said the distance to the location was about a half a mile.

She looked ahead in the indicated direction – up the ever steepening road and slightly to the right.

"What if this is one of the ones that require rock climbing?" she wondered, handing the GPS back to Terry.

"I don't know. Hey Eugene, are there any big rocks around here?"

The dark boy turned, walking backward up the steep road. His oversized sneakers plopped against the pavement with each step. In the shadows of the jungle his eyes and teeth flashed white.

"De rocks over by de water?"

"How about any up this way, in the jungle. Rocks you would need rope to climb?"

"You'll see de waterfall mon. I can climb him wid just my hands."

"Of course, the water would fall over rocks," Terry mused.

"But he can climb it. I'm sure we can, if that's what we need to do.

Let's just see where the GPS leads us."

That turned out to be harder than expected. Once the road was truly immersed in the dense jungle the GPS signal grew less and less reliable. They had to rely on instinct and the device's mechanical compass.

"This feels like the right direction," Beth observed as Eugene led them off the road on a path through the trees and shrubs.

"It's certainly leading to a waterfall," Terry replied, "Listen."

He was right – the roar of turbulent water filtered through the trees.

"I'm jumping in," Beth vowed, although she had forgotten to wear her swimsuit. She brushed her wrist across her forehead and subconsciously wiped the perspiration on the leg of her shorts. The moisture in the air was palpable, carrying the odors of the jungle.

"See dat tree?" Eugene asked, pointing at a massive old creature, its branches a dense mushroom of foliage. They realized that beyond it was the pool at the bottom of the waterfall. The falls themselves were tucked into a far corner of the pool, shielded from view by a rocky, fern-covered outcropping.

Eugene was fixated on the tree. He ran a few steps and leapt up to grasp a low branch, then walked hand over hand along it until he encountered a smaller side branch. Beth took a breath, fearing that he would switch to that branch and fall. Instead he hung from one hand and reached out with the other to grasp an even smaller, leafy branch, then he let go, pulling the small branch with him. It broke off under his weight and he landed on the balls of his feet and straightened, extending his prize toward them. Now they saw the three buttery yellow fruits in among the leaves.

"Nutmeg!" he said proudly. Beth didn't have the heart to tell him she'd picked it before – only a few days ago on Grenada. They thanked him for his effort, tucking the fruit in Beth's bag.

"Now the water!" he declared, picking his way along the rocky bank of the pool toward the sound of the water. They followed, setting their packs on a high, dry rock. Beth leaned against it and slipped off her shoes. The water looked cool and clear, roiled and turbulent where the falls entered, calm at the edge near them.

Terry pulled off his shirt and dropped it on his bag, stepped out of his topsiders, and jumped in with a massive splash.

"Hey!" Beth dropped her shoe and stepped to the water's edge, already dripping from his splash. Further around the pool clinging to the rock wall leading to the falls itself, Eugene was laughing.

"Just jump!" Terry yelled, water droplets spewing from his hair as he shook his head. Beth took a deep breath and leapt, focused on breaking her entry to avoid going too deep. It might be very shallow and the bottom might be rocky.

Eugene and Terry were both laughing when she surfaced gasping, skin tingling from the chill.

"It's cold!" she eyed Terry accusingly.

"You very good mon," Eugene said to Terry. "She never guess."

"Cruel!" Beth protested, stroking overhand toward Terry. He backpedaled, arms extended to fend her off. She swam up on them, laughing as she got her hands on his shoulders and dunked him.

His feet found purchase on submerged rocks. He placed his hands on her waist and surged upward, tossing her back through the water with another big splash.

"Okay, okay," she sputtered. "It's not so bad, once you get used to it."

They explored the calmer parts of the pool further from the falling water while Eugene performed his promised rock climbing feat, scaling the mossy stone wall alongside the thundering waterfall. Watching, they could tell that he had made the climb many times, for his hands and feet sought and found nooks and cracks with ease. He turned and stood on the edge next to the water course, grinning proudly down at them, most certainly feeling assured of a generous tip for providing entertainment as well as the nutmeg treats.

"Jump!" Terry egged him on, stroking backward from the falls to give the boy room.

"Be careful!" Beth added, immediately feeling silly for her misplaced expression of maternal instinct. Twenty feet above them Eugene executed a showy bow, straightened, and then jumped off the edge. He yelled joyfully all the way down, the sound abruptly squelched in a splash that completed with the thunder of the falls.

"Bravo!" Beth shouted and clapped as Eugene reappeared on the surface a few feet from the waterfall. He was still grinning, swimming frog-like to the edge of the pool. Meanwhile Terry had approached the falls, extending a hand into them to test their force. Abruptly he surged forward thrusting his head and shoulders under the water.

"You've got to try this Beth," he yelled out, foamy water streaming over his shoulders and down his chest. Where Beth had expected him to be pushed under by the water he was actually holding his own, obviously standing on something. The water massage was too tempting to pass up and Beth swam over and joined him.

It was closer to a beating than a massage. The force of the water resonated in her bones. She slowly shifted her position, moving the force across her shoulders and upper back, then onto her head. Eyes and mouth squeezed tight she held her breath as long as she could. Then she leaned back, falling through the water into an oddly quiet grotto behind it. She lost her footing and slipped into deeper water. And then Terry joined her, head bobbing on the roiled surface.

"Cool isn't it?" he asked, not referring to the water temperature.

"Beautiful," Beth agreed.

"I wonder how deep it is back here." Terry disappeared under the water. Beth tried to look down into it, but the ripples and foam obscured all clarity.

Terry found the gravely bottom only about ten feet down. With plenty of breath to spare he held himself under with upward strokes of his arms and looked around. The watery distortion gave him little clue to his surroundings: rocks, certainly, and some bits of aquatic plant clinging to them. A darting movement in the shadows that he hoped was a fish.

As his lungs expressed the first hint of complaint something else caught his eye. But he was already pushing upward even as he comprehended that he'd seen a patch of bright red on the bottom.

"What did you find?" Beth asked when he had surfaced and taken a breath. She looked ready for a dive herself.

"Something red on the bottom. Can't be coral in fresh water."

"My turn," Beth said, then took a long breath and did a surface dive. He breathed deeply and followed her. The space narrowed to a well about four feet across. Beth was already head-down in it. He pulled himself down beside her, concerned that she would grab whatever it was and be hurt.

He was right, that was exactly what she was doing. He could tell that she had it in her hands, a rectangular object too regular to be natural. She inverted herself still holding it and pushed off the bottom to the surface. He followed.

"What is it?" he asked as soon as he broke the surface. She was at the side of the chamber, her back to him.

"It's a box," she said, glancing over her shoulder. "It's chained to the bottom, but the chain is long enough to put it up here."

Terry joined her and saw that she had set it on a small rock ledge just above water level. It was a red plastic box, about twelve by six by six inches with a rubber seal and multiple latches to secure the lid. She was working on the latches.

"Does it have a logo on it?" he asked. She nodded. "On the other side." The fourth latch popped open and the lid loosened with an audible pop.

She lifted it, shaking the box a little to separate the top from the bottom. The inside was full of clear plastic bags containing papers, flashes of red amid the white.

Beth removed one bag by its sealed edge and held it up to examine the contents.

"It's the next clue. It's got to be," Terry said.

"I'm sure it is," Beth replied, holding it so he could see the familiar logo on a card inside. She handed him the bag and reseated the lid on the box. She carefully closed each latch and checked the seal all around. A voice cut through the roaring water as she dove down to replace it.

"You find it?"

Clutching the bag Terry pressed through the waterfall and the churning pool outside. He held the bag above his head, trusting the sealed bag, but still wanting to be careful. Behind him he heard Beth inhale and dive, returning the box.

"You knew it was there," he said to Eugene.

"You got de GPS, you going dis way, I figured," the boy replied.

"And have you brought many people here to find it?"

Beth emerged from behind the falls, swimming on past Terry toward the edge of the pool but listening at the same time.

"A few."

"A lot?"

"Well, yeah. Not just me, but the other guys too."

"Why didn't you say something?" Beth asked. She had climbed out of the pool and was standing on a rock squeezing water from her t-shirt.

"Dat would spoil de fun, no?" Eugene shrugged unapologetically.

"No!" Beth laughed back.

"You're right," Terry said at the same time.

"And de company pay us good." Eugene went on.

"They paid you to bring people who asked about the treasure hunt?"

Eugene nodded. "Dey pay us to leave de box alone. Dey pay us to make sure nobody take more dan one."

Terry followed Beth to the edge of the pool where he extended the plastic bag to her before hauling himself out.

Having stopped the worst of the dripping Beth crouched over her pack and pulled out a hand towel she always carried on shore expeditions. It wasn't big enough to dry her body, but it was perfect for hands and face. It was intended for recovering from sudden rain storms, but this situation was close enough. She dried her hands, then handed the towel to Terry before opening the plastic bag. He watched her examine the points card – another one-point find – and the next clue.

"It's a riddle," she said, handing it to Terry.

"Did anyone solve it while they were here?" Terry asked Eugene with a sly grin.

"No mon," the boy laughed. "Dey all had ideas, but I don think anyone come up wit de answer."

"Nice try," Beth said, leaning close to Terry to re-read the clue.

"Twin Peaks. Wasn't that a TV show?" he asked.

"Um, yeah. David Lynch. Very strange. Kind of opened the doors for weird TV."

"I can't imagine how that applies."

"I can't either. Let's go back to the boat. We can do some research in the guides."

Terry fished a handful of Eastern Caribbean coins from the front pouch of his pack and offered Eugene twenty – the equivalent of about five US Dollars. The boy accepted it with a shy thank you, quickly pocketing it.

About half way back to the beach their plans were altered by the weather: a clap of thunder was the early warning for the deluge that followed. In moments the road was slick with running water and the foliage all around them was rattling under the force of falling drops.

"Crazy!" Beth cried, pointlessly holding her pack over her head.

"At least we were already wet," Terry pointed out.

"Always the optimist."

"Time to run!" Horace declared, then did so, quickly leaving them behind.

Around the next bend they saw a group of five people trudging up the road. Four of them were wearing red or yellow foul weather jackets.

Their dark-skinned leader wore only cargo shorts and ragged sneakers.

They exchanged "hellos" in passing, but the drenching rain was more than an adequate excuse for not stopping for a more thorough greeting.

Eugene had disappeared by the time they reached the beach. They paused at the border of sand and pavement and looked across the beach at their dinghy. It was fine, still securely tied to the rock above the waves that were breaking in little hollow tubes behind it. They would be hard to launch the boat through, but that wasn't the largest deterrent: the new stream flowing across the sand between them and the boat was. It was a torrent of rainwater carrying branches and sediment out of the jungle.

"It must have started raining much sooner higher up," Terry observed. That's been building for a while."

"The dink's fine. Why don't we go see if the bar is open and wait it out. The stream wasn't there when we came, so it will have to dry up a bit."

"If it stops raining."

"We'll cross that stream when we come to it."

Terry snorted at her bad joke and led the way along the beach toward the few buildings that represented the town of Wallilabou. The customs building was dark and shuttered, but there were a few guests on the veranda of the restaurant next door. The area was surprisingly free of locals.

They stepped up onto the porch and selected an outside table. They could see *Trouble* moving side-to-side in the wind, mostly restrained by the long line tied to the tree on shore. There were no local boats anywhere near it, which eased Beth's mind.

"I'm beginning to appreciate this type of anchoring," Beth said.

"It does have its uses," Terry agreed.

"That boat is new," Beth nodded at a sleek hull at the end of the row of boats. "Must be the people we passed on the road."

"It's a beauty."

"Yeah. Not your typical charter boat." Beth's gaze moved to another sailboat a few yards from *Trouble*, secured in the same way, its stern facing them. "Hey, it's *Great Escape*."

"So it is."

SEVENTEEN: *PETREL*

They ordered beers and drank them from the bottles sitting on the bar's verandah while watching the rain pelt everything around them. They had just ordered a second round when the four sailors they'd passed on the road trooped onto the verandah dripping rain all over the floor and closest tables. Beth slid the treasure hunt clue off the table and into her bag, noting Terry's amused look at her.

"Hello!" one of the group said, lowering the hood of a yellow slicker to reveal damp blonde hair. She was looking toward Terry and Beth's table.

"Hi," Beth replied. "Did you make it to the waterfall?"

"Oy, yeh," one of the others said with an unmistakable New Zealand accent. He was removing a worn red Musto foul weather jacket. Beth couldn't help noticing that it was one of the expensive offshore models, and it had seen a lot of use. The rest disrobed and hung their wet gear, all of which was more common coastal cruising gear, on the backs of chairs, revealing that the group comprised three men and the one woman who had greeted them.

"Wet trip, but not so bad in the grand scheme of things, I guess," another of the men said, eying Terry. His accent was Ivy League. Beth immediately placed him on the verandah of a Connecticut yacht club, maybe the same one that her friend Ori's father belonged to. He was mid-forties, shots of grey at his temples, deep tan, sun-wrinkles at the corners of his eyes and a round mouth. His nose was a bit oversized and looked like it had been broken more than once. His hazel eyes were close-set, which gave the impression of a focused robot. "One of those boats yours?"

Terry looked at Beth. "My boat is *Double Trouble*," she said, looking out toward *Trouble*'s stern where the name could be clearly seen.

Unfazed by the possessive nature of her claim, the other sailor followed her gaze as he took a seat at the table that the group had claimed. "Oh yeah. Nice little cruiser. Mine's *Petrel*, over there," he pointed to the right to the last boat in the line. It looked almost twice *Trouble*'s size, with broad teak decks and a second mast at the very back of the cockpit. *A great, big yawl, and not a charter boat*, Beth told herself.

"Who wants a beer?" The third man asked the group. His accent was mid-western United States. Everyone nodded, and he went into the bar through the open doorway at the back of the verandah.

"Nice," Terry was saying. "How old is she?"

"1964. Sangermani – Italian make, heard of it?"

To Beth's surprise, Terry nodded. "I've seen them listed, that's about it. It's a real commitment."

"You mean upkeep? No more than a home, just different."

That struck a chord for Beth and she said so.

"You live aboard?" The other skipper asked her.

"Yes. It was hard to explain to my family. It told them it was the same as maintaining a house."

"Did they get that?" He asked with genuine curiosity that made Beth wonder about his story. She shrugged and glanced at Terry.

"Not really. They just pointed out that I wasn't buying a house so it's not the same, and a house isn't floating on water. They know nothing about boats."

The other skipper nodded and chuckled. "Probably for the best. They can imagine disaster, but they don't know what can really go wrong, so it stays abstract for them."

"True."

"Is this just a stop, or are you staying the night?" Terry asked.

"Staying!" The woman declared with a pointed look at the guy with the New Zealand accent. Beth wasn't sure whether she was enlisting his support for her cause or defying him.

"Introductions are in order," the skipper said. "I'm Evan. This is Marnie and Connor. The waiter is my son Max."

As Marnie and Connor nodded formal greetings Terry introduced himself and Beth.

"Marnie wasn't feeling well today," Connor said as if making an excuse for her earlier declaration. His eyes were on Evan when he said it. The skipper seemed to pay no attention.

"*Petrel* is a handful, I've never re-rigged her for single or double handing. So Max and I decided we wanted another pair of hands."

"Mine," Connor said, holding them up to illustrate.

Just then Max returned with four bottles clutched between his hands, which Beth noticed were particularly large. She had also noted that Evan had not explained Marnie's presence. Her guess was that Connor came with a plus one, and that Connor must have such a strong sailing resume that Evan was willing to take his girlfriend as well. He probably expected her to cook, and probably, at least today, she had not.

"Max, this is Terry and Beth," Evan said as his son placed the bottles on their table. "They're on *Double Trouble.*"

Max straightened and turned toward them. "Hello. Nice to meet you. Cute little sloop."

Beth caught the single eyebrow raise that Evan aimed at his son, but she didn't think that Max, who was seating himself, noticed. The "cute" comment expressed an aloofness that Max's father showed no sign of. Beth was thick-skinned, and she knew that *Double Trouble* was a small, simple boat in a world of yachts. The comment had already bounced off.

"Where are you headed next?" Terry asked.

The skipper flashed a toothy grin and glanced at his companions as he replied, "We're not sure yet."

For Beth that sealed it. *They're on the treasure hunt.*

"Have you already solved the clue?" Marnie asked. The annoyed looks that both Connor and Max aimed at her sparked Beth's competitive side. Marnie was a disunifying element in this crew. *Can I use her to slow them down? Stop it!*

Evan had also caught his son and crew's looks. He seemed to chuckle to himself as he looked again at Beth and Terry. "Some of my crew seems to believe stealth is an important element in the *Gunkholing* treasure hunt. Are you aware of it?"

"We are," Terry replied.

"And no, we haven't solved the puzzle yet," Beth added.

"Have you met many others on the hunt?" Terry asked. Beth could follow his thoughts easily: *Petrel*'s crew had to have started after they did. The only other people they knew for sure were behind them were Laurie and Joe and the boys. Terry was trying to gauge whether they were really at the back of the pack, which the estimate of fifty teams ahead of them at the brewery, suggested.

"Oy, there were four other groups at that waterfall on Grenada. We were like a fuckin' parade from the Information office," Connor said.

"But there were only two others at the bar at Petit Quaf, and the distillery," Marnie added sounding pleased. Beth wondered whether her illness today had anything to do with the distillery.

"So at least four," Terry said thoughtfully.

"Was there a family of four? Two boys and their parents?" Beth asked.

"Yeah. They couldn't get the boys out of the waterfall on Grenada," Evan replied with a smile. "Nice people. Friends of yours?"

"We were in the Tobago Cays together for a while. They started on the hunt the day after us."

"Well, we last saw them at Orion. I half expected to sail in here with them," Evan said. "But the boys seemed very interested in doing some scuba diving on the south end of the island."

"They're fixated on finding sunken treasure," Terry nodded with a fond smile.

"Are you planning to follow through to the end?" Max asked, apparently disinterested in other cruisers.

"Not sure. Are you?" Beth countered cagily. Evan smiled appreciatively.

"I'm not sure how many more points we'll accumulate," he said. "But I'm fairly certain that we'll see you at the party."

"Cheers to that," Terry replied, lifting his beer.

The conversation moved on to favorite anchorages in the islands, and then Evan described the passage from Spain that he'd made with Max's mother and another couple. It made Beth want to ask why Max's mother was not with them now, but something about the way he spoke of her made Beth hold her tongue. Instead she focused on the details that he described: the weather they'd encountered, how long it had taken, their first landfall on this side of the Atlantic. She filed the tidbits away to be typed up later in her log.

When they finished their second round Terry walked along the beach to check on the dinghy and returned soaked all over again. By then *Petrel*'s crew had put their rain gear back on and gone to wander around the tiny village.

"It's still fine, and the stream is still raging," Terry reported.

Beth sighed, patience waning.

"Maybe we should try to cross it."

"It gets wider nearer the water. Might be shallower."

"What's the worst that can happen? We get knocked down? Wet?"

"I guess the worst of the debris has already been washed out," he agreed reluctantly.

"Let's at least try. I can't handle another beer, and dry clothes sound delicious."

As they approached the stream a dozen children materialized out of nowhere.

"You crossing?" one boy asked.

"We're going to try," Terry confirmed.

"We help."

"I bailed your dinghy mister," another boy said, holding up the cut off plastic jug that they kept in the dinghy for that purpose. Beth felt a rush of anxiety at this small violation of property. It's just a bailer, she reminded herself.

"I carry your bag miss," a small girl said, tugging on the hanging strap of Beth's daypack.

"No, that's okay," Beth replied, shifting the pack to put both straps on her shoulders.

"Carry your bag mon?" a boy was asking Terry. He shook his head, eyes focused on the dinghy.

"De water really fast," someone said.

"Well, we're big and strong," Beth replied, noting Terry's puzzled glance.

"I can carry your bag," yet another child offered. Beth didn't answer him. They came to the edge of the running water just above where it joined the small breaking waves. The rain, to their relief, had stopped.

Suddenly small hands were grasping Beth's. With a child on each side she stepped into the water, thinking that if these urchins could make it across there was no question that she and Terry could. And then resenting their interference even more.

"You think Eugene sent them?" she asked, directing her comment to Terry over the children's heads, although she was annoyed enough that she did not care if they heard and understood.

"Who knows," Terry replied, equally annoyed.

The children surged around them as they finished the difficult but not treacherous wade and walked the last few yards to the dinghy. Terry started to remove his pack to put it in the boat, then thought better of it. He went to the rock and removed the painter, then carried it back to join Beth at the bow of the little boat.

"Swing it around to go bow first?" she asked.

"I think so. It should pivot easily enough. And we've got all this help," he grimaced at the children, who were standing around the boat. A small girl was sitting on the gunwale. "Keep an eye on the motor though — don't want to dig the propeller into the sand. Please get off," this last was to the little girl.

She gave him an angelic smile.

"Now, please," he added, unmoved by her charms.

She slid off the boat, expression turning surly. Beth and Terry heaved and pushed, Terry staying near the bow and Beth moving toward the stern as it rotated. When she got there she put both hands on the propeller shaft and lifted up and forward, bearing some of the weight of the outboard engine while helping to slide the boat down the sand toward the water.

Nearly a dozen pairs of small hands were also on the soft rubber sides, pushing, pulling, and generally interfering. Beth was concerned that one of the children near the bow would fall and the boat would run over him or her. Visions of being accused by the local adults of hurting a child filled her head.

"We can handle this, thank you," she heard Terry saying as he gave up hauling on the painter and moved in beside the boat, wrapping his left arm around the forward gunwale and heaving, displacing two little boys who'd been shoving ineffectually in that position. The breaking waves shoved at the bow of the boat and it started to pivot again. To Beth's horror a little girl on the opposite side from Terry did lose her footing and fall into the water as the boat shifted away from her. She came up screaming and the bigger girl beside her wrapped an arm around her.

Meanwhile Terry had muscled the boat to point its bow into the surf again and was holding it, waiting for the next small wave to break around him and it. He was soaked again, and Beth could see there was no way they were getting the boat launched and them in it without getting wet. The children were still clinging to it with them, curious faces watching both of them. Beth got the feeling that they all knew how to launch a boat in these conditions. They were like a small jury, waiting to see how the white grownups did.

The stern of the boat was still resting on the hard sand, although as each wave surged up the beach it rose and floated, trying to swing broadside to the sea just as the bow had. Beth held onto the motor, feet planted in the sand, resisting the force of the water.

"Now!" Terry said as the next wave lifted the bow. He moved forward nearly dragging the motor out of Beth's grip. She stumbled with it, leaning heavily on the stern of the boat and causing it to sideslip just as Terry was trying to climb in.

He fell to his knees in the surf as the boat slipped out from under him, surprised eyes looking back at her.

"I'm sorry!" she cried, recovering her own balance. "I wasn't quite ready. Please move away now," she added to a little boy who had just taken a grip on the motor. The boat lifted on another wave and slammed into Terry's chest as he struggled to stand up. A boy and a girl were on either side of him, the girl pushing upward on the daypack on his back as if that would help him rise.

Holding the boat against the waves with one hand he dug into the pocket of his wet shorts with the other and drew out more of the change he'd used to pay Eugene. He opened his palm in front of the little boy beside him.

"Here," he said. "This is for you and your friends. Take it up on the beach and split it up."

The boy snatched the money and made for the dry sand, the girl immediately behind him. All around the boat the other children shouted and yelled and almost as one took off after the boy with the money.

"Let's go," Terry snapped, this time looking to see that Beth was ready. She nodded in total agreement.

As the next wave broke around its bow Terry heaved the boat into deeper water and then climbed in while Beth continued to push it out. Terry freed the oars from where they were tucked in under the rounded sides on the floor of the boat and started to paddle with one, both directing the boat and moving it forward into the next wave. Beth held on, pushing as long as she could still touch bottom, knowing that once they got it through the surf line they could stop and she could climb in.

The bottom dropped off just before they got through the last of the waves and Beth found herself holding onto the gunwale kicking, although her meager effort wasn't enough to push the boat. At least she'd tossed her wet deck shoes into it just before entering the water.

"You'd better get in," Terry was saying, shifting to one side to counterbalance her.

"Okay. I'm not great at this," she replied, first slipping the straps of her pack off and dropping it on the floor of the boat. She kept anything that shouldn't get wet in sealed plastic bags inside the pack, which was fortunate since it was doubly soaked.

She planted her hands on the inflated gunwale and heaved, kicking with her legs to get her torso up on the side. Teetering there she got her right leg up and threw it awkwardly over the side. And then she was sprawled on the floor, her feet sticking out over the bow, her face next to the red plastic jug of gasoline. Oily, gritty sand coated her cheek.

"Thank goodness we didn't rig the seat," she said as she pulled her feet in and sat up, then pushed up onto the side. Terry was already moving into position to lower the motor.

"Grab the oar and keep us pointed out," he said. "We'll surf back in if we don't get moving."

She did as he asked, using the paddle to counter the pull of the surf toward the beach. He checked that the engine had fuel and pulled on the starter cord. And pulled again. Beth was getting ready to get the other oar and start rowing when it finally caught.

"Thank God."

"I know. Let's get home."

Despite Beth's concerns about the behavior of the locals *Trouble* was exactly as they had left her. To her relief they were unescorted as they climbed up from the dinghy and opened the companionway into their private world below.

The water in the hot water tank was just lukewarm so they decided to turn on the engine, which would heat it back up as well as charge the refrigerator for a while. They both stripped out of their wet clothes and Beth wrapped herself in a towel in anticipation of a hot shower. She dumped the sodden contents of her pack in the cockpit and brought the plastic bag with the clue below, settling on the settee at the salon table.

Terry pulled on dry underwear and shorts, opened another beer, and pushed in next to her, forcing her to scoot over. She didn't mind, his warm body was comforting after their difficult adventure.

They re-read the riddle and looked through the St. Vincent cruising guide local descriptions. They didn't see any place names related to "twin peaks." Closing the cruising guide in frustration Terry looked at the photograph on the cover of a sailboat under full sail with St. Vincent's volcano in the background. Abruptly he got up and went to the bookshelf. He returned with a different guide, which he plopped on the table in front of Beth.

"Twin peaks," he said pointedly.

"Well duh," she replied, picking up the guide to St. Lucia. Its cover was similar to the St. Vincent guide, but the mountains behind the featured yacht were the Pitons, the island's twin volcanic cores. They rose nearly vertically from the water on the island's southwest shore. A bay in between provided an idyllic harbor for visiting boats.

"I feel silly for not thinking of it," Terry admitted, sitting back down.

"It is pretty obvious, in hindsight," Beth agreed, opening the guide to the pages that described the harbor between the pitons. "We should be able to get there mid- to late- afternoon tomorrow. We'll have to go back ashore and check out of here this afternoon. Now I wish we'd taken the paperwork ashore the first time just in case," she added.

"I sort of regret that we're making this northbound trip as fast as we went south. But I won't mind getting out of this particular harbor – the sooner the better."

Beth's agreement was interrupted by a loud pounding on the hull that made her jump in her seat. Terry put down his beer bottle and turned toward the companionway. He stopped halfway up the ladder and she could hear him talking to someone. After a moment he ducked his head back inside.

"It's Horace and his wife with produce and bread."

"Oh Lord," Beth sighed, really not up for a bargaining session.

"You go get your shower, I'll buy a few things and get rid of them."

"I love you for this," Beth scooted out from behind the table and stood up.

"You'll have to pay, though – I gave all my small change to the kids, and don't want to flash large bills to these guys."

"Sure, um," she paused, looking around the cabin, then remembering, "I guess I dumped my wallet out with the rest of my soaked stuff – in the cockpit," her eyes widened at the riskiness of her rash move. Terry raised his head, looking at the pile she'd made just outside the companionway opening. He stepped up on the bottom step and reached out to retrieve something.

"I've got it. Don't panic."

"I should have enough in there to satisfy them."

Twenty minutes later Beth climbed out into the cockpit dressed in dry shorts and a t-shirt. To avoid Horace and his wife she'd taken her shower below in the head, something she almost never did because it was a confined space that took a long time to dry. But the refreshed, rejuvenated feeling she brought with her to the cockpit now made up for the damp below. She found Terry sitting on a lazarette contemplating the cockpit table, which supported a pile of produce and bread topped with a primitive figure carved of wood with red bead eyes.

Beth burst out laughing – the little man was particularly well endowed – and then laughed harder at Terry's irritated expression. Struggling to control herself she asked, "how much did you pay for that?"

"I don't know why you're laughing, it was your money," he deadpanned, causing her laughter to surge again. He cracked a smile and reached out to her, drawing her down onto the seat beside him.

"His wife insisted," he said. "Said it would be good for me."

"For you? I think she meant for me."

He nodded, "Probably."

"Did we need all this?" she asked, noting a particularly ripe mango.

"No. But after our adventure on the beach my sales resistance was way down. There is one good thing, though."

"Yes?"

"I arranged with Horace to take one or both of us ashore to customs in about an hour. I was going to take the motor off the dinghy for the sail tomorrow."

"That's a relief – not having to deal with the kids again. I'm sure they don't harass Horace like that. Let's do the motor."

"Well I was going to, then I remembered," he looked across the cockpit pointedly, his gaze extending past *Trouble*'s gunwale. Beth looked too and realized his point.

"I forgot all about *Great Escape!*" she said, standing up too look at the neighboring boat. Because of the lines tied ashore she was positioned exactly broadside to *Trouble*, so it was impossible to tell if the companionway hatch was open. But they could see that the other hatches that admitted air into the boat were standing open, which meant someone must have been on board to open them when the rain stopped. And the dinghy was tied to the stern, its motor mounted and raised.

"I figured you'd want to go calling," Terry said, a hint of amusement in his voice. "See if Bill's on board." He ended with a smile.

"It would be rude not to go say hello."

"They could come here. Why are we the rude ones."

"Whatever," Beth sat back down and studied the fruit again, looking for something immediately edible. She was worn out from the walk, the swim, and the struggle with children and surf. She didn't really want to go calling on the neighbors, but equal amounts of curiosity and courtesy were pushing her toward it.

"How about if I mix up a pitcher of rum punch and we take it over?" she suggested. Terry brightened. He loved her rum punch.

"I won't say no."

Beth went below and mixed orange and pineapple juices with thick, sweet coconut puree and a generous portion of rum. She tucked part of a whole nutmeg and the little metal grater – a curl of soft scrap metal pierced all over with an awl and sold in an island spice market – into her pocket and carried her lidded plastic pitcher back to the cockpit.

"I thought I saw a head poke out of the companionway a minute ago, but that's been the only sign of life," Terry reported.

"Could you tell who it was?"

"The hair might have been red, could be Maggie."

"Well let's go find out." There was an aspect of "get it over with" in Beth's tone.

EIGHTEEN: A FAVOR

"I was so glad to see *Trouble* here when we came in," Maggie Hartford said as she poured three glasses of Beth's punch. She was alone on *Great Escape* and about to explain why, Beth suspected.

"We were up at the local waterfall," she said. "Did you have an interesting trip in – I mean with the locals?"

"Oh God," Maggie groaned. "It's criminal that the cruising guides don't warn you more clearly about them here. They've been this way forever. Very aggressive. And dirt poor, most of 'em. That's the only reason I tolerate it."

"Not like you have much choice," Terry pointed out. "Unless you want a much longer sail."

"I wanted to skip it," Maggie said, sampling Beth's punch and smiling. "Yours is always perfect!"

"Thanks. So why did you come in?" Beth asked, for a moment wondering where Maggie had been heading instead and whether she could have gotten anywhere safe before nightfall, based on what time she arrived. Something about it didn't hold together, but she'd have to look at the charts to be sure.

"My brother Steven got a phone call – we were just on the edge of reception out there," she glanced forward, indicating the open sea beyond the mouth of the bay. "It was breaking up but he could tell it was some kind of emergency. So we brought her in closer to shore and he called back. It's his daughter Angela – she was in a car accident."

Maggie took another sip of punch, as if using it to swallow down strong emotions. Beth was afraid to look at Terry, she was certain he was sincerely concerned while she couldn't put down a sense of deception.

"We were just north of here, so we turned around and came in – I think that threw the boat boys, actually. They had given up on us, and then we came back."

"So what did your brother do?" Terry asked.

"I took him ashore and he spoke to the customs officer. They called him a taxi to go back to Kingstown to the airport. He's going to try to fly out tonight."

"That's awful," Beth said. "He must be frantic."

"He's a stoic guy, but yeah, he's pretty upset underneath. She's his baby."

"So what will you do?" Terry asked, "it doesn't sound like he's likely to resume his cruise with you."

"You're right about that," a shadow of embarrassment crossed Maggie's face. She ducked her head for a moment, took another sip of punch, and then looked up into Beth's eyes. "I think I have to ask a favor. I hate to do it, but I'm in a bind."

"What is it?" Beth replied cagily. *Don't be so suspicious.*

"We were heading for St. Lucia – Rodney Bay. I have to pick up Bill there. He's flying in with the new canister for our life raft. I'm stranded here: I'm not like you Beth, I can't sail *Great Escape* alone."

"So Bill will have to take an Island Hopper to St. Vincent," Terry said, sounding hesitantly sympathetic. Maggie turned her gaze on him and Beth could have sworn there was the hint of a smile at the corners of her mouth.

"I wish he could Terry, that would solve everything – well, except for poor Angela," she swallowed hard again. "But it took him weeks to get the permits to bring the canister on the flight. You know how strict the airlines are these days. He won't be able to carry it on to St. Vincent. I've got to go to him."

"And you need help," Beth concluded somewhat sourly.

"Oh Beth, I feel terrible. I should not have asked. But I'm just desperate."

Beth frowned, thinking over her past experience with Maggie. She was not the desperate type. But on the face of it she did seem to be in a bind. And it was a simple request – experienced crew for the one-day trip from here to St. Lucia. In the cruising community it was not out of line for sailors to help other sailors like this. *If it weren't for the whole dinghy engine episode back in St. Thomas I wouldn't think anything of this*, she reflected, feeling suddenly rather petty.

She looked to Terry, trying to guess his thoughts. He looked troubled, but by what aspect of the request she could not guess. She knew that he thought her suspicions about Maggie were unfounded, the product of a creative imagination. And he was an honorable, charitable guy – these traits were part of what she found attractive about him – so it was likely he wanted to help.

"What do you think Beth?" he asked, turning to her. She peered into his eyes, as always finding their blue depths entrancing and encouraging at the same time.

"I can sail *Trouble* to St. Lucia," she said, more an admission than the statement of the obvious that it was.

"We just decided to go there tomorrow," Terry added, turning back to Maggie. "So your request isn't so far outside the realm of possibility."

"We could sail in company," Maggie suggested, visibly brightening at the prospect of success. "Bill will be so grateful to you."

He better be, Beth thought. She didn't mind sailing *Trouble* alone, she'd done hours of solo sailing and the prospect didn't frighten her in the least. Nor did she resent helping a fellow cruiser in a bind. But something about the way Maggie had maneuvered them into it rubbed her the wrong way.

"And with *Petrel*. They're on the treasure hunt too, so they'll be heading to St. Lucia next, assuming they solve today's puzzle," Terry said.

A flicker of something odd, like anger or strong displeasure, crossed Maggie's face and was gone.

"No need to bring in the fleet for me," she said.

"Say," Beth started, an alternative that touched on the crux of her concern suddenly coming to mind. But she was interrupted for the second time that afternoon by Horace, who had brought his boat rather stealthily alongside *Great Escape*'s cockpit.

"Hello Mr. Terry. I come to tell you de customs office open. You wan to come?"

"We do, yes Horace," Terry turned back to Maggie, "Do you need to clear out?"

"I took care of it at Young Island. We weren't going to stop, remember?" She replied with a pointed look that reinforced Beth's unease. It was as if Maggie needed to be sure they were aware of this minor detail of her journey.

"We'll go in then," Terry said to Horace. He turned back to Maggie, clearly oblivious to her tone, "What time do you want to head out in the morning?"

"As early as we can, from my perspective," Maggie replied, looking to Beth.

"Sure, let's pull out as soon as it's light enough."

"Okay. Great. I can't thank you enough, Beth, Terry. You'll come over in the morning, by dinghy?"

"I'll bring him over," Beth said, and to Terry's curious look, because she knew what he was thinking, "We'll take the motor off tonight. I can row it."

"I've never felt this uncomfortable in an anchorage before," Beth said, placing a final clothes pin on the shirt she'd worn to the falls. *Trouble's* lifelines were festooned with colorful drying laundry rippling in the breeze.

They had watched another boat make a late afternoon entry into the bay. It was a bareboat charter, sailors with just a week or two to enjoy their expensive rented yacht. The swarm of locals had enraged the skipper, who had kicked the carved coconuts off the side deck into the water. This had caused a stir among the locals, who despite their competitiveness were certainly united as a community. From the vantage point of *Trouble's* deck Beth could see the angry looks exchanged between the various boatmen.

Even the boat boy who'd made initial contact with the yacht appeared to be displeased after that. He hung back, pretending to fiddle with something in his boat, while the enraged skipper mounted the motor on his dinghy and went ashore with one of his crew. Beth watched their progress along the beach, and noted numerous nasty looks from the locals they passed. Although she and Terry had done nothing to offend the locals, she felt vulnerable because of this other sailor's actions.

She located a pair of small padlocks in the navigation desk and locked the dinghy motor to the *Trouble's* stern rail where it was mounted for the inter-island passage. Then she climbed down into the dinghy and fished the eight foot steel cable from under the lifejackets and oars. One end was attached to a pad eye on the bow of the dinghy. She fed the other end through the cleat on *Trouble*'s stern and locked it as well. This forced her to shorten the painter, bringing the small boat right up under *Trouble*'s port quarter where it bumped gently against the mother ship. *Well, at least we sleep up in the bow.*

The bay grew ominously quiet after dark, and it wasn't very late when the lights in the restaurant on shore went out.

When Beth climbed down the companionway she pulled the hatch boards from their storage slot and seated them in the opening. She slid the hatch closed, effectively shutting the front door. For the first time she could remember she fitted the padlock into the internal hasp, leaving it hanging open for easy removal.

"What were you doing out there?" Terry asked when she came into their cabin. He was stretched out on the bunk on one side, head on his hand, reading.

"Locking the companionway."

He looked up, eyes wide. She shrugged, pulling her t-shirt off over her head. She'd removed her worn out bra earlier. It was the one where the underarm stays had finally poked through the fabric and started to pinch. As she lowered her arms and loosely folded the shirt she saw Terry's expression go from surprised concern to something much more welcoming. He reached out and stroked a hand along her side from her waist upward.

"You're so easily distracted," she teased, sticking her thumbs in the elastic waistband of her shorts and pushing them down, leaving her underwear on. She shivered as he drew a line from her side to her belly button with one finger.

"You think the natives are restless?" he asked, to prove her wrong. She shrugged again, stepping out of her shorts and letting them fall where she stood.

"I've just never seen such poverty in a popular anchorage. I locked the dinghy and the engine."

"Precautions are never a bad idea," his tone softened. She willingly gave in to the urges of her body, climbing onto the bunk to stretch out. He bundled her against him, his book shoved aside. The warmth blooming between her thighs heated as her breasts pressed against his warm, bare chest.

"I'll miss you tomorrow," he murmured, mouth exploring the delicate skin of her neck. "Let's make up for it now."

"Mom!" Beth's feet couldn't find traction on the kitchen's linoleum floor. Her mother lay sprawled among the castors of the kitchen chairs. Beth hated those chairs. He mother had fallen when the one she was sitting on tipped. Beth was sure that she'd hit her head. There had been a hollow thunk.

"Mom!" she repeated, still trying ineffectively to walk across the room. The hollow thunk came again and Beth shook her head, confused. Then she opened her eyes.

It was a thunk on *Trouble*'s hull: something had hit them. Her childhood kitchen, in a house that was empty and for sale, dissolved into *Trouble*'s dark forward cabin. Truly awake now Beth sat up and then rose to her knees and pushed the hatch above the bunk further open. She poked her head and shoulders out.

"What is it?" Terry murmured, half asleep. Conscious of her nakedness as the cool pre-dawn breeze caressed her skin Beth craned her neck to look all around. As she looked over her shoulder to the north she gasped, her pulse quickening almost before her eyes understood what she was seeing.

"The next boat has come loose from the shore," she said, already calming down as she realized it was a slow disaster, unlikely to cause any lasting damage if they acted quickly. The breeze wasn't strong enough to cause more than light ripples on the water's surface. A nearly full moon rimed the forest fringe and turned the white sand beach into a gleaming path along the sparkling sea.

"Maggie's?" came Terry's muffled response. She thought he sounded slightly hopeful. Not, she was sure, out of any malice, but because it might mean he could get out of sailing with her. Or at least that's what Beth hoped he was thinking.

"No, the bareboat," Beth lowered her head, slipping her feet to the floor where they landed on her shorts. "It's absolutely gorgeous out there," she added.

Terry seemed to ignore that. "Is anyone up on her?"

"I didn't see anyone."

They dressed quickly in yesterday's clothes and Beth unbarred the companionway while Terry retrieved the portable spotlight from the shelf above the navigation desk.

It was as she had thought – the gleaming white charter boat sat with its stern to *Trouble*, the back corner of her open transom just touching *Trouble*'s hull when the breeze and slight swells combined to bring them together. Terry switched on the flashlight and directed the beam down the other boat's open companionway.

"We may have to go aboard if they don't wake up," he said, flicking the light around in an attempt to arouse anyone who might be sleeping in the main saloon. Beth didn't like that idea, given the skipper's reaction to the locals' setting their goods on the side deck yesterday. He had that territorial trait that was common among the bareboaters. Type A businessmen who thought they were getting away from their stresses at work but really just traded their jobs for a different management position, and they applied the same management techniques.

Fortunately Terry's light show was effective. The head and shoulders of a drowsy looking man in a dark t-shirt appeared in the companionway. He raised his right arm to shade his eyes against the flashlight beam while trying to see its source at the same time. As Terry redirected the beam downward at the back of his boat he dropped his arm and took another step outside.

"What –?"

Beth stepped up onto *Trouble*'s side deck and stood holding the frame of the bimini while the man on the other boat stepped in to the cockpit, eyes taking in the sight of *Trouble* so close. He stumbled on something on the deck and caught himself on the cockpit table.

"Your stern line came free," Beth said. There was no telling how experienced a sailor this man was, but she thought anyone would understand that. He moved to the back of the cockpit and laid one hand on the cleat on the transom where Beth now saw that the stern line was still attached. She shivered, knowing it wasn't the breeze chilling her through her thin clothes but the idea that someone had untied, or cut, the line on shore. Her eyes rose to the beach, half expecting to see dark figures there picked out by the brilliant moonlight. But there was no one.

"You'll need to go ashore and re-tie it," Terry said, stepping up next to Beth. The man on the other boat turned his gaze from the shore to Beth and Terry.

"Can't we just put out some bumpers?" he asked. Beth revised her earlier opinion – his quick identification of the cleated line had deceived her into thinking he was a sailor. But no sailor would suggest simply padding the boats, and no sailor called fenders "bumpers."

"That won't work. Can you get some help?" Terry replied. Beth appreciated his ability to accept the situation and move on, subtly taking charge.

"Uh, yeah. Hang on – that's okay?" the man turned back toward the companionway.

"Yes, we're okay unless the wind or swells pick up."

The man disappeared down the companionway and they heard voices below almost immediately.

"What time is it?" Beth asked, voice hushed.

"Almost five. It'll be light soon," he replied, eyes meeting hers. "You want to get ready to pull out?"

It was what she was thinking. And then their plan for the day came back to her and her thoughts took a left turn. Not because of this little incident, which to her was nothing but a note in the log but for the charterers would be an adventure story to retell back home. No, her thoughts turned to disappointment as she realized Terry would be leaving. "Why don't you get ready," she suggested sourly. "I'm okay to stay here and work with them if they need it."

Terry studied her face in the moonlight for a moment, then bent close. His lips found hers, a sweet light touch that countered the sourness. "Okay. Remember, absence makes the heart grow fonder."

She snorted a chuckle and patted him on the behind as he stepped back down into the cockpit.

She shivered again, wrapping her arms around herself, but this time it was definitely the pre-dawn chill.

Presently the other skipper climbed the ladder, footsteps clumping rather loudly. Nobody was going to stay in their bunks, apparently.

He surveyed the situation, eyes passing over Beth, then coming back to look at her. He was wearing a polo shirt over khaki shorts – certainly not what he'd slept in so he'd taken time to dress.

"We're going to head out," he said.

"Okay. I'll fend you off," Beth replied. She had no opinion of his decision – after all it was almost the same as hers.

He nodded curtly and started issuing orders to the crew members who were straggling out into the cockpit in various states of preparedness.

A moment later the grumble of the other boat's engine disrupted the serenity of the anchorage. The first crewman had pulled the long line into the cockpit, laying it in random loops on the lazarette and floor. Beth noticed that from behind the wheel the skipper shot a few annoyed glances at the mess. She was sympathetic, but obviously the crewman didn't know how to coil the line properly and she laid that at the skipper's feet for not training him.

The skipper directed his crew to raise the anchor using the windlass on the bow. It took a long time – longer than usual for Caribbean anchorages because of the extreme depth. But as soon as they started pulling it in the boat began moving forward and away from *Trouble's* flank.

"I don't think we're going to get local help with our line at this hour," Terry had come out behind Beth. She noticed that he'd set his daypack on the lazarette, obviously packed for his day with Maggie. It made her wince with discomfort at being so unhappy about their arrangement with the other cruiser. It was nothing: a favor for a friend in need. She decided she needed to do something to take her mind off of it.

"I'll pull the dinghy in to shore on the line, go untie it, and pull back out," she said, knowing Terry had thought he'd be the one doing it.

"Sure?" he asked, not really questioning her but testing her mood.

She crouched to free the ladder from its night lashings on the side deck – she had even taken that in for the night during her lock-up process. "Sure. It'll wake me up."

"Okay. I'll put on coffee and get ready to haul the anchor," he watched her place the ladder over the side and secure it. "What about Maggie?"

Beth stood up and looked over at *Great Escape*.

"If she doesn't look to be awake by the time we're free I'll row over there on the way back."

"Okay. Hey, you should free her line while you're there. I'll keep *Trouble* from hitting her, if it comes to it. And maybe I'll drive over close enough to knock."

Beth smiled at the image, realizing he was right – otherwise someone, probably him, would have to go back ashore. She leaned out under the stern rail to uncleat the dinghy and felt the cold steel cable.

"I forgot. I locked it. Could you get the key? It's hanging over the desk."

Terry disappeared below and the light over the navigation desk came on. He reappeared a moment later, coming to the rear of the cockpit to hand her the key.

"Thanks."

He went back below, presumably to start the coffee, while she removed the lock and tossed the cable into the boat, then brought the boat alongside *Trouble* under the ladder.

"I'm going," she called out softly, directing her voice at the open companionway. Terry's head appeared in the opening.

"Take the light." He nodded at the big flashlight he'd used earlier and left on the cabin top under the bimini. Beth stepped back onto the deck and grabbed it, then started back down.

"I'll keep an eye on you. Flash that thing at me if you run into trouble."

Her eyes just above the toe rail, her foot on the soft side of the dinghy, Beth felt a flicker of apprehension. But Terry had disappeared back inside after his off-hand comment. *What sort of trouble?* She wondered, then stepped down into the little boat.

There was the obvious sort – she couldn't get the line untied, say – and then there was another sort that up until his comment she hadn't considered. It was the sort she'd been preventing by locking everything up last night. What if the locals had untied the charter boat's line? What if they met her in the trees to take out their anger with the rude skipper on her?

She crouched to keep her balance in the small boat and moved to the middle to kneel down. Now she regretted the absence of the seat that they had not rigged. Hanging on to *Trouble*'s toe rail with her hands she walked the dinghy backwards to the stern, then used one paddle to spin it awkwardly around and propel it a bit further until she could reach the long line. It descended at a low angle from *Trouble*'s other stern cleat to just touch the water in its run to shore. Beth realized that it had stretched a little, or *Trouble* had moved slightly shoreward, because it had not touched the water so much yesterday. *Doesn't matter. We're leaving,* she assured herself. Then stopped herself from thinking about the imagined dangers awaiting her on shore.

She amused herself by pulling hand over hand as hard as she could, absorbing bumps with her knees as the dinghy ploughed through the water. She continued pulling even as they rode a small swell onto the beach. As it receded she climbed out of the boat with the painter and dragged it further up. She didn't bother looking for a way to secure the painter: she wouldn't be here very long and wasn't going very far.

She continued to follow the long line up the beach and stopped where it passed through the first line of shrubs to a substantial old tree beyond.

"Ouch! Shit!" she picked up her bare left foot and looked for the source of the sharp pain. Just a rock. But the ground beneath the shrubs and trees was littered with them as well as twigs and other hard debris. "Idiot," she muttered to herself for not thinking to put on her shoes.

She used the flashlight to pick her way to the tree and examine the knot that Horace had made. It was surprisingly proper, a clove hitch with several riding hitches. She easily undid it and dropped the line, which didn't seem about to spring away — she doubted *Trouble* would swing very quickly or radically, and if she started to Terry would use the engine to keep her in position. Beth's only concern was that she planned to use the line to pull the dinghy back out. If *Trouble* pulled it into the water she'd have to row, but she could do it. She left the line to its own devices and started picking her way through the trees to find *Great Escape*'s line. When she didn't come across it after a few yards she made her way back out onto the beach and saw that it was much further along. Distances were deceiving. With that correction made she was able to trace it to its tree and untie the somewhat less organized knot. She emerged from the trees coiling the line as she walked, ignoring the things that poked at her feet.

She thought to carry *Great Escape*'s line over to the dinghy and coil it as she pulled herself out, but it wasn't long enough. For a moment she stood on the beach half way to the dinghy holding the bitter end of the long line, looking from small boat to the end of the line in her hand. The line actually curved away from her through the water toward the big boat. If she could pull on it very hard she could tighten it and have enough to get to the dinghy. But that would require a winch to fight against the drag of the water. Rolling her eyes at this useless contemplation she dropped the line and went to the dinghy.

Fortunately, *Trouble*'s line lay on the sand nearby, the end about half way up the beach. *Trouble* was swinging, pulling the line into the water, but as she had expected the movement was slow. Beth retrieved the line and held onto it while she pushed the dinghy back into the water. The swells were so much lighter than yesterday she had no difficulty. Once the boat was floating in a few inches of water she could turn it easily. She climbed in and started hauling on the line. It worked perfectly. She let the line fall in loops into the dinghy behind her.

"Nice job," Terry said as she pulled near.

"Thanks. I should have worn shoes."

"Oops. You okay?"

"Yeah, I just felt dumb when I realized. Good thing I had the light. What about Maggie? Any sign of her?"

"She poked her head out, so I waved the radio at her. She understood and got on and I told her what happened."

"Good. So we're set. Coffee ready?"

NINETEEN: SAILING IN COMPANY

"I can't thank you enough for doing this, Terry," Maggie said, not for the first time, as Terry stepped into the cockpit after hauling *Great Escape*'s anchor and securing it on the bow.

Much as he regretted missing a day of sailing with Beth, getting to know a new boat was always interesting. Although he was an experienced sailor, he had not sailed on all that many different boats. He'd learned on his father's O'Day 28, an early fiberglass model that had always required an hour of maintenance before they could set sail. As a result he'd come to know every cotter pin and solder, and he'd come to hate them. In college he'd raced on Lasers and Sonars, but those were like speedsters, or soap box racers, compared to the big cruising boats. His partner Jeff's race boat was like a Formula One car – designed, built, and rigged entirely for speed, and dreadfully uncomfortable for its human crew most of the time. At least it had a head, although Jeff usually kept the water tanks empty and carried only enough fuel to get to and from the dock.

He tended to think of *Trouble* as the old family station wagon. In contrast to Jeff's boat, *Trouble* was built to be seaworthy and comfortable, with convenient sailing features almost like a concession to the fact that she was a sailboat. She was a good boat for Beth, and for him: not too hard to sail single handed and just big enough that they could live aboard without killing one another. But add more people or tougher conditions and he'd want something more like *Great Escape*. A number of years ago the French designers had revolutionized the Caribbean charter fleets with wide, open transoms that allowed people to step from dinghy to boat with ease and provided a swim platform for snorkelers. The fabrics and finishes were durable and attractive, the power plants were usually excessive. Bareboat charterers wanted to sail, but they had a limited period of time with the boat, so they wanted to get where they were going. If the wind wasn't cooperative they wanted to be able to use the motor. And they wanted hot showers, and cold beer, and lots of storage space. So boats like *Great Escape*, which had never been a charter boat but was of the same make and model as many of them, were like the fanciest travel trailers. They were laden with heavy equipment like refrigerators and even vacuum cleaning systems, the sailing instrumentation overlayed on it not so much as an afterthought but like icing on a particularly rich cake. The amazing part was that despite all that weight, they sailed, often very well. Indeed, their sister ships – the racing models from the same manufacturers – were known to be fast. But it was remarkable how well they applied the same design principles to these decadent monsters and got such decent results.

But if he and Beth were to consider going beyond Caribbean cruising, he would want a true off-shore boat. Something more like *Petrel*. It was true he'd seen listings for Sangermanis in boating magazines. He was glad Beth hadn't asked why he was looking.

On the whole Terry did not regret the day with Maggie. So far she was pleasant company, making no complaint when he worked his way around the boat examining the many controls that adjusted the shape of the sails and rigging, noting what he might want to adjust once they were under sail.

He stood in *Great Escape*'s cockpit watching astern as Maggie negotiated the wide entrance to Wallilabou Bay. Beth had *Trouble*'s anchor up and was hurrying back to the cockpit. Had he not been busy with *Great Escape*'s anchor he would have asked Maggie a few minutes ago to circle in the bay until Beth was underway. Apparently it hadn't occurred to his host that the other woman could run into a snag with *Trouble*: *Great Escape* was heading directly for open water. He decided that Maggie's assumption that Beth could handle her boat and wouldn't need assistance was a compliment. But it still nagged at him a little: boats sailing in company should look out for one another.

"She away?" Maggie suddenly asked, looking briefly over her shoulder.

"Looks like it," Terry replied, glancing down at Maggie's red curls and noticing for the first time that they weren't natural. From this angle standing above and behind her he could see that the roots were both darker and lighter – some grey mixed in with the mousy brown of her natural color.

He understood the impulse to disguise grey hair. His mother had gone grey very young and it had embarrassed him when his school mates asked if she was his grandmother. He had asked her to dye her hair. He winced at the memory of the fight that had caused. In retrospect he realized that he'd hurt her, but as a nine year old boy it had seemed like a simple solution to his schoolyard problem. Of course, in retrospect he knew that it didn't matter what his schoolmates thought. But it was easy for an adult to say such things to children. It didn't ease the sting of the teasing.

Disguising grey was one thing, changing the color to something radical, like red, was another. Like bleaching to blonde, it made a statement. What was Maggie's message, spoken through her hair?

Terry's ex-girlfriend, a statuesque, drop dead beautiful model with sheets of long blonde hair, had colored her hair too – from blond to blonder, he always thought, for the natural hair on her body was nearly the same color as that on her head. She'd explained in excruciating detail that her hair was basically flat and the colorist added highlights and lowlights and kept her eyebrows in theme. God, Linda – he hadn't thought about her in months. He vowed to return to that blissful state and looked back out at *Trouble*, motoring directly behind them now, bow rising and falling gently as she encountered the larger swells outside of the bay.

He raised his right arm and waved, left hand holding *Great Escape*'s backstay for balance. He was sure he saw a distant wave back although his view of Beth was obscured by *Trouble*'s rigging, dodger, and bimini.

"Shall we put the sails to work?" Terry asked a short time later. Maggie had put *Great Escape* on a northward course far enough off shore from St. Vincent that the wind speed gauge was reading a steady fifteen knots. Terry had watched Beth raise the main on *Trouble* and the smaller boat seemed to be making better speed now than under motor alone. He was sure he'd see the jib unroll at any moment.

"Sure, go ahead," Maggie replied from her position behind the wheel. "Let me know when you need her into the wind."

Great Escape's mainsail was rolled up inside her massive mast, a popular design that was sold as being easier than having sailors up on deck wrestling with the flapping sail. Terry hadn't used such a system before, but Maggie directed him to the right lines to tighten and loosen and he quickly got the hang of it. The main crept out along the boom like a sideways window shade as Terry ground the big winch at the front of the cockpit. Slow coming out was one thing, but he wondered if it was just as slow going back in, and how that would be in sudden rough weather.

The jib employed the same sort of mechanism as *Trouble's* and in a few moments he had deployed it too. Under Maggie's steady hand the boat heeled slightly and found her "groove." It was a point where the trim of the sails met the wind at the perfect angle, where the boat took the bit in its mouth and cantered on, taking only slight direction from the helmsman. A change in wind direction or speed, or an inexperienced hand on the helm could pull her out of the groove as easily as she'd found it. But Maggie was not inexperienced and the wind and sea conditions were consistent. Terry sat down and put his feet up on the edge of the cockpit table, then stretched his arms above his head and let out a contented sigh.

"Perfect!" he said, smiling at his skipper.

"The weather report mentioned squalls in the channel," Maggie said an hour and a half later. "Standard stuff. But that looks pretty dense."

They were coming to the northern end of St. Vincent, where the uninterrupted breeze from the Atlantic built up higher swells, not to mention powerful gusts. And today it seemed to be blowing in some ugly weather from somewhere to the east.

"It could look worse than it is," Terry replied, although he had to admit the ugly grey and greenish clouds streaming westward through the channel north of the island did look ominous. Out of habit he looked around for *Trouble* and spotted her far back, sails brilliant white in the bright sunshine. "It's about time for a check-in. I'll see what Beth thinks."

As Terry started below to use the boat's main radio he noticed a flicker of something cross Maggie's face – annoyance? Anger? He realized he'd taken a misstep: Maggie was in charge of her boat, and Beth's opinion was not welcome. He should have stated it differently, just said he was going to ask Beth what she was going to do. He'd have to talk his way out of that one after he talked to Beth.

"I'm not afraid of a couple squalls," Beth said. "Lots of them on top of each other is another matter, though. Over."

"It's hard to tell. The wind is averaging twenty now and we're just starting to cross the channel. But the forecast is still for scattered squalls. Over."

"*Trouble* can handle twenty. I'll reef now and put on the motor. I've been through worse Terry. Really. Over."

"I know you have. I'm just sorry I'm not there to help. Over."

"Me too. But I guess Maggie will need your help more than I will. Over."

"Roger that. Okay, call if you run into trouble. Over."

"Love you. Over."

"Me too. *Great Escape* standing by on one six."

Terry switched the radio back to the hailing and emergency channel and stood for a moment staring blankly at the unit in its niche over *Great Escape*'s navigation desk. Control center, more like: the boat's power control panel was massive, with dozens of switches and gauges for her batteries, water tanks, holding tanks, and a few he couldn't guess at.

In his very private musing over what boat he and Beth would get next, maybe for when they had a family to fit on board, he considered something like *Great Escape*. But when he looked at the complex systems even his generally comfortable wallet got nervous. And then he reminded himself that this was his little fantasy, he and Beth hadn't even touched on the subject of family, and only vaguely on marriage when he'd tossed out that comment about it a few weeks ago.

What was I thinking? She's never said anything about it. I don't have a clue what that means.

His musing was interrupted by a shout from Maggie. He stepped to the companionway to look out. She was standing at the high side of the back of the cockpit, one hand on the wheel as she used the higher vantage point to see the water ahead. The wind was whipping her hair around her head, blowing strands into her eyes. As he watched she dragged her right hand over her face and held it on the side of her head, pinning the loose locks.

"Need a hat?" he asked, ready to fetch one if she would tell him where to find it.

"I need crew!" she barked back. "We need to reef. Get up here."

"You got it," he replied, but his heart wasn't in it. Her tone was far from that of a woman grateful for his help. She sounded more like a crotchety racing skipper, although even Jeff, who could bark with the best of them, never had quite that tone of venom. The notion that she was envious of Beth – that he had been speaking to Beth – flickered through his mind and was gone. It was too silly to consider.

"Jib half way in. Main one third," she said as he stepped into the cockpit. Without comment he went to the jib reefing line and sheet and prepared for the change.

"I may need you to head up. I'll let you know," he said, not looking to see her reaction. It was a reasonable request. He would try to grind the jib in under pressure, but if he couldn't do it she would turn the boat into the wind. The sail would flap uselessly and he could easily roll up half.

He started cranking the winch with his left hand, controlling the shape of the sail with the sheet in his right hand. It was hard, but the sail started inching in. He expected Maggie to head up without being asked – to see that it was going to take a long time and take action that would quicken the process. But she held her course. Finally, with less than a foot rolled up and seven or eight to go, he gave in.

"It'll go in much faster if you head up for a few seconds."

"Give up?" she seemed to laugh.

"I just think it would be better to sacrifice a little speed to get this done."

"As you wish."

The pressure eased instantly as the sail began to flap, a thundering sound that grated on every sailor's nerves. Terry cranked the winch madly for twenty seconds then readjusted the jib sheet for the new size sail.

"Okay," he said, although he felt the boat already turning back off the wind. She was good, he had to admit. Completely in tune with her boat.

"That's about right," she allowed, eying the smaller sail area. "But she's definitely unbalanced now. Need the main reefed."

"Aye aye," Terry forced a smile and went to the main controls at the front of the cockpit.

"You've got to trim it about fifteen degrees to port so it doesn't bind up going in," she said. "Should be no problem on this tack."

Indeed, the boom was about ten degrees off center now. Terry used the traveler to lower it a little more, seeing Maggie nod approval at the position he selected. Then he figured out the correct sequence of lines to pull and release and threw his shoulders into cranking the sail in.

Four minutes later he knew he was right about the cons of this type of rig. The sail was inching into the mast by centimeters. In this case simply turning into the wind wouldn't help because of the necessary angle for it to go in smoothly. If the sail was flapping about as it entered the mast it would bind.

"Jesus!" He swore after ten minutes and what seemed like no progress.

"I know, it's a pain," Maggie replied, tone once again friendly.

Sadistic, aren't you?

With the sails reefed *Trouble* shouldered her way into the approaching squall line with enthusiasm counter to Beth's. *Great Escape* had become a light dot in the gloom far ahead, and then vanished, revealing that the streaks of yellowish grey were not just cloud cover but vision-obscuring squalls. She could only spare brief thoughts for Terry as she wrestled with *Trouble*'s increasingly stiff helm. After all, he was on a bigger boat with another person. She knew without a doubt that he was thinking about her.

A rumble of thunder startled her and she scanned the sky all around, but saw no lightening. She was in under the edge of the storm now. After having sailed through this kind of weather on her own a few times she had learned to prepare. She was wearing her foul weather gear, which was too warm now, but would be necessary when the rain came. She had stocked the cooler near her feet with drinks and sandwiches in sealed bags. And she was wearing her safety harness, the tether clipped to the binnacle.

"This is going to be a rough one," she said aloud, the comment directed at the boat. As if in punctuation a stray wave splashed upwards against the forward quarter and rushed along the side deck, pouring gallons of seawater into the cockpit around the dodger.

Maggie stood in *Great Escape*'s main saloon rubbing her fingers on her wet scalp. Her short red hair stood out in a damp frizz, but the impromptu massage felt so good she couldn't resist. She glanced out the companionway to see that Terry was holding the wheel with both hands, attention focused on the way ahead. *Good.*

She moved to the navigation station and looked at the lighted display of the VHF radio. Face contorted in a smirk she twisted two d-rings on bolts that secured the wooden panel where the radio was mounted. The panel popped loose and she gently pulled the entire body of the radio out. She grasped one very thick wire at the back and gently pulled it from its socket. She left it laying loose and slid the radio back into its slot, display still showing channel sixteen in black liquid crystal against a blue background. She twisted the two bolts back in and tuned her attention to the other gauges.

"*Double Trouble, Double Trouble, Double Trouble*, this is *Great Escape*. Come in." Terry clutched a vertical support in one hand and the radio microphone in the other as the boat slammed hard against a wave. He'd handed the helm over to Maggie and come below to use the head, but decided to try Beth again. This was the third time since they'd entered the storm and lost sight of land and, more importantly, the small boat carrying his love.

The hailing channel was ominously silent. He flicked through the channels and got only static. Frowning with real concern he climbed back into the cockpit.

"Could the radio be out?" he asked, foolishly leaning out from under the bimini and looking upward toward the top of the mast where the antenna was mounted and getting a face full of stinging rain.

"Shouldn't be," Maggie replied. "No answer?"

"No nothing on any channel."

"Sure, they're all running for cover like us."

Terry thought about that. In fact, they were not running for cover. That would have meant turning back a half hour ago when the true nature of the storm had become clear. He'd mentioned it, not so much a suggestion as a stray thought. Maggie's rejection had been simple and silent. She'd ignored him.

GPS reception came and went under the cloud cover, but the device was clearly showing them that they were slipping westward almost as much as they were moving north, blown by the fierce winds and carried on the current. St. Lucia's south western coast was receding when it should be getting closer. But they had the sails trimmed in tight and the bow pointed as much into the wind as possible. The engine was rumbling away, probably providing the bulk of the forward thrust, Terry reflected. The next step, if conditions worsened and the wind gusts began to overpower the boat, would be to douse the sails completely and rely on the engine, unless Maggie had a storm jib tucked away below. *Great Escape* was, as far as he could tell, well built and maintained. She should be seaworthy in far more extreme weather than anything likely to blow thorough the islands on such short notice, even in hurricane season.

TWENTY: SEA CHANGE

"Damnit!" Beth growled, taking one hand off the wheel long enough to drag the recalcitrant strand of wet hair out of her eyes again. She plastered it back behind her ear, knowing it would be back in her eyes in a moment. *Trouble* had entered the edge of the squall line a half hour earlier, and she had quickly decided that this series of thunderstorms rivaled the one she'd met north of Guadeloupe on her way south. That day had taught her a few lessons, including that when you're alone, avoiding bad weather is the choice of the prudent sailor. For the last fifteen minutes she'd been hosting an internal debate about the necessity of this passage – or rather, of her making it today. Beth was a planner, and changing her goal took much more effort than it probably should. There were elements of admission of defeat in the decision to turn back. And having to retrace her steps and deal with the locals in Wallilabou was a big deterrent. She wanted Terry back, and she wanted him now. Short of that, tonight would have to be soon enough, but creating a greater delay was almost unthinkable.

"Risking everything in this weather is even worse," she said out loud as her hair blew across her face again. "All right. You win. We're turning back." She addressed the looming bruise-colored cloud off the starboard bow.

Executing a turn in extreme weather was more risky than steering a straight course. Turn the bow away from the wind and swells and she risked an uncontrolled gybe, when the mainsail slammed from one side to the other so hard it could damage the rigging. Try to turn the boat into the wind and she could stall out, the wind pushing the bow back harder than the engine could bring it around.

Beth looked up at the reefed main – it was two thirds normal size, but still a substantial spread of fabric to be caught and slammed over by the wind. The choice was clear. Increasing engine RPM to 3200 she turned the wheel to starboard and clenched her teeth. *Trouble* straightened as the sails lost the driving force of the wind. And then the sails began to flap as the bow began to point directly into the oncoming squall. Their thunder drowned out the engine's steady hum, accompanied by a cacophony of rattling hardware and slapping lines. The bow edged up into the wind and was slapped back by a swell that struck on the windward forward quarter. A rush of water ran along the deck and poured into the cockpit. Beth tried again, goosing the engine up just a little bit more. In a moment the bow was pointed directly into the wind; *Trouble* went dead in the water, shivering in the gale. Beth was about to cheer when a stronger gust swept over them, clutching at the high freeboard of the boat and forcing it back, back, back onto the starboard tack.

"Damnit!" Beth repeated, scowling at her own inarticulate vocabulary. Reducing the throttle to cruising RPM she looked again up at the mainsail. It was time for drastic measures. She had to drop the sail then gybe the boat. She could reach back toward St. Vincent under jib and put the main back up when she got out of the squalls.

Unfortunately she could not simply loosen the mainsail halyard and let it drop: the slack folds of cloth would fly wildly and most likely be damaged by the wind. No, she had to secure the sail, no matter how inelegantly, before executing the gybe. And in order to get the sail down she had to point *Trouble* back into the wind, at least partially, to relieve the pressure on the sail.

Praying that the auto pilot could handle the conditions for a short while – it wasn't rated for steering into wind this strong – she turned the bow back upwind and switched it on. *Trouble* shuddered terribly again, spurring Beth to act as quickly as possible.

She unclipped her tether from the binnacle and went to the front of the cockpit. The main halyard – the line that held the sail up – was controlled from the cockpit and would have to be released before she went to the mast to secure the sail. Taking a deep breath and praying that the sail wouldn't beat itself to shreds before she could wrestle it down she slammed open the lever-style cleat. The feel of *Trouble*'s shaking changed immediately, becoming even more violent and less organized. Holding with both hands onto the dodger frame Beth climbed out onto the side deck on the windward side. She hadn't realized how protected she was in the cockpit until the full force of the wind hit her on the exposed side deck. Sudden fear combined with the actual increased air pressure of the storm to make her gasp. Crouching to keep her center of gravity low she clawed her way forward hand over hand on the wooden handrail mounted on the cabin top. The deck rose and dropped beneath her unsteady feet and each step had to be carefully placed and held. When she got adjacent to the mast she held on to the stiff wire shrouds as she straightened, then took a tentative step up onto the higher deck, reaching for the winch mounted on the mast. She immediately clipped her harness tether to one of the taut spare halyards cleated there.

Feeling slightly safer she edged aft a couple feet to where the reefed portion of the sail was already tied down with a sail tie. She had to untie what was already secure in order to bring down the rest and add it to the bundle. And while she was doing it the wind would be trying its best to rip it all from her grasp.

Although it was relatively warm, her teeth began to chatter as she tugged the slip knot in the sail tie. She worked her left hand deep into the folds of sail to hold on and reached up with her right, struggling to get a grip on the slippery fabric flapping above her head. It was impossible. There was nothing to grasp; the sail was too stiff to bundle into her fist. She had made a tactical error, not starting further aft where she could grab the edge of the sail and pull it down. She couldn't even re-tie the bundle of reefed sail now – there was no way to work the tie back through the small grommet-reinforced hole in the sail in these conditions.

Hoping for the best she inched backward, placing her feet carefully on the cabin top, so familiar with the obstacles there that she knew where the vent over the galley was without looking. To her relief the untied bundled sail did not instantly start to fly, but stayed somewhat controlled by its own weight. She quickly undid the next sail tie and reached for the edge of the sail flapping above. Now she could get a grip and pull down on the fabric. It inched downward, the angle of the sail forcing her to move forward to follow it as she worked. When she'd brought down a few feet and stepped about half way back to the first tie she turned around, and threw her right arm over the boom, searching with her left for the sail tie still hanging beneath the bundle of sail. For a moment she flailed about as the boat shook atop a particularly violent wave. And then she had one tie end in each hand. Right underarm wedged against the boom she awkwardly tied a bow over the stiff, wadded sailcloth. Not pretty, but it would probably hold and be easy to untie later. She inched forward, right arm wrapped around the boom holding the roughly folded sail as she pulled more of it down with her left. The farther forward she got, the easier it was as there was less and less sail flapping above her. Retying the second tie was much easier, and finally she was back at the mast straining upward to grab the halyard where it was attached to the sail. She drew the cable down and wrapped it around the winch on the side of the mast so that it exerted downward pressure on the top of the sail. Now she had to hurry and tighten the halyard in the cockpit before the wind caught the head of the sail and knocked the halyard out from beneath the winch.

She unclipped herself, got down on her knees, then lowered her feet to the side deck. She made her way hand over hand again, nearly jumping into the safety of the cockpit and not bothering to re-clip her tether before hauling in on the halyard. She'd been quick enough: the halyard tugged the top of the sail downward toward the winch, preventing the wind from catching it and freeing the cloth from beneath the ties.

There was no time to admire her work. She returned to the helm and switched off the auto pilot, taking control with shaking hands. She turned *Trouble* away from the wind. Just as the forward sail filled again and the terrible thundering of loose cloth ceased Beth stepped to the left and freed the jib sheet. She knew that the starboard sheet was loaded and ready – she always left it that way – so as *Trouble* turned away from the wind she let the port sheet play out enough that the sail billowed with the wind coming from behind, but not enough to let it fly forward ahead of the forestay. And then they had turned further and the wind came from the other side. The sail slid over with the zipping sound of cloth on cloth against the forestay, then filled with a thunderous crack. Beth turned on the auto helm and let the port jib sheet go, allowing the sail to stream forward and flap horribly. She darted to the other side of the cockpit and gripped the starboard sheet with both hands to drag the sail in enough to stop the flogging. She fit the winch handle into the socket to continue pulling it in to a close reach, then retook the wheel and steered *Trouble* onto a reach that matched the trim of the jib.

She took a long, deep breath, and then she grinned. The compass told her they were heading slightly west of south. Good enough for the moment, until they got out of the squalls. She had done it, and Maggie most certainly couldn't have. A lot of people, even sailors with some experience, couldn't have.

Pride and renewed confidence replaced the fear and unhappiness. She no longer worried about re-entering Wallilabou.

Trouble moved along on a comfortable reach in the shelter of St. Vincent's northwest coast. Once far enough south to feel safely out of the storm's way Beth had turned her boat to face the wind and raised the main sail once more. Out of an overabundance of caution she'd put the reef back in it, and rolled out a partial jib, then put *Trouble* on a southeasterly course toward the island.

She kept looking north at the line of squalls, wondering if they had the power to last all day. Maybe she didn't have to give up, just delay. They'd gotten such an early start. Turning on the auto helm she went below and picked up the VHF radio microphone.

"All stations, all stations, all stations, this is the vessel *Double Trouble*. Can anyone provide an update on the weather between St. Vincent and St. Lucia?"

It was an unconventional approach and she wasn't especially optimistic. Leaving the VHF on, she turned to the single sideband radio mounted next to it. She'd spent a few hours early in her cruise studying the manual and fiddling with this radio, but she had yet to become as comfortable with it as she was with the VHF. It had a lot of pre-programmed frequencies with numeric designations that had little to do with the actual frequency number. Or she could tune it to a specific frequency – but that took incredible finesse. When she remembered, she tuned in to the morning cruiser's net, which was on one of the preset channels. And the U.S. Coast Guard did hourly weather broadcasts, but they were too broad for what she was after. *I should at least give it a try*, she thought as she set the radio to the same frequency used on the morning cruiser's net. She made her same broadcast requesting a weather update for the St. Vincent Channel. Silence.

So many of the cruisers she'd met had ham radios she'd been looking into it. As with everything, the expense had discouraged her. Having to take a test to get a license was also a little discouraging. But in times like this, she knew that the ham operators would be on and talking. She still had not gotten beyond the habit of monitoring VHF channel sixteen, the official communication channel in the states. It was used in the Caribbean, but not nearly as actively. It was more important to know what VHF channel the locals in an area used.

Nobody responded to her request for information on either radio. Most likely because nobody heard it. She returned to the cockpit and listened on her handheld VHF radio for ten minutes without hearing a single broadcast.

The forested peaks of St. Vincent grew clearer in the distance. Beth checked the GPS. She was a mile and a half off shore now. She went below and fished her cell phone out of the waterproof bag where she stowed emergency gear whenever she set out on a long passage. It could be sealed up in an instant to become a go-bag. She turned on the phone and counted to ten as it came to life.

"Yes!" The display showed four bars out of five.

Her elation dwindled as she listened to the ringing of Terry's phone transition to his outgoing voicemail message.

Terry and Maggie had switched off on the helm several times by the time the GPS told them they were ten miles due west of the southern tip of St. Lucia. Each time he'd handed the helm to Maggie, Terry had gone below, dried his face and hands, refilled his water bottle, and tried to reach *Trouble* on the VHF radio with no luck. Now that they were sailing out of the band of bad weather his optimism for some communication increased. But there was still nothing on any channel. Even so, he could hardly claim *Great Escape* was incapacitated due to lack of radio reception. Glancing over his shoulder and out the companionway where Maggie was standing at the helm, he leaned a little further into the navigation station and opened the cabinet that housed *Great Escape*'s Ham radio. It was off. And Beth didn't have one, so it was useless to him anyway.

He went to his sea bag and pulled his mobile phone out of a side pocket, knowing even as he did so that it was ridiculous. He turned it on and waited, just so that he could see that it had no service. *Ten miles off shore. Duh.* He shut it off, shoved it back into the pocket, and zipped it shut. Maybe once they got near St. Lucia.

Back in the cockpit conditions had improved dramatically since he'd left fifteen minutes earlier. The sun, high in the sky, was drying the decks. The wind had moderated to a steady twenty knots. At the top of the companionway Terry shrugged out of the foul weather jacket that he'd just put on and shoved it in under the dodger.

"You want a few minutes to dry off and change?" he asked Maggie, who was still dressed for the bad weather.

She tore her gaze away from the jib telltales to look at him, her expression somewhere between anger and scorn.

"What I want is for you to shake out these reefs," she replied. With that she flipped on the auto helm and proceeded to unzip her jacket. Terry's eyes widened at her vicious tone. He inhaled a slow breath, taking the time to try to guess what was going on. It was no use, he couldn't guess why she was in such a bad mood.

"Which first?" he asked, afraid to take any action without specific direction.

She paused in the process of unclipping her suspenders.

"Jib." She replied, her tone suggesting that it should be obvious to any sailor with half a brain. He swallowed a bitter retort and moved to the leeward side of the cockpit.

Fortunately, releasing the reef in the jib was easy, and *Great Escape*'s big sheet winches gave him sufficient mechanical advantage to trim the sail in the moderate breeze without asking Maggie to head up into the wind.

The mainsail was another matter. Terry readied the outhaul and inhaul, then looked back at Maggie.

"I'm afraid I won't be able to grind this out without going into the wind," he said.

"Of course you can't," she replied. "Ready?"

"Ready Skipper."

As she turned *Great Escape*'s bow toward the wind he started grinding the outhaul. The huge mainsail inched out of the slot on the mast. Terry focused on the lines, watching it wind onto the corkscrew gear in the widened portion of the slot in the mast. It was difficult to measure the pace of the sail deploying. Typically someone else – the helmsman had the perfect view – would tell the person doing the grinding how much further they had to go. But Maggie was silent. Terry managed a quick glance over his shoulder and saw that she was indeed peering up through the Plexiglas window in the bimini, watching the mainsail inch out along the boom. He forced himself to keep grinding and not ask for a progress report.

By the time she finally said, "That's it," beads of sweat were running down his face and his arms were leaden. He wiped his forehead with his left forearm as he removed the winch handle from the winch with his right. He took the outhaul off the winch and put the mainsheet on it, opening the mainsheet cleat just as Maggie turned the boat, bringing it onto a screaming beam reach.

"Here we go," she said softly, more to herself than Terry. But he knew what she meant. He felt it as *Great Escape* found the breeze and surged forward. He tidied up the lines and sat back on the leeward lazarette. After a few minutes he leaned further back so that he could see the compass.

"Let me know when you're ready to harden up," he said.

"This is good for now," Maggie replied.

Terry couldn't stop his brow from furrowing. They were sailing due north at six knots. But St. Lucia lay due east. If they didn't tighten the sails and adjust course to northeast they'd end up having to gybe and backtrack to get to Rodney Bay on the northwest coast. Although they could go for a couple hours before that would be the case, it made much more sense to harden up now and make headway toward their goal, rather than make a sharp turn and a ten or so mile slog toward it later.

Terry was waging an internal debate about whether to speak up when Maggie said, "I've changed my mind. We'll head for Martinique instead. There's plenty of daylight. And it's okay if we come into Sainte Anne after dark."

Terry felt his jaw hanging open as he stared at Maggie. She just kept on steering *Great Escape*, eyes flicking from the instruments to the sails to the sea ahead in a constant circuit. On the third circuit they finally included him in their route.

"Oh come on, Beth sailed from St. Thomas to − what was it, Guadeloupe? − single handed. She'll be fine."

Terry settled onto the leeward lazarette and tilted his head, forcing himself to stick with a puzzled outward expression despite his utter shock.

"Maybe I misunderstood," he said in as conversational a tone as he could manage. "Isn't Bill arriving on St. Lucia?"

Maggie's eyes made another circuit, then she took one hand off the wheel to touch a button. The auto helm took over steering. As she shut her eyes and inhaled a long breath her expression, formerly all rigid concentration melted into despair. When she opened her eyes tears spilled down her cheeks.

"Oh Terry, you don't understand how awful it is. I need your help."

"Winds moderating over the afternoon and squalls abating by sundown," the droning voice of a recorded weather broadcast hardly matched the nature of the positive news it delivered. Beth grinned and danced in a circle in the narrow space beside the navigation desk. Then she reached out and shut off the radio and bounded up the companionway ladder.

It was the radio tower on the chart, and up on top of a peak on the island, that had reminded her to try regular old radio for a weather report. She'd checked the cruising guide to find an AM station on St. Vincent that did hourly reports. It was two o'clock and she was off the northwest coast of St. Vincent. Rodney Bay on St. Lucia was nearly fifty nautical miles northeast, but the anchorage at the Pitons was just thirty-one, or Souffriere was thirty-two.

She was sure that *Great Escape* would make it to Rodney Bay, but if she could at least get to St. Lucia then maybe Terry could make arrangements to meet her. The realization that the next treasure hunt clue suggested that they needed to visit the Pitons was also there at the back of her mind.

Looking north she was positive that the ugly weather looked thinner. There were still squalls moving through the passage between St. Vincent and St. Lucia, but there were spaces between them, and they didn't look as dark and dense as earlier. *Trouble* seemed pleased to settle onto a close reach on a starboard tack and head right at them once again.

Sails set and Otto at the helm, Beth paged through the cruising guide to the section on the bay between the Pitons, St. Lucia's twin volcanic cores. The harbor was very deep. She would have to get as close to shore as she dared and take a long line ashore just like in Wallilabou. Hummingbird anchorage in Souffriere was reported to be very rolly and also require a line ashore. Moorings in the national park on the south end of Souffriere bay were described as "unreliable."

"Great." Beth groaned, slapping the cruising guide down on the cockpit table as she stood up to look around. *Trouble* was pointed at a break in the squalls ahead. Even though Beth knew that the squalls were moving east to west and by the time she got there the hole in front of her would have moved, it still felt like a good omen.

She turned and opened the lazarette where Terry had stowed the long line early that morning.

TWENTY-ONE: COURSE CHANGE

"Bill went back to Minnesota on business. We were hoping it would be the last time. His contract was almost done."

"What does Bill do?" Terry asked, instantly regretting interrupting Maggie when her gaze snapped to him. For a moment he thought she might stop talking. She glanced at the compass and then out across the water ahead. Apparently satisfied, she went on.

"He took partial retirement from his firm. He was the CIO – Chief Information Officer?" Terry nodded, he knew what a CIO was. But he didn't know what partial retirement meant. Only this time he picked up on the Maggie's past tense and decided to stop talking and listen.

"He was in the hotel, getting ready to meet our son for dinner – Kevin is also with the firm – when he collapsed." She paused, swallowing, and Terry realized that she was struggling to prevent more tears. "Kevin called and called, and went to his room and knocked. He finally got hotel security to open the door." She swallowed again and took a deep breath. "He was gone." She pressed her hands to her face and shuddered, the tears flowing.

"Bill's dead?" He hated the way that came out, but he couldn't quite believe that's what she meant. He had so many questions, all of them inappropriate to ask of a grieving, weeping widow.

"Yes." It came through in a quavering wail.

"I'm so sorry Maggie. This must be terribly difficult for you."

She sniffed, dragging her hands over her eyes then pressing them against her thighs as she looked out at their surroundings once more. She may be upset, but she was still a sailor, Terry noted.

"It was his heart." Her head was shaking, her tone bitter. "We had no idea. One of his arteries was eighty percent blocked."

"Wow. Had he been getting regular checkups?"

She nodded. "The firm required it. But he hadn't had a stress test because there was no family history."

"It's a terrible thing." Terry said, hoping to transition away from Bill's condition to that of Maggie and the boat. "And your niece was just in a car accident, you said? Did Kevin call you after your brother left, then?" he asked, trying to put together a rational timeline.

"Yes. That's right. After I dropped him off on shore in Wallilabou."

And moments later he and Beth had turned up with a pitcher of rum punch that they'd shared with Maggie. She'd been pleasant, in a good mood, if a little desperate about getting to St. Lucia. She had not behaved like a woman who just learned that her husband was dead. At least not any other woman Terry knew.

"And you need to get *Great Escape* someplace where you can leave her?" he asked, playing along with Maggie's narrative until he could sort out the real story.

She nodded. "I have a slip reserved on Martinique. They'll take care of her while I go back to — to deal with things."

"But Maggie, I don't understand. Why didn't you just tell us you need to get to Martinique?"

She shrugged, head dropping in apparent shame. "I don't know. I guess I was afraid you'd say no, you weren't going to Martinique."

"No we aren't. And I'd have to talk with Beth, but we would probably have agreed to help you out. If you'd just asked."

Even as he assured her a dozen more questions came to mind. So many, in fact, that he didn't think it was wise to start asking them. Something wasn't right.

"Why don't we get closer to St. Lucia — within cell phone range — so I can let Beth know what's up? It would put us on a better course for Martinique, too."

Maggie's face displayed a series of difficult to read emotions. The grief transitioned to definite anger followed by frustration. Finally she settled on tight-mouthed complacence.

"Very well. Ready about."

She switched off the auto pilot and turned the wheel, sending the bow into the wind before Terry had a chance to turn around and prepare the leeward jib sheet. The foresail back winded and the mainsail started to shudder before he could get the sheet off the winch. Once he did, the jib started flogging on the foredeck, but at least the main filled with wind and *Great Escape* completed the turn. Terry scrambled for the other jib sheet, which was already wrapped a couple times around the winch. He hauled in the slack, then heaved on it to get as much as he could in before resorting to the winch handle. Just like before, Maggie steered her new course, the wind filling the jib and making his job very difficult. It was almost as if she wanted to tire him out.

"Want me to spell you?" he asked Maggie as he tidied up the sheets.

"What?" she barked, sounding like she'd been lost in thought. She probably had.

"Shall I take it for a while?"

"Oh. Yes."

She slid to the side leaving space for him to get around behind the wheel and stand with his hands on it.

"Got it." He said, eyes moving from sails to water ahead to instruments and back to sails.

"I hadn't settled on the new course yet," Maggie said, looking at the compass.

"I'll see what she wants to do," Terry replied, making a tiny adjustment of the wheel. Maggie nodded, silent, and turned away.

She made a point of looking around the deck, nudging a line that he'd coiled into a different but no better pile, straightening the binoculars where they hung from the binnacle. Then she disappeared down the companionway ladder.

Beth had the reefed main and jib set for a close haul as *Double Trouble* passed beyond the northern tip of St. Vincent once again. There was no abrupt change in the wind, but over the course of a half a mile the speed rose from the low teens up to eighteen in a series of gusts. Beth steered to them, pointing *Trouble*'s bow into them when the wind accelerated and falling off a little when the velocity dropped. The band of squalls broke up all around her as *Trouble* forged onward toward the distinct twin volcanic cores of St. Lucia. Beth shed the rain jacket she'd put on just in case. It was too hot, even with the wind in the high teens. After the miserable morning, this was turning into a fantastic sail.

The sun was in the western quarter of the sky as Beth sighted Maria

Island at St. Lucia's southeastern tip directly to the East. The wind had come slightly north of its usual east, so *Double Trouble* was nearly sixteen miles west on a course slightly west of north. Fortunately, St. Lucia's southern coast ran southeast to northwest up to the Pitons, then turned due north, so in effect it was coming west to meet her. If the wind would allow her to sail northeast, directly to the Pitons, it would be less than ten miles. Instead she had to tack and head due east, if she was lucky, or slightly south of east if she couldn't get *Trouble* to point that high into the wind, to get closer to shore and a cell phone tower.

The best case scenario was she came in to the Pitons and found *Great Escape* safely at anchor. If that were the case, maybe Maggie would let her raft *Trouble* alongside rather than placing her own anchor and shore line. It would be the courteous thing to do after taking her crew from her for the day. If *Great Escape* was not there, Beth could anchor herself, or head on around the Pitons to Souffriere Bay. With the wind in the northeast, chances were it would not be as affected by swells coming around the island from the south. If *Great Escape* was not at Souffriere, she could head further north to Rodney Bay, the most popular anchorage on the island, but it was not such a great spot with the wind north of east, unless you could get tucked right up near shore. She couldn't get there before dark, though. Anchoring in a crowded anchorage at night was very risky, even if she weren't alone.

There were commercial ports along St. Lucia's coast, but they weren't an option for a small sailboat. The only other possibility was tiny Marigot Bay where one of the big charter fleets was housed. Anchoring was prohibited, but the marina might have room, and there were moorings. But the fees were very steep. And like Rodney Bay, she probably couldn't get there before dark.

Picking up her binoculars, Beth scanned the sea ahead and between herself and the island. She counted seven other sailboats, all too far away to identify. Heaving a sigh, she studied the instruments and noted that the wind had dropped to fifteen knots. Seeing that Otto was holding course easily, she unclipped her harness and went forward, clipping it near the mast so that she could shake out the reef in the mainsail. *Might as well make some way and get to wherever we're going.*

The expanse of Rodney Bay with its classic Caribbean sandy beach lay off of *Great Escape*'s bow. Terry had shoved his cell phone in his pocket last time he was below. Now he was on the helm and didn't want to give it up to Maggie for fear that she would decide to change course. Not that being at the helm was required for the skipper to call for a course change, but having his hands on the wheel gave Terry a false sense of control.

Maggie lay stretched out on the lazarette on the leeward side of the cockpit, her left forearm laying across her eyes. He'd taken a turn for about an hour after hearing her sad story. Then she'd returned to the cockpit in a fresh shirt, carrying bottles of cold water. She'd taken over and he'd tensed, waiting for her to ask him to help tack the boat. But she hadn't. She'd steered them for another ninety minutes, bringing *Great Escape* within five miles of St. Lucia. The twin ancient volcanic cores, the Pitons, were an obvious landmark to the south. St. Lucia's gentler coastline to the north included several inlets and bays, mostly commercial and industrial. If they were to follow Maggie's plan, they would come close to shore at Rodney Bay, then tack again and head west of north toward Martinique. It was already after three o'clock and Sainte Anne, on the western coast of Martinique, was thirty miles away. As Maggie had said, they could arrive there and anchor in the dark. There were not very many hazards, and *Great Escape*'s GPS chart plotter showed their exact location.

As *Great Escape* plowed along through the waves Terry had turned Maggie's story around and around in his head. If Bill had been found dead in the evening – because he was late for a dinner appointment – why had Maggie received a call about it in the middle of the afternoon? Could the time difference between the Caribbean and Minnesota account for it? No. Even if dinner was early, and people in the mid-west did eat early, the islands were at least two, maybe three hours later than Minnesota. He had to have died the day before yesterday, but the news only reached Maggie yesterday. That was the only explanation for the timing. But from there the timeline became very compressed. She must have immediately called the marina on Martinique to make arrangements for *Great Escape*. And then composed herself sufficiently to conceal her loss from him and Beth, who showed up around three o'clock to have a drink before going in to the customs and immigrations office.

He didn't believe her reason for not telling them. It made no sense to reveal only the lesser family tragedy that had robbed her of crew and not the devastating news that would most certainly have spurred them to help her get *Great Escape* to Martinique. The only explanation he could think of made less sense than hers: she'd invented Bill's death to explain her sudden change of plans. And it didn't explain Maggie's desire to skip St. Lucia and leave Beth far behind.

His concern growing, he pulled his phone out of his pocket and checked it. His thoughts raced when he saw three bars. He glanced at Maggie, still laying with her arm over her eyes, and touched the screen to call Beth's phone.

The Pitons dominated the shore ahead as *Double Trouble* glided across the mouth of the wide harbor in between them. The closer they got to the island, the lighter the wind grew, so that now, a half mile off, they were moving along at just two and a half knots. The sun was low in the sky over Beth's right shoulder. The decision about where to go was made, although there were no other boats in the harbor. *Great Escape* was not here, but Beth didn't have time to go anywhere else before the short tropical sunset turned into night.

Wearily, she reached down to the engine console, then back up to check that the transmission was in neutral, then back down again to turn the engine on. It hummed to life, the sound of cooling water splashing off the stern reassuring to Beth. She turned the wheel to point *Trouble* directly into the light wind, which was coming over St. Lucia's mountains between the two volcanic cores. She turned Otto on and stepped to the side of the cockpit to roll up the jib. The wind had grown so light it hardly flapped as she rolled it.

That done, she carried her tether clip up to the mast and attached it, then went to work on the mainsail. The halyard slipped out of her grip, so the sail slid down the mast and piled messily onto the boom. Groaning at her own sloppiness, she worked at organizing the folds of heavy Dacron into neater piles, then remembered that the sail ties were below. *I really am tired.*

She unclipped, climbed back to the cockpit and reached into the companionway to pull them off of the handle where she kept them, climbed back up, and clipped back on before securing the mainsail to the boom with the ties.

Back at the helm, she inched the throttle forward until *Trouble* was plowing through the calm seas at four knots. Otto was steering easily, and the water ahead was wide open right up to the shore. So Beth went up to the bow and opened the anchor locker. She hauled out all of the chain attached to the anchor, piling it on the deck just aft of the locker. Then she hauled out the rope, watching the little yellow plastic tags woven into it until she got to the eighty foot mark. She cleated the rope rode at that length and hurried back along the port side deck to the cockpit. She had studied the chart of this bay for so long during her sail she'd gotten eye strain. Now she looked at it again, matching real life landmarks to the markings indicated by asterisks and dots and numbers.

Her slightly dated cruising guide said that the fancy resort in the bay was closed, but such information could change on a daily basis. There was a row of moorings along the shore south of the resort's beach, but the cruising guide warned that they were not being properly maintained. Ordinarily she would have picked one up and dove down to check the condition of the line and connections. But by the time she got there it would be almost dark, and the moorings were set in forty to sixty feet of water – too deep for her to check without scuba gear that she did not have.

With the moorings out of the question, her only option was to anchor. Except that *Trouble*'s anchor rode was not long enough to hold in such deep water. She would need something like five hundred and sixty feet to be minimally secure, and she had three hundred.

During those minutes spent staring at the horizon Beth had thought through every possible scenario. Combine the spare anchor rode with the working rode? That would give her enough rode, but she'd fret about the knot all night. Deploy both anchors? Two anchors with insufficient rode was no better than one. Risk a mooring? She'd seen boats on beaches that had depended on deteriorated moorings. Drop the anchor, then grab a mooring at the stern? That could work, or both anchor and mooring could fail. There was no way she would risk it. She'd considered every option in an attempt to avoid taking a line ashore, but she'd had to discard each one.

The steep slopes of Petit Piton loomed straight ahead, Gros Piton's slightly gentler slopes off to port as *Trouble* made her way deep into the bay. Beth could make out the resort's sandy beach and with binoculars she could see a string of floating balls in a loop in front of it. A marked swimming area. There was no sign of swimmers, nobody on the beach. The resort, if it was there, was hidden in the lush jungle growth.

She could also see the suspect moorings strung out along the rocky shoreline to the south of the beach. There were not that many, so there was room to drop her anchor between two of them and take her long line to the shore. She'd want to back her boat much closer to shore than the line of moorings, both to reduce the length of line and also to reduce the likelihood of any local boaters trying to go between her boat and the shore and getting tangled in the line.

With wonder she watched the depth gauge reading hundreds of feet when she was a football field's length from the shore. She was beginning to despair, and eying the nearest mooring glumly, when the numbers finally started to go down. Just before she got to the line of moorings the bottom rose up beneath her like a welcoming hand. Engine in forward idle she toured the area, watching the depth go from sixty to forty to twenty to ten with alarming speed. Suddenly it read eight feet, then six. She shifted into reverse and increased the throttle, backing *Trouble* away from shore before even considering turning. In seconds she was back in sixty feet of water.

"Okay, old girl, we're going to have to give it a try."

Fortunately, the mountains almost completely blocked the wind. The waters of the bay were calm, although Beth sensed a slight current running south. She circled to point the bow toward shore again and watched the depth rise up. When it read fifty feet and *Trouble*'s forward momentum was almost gone she turned on Otto and ran forward, ignoring her unclipped tether. At the bow she shoved the anchor overboard and fed out the chain and then the rope. She had to remind herself that she needed nearly half of what she'd measured out just for the anchor to hit the bottom. By the time it was all out *Trouble* had stopped, but she had no illusion that the anchor was set. Still, she had some time now to take the next steps.

She returned to the cockpit and examined the huge coil of line that she'd dragged out of the lazarette a little while ago. She had securely cleated one end to the starboard stern cleat. The rest of the line was piled up right on the stern rail, easily reached from the dinghy. She checked the depth – still forty feet – and made a waypoint on the GPS at their current location. Then she looked at the nearby shore. Very nearby. Without giving herself time to reconsider, she rose and went to the side deck to un-lash the boarding ladder.

While she was doing so she noticed a steady, high pitched hum. As she stood up with the ladder she looked around and spotted a local boat arrowing across the bay from around Gros Piton. A local from Souffriere.

He'd probably seen her come in. She couldn't suppress her apprehension after their dealings with the locals in Wallilaboo. Although she'd had plenty of great experiences with other locals throughout the islands the most recent colored her thoughts most vividly. She knelt and secured the boarding ladder over the side of the boat, then stepped aft to uncleat the dinghy and drag it forward until it was alongside under the ladder.

She returned to the cockpit and checked the depth and *Trouble*'s position. She'd drifted south a few feet toward the mooring on that side.

"I'm going to have to swing you around," Beth said. "And hope you don't turn back while I take the line ashore."

Suiting actions to words, she swung the helm hard over to port and shifted into reverse. She pushed the throttle, bringing the engine quickly up to 2000 RPMs. *Trouble* shuddered, and her stern swung slightly to port. She quickly reduced the RPMs and shifted to neutral. *Trouble* continued to swing around for a few more seconds. Before the momentum was lost Beth spun the wheel all the way to starboard, put the engine in forward, and gave the throttle a shot for a count of two. *Trouble* surged forward a little, but mostly her bow turned to the right. Back to neutral.

The outboard hum had grown quite loud and Beth spared a glance toward the boat, which was wooden and painted in red, green, and yellow stripes. A tall, muscular black man with impressive dreadlocks stood at a center steering console. Seeing her glance, he waved, his teeth flashing in a grin. Beth centered *Trouble*'s wheel and turned to wait for him, noting that his black t-shirt said "Welcome to St. Lucia" in bright yellow letters.

He came along side, the bow of his boat facing *Trouble*'s stern, and grabbed the base of a stanchion.

"Welcome to St. Lucia! I am Toto."

"Hello Toto. I'm Beth, and this is *Double Trouble*," Beth replied, moving to the seat nearest him. She was just a little bit relieved that his arrival delayed her project, although the sun was about to set and running the line in the dark was not appealing at all.

"Hello *Double Trouble*," Toto said with a grin, looking up and down *Trouble*'s side deck. "And Beth." She couldn't help but like him for responding to her introduction of her boat.

"Where you comin' from?"

"St. Vincent. It got too late, I can't get to a port of entry tonight."

His grin widened and he shrugged playfully. "I not de customs man, Beth."

"I know, I know."

"Lots of sailors stop here before going in," he added with a wink.

Beth nodded, appreciating the information. She hadn't really expected her unofficial stop to be a problem, if she didn't go ashore. Except she would be going ashore to set her line.

"You don't like de moorings?" Toto asked.

"I've read they're not reliable."

He nodded, "Dat could be. But if you swing, you gonna' tangle de anchor line wit de moorings."

"I'm going to take a line ashore. That's why I was turning stern to."

Another thoughtful nod, and then Toto said, "You gonna' need some supplies? Sometin' for supper? I got fresh snapper, papaya, fruit."

Beth knew the code. She stood up and looked down into his boat. It contained a pile of papayas, mangos, and bananas, a few coconuts, and two closed coolers.

"You buy some supplies, and I'll take your line ashore for you. Make it nice and tight. You no worry."

His offer, which was not at all surprising, was like a weight lifted from her shoulders. She should have known the moment she saw his boat that she could make such a deal, but in her fatigue she'd remained single minded in her course of action.

"I'll take a snapper, a mango, a papaya, and do you have any ice to spare?"

His grin widened again. "I got it all, miss Beth."

"How much?"

His face went serious, as was so often the case with the locals when the negotiation began. Sometimes they became truly menacing looking, but Toto's broad nose and smile wrinkles prevented him from looking more than just serious.

"Twenty-five EC."

Beth cringed visibly, on purpose. "I've only got twenty, if I'm to pay customs tomorrow." She watched him purse his lips and cant his head sideways for a moment, then shrug again.

"Okay miss Beth. I got to sell this fish, so you got it."

Beth went below to get his money while he stepped to the bow of his boat to collect her supplies. When she got back, the fruit and a whole snapper, about ten inches long, were lined up on the side deck, the fish on a piece of newspaper. She picked up each of the pieces of fruit to inspect them, placing them on the seat beside her to indicate acceptance. The truth was after Terry's purchase yesterday she didn't need any fruit at all, but she knew that just buying the fish wasn't enough in exchange for his help with the line.

She looked at the fish. Its eyes were clear, and it looked very fresh. She nodded and scooped up the newspaper, moving the fish in beside the fruit.

"Ice?" she asked, but he had already bent down to one of his coolers. He produced a half-bag of ice cubes, water streaming from holes in the bag. Pretty much what she expected. In the Tobago Cays twenty Eastern Caribbean dollars would get you just that, no fish and fruit. She took the bag. And handed him two ten Eastern Caribbean dollar notes.

"Now, you give me dat line and I'll find a good strong tree on shore," Toto said.

He maneuvered his boat to *Trouble*'s stern and Beth passed him the coil of line.

"I'd like you to pass it around a tree and bring the other end back, if it's long enough. I think it is."

"Makin' a fast getaway, Beth?" he asked, his grin mischievous.

She offered him an innocent shrug.

"I'll need to back toward shore, and I may need to let out some more scope."

"Okay. I'll take de line. You adjust position while I go. If it ain't long enough, you adjust some more."

"Sounds good. I'm just going to run the fish and ice below.

Moments later Beth had backed *Trouble* until the depth gauge read ten feet and they were the length of a tennis court from shore. Toto had brought his boat right up to the rocky shore and climbed out with her line as well as his boat's bow line. He was scrambling over the rocks toward a pair of palm trees, paying out both lines. She wasn't surprised when he came to the end of his bow line, but she was surprised that he just dropped it and carried on around the trees and back. The water was so still his boat didn't move, and he picked the bow line back up on the way. Soon he was throwing a sizeable coil of line back into the boat and climbing in after it.

"You spaced it just right miss Beth," he said as he came along side on

Trouble's port side. He still had several loops of the coil in his boat that he passed to her. She cleated it.

"I have about a hundred and ten feet of rode out, with the anchor in forty feet. I sort of set it, it seemed to grab," she told him. It was the sort of thing she'd tell Terry, seeking his opinion as to whether they were secure. Toto just nodded thoughtfully.

"Weather calm tonight. You be good here. Nice and quiet, too." He glanced toward the invisible resort.

"It's closed, isn't it?"

"Yeah. Gone outta' bidness again." His sour tone suggested a loss of business for him, and the "again" only added to it. He reached in under his boat's steering console and withdrew a business card.

"I monitor channel sixteen, but it won't reach town," he jerked his head toward Gros Piton, meaning the village of Souffriere on the other side of the mountain. You need anyting, you call my mobile." He passed her the card and she took it.

"Thank you Toto. There's cell service here?"

He barked a laugh and pointed up at the top of Gros Piton. She couldn't see it, but she assumed there was a cell tower up there.

With that he let go of *Trouble*'s stanchion and pushed off.

"Good night miss Beth," he called, waving. "If you go looking for the clue, you don have to wander too far." He laughed heartily and she grinned, not surprised that he had guessed that she was a treasure hunter. Except that because of Maggie, the hunt was going to have to wait, at least until she got in touch with Terry. She waved back, and watched Toto's brightly colored boat accelerate, heading directly into the setting sun. She stood in *Trouble*'s cockpit long enough to watch the orange orb slide down behind the horizon. She hoped for a green flash, but none came. And in moments the water around her had turned dark, the mountains looming ominously over her little boat.

TWENTY-TWO: THE PITONS

There was indeed cellular service. Before even considering what to do with the snapper Beth powered up her phone and found two voicemail messages from Terry. Feeling intensely relieved she played the first one.

"Hey Beth, we're off of Rodney Bay. I hope you got past the squalls okay, but if you decided to go back I understand. Listen, Maggie has a situation here, and I sure wish I could talk to you directly. Bill passed away back in the states, and Maggie needs to get *Great Escape* into a marina so she can fly home. We're thinking of sailing on through to Martinique."

"What!" Beth cried, then realized Terry was still speaking. She rewound the message a few seconds and listened.

"…on through to Martinique. I really wanted to talk to you, make sure you'll be okay with it…" he trailed off, and Beth got the distinct impression he'd wanted to say something else. But she heard Maggie's voice in the background, and then Terry spoke again. "We've got to tack honey. I'll call you again later, before we get out of service."

The message ended.

Bill died in the states? Poor Maggie! Even as Beth thought it, guilt for her suspicions about Maggie filled her. Evaluating the situation rationally warded off the half-formed notion that her suspicions had caused his death. She checked the time stamp on Terry's voicemail. He'd been off of Rodney Bay about the time *Double Trouble* was abeam of St. Lucia's southern tip. *Great Escape* was nearly the entire length of the island ahead of her then, and that was before she tacked east to get closer. Looking at her phone, she remembered the second message. It was recorded ninety minutes after the first one, around three-thirty in the afternoon.

"Hey Bethy, gotta be quick, we're almost out of range." Terry's voice was hushed and there was no sound of wind as in the first message. He must be below. "We're going to anchor at Sainte Anne on Martinique when we get there, then Maggie has a reservation in the marina inside for tomorrow. I'm getting off as soon as we get there. I'll call you again as soon as we get into cell service. It will be in the middle of the night. I hope you're anchored somewhere nice. I miss you so much." He paused and there was a banging sound, like a door slamming. "Love you." He hissed, as if he was trying not to be heard.

Beth frowned. Something wasn't right. She understood that they'd gone on without her, it was the right thing to do to help a fellow cruiser with an emergency. Except there was something about the way Terry was speaking, the way he immediately signed off his first call when Maggie spoke, and the way he whispered his final "I love you" in the second message. But was he in danger? From Maggie? Beth shook her head at the idea and put her phone down.

Across the saloon the snapper was staring at her, and the mainsail was still a bundled up mess. Wearily she opened the drawer under the navigation desk and fished out her headlamp, then climbed up on deck to tidy up the sail in the dark while contemplating how to cook the fish.

Cleaning fish was a skill she'd picked up during their passage from Cuba to St. Thomas, when Terry had thrown a line off the stern and actually caught a fish now and then. In no time the fish head, guts, and bones were back in the sea and the sweet, fresh flesh was poaching in the oven with some dried herbs, chopped onion, butter, and lime juice. She made a tropical salad of the papaya and mango, squeezing on more lime juice and a splash of rum. To round out the meal she put on a pan to cook a half a cup of rice.

Since she had cell service and she was alone aboard *Trouble* for the first time in months, she settled in at the navigation desk where she could keep an eye on the rice and called her sister.

There was no reason for Maggie to try to enter the head where Terry had retreated to make his phone call. Even if she was desperate, *Great Escape* had another head off the forward cabin. He suspected that she wanted to keep him from communicating with Beth, or anyone else, which was why he had resorted to hiding in the three by four-foot chamber. He wasn't sure why, but then, nothing Maggie had done in the last twenty-four or more hours made much sense. He shut off his phone and bent to pump the head. Hopefully she hadn't heard him leaving the message for Beth, and the sound of the head pump would justify his activity below.

The pump handle rose with a squeal – she would certainly hear that! – but resisted his downward pressure. He pushed harder, recognizing the slightly squishy give as symptomatic of a full holding tank or clogged line. Glad that he had only urinated in the head, he shut the lid, opened the cabinet under the tiny sink, and bent over to look inside. He took out and set on the wooden grate over the floor a can of air freshener, a toilet brush, and a sealed plastic box containing miscellaneous junk that he didn't bother to look at. This revealed that the fat hose from the toilet was attached to a Y-shaped valve. One outlet went to an overboard fitting, which was open. The other outlet went to another hose that disappeared through a hole on the other side of the cabinet. He was sure it went to the holding tank. The Y valve was set to send output to the holding tank. That was a standard setting when anchored in a harbor, especially where people might be swimming. But they were in open water now. He changed the Y-valve to send waste from the head overboard. To cover his bases, he stood up and rummaged inside the upper cabinet, where he found a bottle of head lubricant. He poured a cap-full into the head bowl and pumped again. The pump moved much more freely and the bowl emptied. He stacked the items on the floor back inside the lower cabinet and shut it.

Checking that his phone was safely stowed in his pocket, he opened the door and stepped into the main saloon across from the galley. Maggie was just setting a pot on the stove, the burner already lit. An empty can of minestrone soup, sharp edged cut lid pointing upward, sat on the counter.

"There you are," she said, her voice flat, tired sounding. "Go take the watch while I warm this up. I'll take over later and you can get some sleep.'

"You got it," he replied, grabbing the handles to climb the companionway ladder.

Sitting behind the helm while Otto steered he enjoyed a glorious sunset enhanced by the towering storm clouds that had moved far to the west. *Great Escape* was making steady progress slightly west of north on an easy close reach. They would watch for the lights on two high towers on higher mountains and leave them to starboard to find and stay clear of Martinique's southwestern corner. Sainte Anne was in a west-facing bay about ten miles up the coast. But first they had to cross about twenty miles of channel between the islands.

The sky had gone completely black, pinpricked by thousands of stars, by the time Maggie set two steaming mugs of soup on the deck outside the companionway, then climbed up and moved them to the cockpit table. Then, as if in an afterthought, she picked one back up and extended it toward Terry. He half rose to reach around the helm and take it. There was a spoon sticking out of the mug.

"There are crackers too," Maggie said, indicating a plastic bag full of them that she'd carried up with her.

"Thanks." He half rose again and picked up the bag, removed a handful of assorted crackers, and sat back down.

"If I can lay down for an hour, I'll be good for a four hour watch." Maggie said. She had taken a seat at the far end of the cockpit on the side opposite Terry. It felt like her distance — as far as she could get from him — was intentional.

"I'm fine for an hour, this helps," Terry replied, lifting the mug.

"It's just out of a can," she shrugged, eyes drifting out into the darkness.

Terry started to repeat what he and Beth always said: "all food served while under sail is great," but he stopped himself. References to Beth were definitely not welcome.

"Okay, I'm on. I set out a mug and a bag of herbal tea for you. Water in the kettle is hot."

Maggie's arrival in the cockpit shattered a lovely silence. Terry stood up and stretched, rolling his shoulders.

"Heading is three three five, speed over ground holding around five point five. Wind is steady at thirteen knots. I sighted a large vessel to the northwest thirty minutes ago, but it's moved out of sight to the west." These were the standard facts that a helmsman reported to his replacement. Maggie nodded as she moved in behind the helm and studied the instruments.

"Thank you. I've got it."

Dismissed, and not particularly unhappy about it, Terry moved out from behind the wheel and headed down into the saloon. As Maggie had said, there was a mug with a teabag waiting for him. The prospect of a warm beverage before sleep sounded good. He poured hot water from the kettle into the mug and left it steeping while he took off his jacket and shoes.

Hours before when he'd arrived on board he hadn't given a thought to sleeping, or more specifically, where he should sleep – he wasn't supposed to be aboard for more than a few hours. He knew that Maggie used the forward berth, so he opened the door on the aft cabin. The berth had been converted into a workbench with tools all secured on an overhead pegboard and supplies in plastic bins secured to the bulkheads. He could see one or more sail bags crammed further back in the space. He shut the door, wondering absently where Maggie's brother had slept.

The bench opposite the dining table was long enough for him, and he quickly discovered that the back cushions snapped off to give it another four inches of width. He sat down cradling the warm mug in both hands and took a sip of the fragrant herbal tea. In moments the boat's gentle swaying combined with the warm tea had his head nodding. He set the mug on the floor, stretched out, and was instantly asleep.

"So you'll send me what you have so far when you can, right?" Trish asked. It was the third time she'd asked to read Beth's article, despite her sister's attempts to explain that it was still very rough. Beth bit back the hard response that first came to mind and tried once again to explain her position..

"After I've been back through it, yes. It's really barely more than a brain dump right now, Trish."

"I understand that. I –."

"I'm not ready to share it, okay? I have to structure it, self-edit, first. I know that if I don't, you'll start to do it for me, and I'll have to tell you no, I don't want your feedback, and you'll get mad –."

"Beth really! I won't –."

"Let me do it my way. I'll get it into a decent draft form and then you can read it and I'll want your input. That's how it has to be, Trish."

"Okay. I get it. I pushed you to do it so I should back off and let you. That's fair."

Beth grit her teeth in frustration. In the end it was always about Trish.

"Thank you. Give my love to everyone. I need to go out and check the anchor and lines, and try to get some sleep. It was a long day."

"Okay. Love you Beth. Good night."

"Good night."

Beth ended the call and plugged her phone into the charger. She'd been on with Trish for more than an hour, and it had been great to hear that their parents were doing well and Trish's family was too. But her long day of tough solo sailing had caught up with her about half way through the conversation, and Trish's badgering about the article had turned her mood sour. She wanted to just curl up and go to sleep, but what she'd told her sister was true: she needed to check the boat first.

She wearily climbed the companionway ladder and stepped into the cockpit. The night air was deliciously cool. A gentle breeze lifted the ends of her hair, refreshing her despite her exhaustion. She went to the back of the cockpit and leaned out to study the line that ran from the port side cleat to the shore and back to the cleat on the other side. At the middle, both lengths of it touched the water, rising up to the boat at her end and up over the rocky shore to the tree at the other. Beth's eyes rose up over the dark jungle to the ravine between the two Pitons. A blindingly white spotlight shone there, highlighting the tops of huge, ancient trees so that they appeared to vibrate. She stared mesmerized for a long while, trying to convince herself that it was, or was not, an alien visitation, until abruptly the shadowy contours of the Man in the Moon popped out at her. She sat down there at the back of the cockpit to watch the rest of the most spectacular moonrise she could remember. Lunar light began to fill the placid harbor where *Trouble* lay alone at anchor. For a time Beth felt as if the moon were entirely hers, there to illuminate dark waters and make her battered little boat look like a pristine princess of the sea. She also felt more alone than she could ever remember, even during overnight passages when she and *Trouble* made their way south from St. Thomas. This deserted bay, the empty resort, the nearly impassible jungle-covered mountains: they all piled onto her lonely, tired psyche.

And yet, the sensation was bizarrely rejuvenating. She had come here on her own – not counting Toto's help earlier. She had this amazing piece of real estate and that gorgeous moon all to herself. She was the richest woman on earth tonight. She climbed out of the cockpit and walked forward along the deck in the bright glow. *Trouble*'s decks shone, glittering with dried salt crystals. She stood in the fore peak, hand on the stainless steel bow rail. Below her the anchor rode pointed straight down into the black water. *Trouble* was as secure as Beth could make her.

Back in the saloon Beth searched the AM radio dial for a weather report, eventually leaving it tuned to a reggae station while she got ready for bed. At ten o'clock the music broke for news and a weather report that gave Beth no cause for alarm. Conditions would remain calm overnight. And tomorrow was a whole new day.

Terry became aware of heat on his legs. He shifted them and they immediately cooled off, letting him drift back to sleep. But then the boat bounced on a swell and he was awake again, more so now. He opened his eyes to see that the source of the heat was a beam of bright sunshine coming in through the side portal. His hazy mind equated sunshine with good weather and he smiled at the prospect. Then his mind cleared a little more and he remembered where he was. Still fuzzy headed, he stood up and stumbled to the head compartment. Standing there, he peered out the small portal at acres of open ocean. They must still be going north. They must have reached Martinique hours ago, so Maggie must have decided to stand off until daylight. That was good. Neither of them had been there before, so avoiding the nighttime approach was a conservative choice. *But Maggie hasn't been acting very conservative. Why not wake me up as planned? What time is it, anyway?* The sun on his legs came back to him. To shine in at that angle, the sun had to be high in the sky. Dawn was hours gone, and he'd slept on. He usually got up with the sun. He couldn't remember the last time he'd slept so late. No, he could: the morning after a party at which the drinks had flowed.

He turned the faucet and listened to the water pump engage. Nothing came out. He couldn't remember whether he'd gotten water out of this faucet yesterday. Would Maggie really let the tanks run dry? Definitely not conservative behavior.

Back in the saloon he spotted the coffee pot in brackets on top of the gimbaled stove. Putting aside any more pondering, he took a mug from the cabinet and poured himself some of the dark fluid. He could tell before it reached his lips that it was lukewarm at best. And it was terribly bitter, as if it had perked far too long. *How did I not hear her making this? Or smell it?* He wondered. He quickly squelched one possible answer as preposterous.

Taking a step up the companionway ladder, he looked out into the cockpit to find his skipper. Maggie was slouched in the far corner, behind and to the side of the wheel, which turned slightly as he watched, indicating that the auto helm was engaged. She was holding a black object in each hand. One was a handheld GPS. Not the same model as *Trouble*'s, but similar. The other was a hand held VHF radio. At the sight he involuntarily glanced over at the navigation station where the boat's VHF radio was dark. Maggie must have turned it off some time in the night. Either that, or whatever had been wrong earlier had spread to the entire device. Maybe a short circuit?

As he took another step up the companionway ladder Maggie noticed him.

"Morning," she said cheerfully. He knew that his expression was puzzled, but she did not react to it. He was high enough now to see the water around the boat. And that was all he saw: water. There was no island in sight.

"What's going on Maggie?" He asked, forcing himself to smile because he knew it would make his voice sound friendly.

"Oh." Her expression was actually a little guilty. But he didn't buy it. He understood now that she was executing on a plan that she'd had from the outset. If anything, she was proud of herself for her apparent success. "Change of plans."

He climbed the rest of the way into the cockpit and sat down with his back to the forward bulkhead, on the side opposite her. Basically as far from her as he could get.

"So I see. Why didn't you wake me up to take watch?"

It was a silly question and he had to force himself not to answer it: *because you didn't want to have a fight about changing course. Better to hear her answer.*

"I was fine. It was a beautiful clear night. The breeze held, so it was easy sailing. You were so helpful yesterday I wanted you to get your rest."

"So just when did this 'change of plans' happen?" He made sure that the quotes around "change of plans" were clear in his voice.

She grimaced, as if preparing for a difficult explanation. Before she could speak the radio in her hand crackled.

TWENTY-THREE: GOOD MOORING

Trouble's mast creaking and a halyard tapping against it on the inside began disrupting Beth's sleep around dawn. But months of sleeping aboard in all kinds of conditions had trained her to know what was going on without having to wake up, get up, and check. The rising sun warming the jungle was causing a light local breeze to funnel down the mountains and across the bay. *Trouble* was rocking gently.

Until a half hour later when the rocking turned into a series of wider sways back and forth that rattled objects in cabinets. Beth's eyes dragged open to take in the clear blue sky through the hatch above her head. She shut them again and sighed even as the swaying stopped. She had to get up and check.

She stood in the cockpit in t-shirt and shorts to survey her surroundings. Small waves now breaking on the beach were the cause of the swaying. Out beyond the mouth of the bay a medium sized cargo boat – a newer version of the Union Island mail boat –was just disappearing behind Gros Piton to the north.

"Wake," Beth said grumpily before climbing back down below to put the coffee on.

She clicked on the radio while she banged around in the galley, half listening for words related to the weather in the rapid patter of a local news report. News of the school band concert, the death of a well-known local business man in Rodney Bay, and the debate of a law banning plastic bags filtered into her pre-coffee consciousness. At the forefront of her thoughts was what to do next.

The weather report, when it came, told her of another beautiful day in paradise. She switched the radio off and went through her automatic battery check: they were well charged and the trickle from the solar panel was starting to top them off. She grabbed her phone and carried it and her coffee mug out to the cockpit to belatedly examine her shore line. It was unchanged from last night. Before settling down with her coffee she went forward to look once again down into the water at her vertical anchor rode.

Her phone had no new voicemail messages. With little expectation of success, she called Terry. It went directly to voicemail, so she left a message, assuring him that she was safely between the Pitons, and that she'd received his messages and understood. And then she added, "I'm a little concerned. I hope everything is okay."

She immediately regretted it, but she'd ended the call without waiting to see if his system would let her re-record her message. *What if he is in trouble? What if Maggie listens to it? Oh stop it. Terry would be laughing at you right now. You need to stop inventing problems and decide what to do.*

She had consciously avoided looking at the puzzle clue, or even thinking about it, since yesterday. But at the back her mind was the burning notion that the next clue must be right here in this bay.

She half expected Toto to come around in his boat, but she remained alone in the bay as she finished her coffee, ate a slightly soft apple and then a hardboiled egg. Then she stripped and went for a quick swim before dressing. By then she had made the only plan that she could: sail to Martinique. The treasure hunt would have to wait until she and Terry could come and look for the clue together, even if it put them in last place.

She dragged her damp hair into a pony tail and pulled on her gloves to haul in the shore line. There was a lot more resistance than she expected when she began, but once she had dragged enough of it aboard to reach the sheet winch she wrapped it around and used the mechanical advantage. *Trouble* was dragged back toward shore by the tension on the line for a while, but eventually she saw the end of the line drag across the shore and into the water, and *Trouble* sprung forward again, pulled by the anchor rode.

She took a few minutes to coil up the long line and cram it back into the lazarette before turning on the engine. On her way to the bow she removed the ties that secured the main sail and freed the halyard from under the mast winch. Then she stood on the bow and looked once more at the anchor rode. There was a reason that this was usually Terry's job, but she'd done it many times herself, too. She rolled her shoulders and crouched to take up the heavy rope. Leaving it cleated in case she lost her grip, she started hauling it in. Soon enough the angle of the rode rose and she was pulling the entire weight of the boat forward toward the anchor. Fortunately, the light breeze helped, pushing *Trouble* toward the deeper water, but also causing her to turn. After a few minutes of hauling the bow was facing the shore and Beth suspected that the anchor was off the bottom and dragging through the water. The risk now was that it would snag the line of one of the moorings that Beth had avoided last night. She continued to heave, squatting to grab more line and rising as she pulled to bring in a length as long as she was tall. She'd forgotten to count her heaves, so she had to guess from the amount of line piled into the anchor well that there was about thirty feet left when she heard a thump on the side of *Trouble*'s hull.

A mooring. No reason to panic. Just keep heaving.

And she did as she heard the thumping continue along the hull – *ka-bump, ka-bump, ka-bump* – getting closer. The join between rope and chain passed through her grip indicating that she had twenty feet to go. She heaved again, chain rattling in over the anchor chock, and again, and then she was stopped short. The chain wouldn't budge. Holding the chain in her right hand she mopped sweat from her brow with her left forearm, then leaned over the side of the bow to see what was going on.

The white mooring ball, about the size of a kid's beach ball, was tucked up against *Trouble*'s bow. The anchor chain ran down next to it and she could just see the shadowy anchor in the water below the ball.

Inhaling a deep breath as if it would re-energize her, Beth repositioned herself right next to the furled jib where she could see the water below. She tugged on the chain. The mooring ball lifted, rubbing against the hull.

Okay. Give it some slack and it will unhook.

She lowered about five feet of chain back into the water. The anchor did not descend.

Crap.

Trouble continued to drift backwards in the light breeze. The mooring ball was soon a few feet off her bow, the chain in Beth's hand going taut. She tightened her grip and felt the tug increase as the mooring ball started to rise from the water. She couldn't cleat the chain. Trying to hold it with one hand she found the splice where rope joined chain and secured the rope on the starboard cleat. Then she let the chain pay out, putting twenty feet between *Trouble*'s bow and the mooring that had snagged her anchor.

Now what?

She could use her boat hook to grab the line that secured the mooring to the bottom. But to do that she had to get *Trouble* next to it again, and she wasn't strong enough to drag the boat forward into the breeze using the chain. The obvious choice was the motor, but she couldn't drive forward from the cockpit, then run back to the bow fast enough to catch the mooring before *Trouble* drifted again. If she wanted to pick up the mooring, she would normally drive *Trouble* up to it until it was next to the stern, then leave the helm long enough to grab it with the boat hook there at the stern and walk with it up to the bow to secure it. But *Trouble* was thirty-six feet long, so her twenty feet of chain running from the bow to the mooring ball was too short. She had to put another fifteen or twenty feet of rope in the water, and then she had to be very careful to avoid the line as she used the engine to reposition *Trouble* with the mooring next to the stern where she could haul it, and the anchor, up with the boathook.

That last part was a big question mark in her mind even as she got ready. She wasn't sure that she could lift the combined mooring and anchor that way. But she had to try.

While *Trouble* drifted back another fifteen feet on the line she'd let out, she hurried back to the cockpit, collecting the boat hook from its spot under the boom as she went. Before starting her maneuver she got a length of dock line out of the lazarette. It was always a good idea to have some extra line on hand in a tough situation.

Standing behind the wheel she shifted the motor into slow forward idle and pointed the bow to the right of the white mooring ball. She needed to take up the slack of line and chain, but keep it to the side so there was no chance of it coming into contact with the propeller. She visualized how she wanted it to work: the anchor rode led out over the bow chock and then directly back along the port side, transitioning from rope to chain up near the mast, and leading to the white ball that she wanted directly to her left, right next to the boat.

But because she had aimed to the right of the ball, *Trouble*'s stern didn't come close enough to the ball when the combined rope and chain ran short. The ball was a boat length off to port, and she could not get *Trouble*'s stern to swing sideways into the breeze.

"Okay. It's okay. Just try again."

She put the engine in neutral and let *Trouble* drift back, leaning over to port to watch the chain and line extend away. She bit her lip and pointed *Trouble*'s bow right at the mooring buoy.

This time she heard the mooring ball bumping along *Trouble*'s hull getting closer and closer. The moment she felt *Trouble*'s forward progress inhibited she moved to port, leaning out beneath the lower lifeline as she snatched up the boat hook.

She plunged it over the side like a spear and snagged the ring on the top of the mooring ball. She dragged up on it, but, as she'd feared, it was too heavy. She could just reach the ring, so she grabbed it and removed the hook, then flailed with her other hand for the waiting dock line. Grunting, *Trouble*'s combing digging into her tummy as she leaned out and over it, she fed the line through the ring and pulled it back up. She got up on her knees and wrapped both ends of the line around the jib sheet winch, then inhaled a breath as she paused to think. The engine was still in forward idle, and *Trouble* was starting to pivot around the mooring ball. Holding the two ends of the line in her left hand, she stretched across the back of the cockpit to shift the engine into neutral. *Trouble* immediately stopped straining to make progress and settled into a stillness that transmitted to Beth. *Take it easy. Step by step.*

She took a heavy steel winch handle from its pocket and returned to the sheet winch. Grinding with her right hand and hauling on both ends of the dock line with the other, she slowly lifted the mooring ball up out of the water against *Trouble*'s hull. She cringed at the sound of the anchor scraping against the hull along with the ball, praying that it wasn't doing any serious damage.

When the top of the mooring was at the height of the deck and the line went straight from it to the winch, she could grind no more. She jammed the lines around the sheet cleat, which was too small for her to properly cleat them. She flopped down across the combing and narrow side deck just forward of the ball and leaned out under the lifeline to see what was going on.

And just as she reached out to grab the anchor's shaft, it slipped downward beyond her reach and splashed into the water.

"Seriously?" she groaned as she hauled herself out from under the lifeline and hurried along the deck to the bow. "If you snagged again down lower I'm going to cut you, do you hear me?" she shouted into the water as she picked up the rode and heaved. Of course it wasn't true, she couldn't afford to lose the anchor. But it felt good to yell.

The rode came in much more easily than it had before, and after four heaves she was hauling on the chain. Even that came aboard with little resistance, as if it had had its fun and was now ready to relax. Another seven heaves and the anchor was rattling up onto the bow looking all innocent and benign.

Trying to stop her trend of anthropomorphizing, Beth hooked the retaining line to it like a leash on a misbehaving dog. She uncleated the rode from the starboard cleat and the cleat in the anchor locker, knowing that the very end of the line was still shackled to a ring down at the bottom of the locker. She closed and secured the cover and hurried back to the cockpit.

Her hasty semi-cleat with the dock line was holding and the mooring ball was still hanging off the side. Before releasing it, Beth stretched back out on the deck and leaned out once more to look at *Trouble*'s side. A three inch wide gouge in the gel coat – the shiny finish on the hull – was *Trouble*'s scar for this adventure. Just a cosmetic injury. Beth patted the hull above the mark. "It's okay. We'll get it fixed. Eventually."

She got up and looked around, spotting the other nearby moorings so she would know to avoid them. The bay was still all hers – indeed, only a few minutes had passed since she'd started to pull up the anchor. She freed the dockline from the cleat and unwrapped it from the winch, lowering the mooring ball back to the surface. Then she released one end of the line and pulled on the other. When the end popped up over the side she dropped it and moved behind *Trouble*'s helm. She put the engine in reverse and backed away from the dreaded mooring, continuing to back until the entire row of moorings was visible half a football field away. Satisfied that she was clear of any possible entanglements, she swung the helm over and turned *Trouble*'s bow toward the mouth of the bay.

Once she was in the middle of the bay where the depth gauge read 200 feet, she turned *Trouble*'s bow to point into the light breeze and turned on Otto. The mainsail ran easily up the mast and she was soon turning the boat back on course. Comfortable for the moment, she let Otto drive while she sat behind the helm reviewing the cruising guide and charts. She found Martinique's Sainte Anne. It was a large, open anchorage at the mouth of a deep, protected bay with a marina complex at the end. So that matched Terry's message. Leg by leg she entered waypoints into her GPS and created a route from her current position. The distance was forty-four miles, and her ETA at her current, pokey, speed was a couple hours before dawn tomorrow.

She looked up at the mainsail, which hung limp. She had tightened the mainsheet to minimize the boom's rattling. She looked at the fuel gauge and smiled at the memory of their long hours of sailing after their last fill up far to the south. She had three quarters of a tank. Sighing at having to give in and use the motor, she increased the throttle to 2500 RPMs and watched her boat speed increase from three knots to six. The GPS now happily reported that her ETA was now around four-thirty p.m. Resigned to motoring for a while, she went below to fetch a book and another apple.

While she was there she noticed the time and switched on the single sideband radio, tuning it to the usual cruiser's net frequency. She hadn't listened or checked in yesterday morning, and she hadn't reached anyone yesterday afternoon when she was trying to get a weather report. There might not be a local cruiser's net, or it might be on another frequency, or VHF. Just in case, she scanned the VHF radio through the usual channels, listening for cruiser voices.

After a minute she turned up the volume on the single sideband and carried her apple and book back to the cockpit to keep an eye on where Otto was taking her. She continued scanning the channels on her hand held VHF, keeping one ear cocked below for voices on the other radio. And sure enough, at about five minutes after nine a male voice that sounded rather elderly came on offering a cheerful "Good morning sailors! It's Jerry, back on to check in with everyone here in the lovely Windwards."

Smiling at his jolly tone, she stepped onto the companionway ladder and sat where she could see out, but hear the radio clearly. Their host read a weather report that promised more settled conditions today than yesterday in the channels between the islands. Then he read announcements ranging from a lost cat in Marigot Bay, St. Lucia to tie-dyed fabrics for sale from s/v *Marigold*, based in Rodney Bay. Beth pictured steaming pots of dye in her galley and shuddered. One by one the cruisers in the area answered a roll call, some reporting their departure, some sending quick greetings to others. When he asked for any newcomers Beth took a last look around the boat and, seeing no traffic nearby, climbed down the ladder and picked up the microphone.

Another skipper had introduced himself, and she belatedly realized that it was Evan from *Petrel*, heading north from Wallilabou. When he finished she depressed the key and spoke. "This is sailing vessel *Double Trouble*, skipper Beth speaking. I just departed the Pitons on my way to Sainte Anne. Hello *Petrel*."

"Good morning Beth, glad to hear you're well," Evan replied.

"Good sailing Beth. How many aboard?" Jerry asked.

"Just me for now. In fact I loaned my crew to a friend back in Wallilabou, and we've lost touch. Has anyone seen *Great Escape*? She's a Jeanneau 45."

"Kidnapped your crew, huh?" Jerry's joke hit a little too close to home, but Beth forced herself to smile as she replied.

"*Great Escape*'s master had an emergency, so we were happy to help. If anyone sees them, at Sainte Anne or anywhere else, can you tell them I expect to reach Sainte Anne late today?"

"Hear that folks, be on the lookout for s/v *Great Escape*, and tell them that skipper Beth needs her crew back." Jerry said. "Are you good single handing Beth?" He added, his tone sincere, but not a bit skeptical as some men might be.

"I sure am. *Trouble* and I are a team."

"I'll bet you are skipper," Jerry laughed.

TWENTY-FOUR: WAITING

Mouth open, Maggie stared down at the radio in her hand as a thickly accented voice repeated "*Escape, Escape, Escape*, dis is *Jericho*. Come in."

One brow raised, Terry said, "Do you need to get that?"

Maggie's eyes darted to him as her mouth snapped shut. She pulled herself up to sit straight in the back corner of the cockpit and cleared her throat before raising the radio to her face.

"This is *Escape*. Come in *Jericho*."

Terry noted her use of the truncated version of her boat's name with curiosity. Was she catering to the caller, which would suggest fear of him? Or was the shortening an agreed upon lame attempt at disguise?

"Hello *Escape*. We have you on radar." Hispanic, but with a hint of creole, Terry thought. The caller was an islander. "Please hold your position. We will be there in forty minutes. Over." He was also a mariner. He knew proper radio etiquette and used proper terminology. A down on his luck captain looking to earn some cash?

Maggie looked toward Terry and he realized that she was about to order him to douse the sails. He shook his head and raised his mug of cold coffee to his lips, although as it touched them he decided not to drink. In fact, he wouldn't be eating or drinking anything else that Maggie had a hand in preparing.

Maggie acknowledged the request over the radio, then set it down and stood up.

"You have to at least hold her into the wind," she said, having understood his silent refusal.

"I don't have to do anything. You're on your own, Maggie." He replied with another shake of his head. "I think you've been single handing this boat since Carriacou, or earlier. Right up until you decided to Shanghai me. Why did you, by the way?"

"Terry please, I can explain –." It was the grieving widow again. His stomach almost turned at her tone of voice. Or maybe it was the smell of the nasty coffee.

"Save it Maggie. Your explanations are worthy of a novel, but you don't have time for that now. You have to douse the sails. As of now, I'm retired as your crew."

She barked a strange little laugh, her demeanor shifting once more as she adjusted their course into the wind and left the helm under the auto pilot's control. "You can retire, but you're not out of this," she shot at him, all business now. "Unless you want to go overboard before they get here."

Terry frowned, but did not reply. Mostly because he knew she was right.

Rather than sit and watch her rolling up the jib, he climbed back down the companionway ladder to the galley. After dumping his awful coffee he opened the refrigerator and found a sealed plastic water jug, one of many that he suddenly realized Maggie had been using since yesterday for cooking and drinking. He broke the seal and poured some into a plastic cup sitting on the drying rack next to the sink. He listened to Maggie moving around in the cockpit and recognized the ratcheting sound of the main winch as she slowly rolled the sail into the mast.

His imagination ran wild with possibilities, but there was one that seemed the most likely: the islands were rife with drug traffickers, and law enforcement agencies monitored vessel traffic, watching for suspect vessels: usually fast moving powerboats or small cargo vessels carrying produce and other ordinary goods on unusual routes. Clever traffickers found transport vessels that didn't fit the profile. A modern cruising sailboat with a lot of storage space below was certainly a candidate. He looked around the saloon, thinking about where he would hide a lot of drugs. He took another gulp of water and paused, looking at the plastic bottle on the counter. Then he reached out and turned on the galley faucet. He could hear the water pump humming somewhere under a floorboard, but no water came out. Just like the faucet in the head.

Above his head the boom rattled noisily for a moment and then stopped as a winch ratcheted loudly. He glanced out and saw Maggie moving back to the helm. *Great Escape* wallowed awkwardly in the two-foot swells, forcing him to grab the edge of the galley counter with one hand.

Should have hove to instead of dropping sail, he thought. Then returned his attention to their reason for stopping. *So if there are drugs, how are these guys on Jericho going to move them off? Or are they?*

The possibility that he and Maggie were about to be replaced by new crew made him shiver. He had absolutely no confidence that Maggie had made a deal that protected herself, let alone him. Without another moment of hesitation he started to prepare for the worst.

He had about forty minutes before *Jericho* would reach them. They would want to keep the encounter as short as possible. Maggie's suggestion that he go overboard lingered in his consciousness as he checked that all of his belongings were in his daypack. This included a pair of trousers and a fresh shirt, his foul weather jacket, and his wallet and passport. He had adopted Beth's practice of cramming his stuff into gallon size Ziplocks whenever there was a chance of his bag getting wet. He pictured her crouching on the ground next to the waterfall at Wallilabou, sealing the treasure hunt clue in a plastic bag. The memory spawned a surge of emotion that stopped him short.

Beth had been suspicious of Maggie for days – months, actually, since they'd shared an anchorage in St. Thomas. But he'd discouraged her, told her there was nothing strange about the other woman's behavior. It wasn't as if he didn't respect Beth's opinions and trust her intuitions, he did. But this thing with Maggie had seemed to be based on nothing. He owed Beth something more than just an apology now. He owed her his complete trust. The terrifying possibility that he would not be able to pay that debt froze him. But then *Great Escape* lurched on a random swell and he flailed for a handhold.

Be ready for anything. You will get through this.

He put his phone in its waterproof case in the pocket of his shorts. He had his rigging knife on his belt. His wallet and passport were in a plastic bag in the front pocket of his day pack. After hesitating for a second, he pulled it out, crammed it into his left back pocket, and buttoned the pocket closed. He had an even more important item in mind for the cargo pocket on that leg of his shorts. He'd located it when he came on board in the compartment just forward of the galley. He climbed on his knees across the settee and retrieved the bright orange canister. The flare gun inside easily fit into his pocket along with all six of the cartridges that he found with it. He returned the canister to the compartment, glancing out the companionway to see if Maggie might have seen his theft. He couldn't see her, so she probably had not seen him. His final step was to put on his auto-inflate life jacket harness and wrap the tether line around his waist to keep it from dragging.

Setting his daypack next to the companionway ladder, he stood by the galley counter looking up through the opening. From there he could just see Maggie, who was seated back in her corner, watching. She was holding the GPS in one hand, but looking out across the water to port. Terry moved over to the navigation station and looked out the portal above it. He saw only open water. His gaze drifted down to the VHF radio. It was switched off. He turned it on and the liquid crystal display came on with a jumble of black bars that resolved after a moment, some fading out some staying on, to display the number sixteen. He turned the knob labeled Squelch all the way down. Silence. Shaking his head, he turned it back off. Maggie had disabled it somehow yesterday to keep him from speaking to Beth and, in the process, broadcasting their activities. He opened the cabinet to look at the ham radio. It was also off. He switched it on, but soon realized that he did not know how to tune it or what frequencies were commonly monitored. Besides which, Maggie wasn't stupid, she would have disabled it too.

Cut off from communication, he refocused on the purpose for the impending rendezvous. He wanted to make a plan without knowing what to expect. If there were drugs in the water tanks, how were they going to get them out? The tank openings were tiny.

"Unless –." He spoke out loud as he strode through the saloon to the forward cabin and heaved half of the split mattress up and to the side, pulling the sheets up with it. He lifted the large, hinged plank that was under it to expose the forward water tank. He stood there staring at the white opaque plastic surface of the tank, frustrated that his hunch hadn't paid off. He'd thought they had removed the tank and stowed the drugs in its place.

Great Escape wallowed again, swaying drunkenly on a passing swell. Terry frowned, then reached down and tapped on the plastic tank. It thudded dully. The sound of a full tank, not an empty one. But there was no water. Impulsively he felt around the forward edge of the tank, grinding his knuckles against the bunk's wooden frame where the tank was fit closely against it.

There was a seam. He took his rigging knife from his belt and worked the point into it. The top of the tank lifted a little. He twisted the blade to pull it up more, then got his fingers into the crack and heaved.

Layers of plastic obscured the outlines of packages about twice the size of bricks that were crammed into the oddly shaped space. The plastic combined with the top of the tank concealed the drugs from cursory visual inspection.

Intensely relieved, he pushed the top of the tank back into place and lowered the lid, then did a quick job of replacing the mattress and sheets. Maybe these guys would take the product and leave *Great Escape*, and him, and Maggie, alone.

Knowing that was a big "maybe" to pin his hopes on, he worked his way back to the companionway and climbed out into the cockpit. Maggie was staring intently out to sea. Out near the horizon he could just make out a white spot that could be a sail.

"Okay, look, before they get here, what do you expect to happen?" He asked, sitting down in front of the wheel where he could also watch the boat approach. Maggie glanced at him, then resumed staring at the other boat.

"Maggie."

"We need the money. So Bill made this deal with these guys. Except when we met them south of Grenada they changed things. They made Bill stay with them. They told me I had to find a crew to help me get here."

"Bill's alive?"

"I hope so!" This came out as wail that Terry thought was the first sincere emotional response he'd seen her make.

"And why didn't they take you and make him sail here?"

"I don't know," she spat. "They sure didn't think I could do it, that's why they demanded that I have crew. 'No crew, no *Señor* Bill, comprende?' They said it over and over."

Terry shook his head, certain that there was something more she wasn't saying.

"The joke was on them," she went on, her tone turning smug. "I'm the sailor in our family. Just like you and Beth. Yes, you're right. I did single-hand *Great Escape* to Wallilabou. That was my last chance to pick up a crew. And there you were. Dear Terry, always the gentleman. I knew you'd be willing to help a damsel in distress, even if you didn't know what you were helping her with."

Terry shook his head again, the disbelief mounting. He wanted to contradict her, to tell her that he was a very experienced sailor, even if Beth was better. But there was no point. His ego had to be irrelevant if he was going to get out of this. He had to focus on her story – invented or true – to get her to explain. "You barely know me. You know Beth from St. Thomas."

"Terry, the cruising community is large and talkative. Beth's more well-known than she realizes – 'the girl who took off on her own after her lost-cause friend' – and everyone who's met the two of you speaks well of you."

So people talked about him and Beth. That wasn't surprising. His membership in the cruising community was tenuous due to his come and go approach. But Beth was a card-carrying member. Maggie's characterization of her was harsh, but not entirely wrong.

"So they kept Bill, and you sailed the drugs to this rendezvous. Why here? Where are we?"

"Hell if I know why here," she stood up, intent on the distant sail. "But Martinique is about thirty-five miles that way." Maggie jerked her head to the right. East, Terry realized.

"And they're coming on another sailboat?" he asked.

"Apparently." She replied. He stared up at her. She was telling the truth. All they'd told her was to come to this spot to get Bill back, and she'd done it. She'd done it with no water in her tanks and no idea of what else would happen when she got here. And she'd dragged him into it, also because they'd told her to. Her devotion to her husband didn't impress him. He knew that if Beth were placed in this situation, which she never would be, she would not have blindly followed instructions. He'd been frustrated by Beth's wild hunt for her friend, but the same attitude that had sent her on it would prevent her from doing what Maggie was doing now.

Terry didn't realize until crew on the other sailboat had taken down the jib and mainsail that it was a ketch with the cockpit further forward on the boat and a second, smaller mast behind it. It was about the same length as *Great Escape*, but narrower and with graceful lines. If it wasn't old, it was a good reproduction of a classic design.

He felt a visceral reaction to the realization that drug dealers were using it for their perverted purpose. They would probably sink the beautiful craft before they'd be caught with their disgusting cargo on board.

A swarthy man with thick, curly black hair and a stained t-shirt and cut-off denim shorts was standing on the side deck holding a coil of line. He had deployed three fenders along the side at the boat's widest spot.

Maggie put down the GPS and climbed around the back of the cockpit to the port side. Glancing astern to where she'd been sitting, Terry saw the handheld VHF radio sitting on the seat, rubberized antenna pointed toward him. Watching Maggie's back as she gestured to the man on the other boat, he stretched his left arm out past the wheel, leaning way over until his fingertips grasped the tip of the antenna. Eyes locked on Maggie's back, he straightened up and pulled it toward himself. He did not dare even check to see if it was on before sliding it into his second, empty, cargo pocket.

TWENTY-FIVE: *JERICHO*

Sandcastle was up on a plane running north at twenty-five knots. Off to the east Burt imagined that he could see Martinique fifteen miles away, although it could just be clouds above the island. These long runs were one of his favorite things about working the Caribbean. Knowing that the fuel cost was covered by his last charter party made it all the better. The sky was crystalline blue. A few fluffy white clouds drifted high overhead providing occasional periods of shade. The sea was that shade of azure that resonated with something deep inside him – the thing that had pushed him to become a waterman when he'd had so many choices in his life.

He'd be back in Guadeloupe late this afternoon. His next group was meeting him there in a week and a half, which gave him time to give *Sandcastle*'s engines a thorough once over and do regular maintenance. He had considered the treasure hunt: he'd picked up the first clue while his charter party were exploring St. George's. His visit to the brewery on Petit Martinique had been purely coincidence, and while he'd waited for his charter party to finish the tour, the bartender had told him that the leaders were a couple of power boaters who were racing one another. They'd both visited the first four locations in one day, including proper customs and immigration stops as they moved between island nations. At that pace, by now they were probably done. He hadn't had the heart to tell Beth and Terry that, even though it had been clear they had no illusions about being first or even in the top three.

He did plan to contact his broker and block out the days around the final party if they weren't already booked. With the one-point card he had received at the first stop he had the right to attend, and it promised to be the biggest party of the season.

His eyes habitually scanned the horizon all around *Sandcastle*. He'd elected to run some distance off shore to stay out of the coastal sailboat traffic, and he'd seen plenty of them making their way north or south. When a white speck to the northwest caught his eye he picked up the binoculars that were sitting on the console and aimed them at it.

The sight of a white hull rocking in the small swells was barely discernible. At first he assumed they were fishing, then he thought he saw masts swaying above the hull. Still could be a fisherman, or it could be a delivery captain more intent on going in a straight line to get where he needed to be than on sailing to conserve fuel. Like Burt, someone else was probably paying for it. He set down the binoculars, scanned the horizon again, and took a swig of coffee from his covered mug.

A half hour and twelve miles further north a dot appeared at the left outer edge of his radar. Something directly west of *Sandcastle*. He looked to the west at the white spot on the horizon. If it was the same boat, it hadn't moved at all. Even a fisherman would be trawling. Frowning, he picked up the binoculars again.

Something wasn't right. There were three masts swaying at different angles. It was two sailboats side-by-side. And they were not making way. He lowered the binoculars, but kept his eye on the spot as he reached for his VHF radio microphone.

"This is the motor vessel *Sandcastle* proceeding north fifteen miles to the west of Port de France, Martinique calling the two sailboats under bare poles to my west. Are you in need of assistance? Over."

He waited. There was no response. After a minute he repeated the same transmission with the same result. By then *Sandcastle* had covered another five miles. The two sailboats were a puzzle, but there were many possible explanations, and if they didn't respond, and there was no distress signal from them, he had no reason – excuse – to change course. Basic curiosity wasn't reason enough.

Maggie had set up bow, stern, and mid-ships lines while Terry was below. She stepped up onto *Great Escape*'s side deck and took the line that the man held out, handing him her stern line at the same time.

"Make it fast aft," she ordered as she carried his line forward along *Great Escape*'s deck. The man took her line to a stern cleat and made it fast. By the time he'd done so she was up on *Great Escape*'s bow, shouting at him to get up there and take her bow line. He glanced across at Terry before hurrying forward, and Terry smiled inwardly at the man's expression of consternation at being ordered around by the woman. The man behind the wheel of the other boat looked like an honest-to-God pirate. His long, black hair hung in snarls below his shoulders, half covering a long scar of shiny white tissue that ran from behind his right ear around his clavicle and descended under the left lapel of his dark green shirt. The cuffs of his dark trousers were tucked into sea boots that seemed totally unnecessary in the current conditions. As he watched his crew work with Maggie to secure the two boats together Terry noticed a gold earring in his left ear and a gold incisor in his mouth. All that was missing was a parrot on his shoulder. And an eye patch. Catching himself getting distracted, Terry refocused his attention on Maggie and the crewman, who were each currently holding the opposite boat's lifelines to keep them from banging into each other on a particularly large swell.

"These are terrible conditions for rafting," he observed, loud enough for Maggie to hear if not the other captain. She looked back at him over her shoulder, her face red with exertion and anger. In truth, he'd rarely been involved with rafting up two or more sailboats, but he understood now just how essential calm water was to the undertaking.

"That's enough," the other captain shouted, making Terry think maybe he had heard his sarcastic comment. "Jose, get Javier and get started."

The crewman left Maggie struggling to hold the boats apart and stepped into the ketch's cockpit, making for the companionway.

"You, climb up on deck," the other captain ordered, looking at Maggie.

"The rigging will tangle," she growled back, looking up at the two boats' main masts as they swayed near to one another and then away. The captain looked up as well, then at Terry.

"You, ease this line," the captain pointed to a line that Maggie had wrapped around the port sheet winch and tightened. Terry raised both hands and shook his head.

"I'm just along for the ride," he replied.

"You are the crew that she was to bring, yes?"

"No."

The captain glared at Maggie, who was already coming back to the cockpit to ease the line.

"He is your crew?"

"He is supposed to be. Let's get this done and we'll figure it out," she replied, crouching by the winch to ease the line. *Great Escape* moved back, the fenders between the two boat's hulls squealing and rotating.

"Harden your line," Maggie ordered when it had moved about a foot and the two masts were no longer right next to each other. Eyes on his boat's rigging, the other captain fitted a handle into the winch that his crewman had put the other line on and ground it. His boat inched forward and Maggie's line grew taught. Terry was impressed with Maggie's refusal to be cowed by the other captain's attitude. Unfortunately, her fortitude would probably not last when he produced the gun that Terry was sure he must have.

The captain nodded, satisfied. "Now, up on deck. Both of you."

"Where is Bill?" Maggie asked, still crouched by the winch.

"Shut up and move," the captain replied. As he spoke Juan and another man of similar appearance and hygiene climbed into *Jericho's* cockpit. "Get started," the captain said to them, gesturing toward *Great Escape*.

"Where is Bill?" Maggie asked again, not budging. She was determined, Terry had to give her that. He wasn't moving both because it suited his act as disinterested bystander, and because he was rooted to his seat in fear and indecision. Maggie must realize that they had guns, but a need even stronger in her than fear kept her going. And then something occurred to him that made him feel naïve for not thinking of it sooner: maybe Maggie had a gun tucked into her baggie shorts, or her bra.

The captain opened his mouth to speak as a voice spoke from below aboard *Jericho*. Terry didn't hear what was said, but the captain stared down his boat's companionway as the two crewmen climbed over the lifelines to board *Great Escape* and go below.

And then a man with grey, curly hair wearing a salmon polo shirt and khaki shorts emerged into *Jericho's* cockpit and looked across at Maggie.

"Bill!" She yelped. She put one foot out onto the side deck, clearly expecting a physical reunion. But she stopped when Bill made no move toward her.

"Maggie, I'm glad you made it. Who's this with you?"

To Terry he sounded like a man speaking to a business associate, not a concerned husband.

"Terry, Beth's boyfriend. Remember Beth?" Maggie's reply sounded automatic, and Terry realized that Bill's polite, ordinary question had been calculated to diffuse her emotions and put her into her role as his wife. It had worked, at least to some degree.

From below the sound of banging indicated that the two crewmen were not taking care to avoid damaging *Great Escape* to get to the drugs in the tanks. Maggie didn't appear to hear it. She was absolutely focused on her husband.

"Everything is going as planned Maggie. Why don't you sit down?" Bill glanced at *Jericho*'s captain as if to acknowledge that he was countermanding his earlier demand that Maggie and Terry climb up on deck.

"Come over here, Bill. I want to get away from them as soon as we can," Maggie replied. Bill tucked his hands in the pockets of his shorts and rolled on the balls of his feet as *Jericho* rocked. Maggie, hanging on to the stainless steel Bimini support, leaned back and forth in time with the swaying.

"Sit down Maggie," he repeated.

"Bill, I –."

"Sit. Down."

A canvas bag appeared on the cockpit sole, pushed up through the companionway from below. Jose followed it, picking it up to carry it out of the cockpit. Terry watched with detached interest. He thought that the bag held about an eighth of the packages he'd seen in the forward tank. If the other tank had the same capacity the two men with two bags men would make eight trips to get all the drugs.

Maggie had to move out of Jose's way. She stepped down into the cockpit and after watching Jose move out to the side deck, she sat down on the starboard side opposite *Jericho* and near the cabin bulkhead. She'd left plenty of space between herself and Terry, which was fine with him. His hand rested unconsciously on the pocket of his shorts where the flare gun was hidden. The hand held VHF radio felt like it was burning a hole in his other pocket.

Javier followed Jose, carrying another bag across to *Jericho*. Bill watched him disappear below, a wistful smile curling his lips. He looked back across at Maggie.

"As I said, everything is going according to plan. You should be able to reach Martinique this evening. Jose and Javier have been there many times. They will help you find a good anchorage in the dark."

"They'll help me? We don't need them Bill."

"Maggie, do I really have to spell it out for you? We're done. I'm sorry. Truly. But this is it. This whole sailing thing was your idea. The boat we could hardly afford, selling the house to do it. You've been running my life since we got married. You tried to run the kids' lives too – they moved as far away as they could. Didn't you realize that? No, you don't, I can see."

Maggie was shaking her head, murmuring "no, no, no," as if Bill's accusations were pushing her over some emotional edge.

"You treat me like a deckhand. You yell all the time, and you're always belittling me. Sailing with you is a miserable experience and I'm done."

Terry struggled not to smile at Bill's accusation. It was absolutely true, and he'd been feeling for the guy since shortly after joining Maggie on *Great Escape*. But that didn't justify this crazy betrayal. Divorce, maybe, but not this.

He and Maggie both flinched at Bill's tone as he added, "You can keep the boat."

TWENTY-SIX: BILL

Maggie had quieted and Bill was engaged in a subdued conversation with *Jericho*'s captain when Jose and Javier reappeared in *Jericho*'s cockpit and climbed across to *Great Escape*.

Jose tossed the two canvas bags down *Great Escape*'s companionway and then turned around to climb down after them. As Javier, facing forward, shifted his balance onto the first step of the companionway ladder, Maggie rose up and threw her considerable weight at his lower back. One hand grabbed the edge of the companionway, then slipped off as she toppled after the surprised crewman. Javier's yelp whooshed out of him as he fell into the cabin with Maggie on top of him. Terry jumped to his feet just as Maggie's right shin cracked against the lip of the companionway as she fell. She emitted a sound that was much louder and more pain-filled than Javier's. Terry leaned into the opening to see a tangle of bodies on the cabin sole. Jose was dragging his legs out from under Javier, who was twisting around under Maggie. She was practically doing a head stand, pinning his shoulders to the cabin sole while her torso and legs were arrayed up the steep companionway steps. Her right shin was bent at an angle that turned Terry's stomach just looking at it. He found still more respect for her fortitude as, despite her apparent pain, she wrapped her arms around Javier's chest and squeezed.

"Out of the way!"

Bill shoved Terry to the side and took his place, aiming a black-surfaced hand-gun down into the companionway.

"Maggie! Let him go. Jose, get him out from under her."

When Terry moved behind Bill to look over his shoulder, Bill half turned, aiming the gun at him.

"Sit down and don't move. Now please."

Terry raised both hands in a gesture he hoped was placating and backed toward the wheel, resuming his seat near it. Satisfied, Bill returned his attention to *Great Escape*'s cabin.

Maggie was wailing now and Terry winced at what he suspected was the sound of the crewmen dragging her off of the ladder.

"Get her on the settee," Bill commanded.

"She cannot get up," Jose said.

"Lift her!"

"Aye." Jose's word sounded more like a complaint than an acknowledgement. Several male grunts accompanied Maggie's cries.

"Lay down Maggie. You've done it to yourself this time. I can't guarantee how the boys will feel about taking you to Martinique now."

Terry shivered at the man's callousness. How had he allowed himself to remain in this relationship with Maggie long enough for it to turn him into this? Or maybe it hadn't. Maybe Maggie had just aggravated deep-seeded rage.

"Get down there. Help them move her if they need it. The faster this is done, the better for all of us," Bill said to Terry. He was aiming the gun into the companionway, not at anything in particular. He did not appear to be that comfortable with the weapon. Terry wondered whether he could take advantage of that. But as he stood up and moved to the companionway Bill brought the weapon up to point at him.

"Wait."

Terry stopped facing him, dreading a catastrophic change in Bill's plan. "She was supposed to hire willing crew. What did she tell you?" he asked. Terry swallowed, sure that Bill could see how frightened he was.

"She said she needed help getting *Great Escape* to St. Lucia to meet you. Her brother was with her, but he had a family emergency and had to catch a flight home from St. Vincent."

Bill snorted, a disparaging laugh. Seeing Terry's puzzled look he said, "Maggie has won several single handed, multi-day races. She's a better sailor than any of us, including your Beth. She didn't need any help. And she doesn't have a brother."

"Then why did you tell her to hire crew?"

"Why? For me. I wasn't in a position to do it. She was supposed to hire someone who didn't care where the boat went, as long as they got paid. Instead I get you. And I'm going to guess that you're not going to willingly come with us on *Jericho*, right?"

"Good guess."

Bill sighed, his mouth twisting in an expression that Terry guessed was consternation. Then he gestured at the companionway with the gun.

"Get down there. I have to think."

Maggie lay with her left forearm across her eyes. Jose or Javier must have straightened her right leg after getting her onto the settee, because her foot lay at a normal looking angle. Terry turned back toward the companionway to tell Bill that she was going into shock, but the man was gone. Jose and Javier were in the forward cabin loading their bags. Terry went to the galley and filled the cup that he'd left on the rack from the jug of water that he'd left in the sink. It felt like an eternity since he'd stood here thinking about what to do. He crouched next to Maggie's shoulders to put his eyes at her level.

"Maggie, have some water. Can you sit up a little?"

Maggie moved her arm and looked at him. Her eyes were bloodshot, her complexion red and blotchy over grey undertones. She crammed her right arm between herself and the settee back and rose up on that elbow with a grimace.

"Hold on," Terry set the cup on the floorboards and rose, reaching for one of the decorative pillows on the settee around the table. He crammed it in behind her shoulders and watched her ease back onto it. "Now drink."

He winced at a loud bang from up forward as he watched her take a long sip from the cup. If she heard it, she didn't react.

"Didn't I see aspirin in the galley somewhere?" he asked her. She nodded slightly.

"Over the stove, with the spices."

He returned to the galley and found the bottle in among bottles of cayenne, dried sage, and garlic flakes. He shook out two pills and returned to Maggie's side.

"It's not much, but it will help," he said. She took the pills from him and swallowed them with the last of the water.

He stood there looking down at her, listening to Jose tell Javier to shove in one more package. It was the perfect moment for her to apologize to him for getting him into this. She lay silent, eyes shut. And then she took in a long, snuffling inhale through her nose. He shut his eyes, head shaking slightly in disappointment. She apparently felt no remorse.

Javier appeared in the forward doorway.

"Sit. At the table," he ordered Terry. Terry complied, sitting at the edge of the settee with his forearms resting on the table, hands clasped.

"No, all the way in," Javier added.

Understanding his purpose, Terry slid to the right, rounding the corner of the u-shaped settee so that the table, which was anchored to the cabin sole, was between him and Javier.

"*Bueno*," Javier said, then crossed the saloon carrying his canvas bag. Jose followed him, glancing first at Maggie and then at Terry before climbing the ladder.

Terry watched them disappear, his eyes drifting to his daypack sitting on the counter next to the ladder. He worked his way out from behind the table and retrieved it, slipping it onto his shoulders. Maggie was shivering now, going into shock as he'd feared. He picked up a woven throw with an image of a sailboat and seashells on it and lay it over her, tucking the outside edge under the settee cushion so that it didn't drag on the floor. As he finished, a voice coming from his pocket filled the cabin.

"This is the motor vessel *Sandcastle* proceeding north fifteen miles to the west of Port de France, Martinique calling the two sailboats under bare poles to my west. Are you in need of assistance? Over."

Maggie's eyes popped open, traveling from the source of the sound up to Terry's face in an instant. Her expression went from anger – at him for taking her radio, no doubt – to impressed that he'd done it.

"Better turn it off," she whispered.

"I should answer him. He'll come help us. I know him."

"You aren't that stupid, Terry. Think about it," she hissed, eyes darting to the companionway as the boat rocked. There was a thump on the deck. "Hurry. They're coming back. They must have just dumped that load to get it done faster. Turn it off."

Terry was irritated with himself when he caught up with her thought process and realized that maybe he was that stupid, or maybe fear was clouding his judgment. If he responded to Burt, Bill on *Jericho* would hear him. He could only imagine, and he didn't want to, what the man would do. He simultaneously returned to his seat behind the table and dug into his pocket, searching for the knob to turn.

"Hold down the blue button on the front, below the screen," Maggie hissed.

He couldn't feel color, so he had to pull the radio out of his pocket to see it and find the button. Jose's form darkened the companionway as Terry held the radio in his lap watching the screen go blank. He set the radio on the settee next to his leg and looked across at Maggie as he placed his hands on the table and tried to look innocent. The two men climbed down, glanced at him and Maggie, and returned to the forward berth.

His mind worked through possible scenarios while the crewmen reloaded their bags and left again.

"Try channel thirteen," Maggie said. "The commercial ship to ship channel."

"No. If you've thought of it so will they." A lot of non-commercial skippers, including Beth when they were in areas with heavy commercial traffic, monitored that channel too.

Maggie fell silent, which he took as concession. That he'd figured it out and she hadn't bolstered him. But could he outthink a plan that Bill and his companions had had a long time to put together? His only hope was that Maggie's aggression and accident was forcing Bill to reconsider his next step. Or at least, that's what he'd said. Would he keep one of the two crewmen with him and leave Terry with Maggie on *Great Escape*?

No. Apparently he had thought he could trust Maggie not to report him to the authorities. It wasn't impossible, with her ego she might not want to admit that he'd betrayed her in such a terrible way, and she's probably retain hope of getting him back. But Bill hadn't factored in Maggie's vengeful streak. Now that he realized his miscalculation, he had to revise his plan to reduce risk. That's what Terry would do if this were a business deal: eliminate as much exposure as he could.

Jose and Javier came clumping back across the deck and into the boat. Once again they glanced at Terry and Maggie as they passed through the saloon.

Maggie had revealed herself to be a big risk. But, Terry knew, he was an even bigger one. For a moment he allowed himself to regret not playing along. If he'd acted as the hired crew Bill had expected, he'd be over on *Jericho* now waiting for them to leave *Great Escape* behind. But then what? The last place he wanted to be was aboard a drug runner's boat. *Great Escape*, with the drugs removed, was the much safer vessel.

And then there was Beth, who would be waiting for him on Martinique. No, she probably would not wait. When she got there and didn't find *Great Escape* she would turn to every resource she could think of to find him. That gave him a little jolt of hope, but it was tempered with concern for her. She had put herself at risk for her friend Ori. What greater risks would she take for him?

Jose and Javier hauled their bags out once again.

So far, a glorious day of sailing was Beth's reward for her sacrifice of Terry's company. *Trouble* was under full sail, reaching slightly west of north at a steady six knots. The weather in the St. Lucia channel between St. Lucia and Martinique was nothing like what she'd encountered between St. Lucia and St. Vincent. The only clouds in the sky were high, white, and puffy, and she appreciated the occasional patch of shade they provided as they moved along on the upper air currents.

She'd planned ahead, bringing up a couple buckets of bright, clear seawater before raising the sails. Now she sat in the cockpit, letting Otto drive while she washed t-shirts, shorts, and tank tops in one bucket and rinsed them in the other. When everything was rinsed she sluiced the soapy water across the cockpit sole and squeegeed it toward the scuppers with her bare feet, then repeated the process with the other bucket of water. She arranged the clothes on the sole and took out the fresh water shower hose to give them a quick rinse and get out some of the salt.

Undersail she couldn't hang the laundry out on the lifelines – it was bad form, but more importantly, even with clothes pins it might blow off. So she wrung each item as well as she could and laid them out on the cabin top under the dodger. They would take forever to dry there, but if they were still damp when she got to Martinique she would hang them out to finish.

That chore done, she went below to examine her to-do list, which was in a notebook in the navigation desk. She crossed off "laundry." As her hand brushed over her laptop, lying next to the notebook in the compartment under the desk's lift-up top, she realized that she was procrastinating without even realizing it. With a sigh, she picked up the laptop and returned to the cockpit to find a shady spot where she'd be able to see the screen. Trish wouldn't wait much longer to read a draft, and she wanted her article to be closer to finished than it was now before she shared it with anyone.

Realizing that he'd lost count, Terry was trying to reconstruct how many trips Jose and Javier had made. He was pretty sure it was eight – his calculation of how many it would take to empty the two water tanks in the bow. But they were still up there and the banging and sound of splintering wood was worse now than before.

The holding tanks.

The tanks that held raw sewage from the heads were much smaller than the water tanks, but they were a place that no inspector would want to look. So if the holding tank up forward and in the aft head were also full of drugs, Jose and Javier would have to make, maybe, two more trips. Plus the time it would take to expose the tanks in each head compartment. They were obviously making progress ripping out the cabinetry in the forward head.

"Where else did they store it Maggie?" he asked, pitching his voice low so that the men wouldn't hear him. She did not respond.

"Maggie?"

Still no response.

Terry glanced at the doorway to the forward compartment where the banging was still going on along with grumbled curses by the two men. He slid around the table and stepped over to Maggie's side. He noticed now that her left arm had fallen from her face and was hanging down to the floor. Her complexion was uniformly grey. He placed both hands on her shoulders on top of the blanket and shook her gently.

"Maggie!"

Her head rolled back and forth and she mumbled something, but her eyes remained shut tight.

"Maggie!"

"Get away!" Javier was standing in the doorway looking frustrated and angry. Sweat coated his face and his shirt had large dark patches under his arms and on his chest. The tiny head compartment was hot and stuffy for one person, let alone two men exerting themselves.

"She's in shock. Going unconscious. You have to tell *Señor* Bill."

"Get back. We come." Javier said. Realizing that Javier's command of English probably wasn't very strong, Terry returned to his seat behind the table. Javier nodded at him, disappeared for a moment, then returned with his canvas bag. Jose followed.

"Please tell *Señor* Bill that Maggie is unconscious," Terry repeated as they climbed the companionway ladder.

As the two men clumped across *Great Escape*'s deck Maggie's voice came from across the saloon, "I'm not."

"What the hell, Maggie!"

"I need to get him back here. I have to talk to him."

Terry sighed. Her single minded determination was not going to help them.

"And tell him what?"

"That I forgive him. For everything. You have no idea all the things that he's done that I can forgive him for. It's why he's done this: he thinks I can't forgive him, so he has to go."

"Maggie, I don't think –."

"No you don't! You have no idea, so just shut up. Shut up and sit there like the thief that you are. Taking my radio. What else have you pilfered while you've been aboard?"

When he didn't answer she lifted herself up enough to look across at him. He withstood her bloodshot stare until she receded onto the pillow that he'd kindly placed for her.

Jose and Javier's return was heralded by their footsteps on the deck above and then the two empty canvas bags dropping down through the companionway. Terry noticed that both men turned to face the ladder as they descended. If no other good came from this, Javier had learned an important safety lesson, Terry thought, enjoying the irony.

The two crewmen were followed by a third: Bill. He climbed down, also facing the ladder, and turned, his eyes landing on Maggie and then moving over to Terry.

"You told them she's unconscious?" he asked, the question in his voice suggesting that the crewmen's word was suspect, or he thought they'd misunderstood.

"Yes. She's in shock. It's serious. She needs medical attention."

Despite all the time to think, Terry hadn't come up with a lie that seemed more effective than the truth. If Bill still had even a modicum of concern for his wife, he'd want to help her.

Bill stood over Maggie looking down at her, his lower lip between his teeth. Up forward, Jose barked an order at Javier. The crewman appeared in the doorway with his bag. It didn't look full.

"*Excusa, Señor* Bill," he said, gesturing past him. Bill stepped closer to Maggie's settee to allow the man to pass. He went to the aft head compartment, setting his bag on the floor outside the door.

"Maggie. I know you can hear me. Cut it out. This is a difficult situation, but we're going to do what's best for everyone."

When there was no answer Terry wondered if Maggie had changed her mind about talking to Bill, or if she really had slipped into unconsciousness.

"You probably want to know what that is," Bill went on after a pause. Then he looked at Terry, "I imagine that you do too."

Terry held his face impassive, desperate to look as if he hadn't a care in the world, although he wasn't quite sure why. Somehow braving it out was how he wanted to play it, even if it ended up being his last action and nobody ever knew.

Shit. Nobody will ever know. If I don't play this right, I could be fish food in another hour. I should be begging for my life. Except I do not believe it will make a bit of difference, other than to entertain Jose and Javier.

"Here's what's going to happen," Bill went on as Javier commenced banging at the wooden cabinetry in the aft head. "*Great Escape* is going to be lost at sea with all – well, both – hands. It will be one of those mysteries of the sea that you see documentaries about on cable television. Or not. More likely this fine vessel will become another statistic that only the US Coast Guard cares about, if them."

All of Terry's blood was rushing to his heart, which was pumping double time. Bill was going to sink *Great Escape* with him and Maggie aboard. It would cover the evidence of their ham-handed drug extraction. If any authorities had been tracking *Great Escape* they would be foiled in their effort to follow the drugs. Nobody would know that the drugs had been moved off the missing sailboat. *Nobody but those here.*

And Burt. The realization that Burt would be able to put together his sighting of two sailboats tied together with the missing boat – which he would hear all about from Beth even before it hit the coconut telegraph – bolstered Terry for no good reason. Suddenly, her friendship with the man seemed very valuable, even though it would still be too late for him and Maggie.

"Bill, you don't need to do that," Maggie's voice was thinner than it had been a few minutes before, and Terry wasn't sure if it was intentional or if she was weakening. Bill cocked one eyebrow as he peered down at her. He did not appear to be surprised that she was conscious. *Those two know each other far too well for either of them to play the other*, Terry thought.

"I forgive you Bill. For everything. For the years of long hours at the office. For Sherrie Miller — did you think I didn't know?"

Bill's surprised look said it all. *He had an affair. He probably would have done something like this to Maggie years earlier if he hadn't had that bit of release at some point.*

"The point is, I forgive you. Tell your friends to take the drugs and go. We'll take *Great Escape* to Martinique like we planned, and that will be the end of it."

It was hard to believe that she thought her forgiveness was the key. *She is beyond egocentric and well into psychopath*, Terry thought, although he had no formal training to make such a diagnosis. But it seemed to fit the both of them. A couple of crazies acting out their drama and pulling in innocent bystanders. If you could call guys like Jose and Javier, and *Jericho*'s captain, innocent.

"*You* forgive *me*?" Bill exploded with ugly laughter. He turned to Terry, his face going crimson as he gasped for breath between guffaws. "She forgives me, did you hear it?" he asked. Terry nodded. Bill's laughter went on as Maggie tried to regain his attention.

"Bill, sweetheart, it's all right. Bill."

When he finally calmed down and refocused on her he was grinning broadly and shaking his head.

"Oh Maggie, how little you understand. Let me spell it out for you. I married you because your father promised me a job. He delivered, and I held up my end of the bargain. I worked hard, made his business more successful, and put up with you. Do you know how Kevin managed his rent in Chicago on a hardware store manager's pay? Your dad. He knew that Kevin needed to get away from you so he helped him. And Cathy? The job in the Orlando office? She's terrible at sales, but he keeps her there to keep her away from you. His own daughter. Well it's been twenty-seven years, and the way I see it, I've done my part. I'm out."

"That's nonsense Bill and you know it," Maggie replied.

Bill just shook his head at her, then turned to Terry.

"You, slide out here," he said.

Terry complied, fearful that he'd finally be searched. He still had his rigging knife on his belt, along with the flare gun and radio in his pockets and his daypack over his shoulders. He was also wearing his auto-inflate life jacket, although the pack would interfere with it if it came to using it.

"Stand up. Turn around." Bill ordered.

This was it. Terry was certain that Bill was going to tie his hands. Panic took over before Terry even realized it was coming. He couldn't let his hands be tied. He had to get out of here, get off of this boat. He would rather swim for it than be tied up on a on a sinking yacht.

Hours at the gym kept him in shape, but he was no fighter. He tried to back away into the galley to get some space. Surprised, Bill tilted his head to one side and took a step toward him, then smiled and nodded. Terry looked at him curiously an instant before a weight slammed into his head and everything went dark.

"Terry! *Terry.* Jesus, you have to wake up *now* Terry!"

Water sloshed into Terry's nose and he snorted it out, annoyed that it disrupted his nap. The way *Trouble* was swaying had brought him a lovely dream, but it was already fading because of the water on his face and the annoying woman yelling at him. Why didn't she shut up?

"Terry, you have to wake up. *Now!*"

It wasn't Beth. He wasn't sure who it was, but she was awfully bossy. He was not going to respond. As he smirked at that thought, the water ran up his nose again and he half snorted, half sneezed. *Damnit.*

Giving in to the discomfort, he raised his head, then planted his hands on the floor and lifted his torso up out of the water.

Great Escape. He was on the cabin sole of *Great Escape*, and there was water.

"Yes, that's it. Get up. We have to get out," Maggie was saying.

Maggie.

Shit. Maggie.

Burt glanced at the radar again. The two sailboats had separated. One was moving north now on a heading similar to his but behind him and further west. The other one was in the same position. *Odd.*

He picked up his binoculars and turned to look for them. The moving sailboat was under sail, making it much easier to spot. He looked further back along its course and finally spotted the other boat, still under bare poles. He studied it as carefully as he could, but at this distance there was hardly any detail, even with his military grade optics.

It didn't take military grade optics to spot the flash of orange that streaked into the sky from the distant hull. Burt lowered the binoculars and watched the flare arc into the sky. It had not even reached its zenith before he had *Sandcastle* executing a wide turn.

TWENTY-SEVEN: WATER

"What did they do? Where's the water coming in, Maggie?"

The woman rolled her head from side to side. "You didn't hear it? He blew six or seven holes right through the hull with a shot gun. I guess he thought I was faking my leg."

Terry had dragged himself up on to the navigation station seat and was feeling around the back of his head. Pain radiated from the base of his skull. When he pulled his hands away they were wet, but not bloody. He felt like he'd been hit by a dock-cart full of bricks, and his stomach was heaving.

"But he didn't shoot you," he said, immediately regretting it as callous, although maybe not unwarranted. He didn't bother to look for her reaction and she didn't reply. "How long was I out?"

"Fifteen, twenty minutes. He knocked you out, then shot up the boat. He must have brought the gun over. He was planning to do it all along." For the first time she sounded bitter, as if she was finally accepting that she'd lost her husband.

"They got all the drugs?"

"I guess so. Jose pulled a bunch out of the aft head."

Knowing that there must be something more important that he should do, but unable to concentrate on more than one idea at a time, Terry eased to his feet and looked at the aft head. The door had been broken from its top hinge so that it hung at an angle into the small space. He looked past it at the shambles that was Javier and Jose's handiwork. It angered him to see the hardwood trim and cabinet doors splintered. Someone, probably Bill, had kept that woodwork varnished and clean, had wiped away mildew and kept it looking good. And then it occurred to him that it was Bill who had probably instructed them to tear it apart. Rather than packing the drugs into the used holding tank, they had removed it entirely and filled the space. As he looked at the mess, Terry absently wondered if Bill had brought the tank aboard Jericho so Maggie could have it reinstalled. Looking into the space where the tank had been, he saw something at the bottom. He reached in and grabbed it: a plastic wrapped package about the size of a pound of flour.

"They missed one," he said out loud.

"What?" Maggie asked.

Holding the package, Terry backed out of the head and turned toward her. Water sloshed over his shoes.

"They missed a bag."

"So what? Leave it. You have to get me out of here."

Appalled at her ego, and then at himself for being appalled by her self-absorption, Terry shook his head and unshouldered his day pack.

"What are you doing? Don't take it! I knew you were a petty thief."

"Shut up Maggie. This is insurance, in case Bill tries to deny his actions."

"He'll just say that you're a druggie."

"Addicts do not carry their stash in this form. And dealers carry a lot more than one package. As for having to get you out of here, I'm thinking you just wait until the water is high enough and swim out."

"What?"

Terry was almost as surprised at his cold blooded suggestion as Maggie was. But in fact, it was the only way he could think of to get her up the ladder.

"Here," he picked up two pieces of wood from the floor of the head. "I need to splint your leg."

Maggie bit her lip in silence as he found two lengths of line in a drawer and laid the two pieces of wood on either side of her right shin.

"It's going to hurt. I can't help it. But it will be better in the water if it can't wiggle around so much."

"You're serious, aren't you?" She asked.

"I am totally serious. *Great Escape* is sinking slowly. You'll float over to the companionway and get out when you can. Now get ready."

He meant for the pain as he slipped the lengths of rope under her upper and lower shin, but the warning didn't prevent her from wailing in pain. Working as quickly as he could, he straightened her foot, aligned the wood pieces, and tied the line around them and her leg in two places.

"That's it, all I can do. Now I have to go up on deck. Try to stay calm."

"You're going to leave me here, aren't you?"

"For now."

He turned and climbed the companionway ladder, ignoring her additional protests. For a moment he considered doing what she was accusing him of: getting in the dinghy and heading for Martinique. But even as awful as she was being, he couldn't do it. Instead, he climbed up onto the forward deck, took the flare gun from his pocket, fitted a cartridge into it, and fired into the air.

Burt pushed *Sandcastle*'s twin 1000 horse power diesel engines to their maximum, pushing the cruiser up above thirty knots on a straight line toward the lone sailboat. While Burt was picking up the microphone of his single sideband radio he watched another flare arc into the sky. He tuned to the emergency frequency and contacted the Martinique coast guard. The officer who responded to his report of a sailboat in distress asked him to continue on his course to render assistance.

As if I wouldn't, he mused after ending the call. He looked off to the west toward the other sailboat. He was abeam of it now, and could see that it was a ketch under full sail making good speed – for a sailboat – north. If his sudden course change toward the other boat was a concern to the skipper there was no sign of it. Not that he could do anything to stop *Sandcastle*, or even get back there first. Burt stared a long time at the boat through his binoculars, but he wasn't able to see its name or any other distinguishing markings. Hopefully whoever was firing the flares would explain what had happened that had caused the skipper of the ketch to leave another boat in distress.

Jericho was a receding white blur on the northern horizon. But another boat, a motor cruiser throwing up a wide bow wake, was approaching *Great Escape* from the north at speed. Terry had known that the chances of Burt seeing the flares were slim, but he'd been afraid to call on the VHF radio because Jericho would also hear him. He knew that the sailboat couldn't get back here faster than *Sandcastle*, but the flares would inform Bill that he and Maggie were alive. Terry had little doubt that Bill wouldn't make the same mistake a second time.

Tempting as it was to stand and watch his rescuer, Terry forced himself to go to the back of the cockpit and bring *Great Escape*'s dinghy up close. As he loosened the bolts clamping the outboard motor to *Great Escape*'s stern rail he noticed that the rising water inside *Great Escape* would make lowering the motor into the dinghy easier. From inside the cabin he could hear Maggie calling to him, her tone alternating between pleading and demanding. She was easy to ignore.

The stern swim platform was awash, with as much as six inches of water covering it and draining off as the boat floundered over the ocean swells. Terry stood on it, knees flexed, and lifted the motor up and off of the stern rail above him. He set its bottom fin on the step beside his feet, and then lifted it again up and over the dinghy's inflated side, laying it half on the bench seat with the propeller on the rigid floor of the little boat.

He climbed into the dinghy and shrugged off his daypack, setting it on the floor in the bow before stepping over the bench to lift up the engine. In one heave he got the motor up, out over the stern, and positioned on the support. Fighting a wave of nausea he exhaled a held breath and twisted the bolts to secure it. His head was throbbing, the pain at the base of his skull almost impossible to ignore.

I'm running on pure adrenalin, and it's going to give out at some point.

The dinghy rocked on a swell, banging hard against *Great Escape*'s stern. It had subsided several inches just in the time he'd taken to mount the motor. The boat was sinking faster.

"Maggie," he called out, stepping over the dinghy's gunwale and down onto the sunken swim platform. He heard her reply: an angry wordless shout that might have been a distorted form of "get back here."

Water was sloshing around on the cockpit sole, lapping up over the bottom edge of the companionway. Maggie would be able to get out very soon. He stepped into the cockpit and went to the opening.

She was there, splashing erratically and yelling non-verbally in the middle of the flooded saloon. Her auto-inflate life jacket had inflated, probably saving her life since she appeared to be in an out-of-control panic.

"Maggie!" he tried again, reluctant to re-enter the sinking boat. "I'll get the boat hook," he told her, knowing that she wasn't listening. He scanned the deck, knowing that he'd seen the boat hook secured there.

He spotted it beside the starboard handrail with the hook tucked underneath. He stepped to the side of the cockpit, about to climb out onto the deck to get it, when the boat exploded.

"May day, may day, may day, this is motor vessel *Sandcastle* reporting an explosion at sea at the location of my previous report. There has been an explosion on the vessel in distress that I am approaching to render assistance."

"Acknowledged *Sandcastle*. What is the condition of the vessel now? Over."

Burt frowned at the microphone in his hand, wishing the speaker could see his expression. Then he took a breath and answered.

"I do not know. I see burning wreckage. The mast is down. My estimate is that the main wreck will sink in minutes. Over." *If it takes that long*.

"Captain, do not place your craft in danger. Do not approach the burning wreckage. Over."

"Acknowledged. I will look for survivors in the water. Over."

He did not believe that anybody inside the boat could have survived the blast, but if whoever had fired the flares was still outside, they might have been thrown clear.

Terry snorted water out of his nose again and wondered why he kept dreaming of being wet. There it was again, cool and silky, leaving the tang of salt on his lips. But something smelled like chemicals. He turned his head and lightening exploded behind his eyeballs, sparkling like crazy inside his head. His nose wrinkled and he opened his eyes. He couldn't focus. A red blur was coming at him, but he couldn't tell what it was. He shut his eyes and listened to the crackling, then reopened them and tried to focus through the pain. It was a red plastic fuel jug floating six inches from his face. He was in the sea, supported by his life jacket that had inflated just as it was supposed to when it got wet. Everything was quiet, even the flames consuming bits of floating debris around him. The pain in his head was still the worst, but he hurt all over now, which actually made it more bearable.

"Maggie?" he croaked, intending to shout. His head throbbed and he felt nauseous, so he didn't try to shout again. He pushed away the red jug, which sloshed heavily. It was half full of fuel. Cushions and life jackets floated around him amid burning canvas and fiberglass attached to Styrofoam floatation. He reached for a singed lifejacket floating beyond the fuel jug, struggling to ignore the lightening striking at the back of his head. His elbow protested as he bent it to pull the jacket to himself and he noticed the ache in his chest when he tried to submerge it. Jaw clenched, he forced the jacket down between his legs so that it lifted his head and shoulders out of the water. Now he could see even more burning wreckage. He dog-paddled slowly toward the largest concentration of debris, trying to spot *Great Escape*'s hull.

But there was no hull, only floating pieces blown off of the boat in the blast. The bulk of the boat was gone.

"Maggie," he tried again, managing only a slightly louder croak. He scanned the debris field for the streak of dark red hair, certain that it was pointless. She could not have been thrown free like he had been.

Even so, he forced his aching arms to paddle through the wreckage. He splashed at a burning cushion to extinguish it, and then he spotted it: the dinghy. He abandoned his hunt for Maggie and swam for the little boat, which was blowing west on the steady breeze. It should not have been a hard swim, but it was. The awkward inflated lifejacket got in his way, but he was afraid to deflate it, afraid that he wouldn't keep afloat without it. His loaded pockets and sandals didn't help either, and he had to do most of the work with his arms. But he didn't dare abandon any of his meager possessions.

He was almost there, ten feet to go, when he saw her: the splotch of rust-colored hair and brighter orange lifejacket. Between strokes he looked from Maggie to the dinghy drifting away from him, back to Maggie, and then turned and stroked harder toward the dinghy.

TWENTY-EIGHT: SALVAGE

Burt brought *Sandcastle* down off plain about two hundred yards from the outer ring of wreckage, shifting into idle as he picked up his binoculars. There was no boat, only floating wreckage. The many small fires were dying out as their fuel became soaked. One by one the bits of charred boat would sink as the main hull had. It was a grim sight, one that no boat owner wants to see. He could tell from the jetsam that this had been a lived-in boat, no clean, empty charter vessel. There were scraps of clothing, plastic containers from the galley, the odds and ends of life aboard all cast across the waters to float away, or descend to the depths that someone had worked hard to keep them from.

His heart was growing heavy with guilt for not acting out of curiosity an hour earlier when he spotted the large black dinghy. And then he spotted the figure in bright orange struggling to climb into it. Jolted into action, he steered a wide arc around the edge of the debris field and toward the small inflatable boat. Curiously, the man who had finally managed to get in and was laying athwart the bench now, did not seen to hear *Sandcastle*'s engines.

"Lucky bastard. I hope it's not permanent," Burt muttered as he placed *Sandcastle* downwind from the dinghy so the bigger boat would stop the smaller one. Then he hurried down to the aft deck, grabbing a boat hook from its rack by the ladder as he went.

"Hey," he shouted as he climbed up onto *Sandcastle*'s side deck, leaning out and down to snag one of the rubber handles on the side of the dinghy. "Can you hear me?"

The man roused, but did not look to his left at *Sandcastle*. He pushed himself up to kneel in the stern of the small boat, then scanned the water off to starboard as if looking for something there. Burt started to drag the little boat toward *Sandcastle*'s stern. The motion set the man off balance and he finally looked to his left.

A burly, bearded man was using a boat hook to hold the dinghy alongside a massive powerboat. He was staring at Terry, mouth moving. Terry shook his head and reached out toward the boat hook.

"Maggie's over there. Let me go," he pointed to starboard, looking as he did for the streak of rusty hair. He couldn't see it now. He looked at the hook holding the dinghy's handle as if it were a confounding puzzle. Then he figured it out. He grasped the aluminum tube of the hook and yanked downward. It came out from under the handle. He pushed away from the big boat, not even looking at the oddly silent man, and moved awkwardly into the stern of the dinghy. He grasped the cord and gave it a weak yank. He was shocked when the outboard motor issued a puff of smoke and started to vibrate but remained silent. Unable to work through that puzzle, he put it into gear and pointed the boat toward the spot where he had last seen her.

"Terry. What happened. Where's Beth?" Burt said even as the other man struggled to free the dinghy from his boat hook. Burt scanned the wreckage again, desperate now to spot Beth, who he had come to think of as indomitable. It shook him to his core to think that she might already be in the depths beside the charred hull of her beloved boat.

He watched Terry steer the dinghy back through the diminishing wreckage field and then figured out his target: a person floating unmoving in a lifejacket. But it wasn't Beth. The hair was the wrong color.

Terry had spotted her too. He brought the dinghy alongside her and left the motor idling while he leaned over the gunwale to reach for her. Burt watched for a long moment, mentally laying odds of whether Terry would be able to pull the other person aboard the boat. How injured was he? How heavy was the other person?

"Damnit." He growled as he put *Sandcastle*'s engines in slow forward and pointed her into the wreckage field.

"Maggie, can you hear me? Maggie?" A detached part of Terry's mind watched his desperation curiously. What drove him to rescue this woman who'd brought him to this disaster? Humanity, he supposed. A hope that others would do the same for him even if he had exercised awful judgment.

He rotated Maggie in the water so that he could see her face and grab the nylon webbing straps of the lifejacket beneath the inflated chambers.

"Maggie!" he repeated. He couldn't tell whether she was breathing. She might not be, and if not, what was the point trying to drag her aboard? Bill didn't care whether her body was recovered.

Her children. Who knew whether what Bill had said about them was true? It wasn't up to him to decide whether to let their mother sink away to the bottom if he could pull her aboard.

"Come on Maggie," he heaved, leaning back as he dragged her inert form up the inflated chamber of the dinghy's side. He got her head and shoulders on top of it at the expense of a massive pain in his chest on top of nausea and headache. He had to shift his own weight further to the other side while still holding her so that the little boat wouldn't flip over. With his feet braced beneath her against the flexible chamber and his own behind on the opposite gunwale, he heaved again, gritting his teeth against the pain. Her torso slid up over the side as her head and shoulders landed on his legs. Her face remained impassive, her jaw hanging limply.

He scrambled to get out from under her, leaving her laying on the floor with her thighs up on the inflated side of the boat. As he leaned across to bring her legs aboard the sight of the cruiser slowly approaching distracted him. And the stillness of everything finally struck him. The crackling and the lights in his head had diminished, but the sound had not been replaced by that of the sea, the burning wreckage, or, most obviously, the motor of the cruiser idling closer to the dinghy.

The sudden realization that it was *Sandcastle*, and the man he'd pushed away from a few minutes ago was Burt frightened him. Had he forgotten that Burt had seen them and called on the VHF? Had he been so single minded about finding Maggie that he hadn't recognized a friend? He lowered his behind to the dinghy's soft gunwale near Maggie's legs, his plan to bring them aboard forgotten as he struggled with his own condition.

You're deaf. You're not observing your surroundings. You need to let Burt take care of Maggie. And you.

"Terry, can you hear me?" Burt called. The other man had seated himself on the dinghy's gunwale and was staring vacantly at *Sandcastle*. The deafness was probably from the explosion. The vacant stare was likely shock. Just because he'd been physically active didn't mean he wasn't seriously injured. Burt carefully maneuvered alongside the dinghy once again, this time placing the tiny boat at the larger one's stern.

He went back out on deck and took up the boat hook, using it to capture the dinghy and bring it broadside next to *Sandcastle*'s swim platform. Terry automatically reached across the platform and grabbed onto a handle, helping keep the boat in place while Burt fished the painter out of the water and secured its charred end to a cleat.

Crouching on the platform, he took hold of one of the dinghy handles with his left hand and tapped Terry on the shoulder. When the other man looked at him he said, with great enunciation, "get out. I've got it." And tilted his head toward *Sandcastle*. Terry nodded, relief suffusing his face, and he planted his hands on the swim platform. He crawled awkwardly from the inflatable to the swim platform and turned, still kneeling, to reach toward the woman in the dinghy. Burt waved him away, pointing emphatically to the steps up onto *Sandcastle*'s aft deck. Terry obediently backed away and climbed to his feet using every handhold he could find.

Burt turned to the woman. That's when he noticed the makeshift splint on her right leg and the odd angle of her foot. She looked familiar, but Burt could not place her. The question of how Terry happened to be here with her, and where Beth was, pushed at his focus as he knelt next to the dinghy.

The woman was absolutely still. One hand on the dinghy's nearer gunwale he reached out to touch his fingertips to the side of her neck. Her flesh was cold and damp. It felt as lifeless as it looked. He moved his hand around, hunting for the carotid artery and finding nothing. He raised her left arm to touch her wrist and felt for a pulse there too. Nothing. He straightened and looked back over his shoulder to find Terry standing on the aft deck looking down at him.

He shook his head.

Terry raised one hand to his mouth, covering an expression between a gasp and a sob. He sank down onto a settee, his head in his hands.

Burt started to tell him the he would get her body aboard, then realized there was no point: Terry couldn't hear him.

He put his left arm beneath her legs and reached down to grab the nearest webbing strap of her harness with his right hand. He put everything he had into hauling her up. When he got her rump onto the side of the dinghy he took a breath, then scooted back on the swim platform to make room for her before heaving again and getting her up onto it. Freed of her weight, the dinghy bobbed away and for a moment he held her torso suspended over the water. He leaned back, hauling her bottom across the deck far enough so that she was sitting securely on the platform.

"Okay," he grunted as he stood up. "Gotta get you up on deck so you don't roll off."

He found the air valve on her life vest to deflate it. Then he wrapped both arms under hers and dragged her upward, gasping at the effort required. She lolled against him, threatening to bring them both back down as the boat rocked. Suddenly, a pair of hands came from above and grabbed the shoulder straps of her harness. Burt looked up at Terry, who must be kneeling on the settee up on the aft deck to lean down to her.

"Thanks," he said, knowing the other man wouldn't hear and certain that he was expending energy he didn't have. The need to tend to Terry spurred Burt to move as quickly as he could. He repositioned himself to heave her onto his shoulders. His knees quivered under the weight as he took short steps across the platform. He resisted the urge to drop her with each one. But the thought of picking her back up was enough to motivate him to keep going. He climbed the steps one at a time, wondering whether his and Maggie's combined weight would be too much for their structure.

At the top of the steps he stopped next to the nearest settee and lowered the body to it with a grunt. Terry came to stand next to him, one hand pressed to his chest, mouth open gasping for breath as he looked down at her greying flesh and limp limbs.

Burt touched him on the shoulder and he looked up. "Was she close to the explosion?"

Terry watched his lips, trying to read them. Guessing at the question, he said, "She was inside the boat. I told her to wait until she could float out, because of her leg. I don't know where the explosion was, but it could have been right next to her."

"The water might have cushioned the force, distributed it to a larger area. Otherwise she probably would have been blown to bits. But Terry, where is Beth?"

Terry stared at Burt's mouth, not understanding. Burt frowned, frustrated, then swung around and entered *Sandcastle*'s main cabin. He came back a moment later with a pad and pen. He had written one word: *Beth?*

"Oh. On her way to Martinique, I hope. Did you think? – Oh God, Burt, no, this wasn't *Trouble*. This was Maggie's boat, *Great Escape*."

The relief on Burt's face answered Terry's question. He nodded, and then smiled, patting Terry on the upper arm. He scribbled, *Call Martinique Coast Guard.*

"*Double Trouble, Double Trouble, Double Trouble*, this is the Windward Cruising Net, come in."

Beth looked up from her laptop, eyes scanning the waters around *Trouble* as she listened to the radio. She thought she'd heard someone say *Trouble*. If they wanted her, they'd repeat. And he did. She had set the laptop down and was down the companionway ladder before Jerry had finished his repeat call.

"This is *Double Trouble*, go ahead."

"Hello Beth. Are you still looking for a sailboat named *Great Escape*? Over."

"Yes I am. Have you heard something? Over."

"On the SSB emergency frequency, a vessel reported a mayday. A sailboat named *Great Escape* had an explosion and sank, about thirty miles west of Fort du France."

Beth's knees gave out. She slumped onto the navigation seat, her mouth too dry for her to speak.

"Beth? The reporting vessel said that he recovered a man from the water, and a woman's corpse. Over."

An uncontrollable shiver wracked Beth, a physical manifestation of the total relief his words brought her. "Acknowledged," she croaked. And then swallowed and managed, "Was there anything more? Is he okay? Over."

"The man has hearing loss. Over."

"Hearing loss." Beth repeated, unable to wrap her head around the notion.

"*Double Trouble, Double Trouble, Double Trouble*, this is *Petrel*, sorry to interrupt. Over."

When Beth did not respond, Jerry did. "Go ahead *Petrel*."

"Beth, where are you? Over." Evan asked.

Beth roused herself. "Hello *Petrel*. I'm in the St. Lucia Channel. I'm going to anchor at Sainte-Anne tonight. Over."

"Very good. We will join you there in the morning. Over."

"You don't have to – I'll be okay. Over."

"If you don't mind my saying, Beth, I think you should accept *Petrel*'s offer of company. Over." Jerry put in.

"It wasn't an offer," *Petrel*'s skipper replied. "We are getting underway shortly and will be there in the morning. We'll contact you then, Beth. Over."

"Okay. Thanks Evan. Over."

"A word of advice Beth? Over." Jerry said.

"Yes? Over."

"Don't go monitoring the emergency channel. I'll do that, and I'll call you on this one if there's any more news. And the rest of you cruisers listening in out there, if you're at Sainte-Anne, keep an eye out for our Beth on *Double Trouble*. Cruiser's Net standing by."

For the first time in her sailing career Beth felt like a trapped animal, isolated on her boat at sea. She couldn't work on the article. She couldn't call anyone until she got closer to Martinique. And she couldn't squeeze any more speed out of *Trouble*'s sails and heavy hull. But she tried. She examined the sails, adjusted lines, checked the speed, and adjusted again. Then she went below and took the water-stained copy of *Chapman's Piloting and Seamanship* off the bookshelf and turned to the chapter on sail trim. For the next three hours she read theory and put it into practice to see if it worked on *Trouble*. Whether it did or not, she tried something else, and something more. In the end she had increased her speed about a half a knot, but she was not certain whether it was due to her tinkering or that the wind had picked up.

Before Burt could get *Sandcastle* underway Terry insisted that he retrieve the daypack that was sitting in the bow of *Great Escape*'s dinghy. Burt climbed aboard the small boat and got the bag. Then he rigged fresh lines to its bow and stern to secure it across the swim platform while he removed the outboard motor. He stowed it behind the engine room hatch in *Sandcastle*'s stern above the swim platform. It took him a few minutes to haul the dinghy up onto the platform by alternately dragging the bow up and securing the line, then the stern. When he was done the little boat was lashed securely on the swim platform.

"You have salvage rights," he said to Terry when he returned to the aft deck. Terry shrugged indicating that he didn't understand and Burt shook his head. "Not important."

He wanted to climb up to the flying bridge to get underway, but Terry grabbed his sleeve and held up a plastic wrapped brick of what looked like heroine Burt snatched it away to examine it. He recognized the symbol stamped in black on the plastic as the sign of one of the biggest dealer organizations in Central America.

"What is this?" He asked, then sighed as he shut his eyes for a moment before taking the pad and pen from Terry.

Inside. Explain.

He gestured to one of the comfortable settees in the saloon and headed for the galley. Glancing back he saw Terry still standing.

"Sit. The upholstery isn't hard to clean." He lowered one hand, palm down.

Terry subsided onto a settee. Burt took out a jug of water and filled a cup, then poured one for himself. He carried them to Terry and sat down. Nodding at the other man to begin.

Terry started in Wallilabou, struggling to edit his story to convey only what mattered, omitting Beth's suspicions and the bareboat's freed line. He described Maggie's unpleasant and ungrateful behavior on board, and how she'd changed course while he was off watch. Burt got up and refilled his water glass while he spoke. His throat hurt, but he kept going, abbreviating more and more to get through it. Finally he nodded at the brick of drugs that Burt had left on the galley counter.

"They missed one. I figure it supports my story," Terry said, looked to Burt for his opinion.

"You think it needs support?" Burt asked, then scribbled his question on the pad.

"Bill wanted both of us dead. He might come looking for me. I think I may need to prove that he's on the wrong side of the law." Burt nodded, looking from Terry to the brick of powder. He picked up the pen and wrote: *Okay. But let me lock it up. We can stage reveal to authorities. Don't want them find on you.*

Terry nodded. "Makes sense."

Burt took the package to his cabin where he kept valuables and certain other useful objects in a large safe. When he returned to the saloon Terry was gone. He climbed up to the flying bridge and found him sitting in the second seat looking out toward Martinique. Around them the burning wreckage was mostly extinguished and had spread to a much wider circle. Soon there would be no sign that *Great Escape* had foundered on this spot. Before engaging the motors, Burt recorded a waypoint in his GPS, marking their position. He didn't know if *Great Escape* had an emergency locator beacon on board, but even if it did, it might have been damaged, or it might be drifting with the other debris. If there was any reason to try to find *Great Escape*, the way point would be necessary. That done, he gradually accelerated the engines, bringing *Sandcastle* up on a plain.

"I'd offer you my satellite phone, but from what you've said, Beth won't be in cell range until late this afternoon," Burt said. Then he looked at Terry, who was peering ahead toward where Martinique wasn't quite visible. He couldn't help but laugh. "Except that you couldn't hear her anyway!"

As if sensing that Burt was speaking, Terry looked at him, then said, "I think it's coming back. I can hear the engines."

Burt nodded, withholding any response. Maybe Terry's hearing was returning, or maybe he was feeling the engines through the hull and his brain was interpreting the vibration as sound. Either way, Burt hoped that the damage was only temporary.

Fifteen minutes later they both spotted a large, grey vessel steaming toward them from the brown-green smudge that was Martinique. Burt nodded toward it. "Martinique coast guard. They said they'd meet us on their way to inspect the wreck. Not that there's anything left to inspect."

Terry watched the side of his face, but couldn't guess at what he was saying. He held the pad out over the instrument panel pointedly.

"Right," Burt said, taking it. He scribbled key words that Terry read as he wrote.

"Can you take me to find Beth? I don't want to go with them."

I try. They may question you. You need doctor. Have to hand over Maggie.

Terry read it and sighed, apparently resigning himself to dealing with French red tape.

Try get you out.

Terry's brows rose. "Out? You think I'm going to jail?"

Burt shook his head, lips pursed as he struggled to think of the shortest way to write what he meant.

Statement now. Will insist you need hospital, try take you myself. Then find Beth.

"I don't need to go to the hospital. I need to see Beth."

Burt shook his head emphatically and reached out to touch Terry's right ear and then the back of his head. He started as a bolt of lightning shot through his temples.

Burt scribbled, *Sry. might be concussed. Maybe internal injury. Need ears checked.*

"My chest hurts."

Burt knew that Terry had conceded the point. He nodded and returned his attention to the oncoming vessel.

He could tell from its reduced bow wave when the coast guard patrol boat slowed and he brought *Sandcastle* down off plane as well. She settled down into the water and continued forward at a sedate ten knots. The two boats both slowed to a stop when they were side by side, a few boat lengths apart. The patrol boat was not much larger than *Sandcastle*, but with more open deck and impressive guns mounted fore, aft, and on the sides. Crew stood at the guns, but they looked relaxed, simply holding their assigned positions.

The VHF radio crackled and a voice hailed *Sandcastle*. Even though they were only yards apart, yelling would be much harder than simply using the radio.

Burt picked up the microphone and responded.

"What is your situation? Over." The other skipper asked.

"I have recovered one body and one survivor, who is here with me on the bridge. Over," Burt replied.

"Where is the body? Over."

"On my aft deck. Over."

"Very well. We will transfer the body to our vessel. Please put the survivor on. Over."

"I'm afraid I can't. His hearing is still gone. With your permission I will take him directly to the hospital in le Marin. Over."

After a pause, the other captain responded. "Very well. Please prepare to be boarded. Over."

Terry looked quizzically at Burt as he replaced the microphone, rose and went to the ladder. Burt shot him an encouraging smile as he descended to the aft deck. He was in a hurry to deploy some fenders before the coast guard vessel came along side and scratched up *Sandcastle's* hull.

Three crewmen crossed to *Sandcastle's* side deck, one carrying a long board with straps. They went to the aft deck where Maggie's body was laying and laid the board on the deck beside the settee. Looking down at the corpse Burt thought it already looked sunken, empty. He'd seen his share of corpses, including some of friends. He'd been trained to look at such things analytically, and he had no trouble doing so now. He was glad Terry had stayed up on the bridge.

When the three men lifted the corpse it illustrated the origin of "stiff." Rather than sag between them, it was so rigid the backboard that they placed it on was unnecessary. But they fastened the straps anyway.

Within moments they had transferred the body to their vessel. The other captain had come to stand on the side deck opposite Burt.

"The police will meet you at le Marin and assist with the man's transfer to the hospital."

"Is he under arrest?"

"No, of course not. But the investigation must be conducted." The captain paused, eyes studying Burt. Then he asked, quietly, "Are you under duress captain? Is there just the one man?"

"There is just the one man, and I know him. He is a cruising sailor. His girlfriend is on their boat on her way to Martinique. He sailed on *Great Escape* to help its owner. He will explain in his statement why they were out here, and all that he knows about what happened."

"You reported that there was another sailboat. We have dispatched air support to look for it."

"Good. I suggest that you try to intercept it. Terry told me that they are responsible for the explosion and the woman's death."

The captain studied Burt once again, and Burt had the familiar sense that he knew something about him. It happened often enough.

"Very well. We will speak again, I believe."

"I suspect so. Good luck," Burt moved to stand where one of his fenders was tied, signaling that he was ready for the other boat to move away. The captain watched him as if considering further discussion, then nodded curtly and gestured to the helmsman to get underway.

Burt held his position until the other boat was several yards away and accelerating, still heading west toward the site of the explosion. Then he retrieved his fenders and returned to the bridge where Terry was sitting watching the other boat.

He picked up the pad and wrote, *Hospital. Police will meet us. Want your statement. Not under arrest. Coast Guard going after* Jericho. *They sent chopper.*

Terry read these notes as Burt put *Sandcastle* into gear and eased forward, accelerating gradually until the big boat rose up out of the water. He loved that feeling. It was almost like flying.

TWENTY-NINE: SAINT ANNE

When *Trouble* was about ten miles from Martinique's south coast Beth turned on her cell phone and found that it had a signal. She waited a moment, but there was no indication of any voicemail. Disappointed, she dialed Terry's number. If he couldn't hear, he couldn't talk on the phone. She knew that. But she was hoping he was able to have someone else speak to her. Somewhere off in the distance the phone rang. Once. Twice. Three times. Her disappointment deepened and tears flooded her eyes. Shocked at her fragility, she dashed at them as she listened to the fourth ring, knowing it was about to go to voicemail.

"Hello, Terry's phone."

"Grrrk," she gasped, her throat constricting.

"Beth?" The male voice asked. It wasn't Terry. How did he – caller ID, of course.

"Yes. Who is this?"

"It's Burt."

"B-Burt Adams? Why do you– what are you –?"

"Hush. Terry's okay. He's being examined. There was – ."

"An explosion. I know. I've been desperate for hours waiting to get into phone range."

"How did you know?"

"Cruiser's net. But they didn't know much. How are you there? I can't believe that you're there. I'm so relieved that you are."

"I'm the one who reported the explosion. I pulled Terry out of the water."

"I –," Beth forced herself to look out across the water, to turn her

271

focus external so that her mind could work. "He's really all right? They said that you reported he couldn't hear."

"That's true. It's from the explosion. It could just be inflammation, or there could be real damage. I'm sorry Beth, that's all I know so far. He was on deck when it happened, so he was thrown into the water. He had his life jacket on. He has a couple cracked ribs and some bruising. And he has a head injury. That's what they're concerned about."

"Oh Burt, I can't believe you're there. I'm so grateful. Thank you so much."

"Where are you Beth?" He asked, clearly not comfortable with her heaping gratitude. She squeezed her eyes shut, tears running down her cheeks, and concentrated on facts.

"I'm ten miles out, heading for Sainte Anne to anchor. It will be too late to try to find my way into le Marin."

"Agreed. Call me when you get closer and I'll go out to the anchorage and anchor. You can raft up to *Sandcastle* if you don't want to anchor."

"Really Burt, that's a lot to ask."

"You didn't ask. I offered. I'm thinking of the safety of the other boats in the anchorage, with you being upset and tired and anchoring at dusk." The levity in his voice was a tonic. She had to smile.

"You're right. Who knows what a mess I'd make of it?"

"None at all, I expect," he replied very seriously. "Just call me. You have my number, right?"

"Yes. I'll call you. It will be a couple hours."

"I know. See you soon."

With a lighter heart, Beth adjusted her sail trim again, squeezing another tenth of a knot out of the breeze, and forced herself to eat a sandwich and drink a bottle of water. She got out the cruising guide and reread the section on le Marin, confirming that there was a hospital very near the marina. That had to be where Terry was. Her terrible command of French was enough to dissuade her from trying to call the hospital. She trusted Burt to have told her as much, or more, than they would anyway.

Instead she set about preparing for either possibility when she got there: lines to tie *Trouble* to *Sandcastle*, and the anchor if for some reason they didn't find one another.

The wind began to abandon *Trouble* as they passed Martinique's southern tip. When boat speed had fallen to four knots from just over five, Beth gave in and started the engine. In a few minutes she had the jib rolled up, the mainsail trimmed in, and the engine revved to 2800 RPMs – optimal for long haul motoring. She watched the numbers on the knot meter increase again, settling at 5.8 knots.

During the last hour of her trip Beth's thoughts returned to Burt being in the right place at the right time to rescue Terry. Was it really just coincidence? If not, why had he been there? Then she didn't realize that she did not actually know where "there" was. Probably Sainte Anne, just like Terry had said they would be. Something must have gone wrong on board. There were plenty of systems on a boat that could catch fire, and other things that could explode, if not properly maintained and inspected. A propane leak could have allowed the heavier than air to gather in the bilge and been set off by lighting the stove. An electrical short could turn into a fire fast, and then the propane in the tank might explode. But somehow Maggie the life coach didn't seem like someone who would miss inspections of vital systems like these. And why was Terry wearing his life jacket at anchor?

Beth resisted the strong urge to call Burt and ask more questions until she was off of Point Dunkerque, a mile south of the anchorage at Sainte Anne.

"Hello Beth. You must be that lone sailboat off the point."

"Yes, that's me. Are you in the anchorage already?"

"I came out about an hour ago. The hospital kicked me out for loitering. I'll turn on my lights to help you find me."

"Thanks. I need to drop my main. I'll look for you when I get closer and call on 16 if I can't spot you. Okay?"

"Yes, that sounds good. See you soon. I'll have a cocktail ready."

Sandcastle was a blazing eyesore against the darkening shoreline as *Trouble* made her way into the placid anchorage just before sunset. Beth wondered what the neighboring sailors thought, and how soon they'd start complaining about Burt messing up their sunset views. That made her smile as she slowed *Trouble* to less than a knot and pointed her bow at *Sandcastle*'s stern quarter. She had placed the coiled mid-ships line right on the toe rail. Now all she had to do was bring *Trouble* close enough alongside for Burt to grab it. He stood waiting on the side deck just forward of the stern, a boathook in hand. Beth challenged herself to put *Trouble* within his reach without the hook, and she did it, turning the bow away just enough – and at just the right moment – to bring *Trouble's* mid-ships up next to her friend.

Within minutes bow, stern, and spring lines were secured and both boats' fenders were squeaking under pressure between the two hulls.

"Come on over," Burt said, putting a hand on the ladder up to his bridge. "I just need to kill the lights before the neighbors complain."

"I was thinking that," Beth chuckled. She went below to retrieve a sweatshirt against the evening breeze, then climbed easily from *Trouble's* deck to *Sandcastle's* just as the bright spotlights that had illuminated the decks went out.

Burt had set up a folding cocktail table and two director's chairs on the aft deck. Two glasses sat next to a pitcher full of amber liquid, ice, and chunks of lime. She sat down on the settee next to the table. Burt descended the ladder and suddenly Beth was on her feet, stepping to him and into a warm, fatherly embrace.

She held on for a long while, hearing his heartbeat, feeling his chest rising and falling. He was warm and he smelled of coconut and lavender laundry detergent.

"Thank you Burt."

"You looked like a girl who needed a hug."

Beth smiled, separating from him. "I guess I was. I didn't even know it."

"Sit down. Have a dark and stormy. I have a story to tell you."

Beth sat and watched him pour, saying "First tell me again that's he's okay."

"He's okay. He's going to be a little worse for wear when you get him back, but he's still your Terry."

"And I'll do whatever he needs me to."

"I'm sure you will. But no need to fret about what's next when you have no idea what it will be. Let me fill you in."

He paused to take a sip of his drink, so Beth did the same. The rich, sweet rum and ginger warmed her insides and the lime tasted like sunshine. She took a long breath and let it out slowly, eyes finding the sun that was already halfway into the sea far to the west.

Burt followed her gaze and they both watched as it slowly diminished, form elongating into an oval and shrinking, shrinking, until, just as it disappeared, the last remnant of it flashed from dark red to green.

"Oh!" Beth cried. "Did you see it?"

"I did. That's a sign of good luck."

"I'm not sure I've ever heard that, but I'll take it. Now tell me what happened to *Great Escape*. And Maggie. Last I heard from them they were coming here."

When he'd finished the story Beth was astounded by the extent of Maggie's deception. She couldn't believe that she'd been right all along, at least in her suspicion if not the facts. Most of all she felt guilty for not insisting that Terry refuse to go with the woman on *Great Escape*. She was more desperate now than before to see him, but Burt exerted a rational influence and picked up his telephone first. When the hospital receptionist answered he requested an update in French and put the phone on speaker while they waited for the reply. Beth appreciated the gesture, not that she would likely understand the response when it came.

The call had been transferred and when an attendant on Terry's ward answered Burt repeated his request. The attendant confirmed Burt's identity, and then provided an answer in rapid-fire French. Burt nodded, mumbling *oui* a couple times and concluding with a *merci beaucoup* before ending the call.

"In case you're wondering, Terry had them note me in his chart as a relative so that they'd give me updates. I'm his uncle Burt, his only relation in the islands."

"Uncle Burt. I like it."

"Did you get any of what she said?"

"Not really," Beth shrugged. She'd caught some words, but the French was heavily infused with creole so the pronunciation was very difficult for her.

"You have to get used to the island accent," Burt said, as if that was Beth's only problem with understanding French, which she appreciated. "He's asleep. They did an MRI on his head. There is some swelling where he was hit, but no fracture. Other checks for concussion were positive, so he's going to have to be inactive for a while. His left eardrum is torn. There's no apparent damage to his right ear, but it was full of seawater. It's been drained, and they expect his hearing to be back in that ear when he wakes up. He also has two cracked ribs – I think I mentioned that before. Visiting hours are at nine a.m. We should leave here at eight."

Beth smiled at his assumption that she'd want to see Terry as soon as she could.

"Why don't you let me make you some supper, then get a good night's sleep?"

Beth didn't have to think too hard about that offer. Already the rum was making her limbs heavy.

"Thank you Burt. For everything."

The first thing Terry noticed when he woke up was birds. The sound was lopsided, though: he could only hear them in his right ear. Still, it was better than not at all. The hospital staff had a lot less tolerance for having to write everything than Burt, so he had only a vague idea of his condition and prospects, and most of that was from secretly reading his chart when no one was looking. Unfortunately, while he could read French, he could not read most of his care givers' handwriting.

The birds were soon augmented by the sounds of the waking hospital: clattering trays that meant breakfast was being served, quiet voices of nurses conferring in the hall, the squeak of crepe soles on the linoleum floor.

He knew that the delicious sense of well-being he was experiencing was mostly drug-induced. But he still attributed part of it to being safe and away from *Great Escape*. Whenever his thoughts veered toward the last moments on that boat he dragged them away by consciously visualizing a cowboy dragging his horse's head around by the reins, and then grinned when he realized that his brain had made Beth the cowboy. That made him wonder if she could ride, and his thoughts would be off on a safer tack.

A serious but courteous police officer had tried to take his statement yesterday, but had given up after a few minutes of having to write out every question. Terry had found his handwriting hard to read too, so he'd had to ask for clarification on practically every phrase. After speaking to the doctor who had examined Terry's ears, the officer took his notebook and files and left. Terry figured he'd be back today. Maybe if he faked continued deafness he could get out of it all together.

Eventually an orderly came in carrying a tray of covered dishes. He walked past Terry's bed to one on the other side of the room and dragged aside the floor to ceiling curtain. Terry only now realized there was another patient in the room. He was an elderly man with a grizzled white beard encircling a wide, red mouth. He looked like his hair had abandoned his head in favor of his face, for his scalp was bald and shiny. His eyes sparkled at the sight of the tray. The orderly placed it on a bed table and rolled it into position, then moved to the other side of the bed to crank the bed up so that the man was sitting. All the while they conferred in light tones, speaking a rapid patois that Terry couldn't follow.

The orderly left, nodding at Terry as he passed, and then returned with another tray. He rearranged things for Terry as he had the other man, leaving him to examine the tray of food. Across the room, the other patient was alternately sipping from his café bowl of coffee and dipping in the length of crusty baguette. Examining the tiny pots of preserves, honey, and butter, the length of baguette and pair of aromatic croissants, Terry thought this was possibly the best hospital meal he had ever seen. And, he realized quite suddenly, he was very hungry.

He was completely focused on the glistening red strawberry preserves that he had spread on one of the croissants when an even better sight drew his attention to the open door.

"Beth!"

She rushed to his bedside, leaning in between the rail and the tray table to place her hands on either side of his face and place a kiss on his mouth.

She smacked her lips as she pulled away. "You taste of strawberries. And you need a shave."

"Good morning to you, too," he replied. He was unable to take his eyes off of her, taking in her white t-shirt and hastily combed hair, still damp from her morning swim, he suspected. Dark crescents under her eyes were evidence of stress over the last two days.

"I was going to say I've been worried since you left St. Vincent, but it's not really true. I was frustrated with Maggie for changing plans, and I missed you. But I didn't start worrying – really worrying – until Jerry from the cruiser's net called me and told me that someone reported *Great Escape* had exploded."

"I know, it's been a bizarre couple of days. Beth, all I can say to you is that I'm sorry. You were right all along. I should never have gone with her."

"No, no, that's not right Terry. It was right to help out a fellow cruiser, and my suspicious weren't based on any real evidence."

"I think the lesson for us all here is to trust in Beth's intuition."

Burt had stayed back, just inside the doorway, but now he rounded the end of the bed to stand across from Beth.

"That's for sure," Terry replied, smiling at Burt.

"You should finish your breakfast, we don't mind," Beth said, nodding at his tray. "Hey! You can hear us!"

"I know. What a relief. My right ear is clear. I guess they can tell me about the left one now that I can hear what they're saying."

"They weren't so patient with writing after I left?" Burt asked.

Terry shook his head, taking a sip of coffee and picking his croissant back up.

"So did you understand that you have a concussion, and a ruptured eardrum, and two cracked ribs?"

Terry's expression said no. "I was hoping the left ear was just water, too. And I should have guessed about the ribs, my chest was hurting a lot. I was afraid it was much worse."

"But you hauled Maggie's corpse out of the water anyway."

Terry held Burt's eyes for a long moment, seeing puzzlement and respect in them. Then he looked at Beth, who looked decidedly annoyed, and was clearly waiting for an explanation.

"In the dinghy, when I tried to drag her aboard and it hurt. But I wasn't thinking about my condition then. I was only half conscious myself, I think. Anyway, I thought about leaving her. I couldn't tell if she was dead or alive. I couldn't leave her if she was alive, and I thought about her children. They deserve to decide what to do with her remains if she's dead. But if I hadn't gotten her on the second try I think I would have had to give up."

He took a bite of the croissant.

"I would have hauled her in, but you got to her first and got it done," Burt said. "It was the right thing to do."

"I'm glad you handed her off to the authorities," Beth said with a shudder.

"Speaking of whom, did they get your statement?" Burt asked.

Terry swallowed and answered, "No. The officer gave up. I'm sure when the doctors tell them I can hear today someone will be back. I'll be glad to get it over with."

"I guess they haven't told you when you can get out of here," Beth said.

Terry shook his head around another mouthful of croissant.

"They told me they would want to observe him for at least another day because of the head injury," Burt said.

"I guess they'll tell me today," Terry said. "Where is *Trouble?*"

"Rafted to *Sandcastle* out at Sainte Anne."

"Why don't you arrange spot in the marina?" Burt asked. "It will probably be better for Terry not to have to do the long dinghy ride, and he's going to have to be pretty inactive for a while."

Burt and Terry could both read Beth's expression, which shouted reluctance to incur the expense followed by resignation, and then a flash of guilt for resisting doing whatever Terry needed.

"Burt's right. You know I'm good for it," Terry said, reaching out to take Beth's hand. The warmth of his flesh against hers brought a sudden rush of relief and she blinked her eyes to prevent tears.

"Okay. Of course. I'll take care of it when visiting hours end."

Burt and Beth stopped at the marina office on their way to the dinghy dock where Beth made arrangements to bring *Trouble* in to the marina in the afternoon. She handed over her credit card to cover a deposit, depending on Terry paying the final bill, which was probably going to be more than her meager credit limit.

With directions in hand she and Burt strolled the docks to look at the place she'd been assigned. As they strolled along the long dock she realized something that she hadn't even noticed before: all of the boats were backed up against the main dock, and there were no finger piers in between them. What's more, each boat had its anchor out to hold its bow, with only stern lines to secure it to the dock. She was relieved when they got to the spot she'd been assigned to find that it was in a stretch of empty dock. She would have room for error as she backed up to the dock. Still, the process presented a new challenge. She swallowed down her uncertainty and headed back toward the dinghy dock. They were just setting out on the two-mile trip to the anchorage when the VHF radio on Burt's belt crackled to life with a familiar voice.

"*Double Trouble, Double Trouble, Double Trouble*, this is *Petrel*. Come in."

Beth's gaze focused on the radio as Burt reached for it. He unclipped it and handed it to her, then slid aft to take over driving while she spoke.

"*Petrel* this is *Double Trouble*, go seven two."

"Seven two."

Beth punched the channel button to change to the recreational channel and waited to hear from *Petrel* again. Even's voice came through calling *Double Trouble* once more.

"Hello Evan. I'm glad to hear from you. Over."

"And you Beth. How is everything. Is that you I see tied up to that stinkpot in the anchorage? Over."

Beth glanced at Burt, who assumed an amused look of insult, making her smile.

"It is, Evan. But I'm in a dinghy with the skipper of the stinkpot heading back out to the anchorage right now. Over."

"Oops. My apologies to Captain Stinkpot. Have you connected with your crew then? Over."

"Yes. He's in the hospital. Over."

"Oy, sorry to hear it. Over."

"He'll recover. We've just left there. Are you anchored? Over."

"We will be shortly, off your starboard quarter looks good. Over."

"When you see us get back come over for a drink and I'll tell you what happened. Over."

"Exactly what I wanted to hear. See you soon. *Petrel* standing by on sixteen."

When Evan and his crew learned that Beth needed to move *Trouble* in to the marina they insisted on helping. Beth had been thinking through how she would do it on her own: the timing needed to drop the anchor and motor in reverse to the dock, then get her dock lines ashore and secured was going to be hard. But even so her initial reaction was to decline. Fortunately, Evan was persistent and Burt gave her a look that said, "don't be an idiot." So in the early afternoon they cast off the lines that secured *Double Trouble* to *Sandcastle* and she pointed the bow toward the channel to le Marin.

Having so much crew felt strange to Beth as she maneuvered *Trouble* into alignment perpendicular to the dock and signaled to Max and Marnie to drop the anchor. She heard it splash and could see Max paying out the line, so she turned her attention to the dock behind her and put *Trouble* into reverse. *Trouble* never backed in a straight line, but she had learned to compensate. Fortunately, the breeze was not too strong so she didn't have to compensate for that too. As she inched her way backwards Evan and Connor climbed monkey-like out over *Trouble*'s stern rail and balanced there ready to jump off with the stern lines. At the same moment that Beth felt the fender that she'd hung on the stern bump the dock she heard the thump of Evan and Connor's feet hitting it. Their lines were cleated so fast she barely saw their hands move. She signaled Marnie on the bow to take in the slack on the anchor. By the time she had the engine shut down, her impromptu crew were standing on *Trouble*'s deck looking around at all the boats in the marina. Something about their intent survey of the place felt odd to Beth, but she was too concerned about getting back to Terry to give it much thought.

"Thank you guys. That was so much easier with help. I'm going back over to the hospital," Beth told them as she collected her bag with her laptop and phone and put the washboard into *Trouble*'s companionway opening to secure the boat.

"Would you like to join me for dinner later, to thank you for your help?"

"This? Doing a Med Moore is nothing with four hands. No. But you can join us," Evan replied. "Let me have your number and I'll call you when we know where."

"Okay. Thanks. I'd love to."

THIRTY: *RAVEN*

Climbing the steps to the broad wooden patio of the restaurant Evan had identified, Beth saw a large group taking up three tables at the far end, and wondered if he'd been able to get them a table outside. But then someone in the group waved and someone else stood up and she realized that they were gesturing to her.

"Here she is, the lady of the hour," Evan said as she approached, reaching out to draw her into the group. She scanned the faces, knowing that they must all be cruisers, but shocked that they seemed to all be here for her.

"Hi everyone," she said, and then made eye contact with a woman at one of the tables and added, "Laurie! Hello!"

Laurie and Joe and their two boys were all there, as was Burt. Some of the other people were familiar from other harbors, some were completely new. Then a lanky, white-haired man with a ragged white beard came around the table to where Evan had indicated Beth should sit. He extended his hand and introduced himself.

"Beth, I'm Jerry. It's a pleasure to meet you."

"Jerry! Me too. Thank you again for calling me yesterday."

"We take care of our own in the Lesser Antilles. While you were visiting your man in the hospital, the net was on fire with plans. Somehow it all came together and here we are. Let me introduce you to as many of the rest of this crowd as I can."

There was no way Beth could remember all of them, so she focused on the people closest to her as a round of drinks was ordered and menus distributed. It soon became clear that she would not be allowed to pay for

282

anything. Surrounded by sailors who understood her situation and cared, she finally felt herself relaxing and even enjoying the company.

Clearly unable to sit still for the entire meal, Aiden and Michael came around the tables to stand by Beth's chair as she was finishing her grouper. They asked how many of the treasure hunt clues she and Terry had found, and whether they were they going to keep hunting. Beth told them about visiting the waterfall at Wallilabou and explained that although she'd stopped at the Pitons on St. Lucia, she had not had time to hunt there. That caused the boys to exchange a look, and Michael hurried back around the table to Laurie and Joe. He conferred with them briefly, getting nods of approval from both, and returned.

"We want you to come with us to find the next clue," he said.

"But I didn't find the one at the Pitons," Beth replied, although the offer excited her.

"I don't think that really matters," Evan put in, having heard the boys' offer. "I agree. Let's all look for the next one together." He directed this last suggestion at the boys, then looked across the table at Joe and Laurie.

"Isn't it cheating?" Beth asked.

"Hah!" Max said. "The kid in Wallilabou told us that one guy tried to take all of the clues the other day. You skipping a clue and getting help from the rest of us is hardly a big cheat."

"Are you guys seriously doing that treasure hunt?" Someone else asked. That sparked a series of questions and comments from the gathered sailors. Some of them were also participating, others thought the whole thing was ridiculous and one woman declared it to be dangerous. Her position was countered by sailors from both of the other camps as extreme. While the discussion heated up Beth half turned to Aiden and Michael and said, "The hospital is keeping Terry tomorrow, and after that he won't be able to hunt for a while. So I'd love to join all of you guys. Let's figure it out after dinner."

"Excellent!" Aiden crowed. "Come on Michael. Gum, remember?" He dragged his brother away from the table, off on his next errand.

"At the Pitons there was a treasure map on a sign at the edge of the resort grounds. It led to a vending machine of clues — we actually had to put in a coin to get one," Evan explained the next morning. They had agreed the night before to gather at the marina gate, and Beth had a feeling that at least Evan and his crew thought the next clue was inside the marina itself.

"Did you notice that it said the money was going to be donated to a charity?" Joe asked.

"Yes. But I think they did it to discourage anyone from taking all the clues."

"I know. If I'd had more money I would have bought them all!" Michael declared.

"No you would not have," Laurie said firmly, giving him a firm look. He seemed unfazed.

"Did you guys use the moorings there?" Beth asked.

"Yup."

"Sure."

Beth groaned. "I didn't trust them."

"What did you do?"

"I anchored and a local took a line to shore for me."

Evan looked thoughtful, then said, "You might have been the wiser. I have heard of those moorings failing. We stood watches."

Joe looked surprised at that, probably because he and Laurie and the boys had not. Beth decided to move things along to prevent Evan and his crew from asking them.

"What does the Pitons clue say?"

"Here, have a look," Evan held out a glossy, colorful brochure to her.

It was a brochure for the marina where they stood, so that explained Evan and his crew's behavior. Beth unfolded it to find a cartoonish map of the docks and waterfront with shops and businesses identified, and many, many boats.

"See it yet?" Michael asked. Beth glanced up at his intent face, then back at the brochure, turning to the other side. "Getting colder," he added smugly.

"Have you found the next clue?" she asked pointedly. He shrugged.

"But he does have a point," Evan said, grinning. "At least that's what we think. Focus on the map."

Beth turned the brochure back over and studied the map, scanning the rows of boats on the several long docks. Far out on the southern end, on a dock that branched off of another dock, she found a boat that looked like a pirate ship and sported a simplified version of the hunt logo.

"I see it. If it *is* it. Is this what you mean?" she put her finger on the boat and held up the brochure for the others to see. There were nods and murmurs of agreement from both teams.

"Let's go find out."

The boys dashed ahead of the adults along the wide wooden dock and quickly disappeared around the first right hand turn. The adults walked purposefully, commenting on the abundance of very large yachts as they passed them. Many looked as if they didn't move very often.

"I'm surprised the boys didn't make you come yesterday," Beth said to Laurie.

"We only got here a few minutes before dinner," Laurie explained. "They did want to come running out here, but we declined. I suspect that they did it anyway, last night when they left the dinner table." She looked at Joe, who replied with a purse-lipped nod.

"What about you guys," Beth looked to Evan. "Are you sure you didn't come out here yesterday afternoon?"

"We decided to wait for you, and we needed some supplies. Then when we met Laurie and Joe and the boys and remembered them from the waterfall, and we'd heard Joe on the radio in the dinner planning. It was obvious that we should proceed together."

"It's not like we're going to win the top prizes, so competing is silly," Beth observed.

"What? Are you saying we're not in first place?" Joe laughed, then amended, "First, second or third, that is."

The others laughed.

"I'll concede first to you and your boys," Evan said. "They're far more eager than me."

"And Terry and I wouldn't be doing it if it weren't for them, so among this group you guys can be first."

"That's very kind of you, if only to keep peace on our boat," Laurie said, taking Joe's hand. The simple gesture sent a shiver of longing for Terry through Beth and she swallowed back a flash of sadness.

"Why didn't your friend Burt come?" Evan asked.

"He's not doing the hunt. He said he had some things to take care of today, as long as he's stopped here. He was on his way to Guadeloupe when he saw *Great Escape* in distress."

"Right, he mentioned that last night. Hey, check out that trimaran." Joe diverted them to the right side of the dock where a boat that was as wide as it was long floated like a majestic swan.

Eventually they rounded the last turn onto the extension of the extension of the main dock. Their target was about half way down on the left side, and they could already see it. The hull was black, which was notable among all the whites and blues, and there were colorful flags flapping from every possible attachment point. There were so many it was difficult to determine the shape of the topsides beneath them. As the group came up to the vessel they heard the boys shouting piratical phrases and the clack of plastic swordplay.

They were running madly around the deck of the small pirate ship with two other kids, a boy and a girl. All were armed with plastic swords and wore assorted pirate costume pieces. A rotund man in a complete pirate outfit – Beth wasn't certain whether it should be considered a costume or regular attire for this guy – was loosely supervising.

"Ahoy mateys," he called to the group on the dock. "Be ye attached to these rascals?"

"Two of them, yes," Laurie said, stepping to the edge of the dock to peer up at the man. There was a boarding ladder on the dock that was tall enough to step from it to the boat's high stern. It made Beth wished she had one for *Trouble*.

"Permission to board?" Laurie asked, grasping the ladder and placing a foot on the first step.

"Aye, aye, get 'cherselves up here," the man replied.

When they were all on deck the man surveyed them through his unpatched eye. "I be Captain Cyrus Deepcurrent, skipper of the *Raven*, this fine vessel. Ye be more than one team, I suspect."

"Aye, we be three teams working together for this leg," Evan replied, getting into the spirit of things.

"A temporary alliance is it? Who be yer skippers then?"

Evan, Beth, and Joe raised their hands, Joe taking a half step forward. The man focused on Beth.

"Shiver me timbers, we have a lady captain! Cabin boy!" this last was delivered in a yell over his shoulder. The boy and girl immediately deviated from their course across the forward deck in pursuit of Aiden and Michael and returned to the aft deck. The boy disappeared down the boat's main hatch. The girl stopped beside the pirate.

"Aye captain sir!"

"Fetch a flag for the lady captain and be quick about it."

"Aye sir." The girl scrambled up onto the deck house where there were flags fastened to every shroud. The pirate swiveled to watch her, then glanced over his shoulder at the hunters.

"Bring me three, girl!" he shouted.

"Aye sir," the girl's cry came back.

"Now, I suppose ye be wanting some points," he said to the group.

"We sure do!" Michael gasped, out of breath from his running battle. The pirate eyed him for a moment, clearly trying to intimidate. It did not work.

"Very well then." He slipped his right hand inside his black vest and withdrew three familiar looking cards, handing them to the three skippers.

They all waited a few more minutes while the girl unclipped the three flags and brought them to him. He shook one out and presented it with a half bow to Beth, then did the same with the other two for Evan and Joe.

"I bid thee luck on the next leg, mateys," he said. "Now, let's toast yer success so far, eh?"

The three of them must have been through this ceremony a lot Beth thought, for at just that moment a tray of plastic cups appeared from below, carried by the boy. He brought it to the pirate and held it as he served each of them.

"Rum for the able bodied seamen, and women, and a special punch for the deckhands," he said as he handed different colored cups to the adults and the boys. The adult drink was a dark and stormy – the blend of rum and ginger beer with a squeeze of lime that Beth favored. Despite the early hour of the day they all drank Captain Deepwater's health.

"Thank you all for that," Beth said when they had reached the head of the dock. The boys had carried their flag on ahead to study it and Beth had tucked hers in her bag to take to the hospital. Connor and Marnie held Evan's between them with Max looking on as they studied it. "I can see that I'm going to fall behind the rest of you – I really have to go see Terry and I know you're going figure out this clue right now."

"Who knows, maybe the next one is around here," Laurie pointed out. "If it is, we'll wait and you can come with us."

"Yes," Evan added, glancing at his crew. Max looked up and nodded. "Sure."

"You guys are great. I want Terry to have a chance at trying to solve it. Can we touch base later this afternoon? But I will totally understand if you decide to carry on."

"We'll talk to you later Beth. We're going to make the boys absorb some local culture and history before we do more hunting." Laurie said, patting her arm. "Now you should go see Terry. Say hello for us."

"Us too," Evan added.

"I should have expected to find your hand in this, Burt."

Burt half turned to look at the speaker approaching along the fuel dock. The police officer with the shouldered assault rifle standing further along the dock turned too. Burt watched the speaker step daintily over a diesel hose, nose wrinkling ever so slightly at the odor of the fuel that permeated the dock. He was tall and slender with the stooped shoulders so common among tall men who had not been athletic children. His narrow, pointed face always made Burt think of a weasel.

"Lou. I never think of marinas as your element," Burt replied, wondering if the other man would realize this was a veiled insult.

"Can't avoid it on this detail. But the rest of the perks of the location make up for it."

"Did this one drag you off of the beach?" There was nothing about the man's appearance, which included a light grey suit, button down shirt with the collar open, and brown leather loafers, that suggested the beach.

"Not this morning, no. Maybe later."

As usual, Burt was astounded by the man's complete inability to detect sarcasm. Lou was with the Drug Enforcement Agency, on loan to the French government to help track down and seize the drugs before they got to the US. And arrest the people involved, of course.

Burt had known him in various capacities for more than a dozen years – pretty much ever since Lou had joined the agency.

"So, you saw a flare." Lou said. He had obviously already read the statement Burt had given to the police that morning. Burt was impressed, even though Lou was a generally efficient, dedicated civil servant.

"I'd noticed the boats sitting dead in the water. But I didn't have cause to check them out. In fact, I radioed them to ask if they needed assistance and got no answer."

"Yes. And you were on your way back to Guadeloupe?"

Burt hated officials who asked questions that they already knew the answer to. It felt like a need for dominance – make the suspect repeat his story just because you ask.

"I am. But my next charter isn't for a few days, so I have time to assist in this."

"Good. Very good."

Again, no reaction to Burt's veiled suggestion that he was doing Lou a favor. Too much of this and Burt would develop bad habits around more perceptive people.

"This is a lovely yacht," Lou said, looking at *Jericho*, which was tied up at the fuel dock. She was the reason for Burt's visit. "It should help the budget, when it sells at auction."

"It's a classic," Burt replied. "Beautiful lines and beautifully built."

"High praise coming from a power boater. I understand that the other one wasn't nearly so special.

"It was a stock cruising sailboat. There are probably dozens exactly like it in this marina. But it was somebody's home."

"Somebody who decided to carry cocaine for the cartels."

Burt nodded, hesitant to defend either Maggie or Bill Hartford. But then he said, "She was a victim of her husband. Not a very nice woman, it seems, but still not the one who made the deal to carry the drugs."

"She knew they were on board."

"Yes. Fair point. She was not without guilt. I'm just not sure she deserved all that she got. But it doesn't matter. I'm just glad that my friend Terry survived."

"Yes. Your friend Terry. Coincidence that he was aboard?"

"Complete," Burt shrugged, arms spread and palms up. "Terry and his girlfriend Beth are participating in the treasure hunt – you know the *Gunkholing* thing?"

"Yes. Every police agency in the islands is well aware of that craziness."

"Oh come on Lou, it's just a fun time."

"Whenever the – ahem – 'gentlemen' from *Gunkholing* stage an event we all sit up and watch. It's always a gathering of boat bums."

"I'm planning on going to the party, Lou."

"Good. That will raise the level some."

Burt emitted a small sigh and focused on *Jericho* to avoid looking at Lou.

"Anyway, I last saw them down in the Grenadines. We even talked about how they'd seen *Great Escape* and Maggie at Carriacou."

"So you're saying it's a small world for you boaters."

"I am saying that," Burt nodded. "Terry is a business man from Washington. Do a background check. He's got no connection to this business."

"Yes, we will. And since the doctors don't want him very active for the next couple weeks, I expect if we learn differently we'll know where to find him."

Burt shook his head, turning to look at Lou this time. "He's a good man, Lou. Leave him be."

Lou's eyes narrowed for a moment, and Burt wondered if he was trying to decide if Burt himself was trustworthy. But they both knew that was a non-starter: Lou would never unearth anything on Burt, and his direction from above was to trust, and expect cooperation from, the charter skipper. Burt was well aware of this. It was, he reflected, probably why he was forever trying sarcasm on Lou.

"So the crew are all in custody?" he asked.

"All four," Lou nodded. Their statements are much less believable than yours and mister Faughnan's. The patrol boat had to put out a launch to scoop up as much of the product as they could – those guys were throwing it overboard. The chopper must have tipped them off."

"Did they recover it all?"

"Hard to tell. The suspects aren't willing to tell us just how much there was, and without the other boat we don't know the volume of the spaces it was stored in."

"Manufacturer's plans? The dozens of other boats just like *Great Escape* around here?"

"Yes, yes, in time we'll nail it down. But best we can figure we got about eighty percent of it. There was still a lot on board."

"That's good. No ambiguity about their guilt." Burt forced himself not to think about the brick of cocaine in his safe. "Any guess as to who set the bomb?"

"Based on Mr. Faughnan's statement, it was most likely Hartford. He did not see the other skipper board *Great Escape*, and the two crewmen were occupied with moving the drugs. It's possible one of them did it, but it feels more like the act of an angry husband."

"Yeah. It does," Burt nodded thoughtfully. "Did Terry mention a bomb in his statement?"

"No. He described an explosion and did not speculate on the cause."

Burt nodded again.

"What are you thinking?"

"Only that he doesn't realize. He thinks it was a – I was going to say natural explosion. He thinks something on board blew up from the rising water."

"How likely is that?"

"Not very, with the engine and electrical systems shut down. I imagine he'll come to realize that at some point and wonder. But let's just leave it alone for now. His girlfriend doesn't need to know there was a bomb."

Lou looked at him for a moment, eyes narrowing again. "You're fond of her."

Burt frowned. "I like them both. There is nothing untoward in this Lou and I don't appreciate even the hint of it you just made. She's a lovely woman, and they are a happy couple."

"All right, all right," Lou raised both hands in a placating gesture. "It's just not like you to be protective."

"You don't know me very well."

"Huh."

They both stared at *Jericho* for a moment.

"Faughnan said you hauled the other boat's dinghy aboard, brought it back. What did you do with it?"

Burt chuckled. "You're the first to ask. I still have it. I was thinking of giving it to Terry and Beth. It's in much better shape than hers."

"Technically the Hartford's children could claim it."

"What if I claim salvage rights? It was adrift in international waters with an injured man aboard. I helped him and took the craft under my command. I can do whatever I please with it."

Lou shook his head as if this one detail was not worth his trouble. "Do what you want with it. I won't include it in my report."

"Thanks Lou."

"As long as you aren't trying to claim this one," Lou shot him a thin-lipped smile as he nodded at *Jericho*.

"It's got to be something to do with the volcano," Terry said, leaning back against his pillow to shut his eyes. The flag was spread out on the tray table across his bed. He'd been excited when Beth brought it for them both to study, but after a few minutes he was having trouble concentrating. The bright colors on the black background made his head ache.

"I think so too. I should have brought the cruising guide with me. Maybe there's a tour."

"Probably," he replied, pinching the bridge of his nose with one hand."

"How are you feeling?"

He removed his hand and opened his eyes. "I'm sorry Beth. My head hurts. It hurts to look at this," he set his hand on the flag.

"Why didn't you say? Don't look at it. They said you'd have trouble reading and concentrating for a few days."

"I hope it's just a few days," he muttered.

"Stop. I'm sure you will be reading easily very soon. Especially if you do take it easy now. So let me tell you about our find this morning instead, okay?"

"Okay," he smiled, reaching for her hand. She squeezed his lightly and launched into a description of last night's surprise gathering and hunting for the treasure with the other teams. He lay with his eyes shut, smiling and commenting as she spoke.

"You definitely have to go with them for the next clue, if you all decide it's here on Martinique," he said when she finished.

"You're sure you don't mind? I'd rather do it with you."

"But if you wait for me to able to go, it will be too late."

When she didn't answer right away he opened his eyes to look at her. Noticing, she shrugged.

"I was just thinking, too late for what? We're not going to win, we know that. I love the puzzles, and going to places we might not go to otherwise. But I've got to balance it with the rest of my – our – life. Right now I'm more concerned with taking care of you."

"We never said we were going to go the whole way. It was always 'do it until we don't want to anymore.'"

"I know. But I also hate to give up on something I start."

He took her hand again and gave it a squeeze. "That's for sure. You're the queen of living up to your commitments. That's why you're so hesitant to make them."

"I –," Beth's objection died on her lips. He was right. And the fact that he knew it about her was at once unsettling and comforting.

"It's okay Beth. It's one of the things I love about you. So let's give ourselves permission to be slackers when it comes to this treasure hunt.

As long as we agree that we're going to the party. Right?"

"Absolutely."

THIRTY-ONE: ANTIGUA

Burt reckoned that the wind carried the sound of the band at the *Gunkholing* Treasure Hunt party all the way across Falmouth Harbour to the expensive homes on the opposite side of the protected bay. No doubt somebody would be calling the police to complain before the day was out. But the boys from the magazine always managed to invite the right local authorities to deflect the worst of the local complaints. A few free bottles of the sponsoring rum was probably the key.

Floating on the harbour's calm waters just beyond the crowded marina docks was an enormous collection of small boats all rafted together at every imaginable angle. As Burt watched, three additions joined the outer edges of the raft and two detached. One motored toward shore, the other was rowed toward the anchorage. The amoebic creation was crowded with boaters, many of them inebriated to a dangerous level. On the outer edge people were diving into the water and climbing back aboard whichever boat they surfaced near. Further in, large plastic coolers full of ice and beer were secured between the boats. Near the middle a guy with tattooed sleeves wearing a denim vest over ragged denim cutoffs was standing, holding forth about something while waving his beer bottle around. He was far more steady on his feet than he ought to be, which suggested to Burt that he wasn't nearly as drunk as he appeared.

These dinghy raft ups were becoming more and more popular. Burt didn't see any harm in it, as long as some of the participants remained sober enough to keep an eye on the rest. He suspected that the magazine, which was big on appearing rowdy and carefree but had pretty risk-averse lawyers, had planted quite a few responsible types to manage the thing. Even so, he was glad when he saw a familiar dinghy coming from the anchorage bypass the raft and head for the overcrowded dinghy dock. It was Beth and Terry using *Great Escape*'s dinghy. Beth was driving, which wasn't at all unusual so it didn't give Burt a clue about Terry's condition. He headed off toward the dinghy dock to meet them.

He'd spoken to Beth yesterday and she'd said that Terry was pretty much recovered. His most recent x-ray had shown mended ribs, the hearing in his left ear was nearly back to normal, and the doctors had declared his brain no longer swollen from Bill Hartford's blow. Still, he wanted to see the man in person to reassure himself. Lou had been right a few weeks ago, he did care about Beth, and for Terry. They were the kind of cruisers that he appreciated knowing here in the islands. He wanted them to stick around.

"Oh man, this is going to be fun," Beth said, eying the dinghies five-deep around the dinghy dock.

"I thought there were a lot out there," Terry replied, pointing over her shoulder at the raft up.

"I know! Okay, it looks a little thinner over here," Beth said, angling their little boat to the right side of the dock. "I'll take it slow, you nudge them out of the way."

Terry leaned out over the inflated bow, gently pushing a path between the other boats so that they could get theirs up to the dock to get off. But he couldn't do it, the boats were too densely packed to get all the way in.

"We're going to have to climb into this one, and then to the dock," he said, indicating the bright blue inflatable that lay between them and the dock. "I'll go first and take the line. Get the motor secured."

Beth resisted the urge to offer to do it. He had started to chafe at her protective behavior a couple weeks ago, and she was trying to break herself of the habit. It had been essential at first – he simply could not do things that required good balance or risked a fall. Since the water under the dinghy was at least three feet deep Beth didn't bother to tilt up the motor – it would just be in the way of other dinghies and was more likely to be damaged. She did make sure the motor was locked to the boat, and she pocketed the safety kill switch. That done, she looked up to see Terry climbing from the other dinghy to the dock with the line in hand. She also saw a familiar form walking out the dock toward him.

Terry crouched to examine a cleat on the dock that was already completely full of lines.

"Lean over the side, there are some vertical supports that you might be able to use instead," Beth said. "Hey Burt, you found us."

Terry looked up along the dock and said hello to Burt before stretching out on the dock with his shoulders and arms hanging out over the edge so that he could see the side. He made quick work of tying a bowline knot around one of the vertical supports Beth had indicated. There were other lines tied to other supports, but they were far less crowded than the cleats.

"Got that?" Burt asked, looking down at Terry.

"Yup," Terry answered, rolling onto his behind to sit on the dock, placing his feet into the blue dinghy. "Come on over," he said to Beth. Keeping her center of balance as low as she could, she slithered across their dinghy's bow and the blue boat's gunwale, feeling Terry's hands on her waist as she completed that stage of the trip. She stood up and placed her hands on the dock, then brought her knee up and scrambled the rest of the way. Burt took her arm as she got to her feet.

"Good to see you both," he said, shaking Terry's hand, then planting a kiss on Beth's cheek. Beth noticed that his look at Terry was longer and more assessing than the quick grin he gave her. "Got your point cards?"

"We sure do. We ended up with ten, if you can believe it."

"Better than my one. You turn them in for the drawing at the entrance. Shall we?"

Beth hadn't thought that their ten points was much, so when she handed them over to a woman in a Hawaiian print bikini top over a clashing sarong the woman's "wow, nice job" surprised her.

"Check it out, Jill, these guys got to ten," she said to her companion, who was in the process of exchanging a single point card for a ticket for another skipper. Jill and the other skipper both looked at Beth.

"You were really serious," the man said with a smile.

"It was fun. But something came up and we had to slow down," Beth replied.

"Yeah, cruising. Enjoying life," the other skipper said, turning to rejoin his companions who were standing nearby.

Beth took her ten ticket stubs, watching that the ten matching tickets went into the fishbowl for the drawing. It was already half full.

"I don't think even our ten give us much of a chance to win anything," she said to Terry while they waited for Burt to get his one ticket.

"Doesn't look that way. What does it matter? The serious prizes are for the top three. The drawing is just for rum and stuff."

"Okay, let's get some swag!" Burt rubbed his hands together in anticipation.

They plunged into the party, weaving through streams of other boaters with different objectives: food, drink, hats, t-shirts, music, more food, more drink. Sometimes making progress required joining a conga line of dancers, or wiggling their way across the dance area in front of the band. Beth realized that she could either let the crowd annoy her, or just get into it, so she chose the latter. Raising her arms to twirl her way through the dancers she felt Terry's hands on her waist again and looked to see him grinning and wiggling his hips as he moved with her. Burt imitated her, a hulking bear dancing through and garnering laughs and claps from the crowd.

They collected complimentary hats and t-shirts and can coolers and bottle wetsuits and a cheap canvas bag printed with the magazine's logo to put it all in. Then they made the rounds of the food and drink stalls, piling up on grilled chicken tenders, hot dogs, and French fries. Beth and Burt got cups of rum punch, but Terry requested a plain ginger ale. Beth was looking forward to the day when he'd be able to enjoy a drink with her again, but the doctors had suggested waiting another month or so.

Along the way they spotted and greeted friends and acquaintances, including Evan and his crew and Michael and Aiden, who said that their parents were "over in the shade," gesturing toward some picnic tables under awnings that looked slightly quieter than the main body of the party.

"I think I could use some shade," Terry murmured into Beth's ear when the boys had merged back into the crowd.

They joined Laurie and Joe, who were nibbling on a plate of chicken while they watched the festivities.

Soon after, the band gave way to a tattooed, bearded man in cargo shorts and bright yellow rubber clogs who garnered a round of cheers and applause from the crowd.

"Okay, okay," he said into the microphone that he held, "Let's get down to business. The business of having fun!"

More cheers interrupted him, which he obviously expected, for he stood grinning and nodding, surveying the rowdy crowd for another two minutes or more. Eventually he pulled them back.

"It's time for prizes!"

The first prize, an offshore certified six-person life raft, went to a crew that had collected fifty-six points and had been the first to more than half of the clues.

"Power boater," Burt commented.

"How do you know?" Beth asked.

"I know him, slightly. And I knew that he was pushing to win. I expect that the second place is a buddy of his. They got a little crazy over this."

"Crazy how?" Terry asked.

"There was some mild sabotage. As the party goes on the stories will come out."

"And how do you already know them?" Beth asked.

"I don't. Only that there are stories."

The winner had finished thanking his crew and the magazine and vacated the stage.

Second prize was a new dinghy and outboard motor, and once again Beth wasn't too sorry not to win, not since taking ownership of *Great Escape*'s former dinghy. She hadn't felt right about it at first, so she'd gotten the address of Kevin Hartford, Maggie and Bill's son, from the police. She'd written to him, explaining that she had the only part of *Great Escape* that had survived. His response was brief and clear. The Hartford family wanted nothing to do with that boat.

The second prize winner did appear to be a friend of the first, based on the barbs he shot at him during his acceptance speech. He was obviously drunk, and their host eventually ushered him off of the stage in order to announce third place. Beth would have liked to have won the water maker, but it went to a sailboat crew that had collected thirty-six points.

After that there were some silly prizes that seemed to be going to insiders, or at least cruisers who'd been to a lot of these events in the past. The crowd grew increasingly less attentive, with a small core gathered at the edge of the stage while the fringes returned to making the rounds of the food, drink, and game stands and the row of hopeful vendors offering gear and goodies.

When the band returned to the stage, Terry suggested to Beth that they take a walk to the customs office at Nelson's Dockyard, which was holding a package of mail for them. Beth agreed, noting that the drawing wouldn't take place until the evening.

Beyond the edge of the party they found a quiet street lined with shops and restaurants. Proprietors of a few stood in doorways or at windows looking across at the party in the marina parking lot. As they walked Beth wondered whether the party attracted more people to the area, and was good for business, or sucked business away from the shops and restaurants.

Nelson's Dockyard in English Harbour was just a ten minute walk across an isthmus. For once the name was not just a marketing gimmick. The protected harbor had served as Admiral Nelson's base, and the remains of the British Navy dockyard were incorporated into the modern marina facility there. They had considered bringing *Trouble* in there to anchor, but it had looked crowded. As they passed through the antique gate that marked the edge of the English fort, their view of the marina and anchorage validated their decision. One of the big charter companies operated out of the marina and it's boats were lined up stern-to the main dock. The rest of the docks were full, and the anchorage beyond was too. After inquiring in the hotel near the gate, they found their way to the customs office where an officer located a thick envelope of mail for them. They had to open it in front of him so that he could determine whether any duty was owed. He looked a little disappointed when the contents turned out to be simple mail, collected and forwarded by Terry's attorney in Washington. Beth was using his address too, which had felt strange at first, but now seemed like the only rational thing to do. After all, it was just a mailing address, and easily changed again if everything in her life changed. In fact, it would be the least important detail if that happened.

The customs man satisfied, they repacked the envelope and stepped out into the bright sunshine.

"How about a cold drink over there?" Terry nodded toward a waterside bar. "We can go through this in the quite before we go back to the madness."

"Yes. Good idea."

Beth could tell that the noise and crowd was almost too much for Terry, and she loved him for trying to deal with it. They took a shaded table at the café and ordered soft drinks and some of Beth's favorite conch fritters.

They nibbled, sipped, and read through the various items of mail that had been worthy of forwarding. This included only personal correspondence and a few much welcome items of reading material. There was a letter from Terry's dad, who refused to use email, and a packet of drawings from Beth's niece and nephew. In a separate envelope from Trish she found a copy of the Alzheimer's association's national newsletter. Terry looked up as she pulled it out.

"Is that it?" he asked.

"I guess so. It must be online too. I didn't know."

"Let's see it."

Beth opened the thin newsletter and found the table of contents. Sure enough, her article was the featured story. She was surprised at how proud it made her feel to see it in print after all those weeks of work on it. She passed it to Terry and looked at the sticky note that Trish had included.

Beth, it's amazing. Mom is over the moon, she's so proud of you. And I am too. Even Dad read it. And the staff at Orange Grove framed it and put it up in the cafeteria. – Trish.

"They framed it and hung it up at Orange Grove Wellness," Beth said to Terry, dashing away a tear.

"That's great! And you know that they'll take extra good care of your folks because of this." He looked at the article for a moment, clearly not planning on reading it now but not wanting to seem abrupt. Beth helped him out by reaching for the newsletter. He handed it back and picked up the last half conch fritter.

"I should call Trish later and let her know we got it."

"Are you thinking you should visit?" he asked. The question took her by surprise. She'd thought of her weeks spent in California as having taken care of her parental duty for a while. But he was perceptive. He'd noticed the tear, and suspected it was a moment of homesickness. *Well, it wasn't*, she told herself. But she knew she was lying to herself.

"I don't know. What are we doing next, Terry?"

"Well," he stretched it out, placing his hand on one of the letters in his pile. "Jeff sent a draft contract for a purchase he wants me to look at. I'm going to have to give him a firmer return date, and it may have to be sooner than November."

Beth wanted to tell him that was not an answer to her question, but she didn't. If he didn't want to discuss their relationship she wouldn't push it. He was watching her intently, waiting for a reaction. She smiled, but it felt wrong.

"I'm not leaving you Beth," he finally said. "So if that's what you're thinking, just stop. Now. I want to know if you mind my shortening our cruise, and if so, where you want to go so that we can get *Trouble* there together. I want it to be somewhere that I can reach you, by phone, by email, by airplane…" With each communications mechanism he moved his hand further up her arm until it was cradling the back of her neck. She leaned into him, eyes locked on his, heart pounding.

"I think it might be best to go back to St. Thomas. I can get a job without a lot of trouble about being a foreigner. Maybe even at the dive shop where I worked before."

He nodded, sliding his hand back along her arm in a caress. "And the shortened cruise?"

Beth tried to focus on it through the roar of blood rushing through her body. She'd known from the start that their idyllic cruise would have to come to an end. And they'd accomplished what they set out to do: sail *Trouble* together, get to know one another, figure out if they could live together in a small space. See some of the islands. The duration, or holding Terry to a specific one, was no longer important.

"I don't mind. I would never insist that you stay and jeopardize your business."

He peered into her eyes for a long while, clearly trying to read her mind. She held his gaze, smiling her sincerity. At last he nodded once and said, "St. Thomas. It's a good plan. Will you stay put this time?" his mouth curved into a mischievous grin.

"That depends on how long you stay away."

-fin-

ABOUT THE AUTHOR

A Southern California native, S. Mia McCroskey started writing when she was in ninth grade. She took up sailing when she was in her twenties as an antidote to an unpleasant job. It was a toss-up between sailing lessons and pottery classes. She flipped a coin; the quarter was a lucky one. She moved from California to New York for a better job a couple years later and continued sailing in Long Island Sound and the Chesapeake Bay. Since stepping aboard that first soling in Marina del Rey she has become qualified to charter large, valuable sailboats in fascinating locales all over the world, and has gotten used to being called "the lady captain" by the locals. In her professional career she transitioned from a magazine and book editor to managing software development. She attributes most of her professional leadership skills to her experience handling crews of friends and acquaintances aboard sailboats. She has never owned her own boat, but she did eventually take pottery classes.

www.ingramcontent.com/pod-product-compliance
Lightning Source LLC
Chambersburg PA
CBHW071248170626
46809CB00001B/132